J U N I  R

R A Y   D O N L E Y

RIVER GROVE
BOOKS

Published by River Grove Books
Austin, TX
www.greenleafbookgroup.com

Distributed by River Grove Books

For ordering information or special discounts for bulk purchases, please contact River Grove Books at PO Box 91869, Austin, TX 78709, 512.891.6100.

Design and composition by Greenleaf Book Group LLC
Cover design by Greenleaf Book Group LLC
Cover images: © iStockphoto.com/vectorcartoons (bee)/Ralf Hettler (clouds)

Publisher's Cataloging-In-Publication Data
(Prepared by The Donohue Group, Inc.)

Donley, Ray.
  Junior / Ray Donley. -- 1st ed.

  p. ; cm.

  ISBN: 978-1-938416-00-2

  1. Bombers (Terrorists)--United States--Fiction. 2. Fugitives from justice--United States--Fiction. 3. Terrorism in mass media--United States--Fiction. 4. Fathers and sons--United States--Fiction. 5. Diary fiction. I. Title.

PS3604.O65 J86 2012
813/.6   2012941762

First Edition

To my mother and father, who pointed me in the right direction and loved me even when I kept getting lost.

To Aileen, who has patiently put up with me for a very long time.

To Kate and Gracie, who make my heart glad.

Foreword

Although millions of people have read and studied this book, it remains in many respects an enigma. For example, scholars cannot agree on when or how the book was given its title. There is also substantial disagreement among experts about whether the entire book was actually written by Joshua Jennings, Jr., or whether sections of the book were instead compiled by friends or compatriots of Joshua Jennings, Jr., or witnesses of the events described herein.

In addition, there is the issue of language. *Junior* was originally written in the language of the Chiricahua Apache, a Native American tribe. Translating this dialect into twenty-first-century English has not been an easy task, as evidenced by the many versions of the book that exist in print today.

Despite these controversies, *Junior* has stood the test of time as a classic study of the human condition. As Professor Ronald Wood of Harvard University concluded in his well-known monograph *Junior: The Son Also Rises*, "*Junior* may not give us all the answers, but it asks most of the right questions. Plus, the chapters are really short, so people with attention deficit disorders can make it through the book with little difficulty."

Although it is impossible to synthesize all the scholarship devoted to *Junior*, I have added footnotes to the text to assist the reader in understanding and interpreting this timeless work of literature.

Dean Wilkerson, Jr., PhD
University of Texas at Fayetteville, Arkansas

Day 1

My best friend Pete suggested I start writing all of this stuff down. "Big Man, if you can somehow ride this puppy out, the written record will be very important." When Pete said this, we were hiding behind two massive granite boulders, watching three guys in white coveralls five miles away shovel dirt on the caskets of my mother and two sisters. Through my binoculars I could just barely make out the lettering on their sweat-stained coveralls: "El Paso Presidio Memorial Cemetery." Camera crews from all the major television networks recorded the scene for posterity.

I love Pete and I have decided to take his advice. But neither of us really believes we will survive this sheepstorm.[1]

Day 2

I'm still alive, but I had a tears and whiskey night, if you know what I mean.[2] I watched snippets from the funeral services last night on television, alternating between crying and cursing.

I am now the last living member of my family. Everyone else has been killed.

This is the second day of my writing project. As you will soon learn, I'm no Joseph Conrad, so don't get your hopes up. This will not likely be a page-turning blockbuster. Just ask Dr. Cathy Hoover, my American Literature professor from college, about my writing skills. The highest grade she ever gave me on a research paper was a C. On second thought, maybe you should not

---

1 The meaning of this word is unclear. Some translations use the phrase "sheep shearing."

2 "Tears and whiskey night" is likely a reference to "Iraqi Nights," a song by the Alcoholic Shrubtones, a musical group popular in the early twenty-first century. It is well known that Joshua Jennings, Jr., was an aficionado of country, pop, and rock-and-roll music of the latter twentieth and early twenty-first centuries. *Junior* contains hundreds of references and allusions to musicians, song titles, and song lyrics. Since this commentary is geared more to the casual reader, only a few of these references will be identified. For a comprehensive analysis of the musical references in *Junior*, see *Junior's Tunes*, by Steve Selbyoski.

contact Dr. Hoover. She probably does not want to be associated with me in any form or fashion, seeing how things have turned out.[3]

In addition to my screaming lack of talent, the fact that I am writing all of this down while being the subject of a worldwide manhunt may also affect the overall quality of the work product. But as my dad used to say, "Junior, if it was easy, any moronic sumbitch could do it!"

My name is Joshua Jennings, Jr. For as long as I can remember, everyone except Pete has called me Junior. (If I live long enough, I may get around to explaining why Pete calls me Big Man.)

When I was a kid, I liked being called Junior, because it linked me to my dad and I idolized my dad. I used to tell people I was helping Dad with his "business." People thought that was real cute. When I reached my twenties, it wasn't nearly as cool. Now that I'm thirty, it is downright embarrassing. Not because I don't still love my dad, because I do. I will always love my dad. However, when you get to be thirty, you need to forge your own trail, you know what I mean? And it is difficult to be your own man when everyone refers to you as "Junior."

Unless you have been flying high stoned or in a coma recently, you know who I am. My name and picture appear on every television news channel at least once an hour. I am wanted by the United States government for treason, mass murder, and all sorts of other evil stuff.

Pete wants me to write down what really happened, so that is what I will try to do. To begin with, let me emphatically state that I am innocent of all charges. I know that is what you would expect me to say, but it's the truth.

Pete says I need to wrap this up because it's getting dark and we need to move. So I guess I will need to explain my absolute and unequivocal innocence later.

Pete says it's best to move at night. Pete also says not to write down where we are or where we're going tonight. I will tell you this much before I finish today's installment—we are in the Chihuahuan Desert,[4] we have only one

---

3   Although Dr. Hoover is mentioned numerous times in *Junior*, there is no record of a Dr. Cathy Hoover ever teaching at the University of Texas at Austin, where Junior attended college.

4   The Chihuahuan Desert is the largest desert in North America. It covers more than 200,000 square miles in Texas, New Mexico, Arizona, and Baja, Texas, the state formerly known as the sovereign nation of Mexico.

gallon of drinking water left, and we are running low on gas for the Porsche. Things don't look real good.

Day 9

It's been a week since my last entry. For a while there I thought Day 2 would be the last day of this project. Shortest book ever written by a wanted mass murderer.

Pete and I got lost in the Chihuahuan Desert heading west out of El Paso because we were trying to stay off the main roads. Seemed like no matter what direction we traveled, we were running into the sun. The Porsche broke down, so we had to start walking. Then we ran out of water.

Pete says I started hallucinating from the heat, screaming that a rabid coyote was chasing me. I don't remember that. What I do remember is stumbling along a two-lane blacktop in the middle of nowhere when a big black Cadillac pulled up beside us. Pete helped me into the backseat (he was not as wasted as I was), and the driver of the Caddie gave us cold bottled water and fruit. I drank two bottles of water, ate a banana, and passed out.

When I came to, Pete told me we had been picked up by Sammy Assassin. I looked into the front seat of the Caddie and saw a huge man with skin the color of a Snickers bar behind the wheel. He extended a hand the size of a canned ham toward me and spoke in a low rumbling thunder of a voice: "Good to see you again, Junior. Feeling better?"

If you are a football fan, you know that Sammy "Assassin" Johnson is an All-Pro linebacker with the Kansas City Almonds.[5] You may also know that the Assassin is a pussycat off the field and has a soft heart for retarded children. His younger brother is retarded. If you are really into football trivia, you may even know that the Assassin has used some of his football wealth to build and operate a home for retarded children in El Paso, Texas, where he was raised.

---

5   The Kansas City professional football team has since been renamed the Kansas City Chiefs. When this entry was written, the original name of the team had been changed to the Kansas City Almonds, to comply with the federal Mascot Anti-Defamatory Act. The law was subsequently repealed, and the original name of the team was reinstated. The "Smoke 'em Almonds!" cheer, however, is still a popular cheer at Chiefs' home games.

What you undoubtedly don't know, unless you are one of my father's lawyers or accountants (and I'm pretty sure they are all dead now) is that my dad put up the original seed money for the Assassin's project for the retarded kids. I don't remember how my dad and the Assassin got to be friends.[6]

You are probably wondering how it came to be that a friend of my father's just happened to be driving through the back roads of New Mexico at exactly the same time that Pete and I were running on empty, bumping into prickly pear cactus, and about to die of thirst. I wish I could explain it, but I can't. Stuff like that has happened to me all of my life. Sometimes I'm grateful; other times it just ticks me off. Today, I'm grateful.

Sammy, Pete, and I talked for several hours as we drove to Las Vegas, Nevada. We talked a bunch about my dad, the Apaches, and the nationwide manhunt. Pete says I should not write down everything we talked about, and I agree. Maybe later, depending on how all this goes and how long we manage to stay alive.

What I can tell you is that the Assassin helped us out big-time. He gave me two money collection chips to use at automated cash machines. He told me that all outdoor bank machines have hidden surveillance cameras, so I should wear a hat and sunglasses when I take out money. He also said I should take out the daily maximum of $1,500, to minimize the number of trips to the machines. He told me not to worry, that there would always be money in the account.

Sammy did not tell me who was putting the money into the bank account and I did not ask him. I suspect it will become important at some point to learn who is financing this adventure, but for now, I intend to remain blissfully ignorant.

When we reached Las Vegas, the Assassin parked the Caddie across the street from the Adidas Desert Resort and Casino. He popped the trunk, pulled out two suitcases, and gave Pete the keys to the Caddie. "This baby gets really lousy gas mileage," he said, "but it has a kick-ass stereo, a satellite phone, and a satellite television. A laptop computer with satellite access is in the trunk. The phone, television, and computer have some special cybergeek stuff on them that makes it hard for the authorities to trace or track you. I can't explain how it all works, but I'm told it's all first-rate spy stuff.

6   The personnel records of Trinity Exploration, Inc., one of Joshua Jennings, Sr.'s companies, indicate that Samuel Lincoln Johnson worked as a roughneck for Trinity during the summer following Johnson's junior year at the University of Texas at Austin.

"Drive carefully. I'm gonna go in here and raise a little hell, thereby establishing my alibi and enhancing my considerable reputation as a badass."

Sammy started to walk away, and then he abruptly turned around and threw something at me. I caught it without thinking. It was a baseball cap. The Assassin then walked across the street to the casino, swaggering like only a badass NFL linebacker can. I put the Duke Blue Devils cap on my head.

Pete and I decided to drive out of Las Vegas immediately, to avoid being recognized. For no particular reason, we headed up State Highway 93. As we approached Caliente, Nevada, the satellite phone rang. It was the Assassin. He might have been drunk—it was hard to tell. I could hear the raucous noise from the casino in the background. A girl was giggling. "Two things," he began softly. "First, don't trust anyone." The line was silent for a moment and I thought the Assassin had hung up. He broke the silence in an even softer tone: "Second, you've got to trust everyone."[7] A series of angry shouts erupted in my headset, and then the phone went dead.

The Assassin's call freaked me out. I told Pete to find us a cheap hotel in Caliente so we could spend the night.[8]

Day 13

I know you're going to find this hard to believe, but Caliente, Nevada, sucks. We are staying in the Hot Springs Motel, which is pretty much a dump. I feel the need to take several showers a day here—the place just has a sleazy vibe to it.[9]

---

7   This statement is known as the Day 9 Trust Conundrum, the first of the Seven Conundrums found in *Junior*.

8   Scholars are divided over whether the Day 9 entry is a literal description of the day or a symbolic message wrapped in iconic imagery. Some interpret the mysterious appearance of Samuel Johnson as a metaphor for divine intervention. Others believe Junior's immediate exit from Las Vegas is a commentary on excessive materialism. A confusing aspect of Day 9 is Johnson's decision to gamble at the Adidas Desert Resort and Casino and not the Vegas Nike Hotel, since he had a substantial endorsement contract with Nike.

9   According to testimony in *Utah v. Warren Jeffs*, a criminal trial that took place in the early twenty-first century, the Hot Springs Motel in Caliente, Nevada, was the site of several forced marriages between underage girls and older men. The hotel was owned and operated by members of the Fundamentalist Church of Jesus Christ of Latter-Day Saints (FLDS Church). Warren Jeffs, who arranged the marriages, was the leader of the FLDS Church at the time.

Pete says we need to lie low, so we may be here another day or two. We have been here only four days, and it seems like a year.

Since I'm in such a lousy mood anyway, I might as well explain why every law enforcement officer in the Western Hemisphere wants my scalp. Two weeks ago, both the president and the vice president of the United States came to the Chiricahua Apache reservation in New Mexico for a rally. It was the first time in history that both a sitting president and vice president visited an American Indian reservation during an election campaign. The media went even more overboard than usual in covering the event. Hundreds of journalists from all over the world converged on the reservation. News anchors went out of their way to include references to Cochise and Geronimo in their coverage of the rally.

The president came to the reservation for three reasons. First, my father invited him, and Dad has been a major contributor to every campaign the president has run since he was elected to Congress thirty years ago. Second, Dad is the primary reason President Carrier is (or was) a millionaire many times over. Although I know it is in bad taste to speak ill of the dead, President Carrier was a blue-eyed knucklehead when it came to business and would probably have ended up in bankruptcy but for Dad's help.[10] Third, the pundits were predicting that the upcoming presidential race would be so close that even the five electoral votes of New Mexico could be crucial.

Pete says I just called the dead president an idiot and maybe I should rethink that statement, given my legal predicament. So for all of you federal prosecutors out there, I do not think the recently deceased president was an idiot (at least not a total idiot) and I did not conspire to kill him. President Carrier was a fine man and I am very sorry he was killed. I liked the man. He was always very nice to me. He just did not have a lick of business sense. End of story.

Shiva on a crutch! Pete says there are some guys outside who look like feds. Pete says maybe it wasn't such a good idea to register under the names of Elvis Presley and Colonel Tom Parker, because the FBI can track stuff like that and might get suspicious. I didn't think anybody remembered the King

---

10 The phrase "blue-eyed knucklehead" is unclear. President Carrier had brown eyes.

any more—the teenage desk clerk with the bad acne did not bat an eye when we registered.[11]

So, I'm gonna have to close for now. The truth about what happened to the president and vice president will have to come in a later installment, if I live long enough to write one.

Pete has gone outside to get the Caddie. Can't tell if this is good luck or bad luck. Bad luck if they have actually tracked us here, good luck if this means we get to leave Caliente. Dad used to say, "Junior, luck is for losers. A real man controls his own destiny. You just need a plan. If you don't have a plan, you won't prosper." Of course, Dad is dead now—blown to smithereens along with the president and the vice president. Somehow I don't think that was part of Dad's plan.[12]

Day 15

We are no longer in Caliente. I'm not totally sure those guys at the motel were feds—they may have just been Jehovah's Witnesses. In any event, we blew out of town and nobody followed us, as far as we can tell. We are now driving on a red, rock-strewn dirt road in the Assassin's Caddie. I have decided that I really love this car, even though Pete says Americans should not drive cars made in China because it hurts the American auto workers. I told Pete I wish I could just say I like something without worrying about the political or economic ramifications.

So that is exactly what I am going to do. I mean, I'm wanted for mass murder and will probably be dead in a few weeks anyway. Who could I possibly offend at this point? So, herein are four things I really like. "Herein" makes it sound kind of official, don't you think?

---

11 Junior's comment regarding Elvis Presley is confusing because Elvis Presley worshippers were prominent and active during this time period. It is unclear whether Day 13's reference to Elvis is intended to be a criticism of Elvis worship. A commentary on *Junior* written by the High Priest of the Elvis Temple in Nashville, Tennessee, construes the Day 13 reference to Elvis as "the King" as an implied acknowledgment of Elvis's deity.

12 The Day 13 reference to luck is significant because the number thirteen was considered by the Chiricahua Apaches to be a lucky number. In fact, Chiricahua children born on the thirteenth day of the month were often honored as prophets. Both Joshua Jennings, Sr., and Joshua Jennings, Jr., were born on the thirteenth day of the month.

First, I really like french fries. I know the health food gestapo wants to ban french fries because they clog your arteries, but I don't care. Eating french fries is really good.

Second, I really like driving fast. I know driving fast wastes gasoline and causes wrecks, but I don't care. Driving fast is really good.

Third, I really like drinking carbonated soft drinks. Dr. Pepper is my favorite. I know that Dr. Pepper had to pay millions of dollars to the government because it was illegally targeting children under the age of six with its advertisements and that the surgeon general has found that Dr. Pepper is addictive and could cause genital warts, but I don't care. Drinking Dr. Pepper is really good.

Fourth, I really like making fun of fat people. I know it is cruel and violates several federal statutes, but I don't care. Making fun of fat people is really good.

OK. I feel better now. Pete says he likes driving fast in a badass black Caddie while eating french fries, drinking Dr. Pepper, and yelling at the fat people he passes. I concur. We are going to push the Caddie significantly over the speed limit until we find a burger joint, while screaming at all the chubsters we pass along the way.[13]

Day 26

Although the president, the vice president, the governor of New Mexico, my dad, and about 1,500 other people were blown up recently, the world has moved on. The National Football League resumed its schedule, according to its television commercials, "to bring the country back to normalcy." This means that Pete's fantasy football league is back in full swing. Today, we both decided Pete could check the fantasy league website to see how his team was doing. The team was registered under an alias and we figured nobody could link us up via the website.

---

13 The Four Really Good Things Declaration has been the subject of great debate. Although many of Junior's followers eat french fries, drive Cadillacs, and drink Dr. Pepper, most eschew ridiculing "fat people," believing that Junior was joking about criticizing the calorically challenged. There are factions of Junior's followers in Montana, however, who engage in the organized practice of heckling individuals with Enhanced Caloric Intake Syndrome.

Pete checked the website from the laptop computer in our hotel room in South Jordan City, Utah. I have never heard of South Jordan before today. Pete decided we should stay here and I did not feel like arguing.

I was tired and decided to take a nap while Pete reviewed his team's progress, made trades, and did whatever else fantasy football goofs do. Just as I was about to nod off, Pete said in a soft voice, "Big Man, I think you should see this." I recognized Pete's tone and knew it was not good. But how bad could a fantasy football website be?

I crossed the hotel room, sat down in front of the computer, and saw a picture of my dad. He was smiling and looked very happy. Beneath the picture was a caption that read: "Pete, wake Junior up from his nap and tell him to hit the play button. You should probably listen as well."

I looked at Pete, who said, "This was attached to an e-mail sent to my fantasy team website. I have no idea how he knew this was my team. I also have no idea how he knew you were taking a nap."

Not knowing what else to do, I hit the play button. My father's exuberant voice boomed over the computer speakers:

Junior! How's it hanging, young man? If you are listening to this, that means I am dead and you are alive, which is of course exactly how I planned it. Yes, I knew the explosion was going to happen, and I made sure you and Pete were out of town when it did. I also had the Assassin in reserve in case you and Pete needed help. I assume by now the Assassin has given you a computer, access to cash, and some wheels. I hope he gave you the Caddie—I am not all that fond of the Chinese, but dadgummit, they make a good car. The Assassin is also the person who sent this e-mail to Pete's fantasy team website.

By the way, Pete, grown men don't mess around with this fantasy league stuff—it's for teenage boys who are still trying to get a girl into the backseat of their daddy's car. Having said that, I need you to keep checking this website because I will be sending future communications. Don't ask how, just trust that I can do it.

Junior, first let me say that I am sorry about what happened. Second, I am sorry everyone is blaming you. Unfortunately, things are gonna get worse before they get better. But you have Jennings blood

running through your veins, boy, and I know you can handle whatever
happens. You are my only son and I love you very much. I am . . .

The voice paused and seemed to tremble for a moment.

I am incredibly proud of you. Don't ever forget that. I will be in
touch with more details later on about what is likely to happen. Oh,
and it's time to ditch the Cincinnati Reds cap. Tell Pete that in the gift
store downstairs there should be a Seattle Seahawks cap. Wear that
one for a while.[14]

The screen then went dead. Pete tried to replay the message but somehow
the e-mail deleted itself.

Then I cried.[15]

Day 28

Pete says I need to calm down, and he's probably right. I think the pressure
of being a fugitive is getting to me.

The whole episode started innocently enough. We were leaving South Jordan and I saw this huge white church. In front of the church was a beautiful
garden, next to a circular fountain spraying water ten feet into the air. I told
Pete to stop because I wanted to go inside the cathedral. I'm not much of a
church guy, but what the heck? It couldn't hurt, right?

My plan was just to go inside the church, incognito, for a few minutes and
sit in silence and see if anything happened. I don't know what I expected to

---

14 Numerous scholarly articles have been written on the significance, or lack of same,
regarding the caps identified in *Junior*. A comprehensive analysis of this scholarship is
located in *Hats Off to Junior!* by Susan Staber.

15 The Day 26 entry, with its combination of strong familial emotion and foreshadowing,
is one of the most famous passages in twenty-first-century American literature. The fact
that Jennings, Sr., appeared to Jennings, Jr., on the twenty-sixth day (26 being a multiple of
the lucky number 13) is seen by many Chiricahua Apaches as confirmation that both men
were prophets.

happen. I just wanted some peace of mind, if only for a few minutes, and I thought sitting in a big white church might help. I mean, is that so much to ask?

Well, it turns out this church is the LDS Jordan River Temple. Pete told me the LDS stands for Latter-Day Saints, the Mormon guys who have lots of wives. I had a vague recollection of the Mormons from one of my college history courses, but not much more.

Much to my surprise, I learned that this beautiful temple is not open to non-LDS people like me and Pete. The guard on duty told me that only LDS members who are performing "sacred ordinances" could go inside. I told the guard I just wanted to sit inside and contemplate for a few minutes, but he said no. I then asked the guard a few questions (Pete says I asked a number of questions and I was rude) and the guard asked us to leave.

So, to the guard on duty at the LDS Jordan River Temple, I apologize.[16] If you ever read this book, I'm sorry I referred to angel Moroni[17] as "Angel Moron" and I'm also sorry about the crude comments regarding a different wife for every night of the week. I was not exactly Mr. Nice Guy. That was totally inappropriate.

Pete and I had a lengthy debate over the pros and cons of multiple wives as we drove away from the LDS temple. To be honest, we got a little crude, so I won't repeat our discussion here. I think Pete started the conversation primarily to calm me down.

The sad fact is that in all likelihood I will never have even one wife. In the back of my mind I had always assumed I would find a nice girl, marry, and have a couple of kids, like normal people do. Looks like that will never happen now. And it's all because of my dad. Bummer.

On the bright side, two more days and I will have survived for a whole month. Stay tuned, sports fans.

---

16 Three different men have claimed to be the LDS Jordan River Temple guard who spoke to Junior. All three wrote books documenting their encounter with Junior. One, John Mark Hicks, was later elected governor of Utah.

17 The Latter-Day Saints believe the angel Moroni provided Joseph Smith with golden plates that were the source material for the Book of Mormon.

Day 31

Well, we've made it a month now. Not bad, when you consider it's me and Pete against the world.

After my unpleasant encounter at the LDS Temple, we left Utah and drove east. Pete was concerned that the guard at the temple would call the police to file a complaint. We didn't need to add the Mormon Police to our enemy list. Today we are somewhere in Colorado.

During the drive to Colorado, I checked out the various news channels on the satellite television. No Mormon Police alerts, which was good. However, I was really surprised to see what everyone was saying about me. It would take too long to list everything, so I will just hit the highlights.

The Starbucks News Channel says that Joshua Jennings, Sr., might not really be my father. Apparently the computer records at the courthouse in Dallas were accidentally erased two days after the explosion in New Mexico and there is no record of my birth certificate. Since my mom is dead, she can't refute this allegation. The America First Channel says that since I can't prove I was born in Dallas, I am not really an American citizen. Therefore, I can't hold public office. Somehow I think my qualifications for public office are not all that important at this point.

The Dallas Cowboys News Channel, citing unnamed sources in Texas, reports that I was hospitalized numerous times for alcohol and drug problems. The Gay and Lesbian News Channel states that it is a matter of common knowledge that I am "queer" (their word, not mine). Finally, the Baptist News Channel says that I am the Antichrist and that the world is ending soon.

Pete says I should refute all of this stuff for the record. I don't know what good it will do, since I fully expect to be dead soon, but here goes.

First, I suppose I can't absolutely prove that Joshua Jennings, Sr., is my dad. Frankly, at this point I wish he wasn't. All I can tell you is that I grew up in his house and he was married to my mom. Before everybody got blown up, nobody questioned who my father was.

On the drug and alcohol issue, I have been known to drink and get drunk, particularly at frat parties when I was in college. I also smoked some weed and chewed some Apache high-grade peyote, even before it was strictly legal to do so. But I have never been in a rehab center. Check the records at the

Laura Bush/Jerry Jones Rehabilitation Center in Dallas, which is where all the rich Texas kids go to dry out. My name will not be on the patient list.

I think the allegation that hurts the most is the gay deal. I know it sounds weird that I am angered more about being called a homosexual than being called a mass murderer, but it's true.

I realize I am offending everyone who lives in the Queer Cities of Refuge, but at this point I really don't care. Why would you care what a mass murderer thinks anyway? So everybody pay attention: I AM NOT GAY. When I am dead, and this book gets read by the public, please note: "I like girls!"[18] Pete is laughing about this as I write it. He would not be laughing so hard if the news anchors on television were calling him a "queer," I guarantee it.[19]

Frankly, I think the Antichrist thing is kinda funny. First of all, let me say that I like most Baptists. You can't grow up in Texas without meeting Baptists. Like my dad used to say, "You can't swing a wet dog in Texas without hitting a Baptist." But do we really need a Baptist News Channel? I mean, come on! Does every news story need to be interpreted as though it has a direct and immediate impact on the end of the world? And why are Baptists so hung up on the end of the world? Most of the Baptists I know drive nice cars and have nice houses. Why are they so obsessed with seeing all of their stuff consumed by fire?

As far as being the Antichrist, I don't see how it could be me. My vague understanding of the whole Antichrist scenario is that the Antichrist is a guy with some sort of complicated plan to do something really horrible that leads to the end of the world. Trust me, I don't have a plan. Never had one, in fact, which I think always kind of aggravated my dad. I'm just a guy with a history degree whose only job has been to take orders from, and do menial jobs for, his famous father.

So listen up, Baptists. It ain't me. I may be the Antiambition, or the Antiworkaholic, but I am definitely not the Antichrist. That would take way too much effort.

---

18 Some scholars refer to this paragraph as the Day 31 Denunciation of Homosexuality. Some gay and lesbian commentators, however, see Junior's vociferously negative reference to homosexuality as proof that Junior was gay. See *Junior: He Doth Protest Too Much* by Andi Bailey.

19 Some scholars have opined that Pete and Junior were lovers.

Day 39

I didn't think it was possible, but things are starting to get even weirder. People are holding memorial services for Senior all over the country. Not the president or vice president, but Dad. Random places like Minneapolis, Minnesota, and Lawton, Oklahoma. Statues are being erected. There's even a story on the Internet that some rich guy is building a Senior temple.

I figured Dad would be hailed as "a great American who died too early," etc., but this hero-worship stuff is getting out of hand. Pete says that to balance things out I should give you a little inside skinny on Senior. (Pete won't admit it, but I think he's still a little ticked off at Dad for his criticism of Pete's fantasy football league fetish.) So, herewith a few words about Senior, from Junior.

Senior was always working, and if the e-mail we got in Utah is any indication, he is still working to this very day, apparently from the grave. The companies Senior founded created jobs for thousands of people. The flip side of that is that Senior was never home. Mom pretty much raised me by herself.

Senior was incredibly successful. His companies made billions of dollars. The flip side of that is that Senior was very arrogant. He was always right. He was a "my way or the highway" kind of boss. Senior fired a bunch of talented people whose only sin was to disagree with him.

Senior was very generous to those who were loyal to him. He gave huge bonuses to employees who performed well. The flip side of that is that Senior was also very suspicious of everyone who worked for him. He was always worried that a competitor was bribing his employees to divulge corporate secrets.

I could say a lot more about Senior (and I will if I live long enough), but looking at what I have just written it occurs to me that Senior was probably like a lot of successful people. The traits that made him successful also made him difficult to get along with at times. So, I am not saying Senior was a bad guy or a bad father. I am simply saying he was no saint, and I don't understand why everyone is making such a big fuss about him now that he is dead. Note to self—at some point, mention what Senior did with the oil.[20]

But to be clear, my father is not to blame for my lack of accomplishments. That is my own dadgummed fault.

---

20 This is the first of seven "note to self" statements in *Junior*.

Boy, this segment took an ugly turn, didn't it? Pete says there's booze and ice in the microblender, so I'm done here. Time to get wasted and hope tomorrow is a better day. Adios.

Day 42

I have never liked cold weather—but Pete and I are discovering that hiding out in a ski town is actually pretty easy. Since my last installment, we have been hunkered down in one of those cutesy Colorado ski villages. The great thing about this place is that nobody thinks you're crazy if you walk around dressed like the abominable snowman. I can wear a parka and a ski mask and nobody thinks that's strange.

Which is a good thing, because now my face is everywhere. Somebody in charge decided that running my picture on television every hour was not good enough, so they have printed Wanted posters. That's right, just like in the Old West. I fully expect to see Miss Kitty and Marshal Dillon pass me on the street any minute now. The Wanted posters are everywhere. Kinda strange seeing your face on a Wanted poster in Starbucks.

The other nice thing about hanging out in ski country is that a number of folks are more concerned with black-diamond runs, girls, and booze than current events. They either don't know or don't care that a nationwide manhunt is being conducted for the murderer of the leader of the free world. This afternoon, I swear to Zeus, Pete and I heard the following conversation as we waited in line for the ski lift:

First guy: Dude, let's do Devil's Razor one more time and then go to Skeeter's for some brewskies. I feel like blowing it out tonight.

Second guy: Sweet. Maybe do some cougar hunting.[21]

First guy: For sure. And if we don't bag any cougars, let's check out that new Wanted *movie.*

Second guy: Dude, those posters are awesome. I hear the movie rocks.

21 This reference is unclear. Virtually every species of cougar in North America was extinct when *Junior* was written.

Gotta love the Rocky Mountain way. Time to throw another log on the fire and watch the snow fall.

Day 45

Since I have mostly whined and complained (but really, who could blame me?), I have decided to write today while I am mellow and happy. Pete drove down to Denver to the Western Regional Drug Center and bought some Bill Clinton Gold, and we have spent the afternoon sitting on the balcony toking, listening to Jimi Hendrix and Rolling Stones tunes, and watching the snowboarders wipe out. A true Rocky Mountain high. Even if the feds catch me tomorrow, at least I had one really good day on the lam before it all went south.

Since I am in a chemically enhanced state, this is a good day to let you in on a little secret about our drug laws. I bet you don't know the backstory on how my dad figured out how to convince the politicians to legalize marijuana and Apache high-grade peyote. Well, sit back, dear reader, and learn how Senior made your purple haze possible.

Some of you may remember the bad old days, when all drugs were illegal and criminals all over the globe made trillions of untaxed dollars selling drugs. Whenever a politician suggested it made sense to legalize and tax dope, the church folks all went biblically postal, and the politician was promptly unelected. Now Senior was no fan of "worthless, shiftless potheads," as he called them, but he was a fiscal conservative who realized that if the government regulated and taxed certain recreational drugs, the tax revenue would be enormous, and the country could also stop spending billions of tax dollars losing the war on drugs.

Senior, like all rich guys, hated paying taxes. He figured if the government got billions in taxes from dope sales, he could keep more of his hard-earned money. Senior also knew that if he could get Apache high-grade peyote legalized for public use, the Apaches would rake in the dough. And Senior loved the Apaches. At some point I will explain Senior's connection with the Apaches.

Anyway, as I was saying, Senior had a vested interest in getting certain drugs legalized. So, he put his considerable influence and money to work and hammered out a deal that, as far as I know, has never been fully reported in the media.

Senior's strategy was brilliant. First, he convinced the right politicians he would back them financially if they pushed for legalization. Second, he brokered a deal with the church folks by making them an offer they couldn't refuse—manna from Washington. Senior got the politicians to promise the biggest religious shepherds that if they refrained from mobilizing their flocks against the legislation, a percentage of the drug taxes would be divvied up and distributed to them under the guise of antipoverty programs. The mainline denominations' objections to the law disappeared faster than you can say "render unto Caesar." The United States Department of Charity was established, and as you know, it distributes billions of dollars per year to charitable programs run by churches.

I know about this because I was Senior's assistant (which means I got him coffee and carried his briefcase) during the negotiations with the church leaders. And I can tell you, the biggest hurdle was not legalizing the dope. That issue was quickly resolved. The most intense discussions centered on the percentage of the tax revenue the churches would receive, and which priests, rabbis, pastors, mullahs, and preachers would be appointed to the Department of Charity.

Senior used the churches' greed to get the deal done, but he did not want the religious heavyweights to be appointed to the Department of Charity because he knew they would abuse the power. So, in a Solomonic stroke of genius, he required all potential appointees to submit to an FBI background check and both a personal and congregational/parish/mosque/temple audit by the Internal Revenue Service. And that is why the Department of Charity is run by do-gooders you have never heard of.

I remember asking Senior if the law diverting the drug revenue to the churches would be challenged by the liberals because it muddied the line between church and state. He told me: "Junior, who do you think works for the ACLU? Worthless, shiftless potheads! Those dope-smoking lawyers will leave this law alone, I promise you." And he was right.

That's all for today, boys and girls. It's time to kiss the sky.

Day 47

Pete and I stayed inside all day today. A blizzard blew in, so we sat in front of the fireplace and watched a Sylvester Stallone marathon on the Diet Channel. Watching the commercials was almost as much fun as watching the movies.

I'm fairly certain that the same fat, hairy, ugly guy appeared as the "Before" picture in the Five-Day Artichoke Diet commercial, the Prune Juice and Avocado Diet commercial, and the Coffee Lovers' Diet commercial. I don't think he appeared as the "After" picture in any of the commercials, so I guess he makes his living being hairy, ugly, and fat. Nice niche. Probably makes more money than I will ever make with my history degree.

While Pete and I were discussing whether *Rocky IX: The Final Chapter* or *Rocky X: Resurrection* was better, a Diet Channel News Alert interrupted our viewing of *Rocky XI: The Second Coming*. At first we didn't pay much attention, because the previous alerts had all concerned the daily weight loss reported by celebrities on one of the promoted diets.

However, when I saw a familiar face on the screen, I told Pete we needed to watch the alert. A clipped female voice with a slightly Hispanic accent spoke:

Sources tell the Diet Channel that former Heisman Trophy[22] winner and current NFL star Henry the Hammer Jefferson will seek to replace deceased President Carrier as the Republican nominee for president. Jefferson, the 525-pound nose tackle for the Dallas Cowboys, has no previous political experience, but stated: "I get kicked, tripped, and illegally chop blocked every week. I have many needless bruises. My job's a lot harder job than sitting in a chair and talking to some dude from Iceland. Politics should be a piece of cake for me. By the way, you got any cake? I'm kind of hungry."

Intrigued, Pete and I quickly switched to the Dallas Cowboys News Channel and watched Ryan Bigelow, the Cowboys' head coach, discuss Jefferson's announcement:

I cannot comment on the suggestion that the Hammer's announcement concerning the presidency is a negotiation tactic. Although the Hammer is in the final year of his contract, he makes

---

22 When *Junior* was written, the Heisman Trophy was awarded by the New York Athletic Club to the most outstanding college football player. This award is now known as the Hamburger Helper Lite Heisman Trophy Presented by General Mills.

approximately fifteen times more money than the president makes.
Threatening to run for president is not likely to make us increase our
offer to him.

I have been so absorbed in my own troubles that I completely neglected
to consider the political ramifications of the New Mexico explosion. The
Republican convention is coming up soon. Who will the Republicans nominate for president? Probably not the Hammer, since I know for a fact that
when he was drafted by the Cowboys out of Stonewall Jackson Mississippi
Valley Technical Vocational Trade School Junior College, the Hammer had
the reading skills of a fourth-grader.

I know about the Hammer's limited reading skills because my dad once
asked the Hammer to make a public appearance at the Chiricahua reservation. Ironically, the Apaches love the Dallas Cowboys. (Dr. Hoover, is that
really irony?)

Anyway, the Hammer's agent, Eric Osterloh, told me about the Hammer's
reading issues because I had arranged for the Hammer to do a photo op reading to kids in the reservation's elementary school. To avoid any embarrass-
ment, the Hammer brought a children's book he knew he could read when
he visited the reservation.

The Hammer's sudden interest in the presidency is further proof that my
dad is still pulling the strings. I wonder what Senior promised the Hammer
in return for making his announcement today.

Day 58

Well, we are no longer safely hiding in plain sight in an expensive, funky ski
town smoking Clinton Gold joints. It's all my fault. Pete is cursing me under
his breath as he drives the Assassin's Caddie east on I-70 toward Kansas. He
really wanted to stay in the mountains a little longer. Actually, I think he
would have been fine staying there forever.

It started out innocently enough. Last night Pete wanted to stay in the
condo and watch the Almonds play the Cowboys on Wednesday Night Football. I needed some fresh air, so I convinced Pete it would be OK if I went
across the street to a bar. Actually, as Pete is pointing out quite vociferously,
I told Pete I was thirsty and just going down the hall to get a Dr. Pepper out

of the vending machine. What happened is that the vending machine was broken, so I decided to get a beer instead.

The bar was called Samara. Apparently the famous architect Frank Lloyd Wright built a house in West Lafayette, Indiana, that was called Samara. I don't know why anyone would name a house Samara. I also don't know why anyone would name a bar after a house in Indiana, but that was the name of the bar.

Samara was crowded, which I thought at the time was a good thing. Two people left a small booth in the back as I arrived and so I quickly moved forward and took their spot. As I was sitting down, I heard a female voice say with irritation, "Are you taking my booth, white boy?" I turned around and saw one of the most beautiful women in the world smiling at me. No joke. She was a stunner. Beauty queen, supermodel, actress-type good looks. I knew this was trouble on several levels, so I mumbled something like, "No problem, I will find another chair," and started to leave.

The no-joke beauty queen took my arm rather forcefully, pushed me into the booth, and squeezed in next to me. She was practically in my lap. "On second thought, sugar," she said, "if you let me share this booth with you, I'll buy you a drink."

I tried to nicely tell her no, but she responded, still with the movie-star smile on her face: "What's the matter, white boy? Don't want to drink with a sister?"

Well, that comment ticked me off, so I forgot that she was beautiful and that I was supposed to be traveling incognito. Stupidly, I said, "First of all, I'm half Apache Indian, so cut the white crap. Second, I'm not a boy. You don't know anything about me, and I think we should keep it that way. I don't know whether you are a hooker, or just a drunk girl in heat. Either way, I'm not interested. Let me out of the booth, and I'm sure you can find another customer in no time."

The last comment was cold, I know, but my intent was to make her just mad enough so I could leave.

Instead, she started to cry. So I had to be nice. Looking back, I should have just walked away and let her cry by herself. I had no business staying in that bar. That last sentence sounds like a line from a country song, doesn't it? Anyway, I digress.

The beautiful, teary-eyed girl then proceeded to tell me her life story, in long and excruciating detail. Her name was Veronica Wells, and she was a television reporter who had come to Colorado for a vacation. Veronica was depressed because she was sleeping with her married boss, who had been promising her for over a year that he was getting a divorce. Veronica's fellow employees did not like her because they thought she was sleeping her way to the top, which, she admitted, she was.

People say way too much when they are drunk.

We spent about two hours sitting in the booth. I mostly listened and tried to say soothing things to make her feel better. Like: "Veronica, I know you are frightened and feel isolated, but you need to have hope and pursue your dreams. If you can break out of this trap you've created, the sky is the limit."

I told her my name was Bruce and I was an ironworker. I was in this snowy paradise because my buddy Wayne's uncle had some business connections and got us a free week in a condo. Veronica nodded like she was paying attention, but the words did not appear to penetrate the fog of booze, guilt, and depression that engulfed her brain.

When the conversation lagged (meaning she stopped talking a mile a minute), Pete appeared at my table. Although on the surface he was pleasant, I could tell he was wondering why I was risking both of our lives by talking to the lovely Ms. Wells. He also looked more than a little confused when I called him Wayne.

As I was leaving, Veronica gave me a hug and whispered in my ear. "You have been so nice to me. Nobody has ever listened to me like that before. Be careful, Joshua."

Damn Wanted posters.

To her credit, Veronica waited until around noon today to broadcast her live, exclusive report. I have watched it on the satellite television in the Caddie several times now. Here is what she said:

My name is Veronica Wells. I am speaking to you from the mountains of Colorado, where so many people come to worship the snow and escape from the drudgery of everyday life. Last night I talked to Joshua Jennings, Jr., who is the subject of a worldwide manhunt. I was brokenhearted over some deeply personal issues and Joshua listened to me. He helped me in my time of trouble with words of incomparable and melodic wisdom. In the depth of my darkness, he was a light. Today I awoke to the chorus of a symphony, and I know there is an answer to all of my questions. Joshua supplied that answer.

I can't believe the man I spoke to last night is a criminal. He spoke the truth to me and lifted my spirits. So please, let him be. Just let him be.

To be honest, I can't decide if I'm mad at Ms. Wells or not. It's hard to be angry with someone who clearly does not yet know what she wants in life and who is struggling to figure out what is important and what is not. Plus, who wouldn't take advantage of a chance encounter with a wanted man to enhance their career?

Pete, who has no problem being angry with Ms. Wells, says we need to stop and get some pizza. We have been on the road since last night, driving hard. Not far ahead is Goodland, Kansas, which, according to my research on the satellite computer, is the Golden Buckle on the Wheat Belt. I didn't even know there was a Wheat Belt. The things you learn being a fugitive from justice.

Pete is angry, so I tell him pizza is fine, even though I am not hungry. I don't want to make him even angrier. He might just leave me in the Golden Buckle.[23]

Day 59

Yesterday, Pete and I stayed in some nondescript motel that I'm pretty sure I saw in one of those horror movies where the teenagers' car breaks down and they have to stay in a motel in the middle of nowhere that houses demons or ghosts or a mass murderer wielding a chain saw. We stayed inside and ate candy bars and drank soft drinks from the vending machine located just outside our door. Pete read a fantasy football magazine. I sat in a stiff green chair covered with who knows what kind of stains and pondered the meaning of my life. I concluded that my life sucks, but not for the reason you might think.

Strange as it sounds, I concluded that having no safe or comfortable place to lay my head, and being chased by every law enforcement agency in the world, has a positive aspect. Now I have something to do, a reason to act. Before the explosion, I just reacted to what Senior or others wanted me to do.

---

23 The Samara Bar in Keystone, Colorado, is now a museum. The booth that Junior and Veronica Wells sat in is now enclosed in a glass case. Before the booth was shielded by protective glass, pieces of the booth were removed and sold to collectors. Remnants from the Booth of Revelation, as it is now known, can be found in museums and religious institutions all over the world.

It's actually kind of exciting to think I am matching wits with the feds and, at least up to now, having some success. I'm sure it will remain exciting up to and including the moment they break down the door and arrest or shoot me.

The sucky part is that I don't know why all this is happening, other than that my father has decided it is important to manipulate my life from beyond the grave. What could possibly be the purpose of all this? Why would my father set me up to be hated by an entire nation and the subject of a world-wide manhunt? I am guessing I may be the only son in history who has ever asked that question.

Pete and I left the motel this morning while it was still dark. Around noon we left the highway and drove the back roads. As we drove through some small town in the middle of nowhere, we decided to live it up and get some ice cream at the local Dairy Queen. I pulled my Utah Jazz baseball cap down low over my head and Pete eased the Caddie up to the drive-through window. I looked away as Pete gave our order. Then Pete whispered that I should turn around. My Wanted poster was taped on the window. At the bottom of the poster the following words were written in a childish scrawl: LET HIM BE.

Well, well, well.

Day 61

OK, then. We are now into month three. And today was a good day.

Believe it or not, Pete and I just left Tom Osborne Memorial Stadium in Lincoln, Nebraska. We, along with 100,000 or so other folks, watched the University of Nebraska Cornhuskers football team defeat United Presbyterian 58–0.

After the Dairy Queen incident, we started driving north and decided to stop in Lincoln. Pete has always been a big Nebraska fan, so we hung out until Saturday so we could go to the game. Before the game, we bought red T-shirts and those strange yellow corn-head hats that cover your face, so we were practically invisible in the crowd.

I knew United Presbyterian had a good team last year, finishing first in the East Jesus Division of the JIL,[24] so I was surprised the Cornhuskers beat them

---

24 The Jesus Is Lord League (JIL) is now known as the Jesus Is Lord and Savior League (JILAS).

so easily. Pete says a bunch of UP's best players went on missionary trips this year and were unavailable to play. I did not even know Presbyterians did mission trips.[25]

Pete also says Nebraska should not have played its scrubs in the fourth quarter because Nebraska needed an even more lopsided victory to improve its position in the polls and increase its chances of playing in the national championship game.[26]

As I write this, Pete and I are in the Caddie. We have been stuck in a post-game traffic jam for several hours now. Pete says I should keep my corn head on, so nobody will recognize me. I hope I don't get arrested today. I don't want the world to see me handcuffed while wearing a corn head.

Day 63

This "Let Him Be" deal may be getting out of hand. There have been "Let Him Be" rallies in Boulder, Colorado, and San Antonio, Texas. The governor of Texas called out the Texas National Guard to break up the demonstration in the Alamo City.

A television talk show host is marketing a yellow ribbon in the shape of a bee. Veronica Wells has filed a lawsuit in federal court against the guy, claiming that the ribbon violates her intellectual property rights.

On a deserted highway, east of Omaha, Pete and I drove by a bunch of hand-painted LET HIM BE signs. We even saw a billboard with nothing but a huge yellow bee on it.

Pete says maybe the bee stuff will sway public opinion and give us a chance for survival if the authorities catch us. I have my doubts, although I confess

---

25 Junior's alleged ignorance regarding the football players' absence has been called into question by numerous scholars. It is now well established that Senior, working with United States intelligence services, recruited football players from the JIL as "religious freedom fighters" who ran deep-cover intelligence and special operations in Muslim countries. Many scholars believe Junior, who helped his father on many projects, likely assisted his father in recruiting these players.

26 The college football championship is now decided by a playoff system, so polls are no longer an integral part of college football. The change to a playoff system was mandated by Congress after thousands were killed in the Playoff Riots, which took place three years after *Junior* was published.

it feels good to believe, even for just a few minutes, that not everybody in the world hates us.

But really, why have people jumped on the bee bandwagon? How could any rational person believe I was innocent, based solely on Veronica's report? Are people really that foolish?

Pete says all belief has a subjective irrational component. Pete is a much deeper thinker than I am. I will have to ponder his theory awhile before I can decide whether he is right.

Day 70

For what it's worth, I am no longer the only suspect in the New Mexico explosion. Veronica Wells reported today on the Plastic Surgery Network that The Bad Jews had claimed responsibility for the explosion. Veronica stated:

> *Today, I received a communication from Ehud Rabinowitz, president of an organization called The Bad Jews. Mr. Rabinowitz told me the following, and I quote: "President Carrier and his anti-Semitic Philistine henchman Joshua Jennings, Sr., have been executed for their crimes against Israel and the Jewish people. We will never forget what these two men did to us. We will also never forgive."*

After Pete and I watched the report in our hotel room in Estherville, Iowa, Pete said, "Veronica looks good. And she's gone national."

It was true. Veronica's chance meeting with me in Colorado had transformed her into a national television star. Pete read somewhere that Veronica had signed a long-term contract with the Plastic Surgery Network for big bucks.

I seriously doubt that The Bad Jews blew Dad up, but I am fine with its acceptance of responsibility. Maybe some of the heat on Pete and me will fade a bit.

Although The Bad Jews are front-page headlines now, I have known about them for a while. It's kind of a long story, but I've got time on my hands, so here goes.

Dad was the guy who convinced President Carrier to offer the state of North Dakota as a place of refuge to the Jews in Israel. From Senior's perspective, it made perfect sense. Hardly anybody lives in North Dakota anyway, and the Jews were crammed together in a small country surrounded by Muslims who wanted to slaughter them. Why not move the Jews to North Dakota, where they could spread out and be safe, and where they weren't surrounded by angry, homicidal Muslims?

Since he was not an elected official, and since he did not care what anybody said about him, Dad was the guy who traveled to Jerusalem to talk to the prime minister of Israel about his idea. At the time Dad went to Israel, both Iraq and Iran were governed by hard-core, fanatic religious leaders who publicly threatened virtually every day to blow up Israel. Israel was on a continuous twenty-four-hour alert status.

The prime minister confided to my father that it was just a matter of time before the Muslims blew up his country. He knew the best Israel could hope to do was to send off retaliatory rockets to blow Iraq and Iran to smithereens as well.

According to Senior, the prime minister told him, "You are a rich, bigoted goy, but at least you are honest. I appreciate honesty. I know many of my people want to leave, especially those with small children. But why North Dakota? Why not someplace warm, like Miami?"

Dad explained that Florida could not easily absorb all the Israelites, but that there was plenty of room in North Dakota. Dad told the prime minister, "I can't give you Florida. Too many rich people there with powerful political connections. But North Dakota works perfectly. Nobody cares about it. You guys can just take over the whole state and run it like your own country."

Senior knew that President Carrier could not propose the resettlement plan, because that would have been political suicide. So when the prime minister told Senior that he would accept the offer of North Dakota, President Carrier asked the prime minister to come to America and publicly request North Dakota as a safe haven for his people. That put Israel's supporters in the United States in a pickle. Who were they to tell the prime minister of Israel that this was a bad idea?

Over 95 percent of Israel's population ended up moving to North Dakota. The rest were wiped out six weeks later by a combined force of troops from Iraq and Iran in the Forty-Five-Minute War. Jerusalem was destroyed by an atomic bomb, which was detonated by the remaining Israeli soldiers in

Jerusalem as the Muslim armies entered the city. Hundreds of thousands of Iraqi and Iranian soldiers were killed by the explosion. The nuclear fallout made the entire country of Israel virtually uninhabitable.

After the resettlement to North Dakota, and before the Forty-Five-Minute War, Dad was interviewed by the *Burger King New York Times* about the move. Dad was quoted as saying: "We just got the good Jews. The bad Jews stayed in Israel." Although Dad vehemently denied ever saying that, the phrase stuck and The Bad Jews was organized soon afterward. The group did not go public until today, but Dad received a number of death threats from the group.

I'm pretty sure the FBI has infiltrated The Bad Jews, which means the group probably did not blow everybody up. However, it's nice to be out of the spotlight, if only for a few moments.

Pete says he is bored and we should go watch the local high school basketball team tonight. Sounds like fun. Pete says Estherville High School's team nickname is the Midgets. Who would name their basketball team the Midgets? Kind of like naming your track team the Slowpokes. Anyway, we're off to the game.

Day 74

Pete and I are now on our way to North Dakota. And no, we have not decided to convert.

I realize that if anybody ever reads this book, memoir, travelogue, or whatever it turns out to be, there is probably some stuff that is going to be hard to believe. I say this because I'm the guy who is living it, and I'm having a difficult time absorbing it all myself.

So, for all of you skeptics out there, I feel your pain. I don't blame you if you think I'm crazy, or a liar, or a crazy liar. And if there is anybody out there who believes that the crazy things I'm writing are true, even though you have not seen them, bless you. I appreciate it.

The latest bizarre event happened after we watched the Estherville High School Midgets defeat the Cherokee High School Braves 59–58 in a double-overtime barn burner. We had a great time. To me, there are few smells sweeter than a high school gym during basketball season. The sweat, the popcorn, the body odor, the slightly burnt smell made by the overworked furnace—I love it.

Pete says I need to stop talking about body odor and move on. So here goes.

After Pete and I left the gym, we were too pumped up to go back to the Cozy Grove Motel, so we decided to walk around a bit. It was dark, so we figured there was not a huge risk we could be recognized.

We knew from reading the local paper that the Snow Globe Winter Festival was in full swing, so we headed to the town square. I have never seen so many snow globes in my life. We saw at least five hundred, ranging from mini snow globes you could hold on one finger to huge two-gallon-sized snow globes.

As you might expect, most of the snow globe exhibitors were older folks, who had the time and inclination to design and build the contraptions. Pete and I listened to a bunch of nice Estherville folks explain how they chose the theme for their snow globes. Most of the snow globes reflected the designer's love for either community or family. I believe I now know the names of every grandchild of every granny in Estherville.

The big surprise for Pete and me came when we reached the end of the exhibition. Three teenage girls sat cross-legged on the cold ground. Spread out on a ragged blanket in front of the girls were about fifty snow globes.

Each of the girls had dyed her hair a color probably not available at the local beauty shop. To make things easier for you, I will call them Blue, Pink, and Orange.

Blue did most of the talking. She explained that the "old farts" (her phrase, not mine) in charge of the festival did not appreciate their snow globes, so they got stuck at the very end of the exhibition. I noticed that many of the snow globes on the blanket contained curse words and rather disturbing images, so I was not surprised. I seriously doubted that the grandparents we had just visited with would have appreciated a snow globe that, when shaken, rained severed body parts.

Pink, who had a black thumbtack in her lower lip, flirted outrageously with Pete while I talked to Blue. The top four or five buttons on Pink's shirt were unbuttoned, and she kept bending over to pick up a snow globe, giving Pete a clear view inside her shirt. (As I write this, Pete is shaking his head, but I know what I saw. Pete's embarrassed grin says it all.)

As we were about to leave, Orange finally spoke up. In a contralto voice that probably kept every mother's teenaged son in Estherville from getting a good night's sleep, Orange said, "Would you like a peek at our best one?"

Pete and I looked at each other. I did not know what to expect. Pink had already given Pete numerous "peeks" and we definitely did not need to go any farther down that road.

While Pete and I were still trying to formulate a coherent response, Orange quickly reached into a scruffy black backpack, pulled out something wrapped in a dingy beach towel, and placed it in my hand. I immediately glanced around to see who was watching, certain that Pete and I were about to be arrested for engaging in some illegal transaction with these Lolitas. (Are you impressed with my literary reference, Dr. Hoover?)

When I unraveled the towel, I saw a snow globe with the words LET HIM BE floating inside. "Shake it," Orange said quietly in her throaty voice. When I did, small yellow bees rained everywhere.

When I looked up, all three girls were smiling at us. Blue walked up to me and spoke very softly. "You guys need to leave town. As in pronto. The old farts don't know who you are yet, but they will figure it out soon enough. We promise we will wait at least two days before we broadcast our report about seeing you. We have to come up with a news report for our television and film class anyway, so we are going to do it on you guys. We should get an A, don't you think?"

Pink walked up to Pete and asked if she could go with him. When Pete declined, she gave him a kiss on the cheek and handed him a snow globe. "I made this one especially for you," she said.

After we said our good-byes to the girls, we walked back to the Caddie. Pete shook the snow globe he'd received from Pink, let loose a few choice invectives, and then showed it to me. Inside the snow globe were the words: "Junior—Go immediately to New Jerusalem. Get rid of the Notre Dame hat. Pete—Stay away from underage girls."

Day 76

I am sitting in Temple Beth-El in New Jerusalem, North Dakota. I am the only person here, as far as I know. I have never been in a synagogue before.

I am typing this because, frankly, I'm a little scared and I don't know what else to do.

Pete is sitting in the Caddie in the parking lot with three really mean-looking guys who I am guessing are Israeli Mossad agents. I don't know what a Mossad agent is supposed to look like, but if I was casting a movie about Mossad agents, I would hire these guys.

Pete did not look happy when I left him in the car, but I was given no choice. I hope he is OK.

The Caddie was pulled over by a police car about ten minutes after we crossed the North Dakota border in a blizzard. Pete asked if I wanted to try to outrun the police, but I said no. I figured if Senior went to all the trouble to have three girls in Iowa with crazy hair make snow globes especially for us, he probably had our arrival in North Dakota under control.

Nevertheless, I am nervous. I hear footsteps and the door to the synagogue is opening. I better close. Hope this isn't the end.

Day 78

Pete and I are still alive—and not in jail. In fact, we are in the penthouse suite of the New Hotel King David, which, according to our Mossad guard Jehu, is a five-star hotel. I believe Jehu—this place is sweet. Plus, if you could see Jehu, you would agree with me that it is not a good idea to disagree with Jehu. He is one of those guys who could probably kill you with his pinkie.

I am not sure why we are here. The rabbi I met at Temple Beth-El was rather brusque. First, he told me to take off my "North Dakota Is for Jewish Lovers" cap. Then, he asked me if I was the gentile mass murderer Joshua Jennings, Jr. I considered disputing the mass murderer part, but I was really scared, so I just said, "Yes, sir. You are correct." The dude was small, but he was really intimidating, kind of like the bus driver on the school bus when I was in grade school.

The rabbi left without saying another word. I sat in the temple for another hour or so and then the Mossad guys brought Pete and me here to the hotel. We came in through some secret underground entrance, so I guess nobody else knows we are here.

I just finished meeting with the prime minister of Israel, which was a trip. When he walked in, he said, "Junior, your dad was one self-satisfied goy son of a bitch." When I didn't respond, he said, "I liked him, though. Sometimes it takes a son of a bitch to get the tough jobs done."

When I still didn't respond, he said with a wry smile, "You look like your dad, but you are not a son of a bitch, are you? Probably just as well."

The prime minister took off his wristwatch, put it on the coffee table sitting between us, and then spoke. "When your dad came to see me in Israel, he told me that Pharaoh's army was coming and that this time the Red Sea was not going to part. He told me it was time for an exodus to America. He also told me we could live in cities we had not built and drink from wells we had not dug. Do you know what he was talking about?"

I had only an inkling, so I guessed. "Prince of Egypt?"

The prime minister shook his head and continued. "Typical, I guess. Your father had read the book. You only know Hollywood's version.

"Junior, your father saved my people. As far as I'm concerned, Jehovah sent your father to save the Jews from the crazy Muslims. We are safe here—we have avoided rivers of tears and constant mourning and death. The old order of things for us has passed away. I owe your father a great debt that can never be repaid, which is why you are here in the penthouse and not in custody."

I told the prime minister I believed Senior wanted me to come to New Jerusalem, but I was not sure why, or what I was supposed to do. Since I did not want the prime minister to think I was insane, I did not mention the snow globe messages.

At that moment the wristwatch on the coffee table started to chirp like a bird. The prime minister picked up his watch and said, "Time's up, Junior. I enjoyed talking with you. I am supposed to give you this disk and tell you to put it in your computer."

The prime minister stood up and walked to the door. When he reached the door, the prime minister turned and looked at me. "Junior," he said, "I feel compelled to say something to you that probably makes no sense now, but may later. I can tell from our brief conversation, and from my research, that you are a good boy and have been a good son to your father."

I did not know what to say, so I just sat there and stared back at him.

The old man could not hold my stare. He looked down at his shoes, and then he looked back at me. He had tears in his eyes. He spoke in a soft voice, as if talking to himself. "Son, your innocence is evident for all to see. But I am afraid your guilt is overwhelming."[27]

Day 80

Have I mentioned yet that Pete's full name is Peter Running Horse and that he is a full-blooded Apache? Or that women (and now teenage girls) find him incredibly attractive? No? Well, I guess it's time I tell you a little about Pete, particularly since Pete is in the next room playing chess with Jehu and doesn't know what I am doing.

Pete and I have been best friends since we were toddlers. Our moms were also best friends, so we spent a lot of time together even though I lived in Dallas and Pete lived on the reservation. Private jets are wonderful things.

Pete has always been a lady-killer—he has that dark, soulful look that women can't resist. He is also blessed with unusual height for an Indian—he is just over six feet two inches tall—and he is muscular. In short (no pun intended, Dr. Hoover), he is everything I am not.

Now, thanks to Blue, Pink, and Orange, Pete is also famous as the dashingly handsome accomplice to Joshua Jennings, Jr., mass murderer. I just watched our teenage snow globe friends' interview on CNN. The snow globe girls mentioned me only in passing. Primarily, they talked about Pete and how handsome he is. Pink said several times that she wanted to have Pete's baby. The CNN reporter said there are multiple websites up showing pictures of Pete, and at least two Peter Running Horse fan clubs.

That's just great. The Gay and Lesbian Channel says I'm a "queer" (their word, not mine), and now Pete is famous as a teenage heartthrob.

Day 82

Well, it looks like our friend Veronica Wells may be in a bit of trouble. In all of her exclusive reports to date, she never mentioned Pete. Now that the snow globe girls have told the world about Pete, the FBI has taken Veronica into custody, accusing her of withholding information.

---

27 The prime minister's statement is referred to by scholars as the Day 78 Guilt Conundrum, the second of the Seven Conundrums found in *Junior*.

The Plastic Surgery Network, which signed Veronica to a long-term contract just a few days ago, terminated Veronica's employment and is running a film clip every thirty minutes showing Veronica's arrest.

The film clip ends with Veronica screaming at the camera: "How was I supposed to know he was with Junior? He was way too cute to be with Junior! I thought his name was Wayne!"

Sorry, Veronica.

Day 84

Thanks to Blue, Pink, Orange, and Veronica, the whole world considers me the ugly half of the world's most-wanted duo. But today I met a guy who makes me look like a male model.

Ebenezer Cohen looks like the kid who got beat up every day in elementary school, junior high school, high school, and maybe even college. He is short, pale, and chubby, with thinning curly black hair. To make matters worse, he wears big square black-framed glasses with incredibly thick lenses.

I met Ebenezer on a yacht in the middle of the New Sea of Galilee. I have never been on a yacht before. It was very nice.

Ebenezer sneezed a lot, like he had allergies. But between blowing his nose every few seconds, Ebenezer told me that he was going to seek the Republican nomination for president at the upcoming convention: "I have never held a p-p-public office, Mr. Jennings, but I believe I could make a great c-c-c-contribution to the c-c-c-country." The stutter was the icing on the total nerd cake.

I felt a bit uncomfortable at this point, because it was unclear to me why Ebenezer felt it necessary to let me, a wanted criminal, in on his plans. Ebenezer must have been reading my mind, because then he said, "The prime minister insisted I meet with you in person to give you this information. He said you would know what to do."

I felt like I needed to contribute something to this conversation, so I asked, "What will be your platform?"

Ebenezer sneezed and nodded vigorously. "We are working on one right now. As you can s-s-s-see, I am rather s-s-s-short in s-s-s-stature, so the p-p-p-platform will need to be s-s-s-substantial."

Oy vey.

Day 85

My instructions from the prime minister were to wait seven days before I looked at the computer disk, so Pete and I looked at Dad's disk tonight. First, Dad gave Pete a hard time about looking down Pink's shirt. I actually enjoyed that part of the message. Dad used pretty colorful language that I won't repeat here.

Dad then said:

Junior, I need you to do me a small favor. I need you to make sure that Ebenezer Cohen gets the presidential nomination at the Republican convention.

Now I know what you are thinking, and yes, Ebenezer is a nebbish and a putz, and if he gets the nomination he will certainly lose. Well, I want the Republicans to lose this election.

I specifically set this up for you, Junior. I can't tell you yet why I want Ebenezer to get the nomination, but believe me when I say it is vital that he does.

I could not have taken care of this if I was still alive, because everyone would have known who was pulling the strings. That's why the explosion had to take place.

You have to take my place on this assignment and speak for me. Don't worry, I will tell you exactly what to do, what to say, and how to say it.

And then he did.

Day 88

To help me with my new assignment, I watched a ton of CNN's coverage of the election campaign. According to CNN, the New Mexico explosion devastated the experienced upper echelon of the Republican Party. Although the blow-dried newscaster on the screen is talking about the effects of the disaster in somewhat neutral terms, it is clear that what he is really saying is:

"Virtually every decent Republican candidate who could win this election was blown up in New Mexico."

The explosion resulted in all the traditional rules for a presidential convention being thrown out the window. After much wrangling, the party decided to name four candidates to be voted on at the convention. The party's by-laws were amended, for this convention only, to provide that once the four candidates were identified, the convention had to choose one of the four as the party's candidate for president. According to the smooth-talking CNN reporter, the Republicans decided on this strategy to insure a candidate was chosen by the scheduled end of the convention. Without this limitation, the party leaders were concerned they would never be able to agree on a candidate in time to run a successful election campaign.

Amazingly, one of the final four candidates is the chubby guy I met four days ago, Ebenezer Cohen. The CNN guy is saying he has no idea who Ebenezer is. All CNN knows is that Ebenezer moved from Miami to Israel when he was a small boy and came back to America in the mass exodus that preceded the Forty-Five-Minute War.

After listening to Dad's computer disk and talking some more to the prime minister, I actually know something CNN does not—that when the North Dakota Israelis agreed to host the Republican convention in New Jerusalem, North Dakota, they gave the Republicans a really sweet price. In fact, the Republicans are not paying a penny to use the New Jerusalem Convention Center and are getting steeply discounted rates for the thousands of hotel rooms rented for the convention. The Israelis figured that the publicity would be worth the price break and hoped their tourism trade would take off.

In return for the price concessions, the Republicans agreed that the Israelis could nominate a "favorite son" at the convention, to foster Israeli pride and enthusiasm. At the time, when it appeared President Carrier would be the certain nominee, the Republicans' agreement to the "favorite son" clause was virtually a throwaway bargaining chip. Now, although nobody believes Ebenezer stands a chance of winning the nomination, the importance of the "favorite son" clause is highly significant. Even if Ebenezer comes in fourth, the Israelis can tell their children that just a few years after the exodus to America, they were already full participants in the American electoral process and were just a few votes short of having one of their own nominated by a major party for president.

The political analysts agree that the odds-on favorite to sew up the nomination is Samson Fairman, the leader of the Methodist Free Militia. Fairman is well educated (a master's in government from Georgetown and a PhD in economics from Harvard), wealthy (he married the sole heir of a computer-designing billionaire), and selfless (he spent two years with the Peace Corps in Africa).

Fairman's greatest claim to fame, however, is that he parachuted into the Hindu Raj mountain range in Pakistan, along with ten other members of the Methodist Free Militia, and rescued twenty Methodist missionaries who had been captured and held for ransom by Abu Abu Mohammed Mohammed, the infamous terrorist responsible for blowing up Hershey's Chocolate World in Hershey, Pennsylvania. Fairman not only rescued the missionaries, he brought back the severed head of Abu Abu Mohammed Mohammed and donated it to the Smithsonian Institution. The head is the centerpiece of the Smithsonian's Islamic Terrorist Severed and/or Mutilated Body Parts Exhibit.

The dark-horse candidate is Georgia senator Bocephus Cowden. Cowden, a five-time winner of the National Bass Fisherman of the Year award, was elected to the Senate four years ago.

Known as either "Bo" or "Lunker" to his constituents, Cowden is immensely popular in Georgia, Alabama, and Mississippi, but, according to CNN, is not well known to the rest of the country.

The fourth candidate to make the cut is, believe it or not, Henry the Hammer. According to the CNN reporter, nobody is taking the Hammer's candidacy too seriously, since he will not even come to the convention. CNN showed a film clip of the Hammer in which he made the following statement:

> *I wish I could come to the New Jew City this week, but coach says we've got a lot of important practices this week that I can't miss, because if we win our next two games we might could still make the nineteenth and final playoff spot. And if we make the playoffs, I get a performance bonus, so that's pretty important. I'm sure everybody understands that. Ain't nothing better for a man than to find satisfaction in his work.*
>
> *Anyway, for all you demographics at the convention in New Jew City, vote for me. I'm a big strong man who's not afraid of contact. I*

would be a great president, particularly if we can get the president's salary increased. It's kinda low.

Let me also say that the people who say I'm a racist are just retarded midgetheads. I have played with and against black Negroes all of my life and many of them are a credit to their race.

They teach 'em up good at Stonewall Jackson Tech, don't they?

I realize this day's entry was a little longer than usual, but writing all of this stuff down has helped me prepare for the next step in Senior's plan. I will try to keep the future entries shorter and more to the point. Is it just a coincidence that when I start dealing with political issues I write more? Probably not.

Day 89

I actually gave some thought to my appearance before I made my television debut today. The prime minister offered to get me a nice suit, but I'm not really a suit kind of guy, and wearing a suit in my predicament (accused traitor, mass murderer, etc.) did not seem appropriate. However, wearing my "Gravity Sucks" T-shirt from the Colorado ski resort did not seem like a good idea either.

After several minutes of fruitless discussion between the prime minister, Pete, and me, the prime minister brought his wife into the room and she just kinda took over. One hour after she arrived, I had a new haircut and a shave and I was wearing a long-sleeved blue dress shirt. "You don't look farputst," she said, "but you don't look like a criminal, either."

After I thanked her, she said, "My husband tells me you are a good boy. I met your father. He was one smug goy, let me tell you, but he saved the lives of my children and grandchildren, and for that I will always be grateful. I am very sorry you lost your father. Good luck with your speech, or whatever it is you are doing." With that, she left, but not before telling her husband that if he was not home by dinnertime he could just eat cold leftovers.

After the prime minister's wife left, Pete and I were spirited out of our nice penthouse in the New Hotel King David and relocated to a nondescript office building that appeared to be still under construction. We walked into a room that contained a simple wooden table and one chair. The wall behind the chair was painted bright white. In front of the table sat some sort of movie camera.

Jehu, our Mossad handler, said, "Junior, sit in the chair. I will operate the camera. We chose this room because nobody will recognize it. The feed from the camera will go live to all the major networks. Our computer geeks will bounce the signal all over the world so nobody will know where you are."

I took about fifteen minutes to catch my breath and go over my notes about what I wanted to say. Then Pete told a dirty joke to make me laugh, and Jehu turned on the camera.[28]

Day 91

Month four[29] and we are still alive—but barely. Apparently the Methodist Free Militia has some really good computer geeks too, because forty-five minutes after my broadcast, the empty office building I delivered my broadcast from was destroyed by some fancy, hydrogen-powered missile. Fortunately, Pete and I were back in our penthouse suite when the destruction occurred.

The Methodist Free Militia did not claim responsibility for the strike—in fact there has been no television coverage of the explosion at all. As far as the rest of the world is concerned, the explosion never happened.[30]

---

28 Junior's thirteen-minute, thirteen-second speech is the fourth most watched video in history, behind (1) the marriage of King Richmond of England to Sir Jonathan Brentwood, (2) the U.S. women's team defeat of Sweden in the first Nude Ultimate Frisbee World Cup, and (3) the explosion that destroyed the 200-mile border fence between the United States and Baja, Texas, the country formerly known as Mexico.

29 In month four, *Junior* returns to its form of seven entries in each month. Month three, with twelve entries, is the only month in *Junior* that does not have seven entries. There has been a great deal of debate on Junior's rationale for using twelve entries in month three. Most Jewish scholars maintain that the twelve entries symbolize the twelve tribes of ancient Israel. Islamic scholars note that the number twelve could refer to the Twelve Imams who succeeded the prophet Muhammad, and some Hindu scholars argue that the twelve entries could be an allusion to the twelve names of the sun god Surya. There are also a number of commentators who see a connection between the twelve entries in month three and the popular song "The Twelve Days of Christmas."

30 Although the explosion went unreported at the time, the biography of the Israeli prime minister and the official record of the Methodist Free Militia both confirm the missile strike.

It took a couple of days full of well-publicized denials and threats, but today Samson Fairman and Senator Cowden both withdrew their names from consideration for the nomination.

Pete and I watched Fairman's comments on the Methodist Free Militia Channel:

I have never met Joshua Jennings, Jr., although I will always have a great deal of respect for his father, may he rest in peace. Joshua Jennings, Jr., is a wanted criminal, and someone is obviously using him to create an even bigger disaster for this country by making false accusations against honorable men who are trying to lead this country in the midst of these troubled times.

The videotapes released by the Jennings criminal that purport to show me . . . cavorting with the wives of the criminal terrorist Abu Abu Mohammed Mohammed have clearly been doctored. I am having these tapes analyzed by experts and I am confident that the tapes will be exposed as fraudulent. I am also confident that the purported affidavits of ten eyewitnesses released by Jennings will prove to be forgeries.

However, these measures will take time and our country cannot wait. We need to move forward immediately. Therefore, I am withdrawing my name from consideration for the nomination.

Finally, let me add that I hope Joshua Jennings, Jr., and those who are assisting him are brought to justice as soon as possible.

Unfortunately for Fairman, he did not know that Abu Abu Mohammed Mohammed used state-of-the-art security cameras to monitor his harem. So when Fairman, showing a remarkably perverse stamina, proceeded to rape six women in succession, the horrific crime was captured in triple high-definition clarity.

Don't ask me how, but Senior knew about the security cameras. After Fairman brought back the terrorist's head and the missionaries to great acclaim, Dad quietly used his contacts in Pakistan to retrieve the tape.

Dad explained his reasoning on the computer disk:

Junior, I did not know if the tape would be helpful, but you can never have enough good information. I did not trust Fairman, in part because I never trust men who marry rich women, particularly if they use their spouse's money to fund their political ambitions. That's just unseemly.

Now I had absolutely no idea that Fairman would defile those poor women, but his actions illustrate a truism you should never forget: Men—be they Christian, Muslim, Jew, white, black, brown, or purple—are stupid when it comes to sex. At least once in his life, and generally dozens of times, a man will do something stupid because the blood leaves his brain and heads south. Never forget that, Junior. Every man you deal with has this defect, and there will come a time when you can use this defect to your advantage—like we are about to do with Fairman.

And one more thing. Truism number two is that all women know Truism number one. Not only are they aware of it, they rely on it.

Nothing like sex education from beyond the grave.[31]

Day 92

I got so wrapped up with Samson Fairman yesterday that I forgot to amplify on Senator Cowden's decision to withdraw from the race. It turns out that Senator Cowden's bass-fishing championships were obtained by fraud. Concurrent (I had to look that word up, Dr. Hoover) with my televised speech, I released film clips and affidavits establishing that Senator Cowden, in collusion with his sponsor, Beijing Bass Boats, planted the prizewinning fish at each tournament the senator won. Lunker Cowden did not use his skills to catch a prizewinning fish after all—he simply netted the planted fish.

Senator Cowden's office issued a short press release announcing that Senator Cowden was withdrawing his name from consideration for the

---

31 The Day 91 Sexual Truisms have been the subject of extreme criticism, particularly from scholars who consider them degrading to women. Since the truisms originated with Senior, it is unknown whether Junior Jennings approved of them. The followers of Junior are divided over whether Junior agreed with the Sexual Truisms espoused by his father.

nomination and was also resigning from the Senate "to spend more time with his family." A few hours later, the Chinese government announced that Cho Dim Wang, the president of Beijing Bass Boats, had been arrested, tried, and convicted of "crimes against the state."

Day 95

I guess Senior is not taking any chances regarding the outcome of the Republican National Convention Presented by Coca-Cola. Today, Henry the Hammer gave a press conference at the Dallas Cowboys' training facility. He met with the media while sitting in a hot tub. His statement was brief:

> *Thanks for showing up, y'all. As y'all can see, I'm getting treatment for my injured groin, which was hurt when Bubba Connolly of the Broncos tripped me so I could not sack his quarterback. It was a typical midgetheaded move by Bubba, who, I might add, is not a credit to his black Negro race because he's a low-life cheater. Anyways, I am withdrawing my name from the election because it appears to me that the Republicans is made up of rapers and fish cheaters! I don't desire to be in the company of wicked men like that. I had no idea those boys was so messed up. I wanted to be a Republican because I like elephants—elephants is big and strong like me.*
>
> *Anyways, I quit. The president's job is not for me. I need to keep my football job, which pays me a lot more than the president's job would anyway. I need to go get my groin rubbed down now. See ya.*

With that, the Hammer got out of the hot tub. Since the event was covered live, millions of Americans then got to see more of the Hammer than they needed to.

Pete and I watched the press conference with Jehu from our suite at the New Hotel King David. Jehu verbalized what both Pete and I were thinking: "Well, the boy has a future in porn once his football-playing days are done."

Senior's plan had worked. The blind-as-a-bat nebbish was going to be the Republican Party's candidate for president.

Day 98

I have never been a big fan of the self-improvement hype. Although Pete and I sometimes watch the Diet Channel, the Skin Improvement Channel, the Abs Channel, the Hair Channel, and the Nose Channel, we mostly do it for fun and to see if the same people are in both the "Before" and "After" pictures. Usually, we conclude they are not.

Today, however, I acknowledge to the whole world (or whoever ends up reading this), that I was wrong. Apparently you *can* make a silk purse out of a sow's ear. The proof? YOUR REPUBLICAN NOMINEE FOR PRESIDENT: EBENEZER COHEN!

Ebenezer came back to the hotel today. Ebenezer's hair was straight, not curly, he was wearing contacts instead of thick-lensed glasses, and he had a golden brown tan. Plus, Ebenezer had lost about fifteen pounds, and his nose looked smaller.

As Pete and I stared like morons, Ebenezer opened his mouth and spoke in a voice one octave lower than when we last met: "Junior and Pete, I sincerely appreciate your help in my successful bid for the nomination. You have my eternal gratitude and I will always do everything in my power to help you both." Direct eye contact. No stutter. The cherry on the successful politician sundae.

Since Pete and I were still dumbstruck, Ebenezer smiled (showing perfect white teeth) and said, "I know it's a shock. My mother fainted when I went to see her yesterday. The technology is expensive, but the party figured I needed the work, which is true, of course." Nobody in the room disagreed.

"Anyway, I know everyone is looking for you. I know you are in danger. But you've got a friend in me, because you basically won the nomination for me. I realize the odds are against me winning the presidency, but as the nominee I will have access to lots of powerful people and a great deal of information. Don't hesitate to call me if you need my help."

I shook Ebenezer's hand—he had a strong, firm grip. I also noticed his manicure. When I withdrew my hand, there was a small computer disk in it.

Ebenezer spoke softly. "About ten months ago I made a presentation on behalf of the Standing Rock Sioux tribe here in North Dakota at the Department of Charity in Washington, D.C. I was seeking grant money for the reservation's elementary school library. It was a boring, horrible presentation. I mixed up my graphics, and I stuttered horribly. I even sneezed on the chair-person of the committee.

"When I was finished, I left the room and sat on a bench in the hallway. I was in tears, because I knew I had let the Sioux down—they are a wonderful people and they had trusted me to help them win the grant.

"Your father appeared out of nowhere and sat down beside me. He did not have to introduce himself—he is idolized here in New Jerusalem for saving the Jews. Anyway, he told me to be strong and courageous. He told me I would eventually get better at making speeches—I just had to keep working at it. He also told me he would personally make sure the Sioux got the grant.

"Two weeks later I received the papers approving the grant. There was also a personal note from your dad telling me he thought I had a future in politics because of my concern and passion for the underdog.

"Today I received an e-mail on my personal computer that said: 'Eb, I hope the Sioux kids are enjoying the new books. Please put the attached information on a disk and give it to Junior today before he leaves.[32] And Eb, I love the new look—especially the hair.'"

Eb paused and smiled his old smile, not his new politician's smile. Then he continued. "I don't mind telling you this absolutely freaked me out." Ebenezer looked down at his pants. "I am embarrassed to say these are not the same pants I was wearing when I got the e-mail, if you get my drift."

Note to self—I put the last sentence in because I want to remember the moment. Be sure and take it out before the book is finished. I like Eb and I don't want to embarrass him.

Pete and I wished Eb good luck and I wondered if Dad had made a mistake. Eb has cleaned up real good—maybe he has a chance to win the presidency after all.

---

32 The computer disk Junior received from Ebenezer Cohen is not mentioned again in *Junior*. The "Second New Jerusalem Disk," as it is referred to in the literature, is a subject of great debate and mystery. Although law enforcement authorities, historians, and scholars have searched for the disk for years, it has never been recovered. Some believe the disk contained damaging personal information on world leaders collected by Senior. Others believe it contained valuable scientific formulas or military secrets.

Day 100

Another milestone. Been on the run for 100 days and still kicking.

We are no longer in North Dakota. Ebenezer put us on a Mossad super-sonic helicopter that flew us out of the state in the dead of night in a blizzard. Pretty awesome.

The Mossad learned that the Methodist Free Militia was monitoring all the highways leaving North Dakota (there aren't that many), and that the militia knew about the Caddie. So, we had to give up the Caddie. I was very sad to leave the Caddie behind.

Pete and I were a little bummed about leaving North Dakota, but since the militia knew we were there, it seemed prudent to get out. Plus, I really like Eb, and I didn't want him to get into trouble because of me.

Pete and I had no idea where to go, however. Jehu said it would probably be better to go a far distance from North Dakota, and also to hang out in a big metropolitan area. He said it would be harder for the authorities and the militia to find us in big crowds of people. Plus, the Mossad was illegally monitoring the feds' conversations and learned that the feds thought Pete and I were in some rural, isolated location in either Alabama or Mississippi. I have no idea where they got that idea.[33]

So we are not in Alabama. We are in the City of Angels. Beautiful beaches. Movie stars.

And, we are driving a brand-new Google XYZZ with tinted windows. This truck is sweet. French calfskin leather seats with inlaid cashmere, feather pillow backrests, minifridge, the whole nine yards. It is absolutely the most outrageous vehicle I have ever driven—and it fits right in with the locals. We would stand out like a sore thumb in Alabama with this truck, but here in L.A. we just blend in with the cool people.

I suppose I should reiterate that I am still a wanted man, scared to death, and incredibly worried—but it's a beautiful day and Pete and I are parked in the Google and watching the waves on Playa del Rey Beach. And the girls on the beach. Oh my. Today, at least, I wish all girls were California girls.

---

33 The search for Junior has been chronicled in numerous books. In *We Could Have Busted Him Any Day*, by retired Secret Service agent David Lacy, Lacy blames the Mossad for planting disinformation with the Secret Service regarding Junior's location.

Tomorrow may be horrible, but I'm going to let tomorrow worry about itself. I think I'm just going to sit here awhile and enjoy the view. Peace and love, over and out.

Day 103

Today was a bizarre day. I know, I know, the last three months have been bizarre. Maybe a better word is surreal. (I admit I had to look that word up, Dr. Hoover.)

Today Pete and I took a leisurely walk down Laguna Beach. Pete had on one of those floppy beach hats that old guys wear to keep their face from being sunburned. I was wearing a Los Angeles Bongs gimme cap low over my face.[34] We were pretty sure nobody would recognize us—and to be honest, there were so many beautiful girls around, nobody was paying attention to us. All the boys were looking at the girls. And all the girls were looking at each other.

Near one of the lifeguard stations we saw a small crowd of fifteen or so people surrounding a guy with a microphone. When Pete and I got closer, we also saw some sort of video camera.

Swear to Jupiter, this is what we heard:

First guy: So Rolf, what did you do to prepare for the role of Junior?

Second guy: Well, first of all, Everett, I drank a whole lot of milkshakes and ate a whole lot of pizza, because I obviously had to put on weight.

First guy (laughing): And you have porked up very nicely, I must say, Rolf.

Second guy: And also, of course, I had to immerse myself in Junior's life. I had to feel the rage, the inadequacies, the personal shame that drove him to kill the president.

First guy: Well, Rolf, there are some people who say Junior is innocent. How does the made-for-TV movie address that possibility?

---

34 The Los Angeles NFL football franchise is now known as the Los Angeles Tokers.

Second guy: I don't want to give too much away, Everett, but rest assured the movie will be an in-depth treatment of all the issues. We have been in touch via e-mail with the snow globe girls in Iowa for their input. Veronica Wells, one of the foremost Junior experts in the world, is also a consultant on the project.

First guy: Wow. Veronica Wells. That is impressive. When do you expect the movie to be released?

Second guy: Very soon, Everett. We want to be first to market. My understanding is that there are two Junior webcast projects in the works, a Junior comic book series that will be published soon, and at least one Junior musical that is in preproduction.

First guy: One last question, Rolf. Does the movie have a happy ending?

Second guy: I don't see any way this ends happily, Everett.

Pete and I left then and walked back to the Google. Pete drove us to our condo and we both got very, very drunk.

Day 106

I am pretty sure that nobody knows we are in sunny California, but I am feeling heat today nonetheless. FBI Director Matthew Lopez gave a press conference in Washington, D.C., today and essentially called me out. Lopez said:

We know you can manipulate the media, Junior. You have proven that. We know you have powerful forces protecting you. If you are really innocent, give us some proof—show us a sign of your innocence. I challenge you, Junior, to publicly show us proof of your innocence. If you refuse to give us some sign of your innocence, the world will know you are guilty.

Pete says this is a test and I need to respond, or we will lose what little "Let Him Be" public support we have. My problem, of course, is that if I told everyone what was going on, nobody would believe it. I can't really tell them that my dad is sending me e-mails from the grave or that, with my dad's help, I just engineered Eb Cohen's nomination. If I tell the world that, everyone will think I am a lunatic and, by extension, probably a mass murderer.

The truth of the matter is that I am just the son of the man who set all of this up, but nobody is going to believe that.

Day 123

Hey everybody. This is your old friend Pete. The Big Man is out of commission for a few more days. I'm not sure exactly what the problem is, but I think he is severely bummed out about all the stupid, mean things everybody is saying about him. Why would these arrogant jokers slander such a nice guy? Trust me, I have been with the Big Man his whole life. He is not a "queer" (the Gay and Lesbian Channel's word, not mine), a druggie (at least not a serious one), or a mass murderer.

I hear the Big Man calling me, so I need to go. He should be back in the saddle in a day or so. Peace to all of you from both me and the Big Man.[35]

Day 130

Whew. Thanks for holding. Month five already. Thanks to Pete for jumping in on the last entry. God only knows what I would do without him. I feel much better now. Tanned, rested, etc. We are still in California and the heat is still on. More later.[36]

---

35 This is the only entry in *Junior* specifically attributable to Peter Running Horse.

36 Multiple theories abound regarding the twenty-four days between Day 106 and Day 130 without an entry from Junior. Some scholars have speculated that Junior was likely clinically depressed and incapable of writing entries in his journal. Others, noting that Day 130 is a factor of 13, the number considered lucky by the Chiricahua Apaches, contend that the entry marks Junior's return to consciousness after a spirit journey. After *Junior* was published, numerous books were written by individuals who claimed they saw Junior during this period of time. These first-person narratives contend, among other things, that Junior was (1) living in a nudist colony, (2) admitted to a drug rehabilitation center, (3) engaging in a drinking binge in seedy Los Angeles nightclubs, (4) living with a popular Hollywood actress, and (5) abducted by aliens. These accounts are catalogued in *Junior's Missing Month*, by Letitia Beverly.

Day 133

I hate to be a downer, but today is a very sad day for me. We are getting rid of the Google. The Google is absolutely the best ride I have ever had, and I will miss it. We are losing the Google because we are leaving L.A., and the Google does not fit in anywhere else but L.A.

I can't say my time in L.A. has been perfect, but overall I have enjoyed myself. I think it is safe to say I have never seen as many beautiful women in one place as I have seen in L.A. Plus, the beaches have been great.

The problem with L.A., at least for me, is that I can't talk to the beautiful women. So which is worse? No beautiful women, or lots of beautiful women I can only admire from a distance? Surely there is a doctoral dissertation analyzing this issue.[37]

Eb Cohen, who is campaigning in California, had one of his Mossad guys bring us a message. According to Eb, the Methodist Free Militia is looking for us in L.A. Eb says the FBI has no clue on our whereabouts.

The Mossad guy also brought us the keys to two Harley-Davidsons. Pete is pumped, because he absolutely loved *Easy Rider*, that old movie where the hippies ride their motorcycles around. Apparently Pete has forgotten that the movie ended with them both getting their happy backsides shot off.

Day 137

It's been a long time since I saw *Easy Rider*. Did Fonda and Hopper mention in the movie that your butt hurts after riding a chopper for hours on end?

Weird thing happened today. After a couple of hours on the road, I told Pete we needed to find a quiet place and get some rest. So, we pulled off into one of those rest stop places by the side of the highway. Pete is having a beer and TOTALLY enjoying his new biker persona. He is even wearing a bandanna. I am minding my own business and wondering where I can buy some cream or lotion or something for my sore butt.

A beat-up clunker drives into the rest stop. Engine is smoking. One of the tires looks really low. Lady gets out to look at the car. Four kids get out

---

37 After *Junior* was published, the United States Department of Personal Fulfillment funded numerous studies on this topic. The findings of these studies are compiled in Volume V of *The Journal of Relative States of Happiness*.

and run around screaming like wild Indians. (Should I say that, since I am one-half Indian? Should I instead say screaming like wild cowboys? If so, my apologies to my Indian half of the family.)

Lady leans against the car and pulls a cigarette out of her purse. She tries to light the cigarette, but her mini lighter won't spark. She sees us. Pauses. Sighs loudly. Pauses again. Sighs. Walks over.

She speaks with the tired voice of someone who has been dealing with four wild Indians on a car trip: "Are you guys really bikers, or are you nice guys having an early midlife crisis? I mean, do you think you could give me a light without raping me?"

Pete steps up, very Brando-like, and without a word, lights her cigarette.

"Thank you. I am having a bad day. Tommy, stop hitting your sister!"

Silence for a moment while she takes a drag. Then Pete speaks up. "I guess we are more life crisis than biker. It shows, huh?"

"You don't look like killers to me."

I am thinking at this point: "Maybe we can get this lady on our jury." Pete looks at me and grins. I can tell he is thinking the same thing.

After several more minutes of small talk, Pete fixes the lady's car and replaces the bad tire with the spare in the trunk. I am worthless at fixing stuff, so I play with the kids. We wrestle around and I pretend they have got me pinned. I scream "Help, Help!" while they giggle and pummel me. The mom tells the kids to leave me alone, but I tell her it's OK. I take them all in my arms and give them a big hug. It feels good to play with them.

The lady calls her kids and tells them to get into the car. They pile off me and run to their mom. All except one. She is probably five or six. Blonde curls. Big blue eyes. Something on her mouth—looks like grape jelly.

She whispers in a kid whisper, with exaggerated seriousness: "I know who you are. You are Junior, the man on TV. All the grown-ups are looking for you."

I can't lie to her. She is just too cute. So I say, "Can you keep my secret and not tell anyone? I did tickle you, after all, and you seemed to enjoy it."

She cocks her little head as if to ponder the trade, and then responds, "OK. You are a great tickler. I won't tell anyone I saw you." Then she runs off to join her siblings.

Praise Poseidon that I'm a great tickler.

Day 140

Did you know that Depoe Bay, Oregon, is the whale-watching capital of Oregon? Or that it has the world's smallest fishing harbor? Neither did I till we landed here. The things you learn as you run from the law.

Pete and I are holed up in the Harbor Lights Inn. I nearly wiped out on my bike on the rainy highway, so we stopped here to rest up. Ate a really good bowl of chowder at the Sea Hag Restaurant. Watched the sun set on the Pacific.

Pete is down on the beach smoking some weed. He is really getting into this *Easy Rider* deal. Thinks he is Peter Fonda.

I have tried to talk about the explosion several times, and I have always been interrupted. Now I am going to try again. If I get interrupted this time, somebody is trying to tell me something.

As I may have mentioned before, the rally at the reservation was both unusual and a big deal. President Carrier, at my dad's request, had planned to deliver a major policy speech on terrorism at the rally. The speech was not distributed to the media beforehand, like most speeches are, and the rumors were flying that the president was going to announce a radical new policy in his speech. I don't know if these rumors were true or not.[38]

I had worked my butt off getting the reservation ready for the event. I spent months coordinating logistics and travel and making sure the reservation's facilities were in tip-top condition. Let me add here that I was actually in charge of a lot of stuff and had a lot of responsibility. I say that not to brag, but to point out that it was unusual for me to be in this type of position. This was the first major project I had ever worked on in which I was more than a gofer.

Which made it that much more frustrating when Senior sent me away to Houston two days before the rally. Senior told Pete and me to go to Houston and talk to some lawyers there who were handling a big lawsuit for one of his drilling companies. Something about a dispute with a bunch of royalty owners. Senior told me the lawyers had a bunch of questions that needed to be answered and the response deadline was approaching. When I protested, Senior said, "Son, I appreciate your work on the rally. I really do. But you are more important to me down in Houston now than here at the reservation. I

---

38 The text of the speech has never been found. All the individuals who had firsthand knowledge of the contents of the speech were killed in the explosion.

can tell you have the reservation ready to go, so things here will run smoothly without you."

Although I was ticked off at the time, I was also proud. I felt like I had turned the corner. That I was useful enough to Dad to troubleshoot several projects without his involvement. Plus, Dad told me to drive his vintage red Porsche 911 Turbo to the meeting. Driving a red Porsche on I-10, where the highway patrol is nonexistent for hundreds of miles at a stretch, is a really, really good thing.[39] Dad knew I could not resist driving the Porsche.

The meeting with the lawyers went well, in part because Wally Douglass and Frank Scott, the two-man firm my dad had long employed to handle oil and gas matters, were good guys who knew what they were doing and weren't, like most lawyers, full of themselves. Frank and Wally worked out of a house near the Rice University campus and practiced law in jeans and cowboy boots. We concluded our meeting by drinking a few longnecks, and then Pete and I jumped into the Porsche for the ride home. Since I had driven to Houston, it was Pete's turn to blow out the turbo on the way back to the reservation. I decided to be a helpful copilot and check the traffic reports on the radio to see what traffic jams to avoid.

As we approached Katy, heading west on I-10, I figured we had cleared the major traffic hurdles and I was about to turn on the traveling music we had programmed into the Porsche's stereo system when the news flash about the explosion was announced on the all-news/traffic station. We had the top down on the Porsche and I was not sure I heard the announcement correctly, so I made Pete pull over. He was not happy with me because I pulled his arm so hard he nearly rolled the car.

We sat in the parking lot of a Kentucky Fried Grilled Marinated Boiled Chicken and listened to a frantic woman reporter who said she was circling the "blast point" in a news helicopter. She was crying. She kept repeating, "Everybody's dead. It's horrible. Everybody's dead."

I confess that from that point on, the rest of the day is a bit of a blur. Generally speaking, here is what I remember. During the 150-mile stretch from Katy to San Antonio, I listened to the radio and made calls on my cell

---

39 Scholars are divided on whether driving a red Porsche fits within the second "really good thing" category of driving fast (see Day 15) or whether Junior intended to create a subset of "really, really good things."

phone. The news on the radio, no matter what station I turned to, simply said there had been a massive explosion at the rally and that emergency vehicles were approaching the reservation. I called my dad's cell phone, my mom's cell phone, and everybody else I could think of who might talk to me. As it turned out, everybody I called was at the rally and was killed in the explosion.

As we exited at the west side of San Antonio, the traffic faded away to nothing. Pete pushed the Porsche up to 130 mph and held it there. I remember thinking, despite my fear, "man, this ride is smooth." What a jerk I am.

Anyway, as we passed the exit to Boerne on I-10, the official announcement came from the White House that both the president and the vice president were dead. The radio station that we were listening to ("KBOE 1560—True Texas Country Music") actually played taps after the announcement. I assumed at this point that Senior was dead, and I feared that my mother and sisters were as well.

As we approached Kerrville, I switched to the CNN radio station. The news at that point was that the FBI suspected that Islamic terrorists had exploded a bomb or bombs at the rally.

We stopped in Junction to get gas, because the towns on I-10 west of Junction tend to be few and far between. Junction was shutting down. We could see the restaurants turning off their lights—even McDonald's was closing. We loaded up on soda and snacks at Jimmie's Exxon. As I paid for the snacks I heard a big man wearing a cowboy hat say something about "those damned towelheads."

By the time we got to Ozona (with all due respect to Jimmy Webb)[40] the "damned towelhead" allegation had lost traction and was replaced by the Mexico is for Mexicans theory. This Mexican terrorist group, formed after Mexico lost its status as a sovereign nation and was renamed Baja, Texas, had previously confined its activities to blowing up tourists in Cancún, but the news anchors said the FBI was interrogating several members of the Mexico is for Mexicans cell located in Beverly Hills, California.

It started getting dark as we left Ozona, but we plunged on into the night. Pete pushed the Porsche hard. We didn't talk much—we just listened to the radio. As we traveled down I-10 we heard the following theories/facts/reports:

---

40 Jimmy Webb was an American songwriter who wrote the song "By the Time I Get to Phoenix," which won a Grammy award. After *Junior* was written, the Baja, Texas, rap group Hard Core Greasers won a Grammy award for "By the Time We Got to El Ozona."

(1) Iran had nuked England and was also claiming credit for blowing up the rally;

(2) Iraq had nuked New York City and was also claiming credit for blowing up the rally;

(3) Iran and/or Iraq had tried to nuke North Dakota and nuked the rally instead;

(4) the Rabid Presbyterians had blown up the rally;

(5) Wall Street speculators had blown up the rally;

(6) the stock market had crashed;

(7) India had declared war on China; and

(8) China had nuked India and Pakistan.

As I sit here in my comfortable room in Oregon, after eating a great bowl of chowder, it is hard to convey the absolute loneliness and incredible frenzy I felt as Pete and I barreled into the pitch blackness at 100-plus mph, stoked by Mountain Dew Plus Extra Rush and sour cream and onion potato chips. There was nobody else on the road. It was like we were the only two sane people left on the planet. We really had no plan at that point other than trying to get to El Paso as fast as we could, because we figured we could use Dad's chopper pilot in El Paso to get us to the reservation.

We stopped again in Sierra Blanca, about eighty miles east of El Paso on I-10, to buy more gas and pee. Sierra Blanca, for those of you who don't keep up with news stories about poop, is the small Texas town that agreed to accept New York City's treated sewage. The good folks of Sierra Blanca figured that since they were out in the middle of nowhere anyway, why not make a little money taking care of Yankee poop? They could bury it out in the desert where nobody could smell it.[41]

I remember sitting in the Porsche that night waiting for Pete to return from the convenience store with my Pepsi Triple X and thinking, "We must be close to the sludge dump; I can smell that Yankee poop from here," when the poop hit my personal fan. My cell phone rang. I picked it up immediately, not bothering to check the number.

It was Frank Scott. He was whispering.

---

41 Not long after *Junior* was written, the methane from the sludge dumps in Sierra Blanca caused an explosion that decimated the town. Soon after the explosion, Congress passed the Poop Runs Downhill Act, which established Federal Poop Dumps in Oklahoma, Louisiana, Mississippi, and Alabama.

"Are you OK, Junior?"

"Yes. I think so. Pete and I are headed to El Paso."

"Did I ever mention to you that my roommate in law school is now a federal judge in Houston?"

It had been such a bizarre day, I took this non sequitur in stride. "No, Frank, you did not."

Frank Scott continued. "Judge King called me in confidence two hours ago and said he had just signed a search warrant for the FBI to search my office. The search warrant seeks any information relating to you and Pete. I am sitting in my car, down the street from our office. The office is burning. Guys in FBI jackets are standing outside of the office, watching it burn. The Houston Fire Department is here, but they are also just standing around doing nothing."

"I'm sorry about your office."

"Don't worry about the office, son. Let my insurance company worry about the office. That's why I pay them all those dadgummed premiums. You need to worry about yourself. It's very clear the feds think you had something to do with the New Mexico explosion and they don't want any evidence around that you were here in Houston when the explosion took place. Get my drift?"

"I guess so."

"Good. I have talked to Wally. Our story is that he and I were fishing down at the coast house in Port O'Connor today. We did not have a meeting with you or any other clients today. I'm sorry about Senior, son. He was a helluva man. I am also sorry about not being your alibi, but it is clear to me that if I try to alibi you, my house will be the next structure to burn, and my wife and I will likely be in it when it goes up in flames."

"OK."

"Here is my last piece of advice, Junior. Don't go to El Paso. Turn off and throw away your cell phone. Good luck, boy."

When Pete returned to the Porsche, I told him what Frank Scott had said. We turned off I-10 onto Farm Road 1111 and headed north toward New Mexico. The only thing I remember about Farm Road 1111 is that we ran over five or six snakes. Hitting a snake at 130 mph can give your heart a jolt.

That is enough of the sad story for now. I am too bummed to write any-more. I may add more details later.[42]

Day 143

Did I mention that some rich guy built some sort of temple to Senior? I can't remember.[43] Well, on the way back from his beach-walking, dope-smoking trek in Depoe Bay, Pete found a promotional brochure for the Joshua Jennings Senior Memorial, "the world's first fully participatory temple," what-ever that means. The JJSM, it turns out, is located in Salem, Oregon, which ain't too far from Depoe Bay. So, we hopped on our hogs, blitzed down the H. B. Van Duzer Forest State Scenic Corridor (as a semi-rude aside, couldn't Oregon come up with a better/shorter/prettier name for this beautiful stretch of country?), and rolled into Salem.

It turns out the rich guy made his money in pet food. The sign on the JJSM says: The Joshua Jennings Senior Memorial, brought to you by Dickin-son Healthy Pet Foods, Inc. It's a really big sign.

I have, to my best recollection (preparing for my trial testimony here), been in only two temples: the Elvis Presley Temple in Nashville and the Troy Aikman Temple in Dallas. Both of these temples have pictures and/or video promoting the accomplishments of the deity being worshipped. Both are huge edifices with many rooms and an auditorium where performances and/or worship can take place. The Aikman Temple, as I recall, has one wing dedicated to his play-ing days and another wing dedicated to his ownership of the Dallas Cowboys after Jerry Jones died in an unfortunate plastic surgery mishap.

Although the JJSM is big (it has to be big just to hold up the sign), there are no promotional videos. There is only one picture—and it looks like

---

42 Pete and Junior's trip from Houston to Sierra Blanca has been dramatized in several television movies, numerous webcasts, and at least one feature film. Although Sierra Blanca no longer exists, there are numerous monuments and statues relating to Junior and Pete located near the former town site. At least twice a year, once in the spring and once in the fall, organized groups of Junior's followers make the trip, many driving red Porsches. The stock prices of Pepsico (the maker of Mountain Dew and Pepsi) and potato chip manufacturers spike during these rallies.

43 See Day 39.

someone copied Senior's obituary picture out of the paper, blew it up, and stuck it in a frame.

Plus, I don't remember having to pay to get into the Elvis or Aikman temples. Pete and I each had to pay twenty-five dollars just to walk into the JJSM.

The JJSM consists of four massive rooms. Pete and I walked into Room 1 and saw a sign hanging on one of the walls. The sign said SENIOR LEGALIZED DRUGS. This sign appeared to be the only official thing in the room. The four walls of the room were covered with stuff people had written on the walls or taped to the walls. Somebody wrote: "Rock on, dude!" There were also a number of "Doobies Rule!" inscriptions. People had also taped rolling papers and roach clips to the wall. I guess this is what the brochure meant by a "participatory temple."

The sign on Room 2 said SENIOR GOT MEXICO FOR US. Someone who was not a very good artist had drawn a crude map of Baja, Texas, on one of the walls and written "Hook 'em" on the map. There were also a lot of references to Mexican food on the walls, like "Cheese and onion enchiladas rule!" and "Guacamole Salad!"

The sign on Room 3 said SENIOR SAVED THE JEWS. The walls in this room were covered with pictures of the Star of David and that candle thing with the seven branches on it. There were about fifty of those weird hats Jewish guys wear stapled to the wall. There were also several inscriptions suggesting that Muslims perform acts that I think are physically impossible.

The sign in Room 4 said SENIOR CURED AIDS. "Queers Love Senior" was the predominant message on the walls in Room 4, although there were also messages suggesting maybe Senior should have minded his own business and let the gays die.

I was not all that crazy about the idea of a Senior temple, but I at least hoped it would be in good taste. This was terrible. How could anybody think Senior would appreciate this?

As we exited the temple, we passed several vendors selling Senior T-shirts, posters, and trinkets. The vendors were selling lots of product. Each vendor had a long line of customers waiting to spend their money on Senior memorabilia.

For some reason, the vendors ticked me off. How dare they profit off of my dead father! I was going to give one of the vendors a piece of my mind, but Pete saw what I was about to do and pulled me away. If I am ever not on the run from the law for blowing up the president, however, I am going to come back here and kick some low-life, in-bad-taste, entrepreneurial butt. Bunch of poop-head buzzards.

Day 149

OK. I have settled down a bit. Pete and I rode north through the Columbia River Gorge National Scenic Area and Mt. Rainier National Park and up to Seattle. Oh man. Spectacular.

Pete suggested we go to Seattle because he knows I have always wanted to see the Jimi Hendrix Museum. He thought that would help me get over my anger with the pet food guy's "memorial" to Dad. Pete is a good guy. Tomorrow we head to the museum, so I can be cheered up by the memory of a great guitarist who drank too much, took too many pills, and died by choking on his own vomit.

Day 151

Welcome to month six. Don't forget to tip your waitress.

Turns out we did not get to see Hendrix today after all. Instead, we watched the Parisian cops blow us up.

As we were eating our room service spelt granola and double-rehydrated organic yogurt (Seattle is such a health food nut place) and listening to a really fine FMDMXM radio station, the disc jockey interrupted a prolonged guitar solo and said, in a voice that sounded like he was on quaaludes: "Dudes. Check out what is happening in Paris. Looks like Junior and Tonto are going down."

Pete, muttering something like "Tonto is gonna scalp himself a disc jockey," switched on the television. The first three channels we looked at had either cartoons or porn on, but then we found CNN, where we saw a bunch of teeny tiny cop cars with flashing lights sitting in front of a small brown house. It was overcast and drizzling—all in all a dreary scene.

The CNN guy said that the Parisian police had surrounded a house in the fourteenth arrondissement of Paris, and the police believed that Pete and I were in the house. Apparently, the police had received several phone calls from folks saying they had seen Pete and me going into the house. The script at the top of the screen read: "SIEGE OF THE TERRORISTS JOSHUA JENNINGS, JR., AND PETER RUNNING HORSE."

Before I go any further, let me first object to being called a terrorist. A terrorist is somebody who has some sort of agenda and kills or maims innocent people because he/she thinks killing or maiming innocent people will somehow further the agenda. As I have stated previously, I have no agenda. Am I leading a rebellion? Absolutely not. I am also not protesting against anything. Everything was just fine in my life until 152 days or so ago. I am just a guy who ran errands for his big-shot dad.

Abu Abu Mohammed Mohammed was a terrorist. He blew up Hershey's Chocolate World because he believed Americans were infidels addicted to chocolate and that blowing up Chocolate World would cause the infidels to suffer from withdrawal and make them easier to conquer.

Dr. Afaf Bahiyaa Hakim was a terrorist. She unlawfully injected drugs into more than 100 Muslim men admitted to the Afghanistan hospital where she worked. The drugs caused the patients' penises to fall off. Dr. Hakim administered these injections to protest the Afghanistan law that required married women to have sex with their husbands at least five times a week.

Oklahoma state trooper Bobby Joe Crankens was a terrorist. He blew up Gaylord Family Memorial Stadium in Norman, Oklahoma, when his beloved Sooners were playing football against their hated in-state rival, the Oklahoma State Cowboys. According to an e-mail he sent to the local newspaper from his phone right before the blast (Bobby Joe was in the stadium and died in the explosion), the trooper was upset about the sanctions that the University of Oklahoma football team received for paying its players royalties from state-owned oil wells and for running a brothel for the players in the athletic dorm. The e-mail ended: "Boomer Sooner!" I don't know if Bobby Joe intended for his last words to be a pun.

I, on the other hand, am not a terrorist. Blowing up the campaign rally in New Mexico does not help me or advance any cause I am affiliated with.

Pete (who is still ticked off at the Tonto slight) says all I have proven is that I am not a terrorist—I could still be a mass murderer. I suppose this is true, but all I am doing now is contesting the script used by CNN. Sometimes you have to just take baby steps.

Believe it or not, after the initial adrenaline rush of seeing Pete and me "surrounded" on television, I got kind of bored watching the next four or five hours of coverage. Basically, all you could see on the screen was the picture of a drab little house. Every now and then some French police guys would move around the house, but you couldn't really tell what they were doing.

Since there was no action worth watching, CNN paraded a bunch of "experts" on screen to talk about the explosion, Pete and me, the search for us, and the legal penalties we were facing. Most of the stuff I had heard before, but I was fascinated to hear how Pete and I had allegedly made our way to France.

According to David Caughey Fair, a private security consultant with contacts in both the FBI and Interpol, Pete and I were in Mississippi or Alabama when I made my speech during the Republican National Convention Presented by Coca-Cola. I guess Mr. Fair did not talk to anyone at the Methodist Free Militia. Those guys definitely knew we were not way down south in Dixie.

Fair went on to opine that Pete and I flew from Alabama or Mississippi on a private jet to either Sweden or Norway, and we eventually migrated down to Paris. After Pete and I stopped laughing, we discussed how in the world this load of baloney was created. Pete thinks Eb Cohen and the Mossad guys are behind it, because it takes the focus off of them. They obviously don't want the world to know they helped us. That could be true, but I think somehow, some way, Senior is also pulling some strings.

The last hour or two of "THE PARISIAN SIEGE: JUNIOR AND PETE'S LAST STAND" (which was the moniker CNN gave the program after it was over) was riveting television, I must admit. We first knew stuff was about to happen when one of the French cops, using a wireless microphone, said something in French in the direction of the house. When nothing happened, a bunch of French cops huddled together for a few minutes, and then a different cop spoke into the microphone in heavily accented English: "Joshua Jennings, Jr., and Peter Horse, you are surrounded. Do you geeve up?"

You could actually hear people laughing in the background. Even the CNN guy smirked, if only for a microsecond. I think it was a combination of the accent, the cop's tinny, tenor voice, and his funny hat. Why do French cops wear those silly hats?

I guess the laughing embarrassed the Parisian police, because there were no more attempts at negotiation. The guys with the funny hats moved back and a bunch of huge men wearing black helmets and black tactical body armor moved forward. As the robot-looking guys approached the house, I heard a weak "pop, pop, pop" sound. At that point, all the big guys went down on one knee, pulled out massive rifles or machine guns, and blasted away at the house. Even on TV, the sound was deafening.

The guns put a lot of holes in the house, but nothing much else happened. No response from the house. No white flag.

To be honest, I did not expect any response from the house, because I knew Pete and I were not there. This whole deal was either a trick orchestrated by you-know-who, or a horrific mistake. I was hoping for the former. I did not want some innocent French guys getting killed because of Pete and me.

Then the house exploded. It caught everyone off guard. The CNN guy actually said "Oh shit!" and the picture on the screen wobbled a bit because the camera guy lost his balance. What was left of the house after the explosion was on fire. Nobody rushed to the house. No fire trucks. No sirens. We all just watched the house burn.

After several more hours of burning house footage, the CNN guy said they were going to stop their live coverage. As the camera took a wider angle and panned the onlookers, my attention was drawn to a large black man standing behind the police barricade. He was wearing glasses and had grown a beard since I last saw him, but I would recognize Sammy Assassin anywhere. Plus, he was wearing a Duke Blue Devils cap. Senior strikes again.

Day 153

I confess it is weird to be dead. I don't know how to act or what to do. Although there were no body parts remaining in the house in Paris, the French cops told the press they found some remnants of clothes that they have linked to Pete and me. How there could be anything left after the explosion and fire is a mystery to me.

Pete and I figure it is just a matter of time before everybody realizes we are still alive, so we have decided to do something we would probably not do if folks were still looking for us. We are going to watch the Seattle Fog basketball team play the Los Angeles Lakers. Seattle just recently got a new NBA basketball franchise and they have a player I have been dying (no pun intended) to see in person: Philippi Julius Whitworth.

At the risk of sounding like a racist (Pete says that phrase already makes me sound like a racist), I have always gravitated to white basketball players.

Maybe it is because I am half white and always got my butt kicked in pickup games by black guys. So, I am not a racist just a jealous half-white guy. The fact of the matter is that almost all the really good basketball players are black guys. Lots of people have speculated on why that is so, but that is a topic for another day.

Anyway, P. Julius Whitworth, who plays for the Seattle Fog, is not only white, he is an albino. White as white can be. And he is good. P. Julius is over six feet ten inches tall, can run like a deer, is deadly from four-point range, and can jump like, well, like a black guy. We are leaving now for the game. Will report later.

Day 154

P. Julius was great. Went five for five on four-point shots. Scored forty-five points and had twenty-five boards. Crazy-looking dude, with the blindingly white skin and the white hair. His skin looked even whiter since he had no tattoos. He was the only guy on the court (and virtually the only one in the building) without tattoos covering his body.

The Fog lost the game, but the Seattle fans did not seem to care. They spent most of the game screaming "Juuuuulius!! Juuuuuulius!" Pete and I had a great time. I almost forgot we were dead.[44]

Day 164

We are on a big boat—and I mean REALLY big. It is one of those supersized yachts that only incredibly rich people have. We are sailing in the Juan de Fuca Strait, which is west of Seattle, near Vancouver Island. Very beautiful.

I can't say exactly how we got here, but in general, when we returned from the Fog game, there were a couple of guys in our hotel room. They were scary-looking guys who said they were our friends and that we needed to

---

44 Several years after *Junior* was written, Philippi Julius Whitworth announced that he was the biological child of Sunday Amir Adebayo aka "The Truth, the Whole Truth and Nothing but the Truth." Adebayo, a Nigerian prince, was an all-American power forward at UCLA who played for three different NBA teams and was a first-ballot selection to the NBA Hall of Fame. Whitworth admitted that he took special drugs to permanently change the pigment of his skin. Soon after the announcement, Whitworth retired from basketball and was later elected as the governor of Washington.

leave immediately. Apparently, the Methodist Free Militia knew we were in Seattle and were closing in. Pete and I looked at each other and decided that we would go with them, although I am not sure we had much choice. If we had resisted, we would have lost.

I REALLY wish I could tell you who owns this boat. I actually got to meet him, and he is so cool. But this huge mountain of a man is watching me type, and he has made it perfectly clear that if I identify the guy who is helping us, the computer will wind up in Mr. de Fuca's Strait. I have never met a guy this big who could actually read Chiricahua. Pretty impressive. He is grinning at me and nodding as I type this.

Pete and I each have our own room. The boat is even big enough to house a gym, so we are getting some exercise. Being on the run and eating room service or fast food all the time is not all that good for my manly figure. I am even chubbier than I normally am. I am going to ask my new friend if he has some fish on board that I can eat for dinner. We are on a boat after all, and fish is healthy, right?

The famous guy whose name cannot be mentioned told me that we need to wait a few days out here on the boat. So, I guess that is what we will do. One quick note about the famous guy—he helped Senior with the oil deal. The big guy just held his hand out over the computer—he is contemplating whether I can say this. OK, he is nodding, so I guess that last sentence stays. At some point I need to explain Senior's oil deal.

Gotta run—gonna work out.

Day 167

The wait on the boat was definitely worth it—almost painfully so. The famous guy himself brought me into his personal stateroom today—and Pete's mom was sitting there. Jane Running Horse is like my second mother. She held me and I cried. I cried for my mom, my dad, my sisters, and myself. I don't think I have ever cried that hard or that long.

Jane, like a true Apache, was calm and unruffled. Her eyes were moist, but no serious tears. We talked for a few minutes, and would have talked for hours, I suppose, but the famous guy interrupted us: "I'm sorry, Junior, but we are on a tight schedule here, for security reasons. Jane, tell him what you need."

Pete's mom looked at me. She did not smile as she spoke. "Junior, Pete's little sister Grace is sick. She needs a bone marrow transplant. The doctor at the reservation says Pete is the best candidate. Without the transplant, Grace will die."

It crossed my mind to ask how Aunt Jane or the reservation doctor knew Pete was alive, since we were just blown up in Paris, but instead I asked why she didn't just talk to Pete about this. "Why do I need to be involved, Aunt Jane? Why are you talking to me about this?"

Her response was terse, and a bit angry: "He won't leave you, Junior. Not unless you tell him to. Not even to save his sister. He is determined to die with you."

Aunt Jane's words and attitude took me back a bit. Hearing someone else say I was going to die made the possibility seem all that much more real.

I told Aunt Jane I would do my best. I went to find Pete and brought him back to the stateroom. I was pretty upset about the whole "you are going to die" comment by my Aunt Jane, so I could not even focus on how to explain this to Pete. So I just punted. I opened the door and simply said, "Pete, here is your mother."

As it turned out, Pete did not put up much of a fight about leaving. He wanted to save Grace and he wanted to please his mother. I wonder if I will ever see him again.[45]

Day 170

Well, it's been three days. Pete is still not back. The famous guy says it will likely be weeks or even months before I see Pete again. That's all for today.

Day 179

Even though I am on this cool yacht, with great food and all kinds of luxuries, I am going crazy. The famous guy can tell I am a bit antsy, plus I think he is ready for me to leave so he won't get caught with me. Can't blame him

---

45 Day 167 is the subject of great controversy, because there is no evidence that Peter Running Horse had a sister named Grace. Some scholars maintain that Pete left because he had a falling-out with Junior. Others believe the Day 167 entry is simply an addition to the book written by someone other than Junior and should not be included in the book at all. For a more comprehensive analysis of the theories relating to Day 167, see *Junior and Pete: The Search for Grace and Truth*, by Dr. Margaret Ratteree.

for that. Looks like I am moving somewhere else tomorrow, although I don't know where yet.[46]

Day 185

Month seven has arrived, and I am freezing my butt off. I am somewhere in the wilderness in British Columbia. I am in a luxury-type cabin surrounded by snow. Remember when I complained about the cold in Colorado?[47] Well, Colorado is Arizona compared to B.C.

This place is so isolated, you have to ride a helicopter to get here. No roads are passable because of the snow. I am here with only one other person. Her name is Hannah, and she is a Mossad agent, so I assume she could kill me if necessary. But she is also absolutely beautiful. I kid you not. Next time I see Eb Cohen, I am going to kiss him on the lips.

So, I am hiding in the wilderness with a beautiful woman. I have food, booze, and legal drugs. I have satellite television access, satellite movie access, and satellite Internet access. I have satellite access to the Library of Congress, if I want to read. I am still wanted by the law and I am still being chased by the Methodist Free Militia, but all in all, this is better than a kick in the head.

I guess I should add that I miss Pete. But Pete is not nearly as cute as Hannah.

I should also add that Hannah, although beautiful, is not exactly my friend. She is guarding me. Although she has never said as much, I think her job is both to protect me from the bad guys and to keep me here and not let me go anywhere. Like I could get very far in all this snow.

Hannah says it is time to eat, so I should go. Yes, she is a good cook, too.

Day 189

I have spent the last few days watching most of the Junior/Pete feature films, television movies, and web movies. There may be some indie movies about us I have not seen, but here are my thoughts and observations on what I have reviewed so far.

---

46 The owner of the "de Fuca Boat," as it is known in the *Junior* literature, has never been confirmed. Indeed, researchers have not even been able to establish that a supersized yacht was in the Juan de Fuca Strait during this time period.

47 See Day 42.

First, *Junior and Pete: A Love Story* was disgusting. For the record, I do love Pete like my own brother. But we never made out in the back of a Ford F-150 pickup truck and we did not blow up the president to prove our love for each other. I understand there is an X-rated version of this web movie, but I refuse to watch it.

Second, I kind of enjoyed *Pete and Junior: The Musical.* The music was good old-fashioned rock and roll, and the snow globe girls were played by absolute foxes.

Third, why am I so fat in all the movies? I realize I am not a hunk, but gimme a break! Most of the actors playing me were obviously wearing fat suits.

Fourth, I appreciate everyone's creativity in discerning my motivation for blowing everybody up. In the movies I have watched so far, I blew everybody up because:

(1) I was high on drugs;
(2) I was angry because Senior did not approve of my love for Pete;
(3) Senior abused me as a child;
(4) I wanted to get Senior's money;
(5) I am a Muslim, Methodist, Presbyterian, Catholic, Mexican, or Apache terrorist;
(6) I felt inadequate because I was fat, stupid, jobless, and/or "queer" (their word, not mine); and
(7) I was hired by the Democrats to sabotage the Republican Party so the Democrats could win the election.

Finally, I really liked the full-length animated feature *Junior and Pete's Exciting Adventure.* The graphics were spectacular, and we came off as just a couple of guys on a long vacation with fun adventures. No mention at all of us blowing everyone up.

I am still waiting on a movie that affirmatively shows that we did not do anything wrong and that we are being chased for absolutely no reason. Guess I will have to wait a little longer for that. Maybe if this book ever sees the light of day, there will be a movie based on what really happened. Dibs on the movie rights.[48]

---

48 There have been a number of feature films based on *Junior*, several of which have won Academy Awards and Golden Globe Awards.

Day 195

The supply helicopter came today. Brought some guns and hand grenades. I don't think that is a good sign. Hannah says it is standard operating procedure.

Hannah also told me something I did not know. The land surrounding the cabin is mined. That freaked me out. She says she knows where the mines are so I don't need to worry. That does not make me feel much better.

In addition to weapons, the helicopter also brought a bunch of T-shirts. Each shirt was either yellow or black and each had a distinctive design that incorporated a black bee and some form of the phrase "Let Them Be" or "Let Him Be." Hannah says there are hundreds more out there—that these are just samples. She says that our public "death" has caused a groundswell of sympathy for Pete and me. I know from watching television that public opinion is divided on whether Pete and I were really killed in the house in Paris.

The helicopter also brought some Hillary Blue Stem Peyote. I know from personal experience that the Hillary is great stuff. Hannah says she won't partake. That's OK. More for me.

Day 196

When I woke up this morning, I was really mellow. The Hillary will do that to you. After breakfast, I turned on the television and was pleased to learn that the explosion in New Mexico was not my fault after all. I was searching for ESPN (I don't have all the Canadian channels memorized yet) and when I came across a station with my picture on it I stopped. Standing in front of my picture was a very large black woman in an even larger black dress with, believe it or not, even larger black hair piled on top of her head. According to the script at the bottom of the screen, her name was Most Holy Reverend Sister Golden Surprise.

Sister Golden Surprise allowed as how the New Mexico explosion was simply GOD'S WILL and not specifically attributable to yours truly:

Brothers and sisters, we all know that Chapter 21 in the Book of Revelation says that the New Jerusalem will come down out of heaven from God, prepared as a bride beautifully dressed for her husband. We further know from John's Revelation that the New Jerusalem will shine with the glory of God, like a precious jewel. The New Jerusalem will not even need sunlight, because the glory of God will provide its light. This is what God intended the New Jerusalem to be!

But what New Jerusalem did Joshua Jennings, Sr., give us? He gave us a dinky little town in North Dakota! And it's full of Jews!

Joshua Jennings, Sr., provoked the Almighty God by creating a New Jerusalem that is an abomination. The New Jerusalem was supposed to come down from heaven after the rapture, after the end of the world. God himself was going to live in the New Jerusalem. John's book says, and I quote: "The city does not need the sun or the moon to shine on it, for the glory of God gives it light, and the Lamb is its lamp. The nations will walk by its light, and the kings of the earth will bring their splendor into it."

New Jerusalem, North Dakota, is a pale comparison to what God intended the New Jerusalem to be. Since Mr. Jennings violated God's plan, God violently struck him down. God did it publicly, so we all would know Mr. Jennings, Senior, was being punished for transgressing God's laws. We all know that things like this happen for a reason. Yes, it was God's will that Mr. Jennings be blown up in a fiery ball of hellfire. God has spoken!

I confess that I have always been intrigued by the "God's will" explanation for tragedy. My experience is that usually it is someone who has not been seriously harmed or injured who uses God's will as the causative event. In other words, when Abu Abu Mohammed Mohammed blew up Hershey's Chocolate World, there were numerous stories of people saying it was God's will that they were late to Chocolate World that day and were thus spared certain death. I don't recall any of the parents of the fifty grade school kids on a field trip to Hershey's Chocolate World who were blown up that day saying it must have been God's will that their children were massacred. I suppose God's will, like beauty, is in the eye of the beholder.[49]

---

49 This sentence was the basis for "God's Will Is Beautiful," a song by the Alabama Crippled Blind Boys Gospel Choir and Drumline, which reached number one on both the pop and gospel charts several years after *Junior* was published.

I am not saying I totally discount the God's will idea, however. Indeed, I hope it is God's will that Hannah the lovely Mossad agent loses all sense of good taste, marries me, bears me three brilliant and beautiful children, and we live happily ever after in the Canadian wilderness. A guy can dream, can't he?

Day 199

I feel a little like Jeremiah Johnson, although I realize I look nothing like Redford.[50] Hannah and I tromped around in the snow today. She had to go with me so I would not be blown up by the mines. I had a big old sheepskin coat on and I kept expecting to see grizzly bears. It is so QUIET out here.

We talked a little. Hannah says she is not supposed to be in North America. "Technically," she said, "I am like you. I am supposed to be dead, blown up in an explosion."

Turns out she was supposed to be in Jerusalem when it was destroyed by the atomic bomb in the Forty-Five-Minute War. Apparently, the Mossad falsely listed a number of agents as being in Jerusalem when the explosion occurred. Now these agents are scattered across the world, hopefully hidden from the bad guys.

Hmmm. Makes you wonder, don't it? Hannah and I could stay here forever and nobody would miss us or ever know the difference. Could something halfway good come out of all of this? Did all of this, as Sister Golden Surprise opines, happen for a reason? Not going to hold my breath.

When I got back from the hike, I turned on the television again and there, big as life (and almost as big as a house), was Sister Golden Surprise standing in front of a picture of the house in Paris where Pete and I blew up. Turns out the Parisian boom boom was God's will as well:

The terrorists Junior Jennings and the Indian deserved to die violently because they violently killed hundreds of innocent people. God wreaked his vengeance on these sinners. God does not abide evil. It was God's perfect will that these two evil men meet a violent end. Like you, I am

---

50 *Jeremiah Johnson* is a 1972 Western film starring Robert Redford as a trapper in the Rocky Mountains.

a little surprised that God used the godless and inefficient French to implement His will, but as we know, God works in mysterious ways.

If Pete was here I would give him a hard time about being the "Indian," but it is no fun ragging on him in absentia. I wonder what Sister Golden Surprise will say if and when she learns we are not blown up? Was it God's will that she was fooled?

Day 200

Today I was messing around on the computer when a note appeared on my screen. I don't know how it got there. The note read: "When the doorbell rings, answer it and don't shoot." I showed it to Hannah, who said, "It would be impossible for anyone to get here without us knowing about it first. Plus, the doorbell doesn't even work." At that moment, of course, we heard a majestic "Ding Dong!" Hannah scrambled off the couch and pulled a gun. I fell off the couch and onto the floor, although in a cool, brave sort of way.

A recognizable, shrill voice rang out from the front door. "Junior, I know you're in there. Junior, please open the door. It's Veronica! I'm alone. Nobody followed me, I promise."

Veronica and Hannah yelled at each other through the door as Hannah checked all the security cameras and sensors. Then Hannah let Veronica in and frisked her quite thoroughly. It's a good thing Pete was not here, because the sight of one beautiful woman vigorously frisking another beautiful woman would have engendered several minutes of inappropriate conversation between us. As it was, I just had to keep those thoughts to myself.

I won't give a detailed back-and-forth of the two-hour conversation between the three of us, because my fingers would fall off. Here are the highlights:

(1) Veronica received an anonymous tip on her computer telling her where I was;

(2) Veronica did not know Pete was gone;

(3) Veronica did not know who Hannah was or that she was at the cabin;

(4) the Methodist Free Militia knows I am not dead and suspects I am somewhere in either the state of Washington or Canada;

(5) the FBI still thinks Pete and I are dead;

(6) Hannah wondered out loud whether we needed to "disable" Veronica so we could safely leave the cabin;

(7) Veronica REALLY needs an exclusive report because her career is in the toilet, and she is basically willing to engage in any kind of subterfuge we suggest if she can just get her scoop;

(8) Hannah told Veronica that she would be VERY SORRY if she failed to cooperate; and

(9) Veronica has a screenplay about me and Pete that she would like me to read.

Like I said, just the highlights. I left out a bunch of the screaming and crying. I actually said very little.

After the lengthy and emotional discussion, Hannah made us supper. We ate some nice grilled fish and drank some tasty white wine. When we finished eating and drinking, Hannah stood up, pointed her finger at Veronica, and vowed that if Veronica did not do exactly what Hannah told her to do, she would regret it for the rest of her short existence. Then we made a deal.

Day 201

Hannah and I did not waste any time getting out of Canada. After dinner last night, a helicopter came and picked us up. I am not in Canada anymore, but I can't tell you where I am. It is a Mossad hideout and I am not supposed to say anything about it.

We left Veronica in the cabin. At noon today, the agreed-upon time, I turned on the television and located the channel for the Plumbing Fixtures Network. Veronica was not kidding about the poopy status of her career. We watched a few minutes of *Toilet Talk*, and then Veronica's face appeared on the screen. She had rigged a camera so that you could see the cabin behind her. Here is what she said:

This is Veronica Wells, for PFN. I'm reporting from a luxury cabin in the Canadian wilderness. Yesterday, in this very cabin, I talked to Joshua Jennings, Jr. Yes, Joshua is alive. I saw him with my own two eyes. We talked for several hours, and I will supplement this exclusive emergency bulletin with additional reports. Because my time is limited on PFN due to the popularity of Toilet Talk, let me make just a few important points. First, Joshua has been eating better and working out, so he is actually quite buff. Second, Joshua was sharing this cabin with a blonde hottie whom he referred to as Mandy, although when they thought I was not listening, Junior referred to her as Sandy, so maybe the Mandy name was a ruse designed to throw me off. Mandy/Sandy is blonde, tall, loves horses, has all the right curves in all the right places, and she dotes on Junior. They are such a cute couple! Third, Joshua has spent a lot of his downtime writing songs and is contemplating starting a band. Fourth, Joshua says he did not kill anybody.

Veronica's report was then interrupted by the sounds of sirens and explosions. The camera (and I don't know how it did this) turned away from Veronica and showed us the woods near the cabin exploding into a fireball. Hannah said, with a nonchalance I found a bit disquieting, "Someone is trying to come through the woods where the mines are." Sure enough, you could see people running out of the woods and approaching the camera. There was also screaming off camera. Don't know if it was Veronica doing the screaming or the screams of people being blown up in the woods.

A tall figure dressed in black and carrying some sort of machine gun ran directly to the camera. He pointed his weapon, and you could hear Veronica yell: "Journalist, journalist, don't shoot!" The man in black lowered his gun and took off his helmet. As he got closer, you could see the letters "MF Militia" on his jacket. It was Samson Fairman!

Veronica recovered quickly. "Mr. Fairman, sir. Veronica Wells, PFN. We are live, I believe, unless we've been cut off for *Toilet Talk*. Would you like to make a statement?"

Fairman paused, then smiled a brilliant, made-for-TV smile, and said:

Yes, Veronica, thank you. The Methodist Free Militia will never give up in its search for the criminal Joshua Jennings, Jr. His fake death in Paris is even more proof that he is guilty. I know some people have been turned off by our tactics in trying to locate Junior. I apologize

again for blowing up the Catholic convent in Montreal. In my defense,
I thought Junior was there for sure, and we did not blow up any
Americans. You can run, Junior, but you can't hide.

Veronica started to talk again, but the screen went black for a second and a voice said, "And now back to our regularly scheduled programming." The next picture on the screen was a commercial for a toilet plunger that "works first time, every time!" Hannah turned off the television. [51]

Day 212

Welcome to the eighth month of our trip. Ask your waitress about today's special.

Believe it or not, Hannah and I are in White Only Settlement, Idaho. Yes, THAT White Only Settlement, where the name of the town is also a description of its inhabitants. White Only Settlement is the brainchild of Ricky "Chuck" Norris, the leader and founder of the Adamic White Power group. The AWP, as it is known in these parts, hates anyone who is not white. And the AWP really hates Jews, which is why it is bizarre that Hannah and I are holed up here. I'm sure that once upon a time it would have been difficult for us to hide here, but the AWP has become so popular that White Only Settlement has over a million people now. It is amazing what the election of two black guys and a Hispanic woman as president will do.

I suppose I should point out here that I basically look like a white guy, even though I am half Apache. The lovely Hannah is a redhead with pale skin and big green eyes, so I don't think anyone is going to point at her on the street and yell: "Demon Jewess!" So, we should probably be safe on the "White Only" front.

When Hannah brought home the groceries today, she also brought the first evidence that our deal with Veronica was paying dividends. According

---

51 Neither the Mossad nor the Israeli government has ever acknowledged the existence of the "B.C. Cabin," as it is known in the *Junior* literature. One week after Veronica Wells interviewed Samson Fairman, the cabin was struck by lightning and burned to the ground. It has never been rebuilt.

to the magazine *We Are You and You Are Us!*, Joshua Jennings, Jr., and Mandy were seen jogging on the beach in Rio. And the best part was the pictures! Someone pasted my head on the body of an Adonis wearing one of those next-to-nothing bathing suits, and next to "me" was a tanned buxom blonde goddess. The perfect couple for White Only Settlement.

Day 220

Since it is cold in Idaho, I can walk around bundled up without much fear of detection. Today Hannah and I walked around Adam and Eve Park. Fittingly, it was located on Eden Street.

Some kids were playing in the park, and I enjoyed watching them have fun. As we sat on a park bench, more and more kids showed up, until Adam and Eve Park was overrun with blonde-headed tykes. And from the looks of the hundreds of baby carriages parked near the moms, there were a number of babies still too small to get out and run around. You could hear them, though. The screaming of the babies in the carriages mixed with the screaming of the kids running around the park seared my brain. I felt as if someone was sticking a dagger in my ear. I said to Hannah, "Let's go somewhere else, before my eardrums burst." So, we left.

We took a different route home from the park. As we approached the corner of Pureblood Avenue and Paradise Street, I saw a red, white, and blue billboard. A picture of P. Julius Whitworth, my favorite basketball player, was at the center of the billboard. The inscription said, "Julius Whitworth says: Do your patriotic duty. Have more white kids."

I told Hannah I did not know it was our patriotic duty to have sex, and I had been hanging out with politicians for years. Hannah said that the AWP is worried because the birthrates of Hispanics, blacks, and even Jews significantly exceed the birthrate for whites. The AWP believes that unless the white folks have a bunch more babies, they will eventually be overrun in what the AWP calls the Great Race War. Hannah says the AWP pays the mothers for having the babies and provides free medical care for both the mothers and the children. Paying people to have sex seems like a political platform that almost everyone (at least the guys) could get behind. Maybe I should mention this to Ebenezer. Might help him pick up a few votes.

Day 223

The time has come, I suppose, to mention the election, since it is going hot and heavy. The Democratic candidate for president is Dr. Kevin Davis, a three-term Massachusetts congressman who has a PhD in biophysics from Boston College. Davis is the first heterosexual white male in decades to win the Democratic nomination for president. To preserve the party's traditional platform on diversity, the vice presidential candidate is Moriah Moonsong Sunset Rodriguez, the governor of Alaska who came to national prominence a few years ago when she announced that she was shutting down the Alaskan oil pipeline because it was interfering with the germination period for the sneezewort weed.

I am still trying to figure out why Senior wants Dr. Davis to become president. I thought President Carrier was doing a fine job, and Dad had lots of clout with President Carrier. My guess is that Dr. Davis would not be a big Senior fan, and I am sure Governor Rodriguez would not take Senior's calls. When the governor said that the State of Alaska was going to shut down the Alaskan pipeline, Senior placed ads in every major newspaper and on every prominent television network calling for "Governor Sneezewort" to be impeached on the grounds that she was a threat to national security and "possessed less native intelligence than a brain-damaged beagle." The governor, under intense pressure, backed down on her threat to shut down the pipeline after only a week.

Hannah and I watched CNN a bunch today. We saw clips of Eb giving a speech in Birmingham, Alabama, to the Swine Farmers of America convention. Although I doubt that Eb will pick up many pig farmer votes, since he does not eat pork, I am amazed at how good he sounded. Eb looked and sounded nothing like the poor guy I met on the yacht in the middle of the New Sea of Galilee.

When I commented that I really liked Eb, but I didn't think he would win, Hannah said, "A lot of things could happen between now and the election." When I asked what she meant, Hannah just smiled.

Day 230

Getting a little tired of Whitesville. Today I was so bored I decided to read the screenplay that Veronica gave me back in Canada. The title is: "The Story of Junior."

The first thirty pages or so of the screenplay follow the life of a black girl from Louisiana who escapes extreme poverty to become a national television sensation by tracking down the mass murderer Joshua Jennings, Jr. Our encounter in the Samara bar in Colorado is not mentioned. Instead, the screenplay describes how Veronica, using experimental satellite technology that she created, tracks Pete and me down in a luxurious condominium on a mountain in Switzerland. Pete and I ski out of the condo and down the mountain, with Veronica in hot pursuit. We shoot our guns, armed with silencers, at Veronica, but she slaloms to avoid the bullets. At the bottom of the mountain, Veronica disarms us and talks us into giving her an interview to tell our side of the story.

The screenplay ends on page fifty with the following notation: "Add sex scenes, more chase scenes, figure out happy ending. Have Veronica be the star witness at Junior's trial? Which states still have the death penalty?"

I am guessing that Veronica's idea of a happy ending for my story is different from mine.

Day 231

Although I was not too crazy about Veronica yesterday after reading her screenplay, today is a better day. The Cellulite Channel ran a special television exclusive today about Mandy and me. Apparently some new beach pictures of us have surfaced, this time from Greece. And Mandy, unfortunately, has some blobby cellulite patches on her thighs. The cellulite expert on the show drew red circles on Mandy's thighs to highlight the offensive cottage cheese. The Cellulite Channel announcer said she was forwarding the pictures to the FBI as soon as the show was over, so the Greek police could be contacted to investigate. I assume the investigation will focus on whether Mandy and I are actually in Greece, and not on Mandy's sudden cellulite issues. Thank you, Veronica, for the red herring.

Hannah just walked in, and without saying a word, took the remote control out of my hand and changed the channel to CNN. At first I thought Hannah was upset about the cellulite thing, since she is the real "Mandy," but it looks like she wanted me to see the picture of Moriah Moonsong Sunset Rodriguez being perp-walked to a police car. According to the announcer, the governor has been indicted for securities fraud and criminal breach of public trust. Apparently, she shorted the stocks of the oil companies right before her announcement that she was going to shut down the Alaskan pipeline to protect the sneezewort. When the stock prices of the oil companies went down, if only for a few days, she made a bunch of money.

I looked at Hannah, who just smiled. I wonder what would have happened in previous elections if the Mossad had a dog in the fight, so to speak. Our history could have been very different, I guess.

Day 235

I was working out today (the magazine pictures have inspired me) when my computer began to play "One Way Out," an old Allman Brothers tune and one of Pete's favorite songs. I stopped running on the treadmill, sat down in front of the computer, and saw one of the pictures of Mandy and me on the beach. There was a small icon located strategically on Mandy's body (I won't say where, but if you knew Pete, the location would be no surprise) that said "Open me!" So I did. Pete's message read as follows:

> *Big Man. How's it hanging? I am SO impressed with the results of your workout regimen. And the girl! Wow! I guess it's true that beautiful women like bad boys. You should have tried this wanted-criminal thing a long time ago.*

Anyway, I hope you are well. I plan to be back later. This is taking a little longer than I thought it would. Remember, Big Man, there are a lot of roads out there, but there ain't but one way out.[52]

I miss Pete.[53]

Day 239

Have you ever had one of those days when nothing seems to go according to plan? I don't mean REALLY not according to plan, like you have been charged with a mass murder you didn't commit, but on a smaller scale, like when events conspire to make you late to something you really wanted to attend. Today has been one of those days for me.

Today is race day in White Only Settlement—the one and only White Power Rally takes place today. The White Power Rally is a stock car race that brings in drivers from all over the world—as long as they are white, that is. The race is a huge money-raiser for the town. Hannah says the income from the tourists who come to White Only for the race pays for the free medical care the residents of the town receive.

The racetrack is located in a valley outside town that is surrounded by beautiful tree-covered hills. Even though it is winter, the track has some special contraption that keeps snow off the track during the race. The bleachers surrounding the track are big enough to hold 300,000 people.

For some reason, Hannah got us VIP tickets for the race. I have never been a race fan, so I certainly did not ask her to get the tickets. Maybe she is just bored. Anyway, even though I was not all that excited when Hannah told me about the race, the publicity about the race on television and in the local

---

52 This statement is known as "Pete's Conundrum," the third of the Seven Conundrums in *Junior*.

53 Scholars who believe that Day 167 was not in the original transcript of *Junior* have relied in part upon the failure of either Pete or Junior to mention Pete's sister Grace in Day 235.

newspaper got me pumped up to see it. Plus, the VIP tickets allow us to sit in the infield, which is the grassy area around which the drivers race. Sort of a bird's-eye view.

Our plan was to leave early this morning to beat the traffic. Nothing, however, went according to plan. First, my alarm clock did not work. Apparently, neither did Hannah's, because we both woke up an hour late. Then, when we were about to leave, my computer beeped and the following message appeared: "Please wait for important message." Since I have learned that these messages can indeed be very important, I waited. And waited. And waited some more. Finally, the "Please wait for important message" was replaced by "Error. Please disregard."

By the time we finally left the house, it was too late to make it to the VIP tent. Traffic was just too stacked up. Hannah knew a back road, however, that allowed us to drive up one of the hills surrounding the racetrack. We found a clearing in the trees that provided us with a nice view of the track. Hannah had purchased a White Is Wonderful baseball cap for me to wear as a disguise while we watched the race from the infield. I decided to wear it even though we were miles away from the crowd.

Hannah and I are watching the children's parade, which Hannah says is a White Power Rally tradition. Before the race begins, thousands of elementary school children, all dressed in white, of course, march around the track and wave at the crowd. Some of the little girls have flower petals which they throw into the air as they walk. It is really a stunning scene. White kids, white smiling teeth, blonde hair, white bows, white snow suits. If you forget for a moment that these people are crazy racists, the whole thing is quite beautiful. As I type this, I am waiting for Hannah, who just went back to the truck to get a camera so she can shoot a few pictures.

I know I started off this entry in a whiny fashion, and I guess I should apologize. Sitting here in the trees may actually be better than down in the infield. It is quieter up here, and nobody will see us.

Hannah is screaming and running toward me. Maybe I should[54]

---

54 It has not been established whether the last sentence of Day 239 was intentionally left unfinished or whether the conclusion of Day 239 was deleted.

Day 241

Hannah says I will feel better if I write. Sweet Jesus. Those poor children.

Hannah saw the helicopters, which is why she was screaming at me to get down. Instead, I stood up. I thought the helicopters were part of the show and I wanted to get a better view. The missiles from the helicopters blew up the racetrack and the infield. Blood everywhere. Screaming. Weeping. Wailing. Sweet Jesus. Those poor children.

Hannah and I had to stay in our spot on the hill outside the racetrack for hours. The roads were jammed with emergency vehicles and AWP militia vehicles. All we heard for hours were screams and sirens. Sweet Jesus. Those poor children.

At midnight, the Methodist Free Militia issued this statement to CNN:

The criminal Joshua Jennings, Jr., was executed today in White Only Settlement, the racist community in Idaho. The criminal was a friend of bigots. The criminal was a glutton and a drunkard. He was drinking and eating with his bigoted friends at a whites-only motorcar race when the wrath of the righteous was unleashed upon him and his perverted compatriots.

So because of me, a bunch of innocent kids got killed. And I would also have been killed, if not for the alarm clock snafu and the delay caused by the weird message on my computer.

Although they may never read this, I apologize to the folks in White Only Settlement. I know I kind of made fun of you, but I would never have wished this horrific catastrophe on you or your kids. I would never have come to your city if I had known this was going to happen. I am so, so sorry.

Day 248

Although I am semi-officially dead again, Hannah says we need to move. The poor folks in White Only Settlement are in an angry mood (who can blame them?) and they are openly talking of attacking the Methodist Free

Militia. The police here are also checking everyone's identification papers. Since I don't have any papers, Hannah says it is time to leave. I am willing.

Although Hannah is also upset about the massacre, she says I should be grateful I was spared. If we had arrived at the race on time, we would have been blown up with everyone else. She did not say I was spared by God's will, which is a good thing, because I would have slapped her. Granted, she would probably have then broken my arm, but I still would have slapped her.

Let me say, without any equivocation, that I am grateful not to be dead. But here is the thing about the God's will argument—it presumes that I am important enough for God to rearrange history for. And I am not. And chances are, dear reader, neither are you.

We all think that the world revolves around our every desire and need. So, if things go well for us, God must be arranging the world to satisfy us, or rewarding us for good behavior. If things don't go well, God must be sending us a message, or doing something for our "own good."

The "God's will" argument is often summarized by folks as "everything happens for a reason." I am not so sure that is true. It seems to me that sometimes, things just happen. The bottom line, I think, is: We are just not that important.

I don't know where all that came from. I am just an accused criminal on the run. I am not a deep thinker. Sorry for the rant.[55]

Day 253

I am down in some underground bunker somewhere. I think we are in Wisconsin. That is what Hannah told me, although she seems a bit distracted. Not sure what is going on there.

According to CNN, even though I am dead (again) I am still at the top of the Criminal Fantasy League standings. I know Pete is into fantasy league football, but I had never heard of the Criminal Fantasy League (CFL) until

---

55 The Day 248 Theory of Unimportance is one of the most controversial ideas in *Junior*. Many scholars see the statement as a form of humility, since Junior became famous worldwide and important to literally millions of people. The Theory of Unimportance has been criticized by religion and philosophy commentators alike, who see Junior's statement as an affront to both humanity and deity. For a compendium of the literature on this subject, see *The Importance of Being Junior*, by Dr. Allie Meredith.

today. The CFL, which was started several years ago, tracks the activities of criminals and inputs them into a database. Each player in the CFL can choose five criminals for their team. Points are allocated based on a variety of methods. For example, a financial criminal gets points for the dollars/rubles/whatever he steals. There is also an interest factor involved in monetary crimes. Murderers and terrorists get points for people killed and maimed. There is also a category for "collateral damage," where a criminal gets points if people were hurt or killed in an incident related to or involving the criminal. I am still on top because, even though I did not hurt the people in White Only Settlement, they count as collateral damage points.

The top five criminals in the CFL are:

(1) Joshua Jennings, Jr.
(2) Samson Fairman—Fairman killed fifteen nuns when he blew up the convent in Montreal. When you add the atrocities in White Only Settlement, he is only a few points behind me. Fairman has also killed a number of Muslim terrorists. In the CFL, you get extra credit when you kill another criminal, and Muslim terrorists count as criminals. Plus, since the CFL is an American/Canadian league, you get additional bonus points for killing Muslim terrorists.
(3) Dr. Ricardo Espinoza—Dr. Espinoza claimed to have developed a cure for women who lacked a desire for sexual intimacy. His product, Liquid Desire, spurred in part by a massive marketing campaign on all ten ESPN English channels, five ESPN Spanish channels, and three ESPN Portuguese channels, flew off the shelves. The Business Channel reported that 100 million units of Liquid Desire were purchased on Valentine's Day last year in the United States. Liquid Desire turned out to be nothing more than a mixture of cheap booze and cough syrup. Dr. Espinoza disappeared, but not before pocketing hundreds of millions of dollars.
(4) The Queer Cities of Refuge Killer (QCRK)—Someone has been killing folks in the Queer Cities of Refuge. This killer has not been identified, so he/she is simply known in the CFL as the QCRK. Since killing homosexuals qualifies as a "hate crime" in addition to murder, the QCRK gets extra points for his victims. Therefore, even though the QCRK has not killed that many people, he/she is in fourth place because of the extra "hate crime" points.

(5) Governor Moriah Moonsong Sunset Rodriguez—Governor Sneezewort's take from her short sales of oil company stock were larger than
originally estimated. Plus, once the authorities reviewed all her financial records, they discovered that she had been diverting some of her
campaign contributions to her personal bank account.

The CNN guy said the experts have predicted that I will likely drop out of
the top five now that I am dead. Most of the CFL players are trying to trade
me or release me from their team to pick up another criminal. I wonder what
happens if anyone figures out I am still alive?[56]

Day 258

Now I know why we are in a bunker somewhere in Wisconsin. The Mossad
guys are worried because the Methodist Free Militia keeps finding me, when
only the Mossad should know where I am. The helicopter strike in White
Only Settlement freaked them out because the MFM should not have known
I was supposed to be in the infield of the racetrack.

By the way, it just occurred to me we are in month nine. A person is very
likely in existence now who was only a twinkle in his daddy's eye when this
whole mess started. Welcome to the world, kid. Whatever you do, don't let
your daddy call you Junior.[57]

For some reason, I feel deader this time. Maybe it's because in my Parisian
death I just watched it on television, nobody died, and I suspected Senior was
somehow calling the shots. The mass murder in White Only Settlement was
very real.

Hannah just walked in and brought me a grilled cheese sandwich. We
have eaten a lot of cheese in Wisconsin. Not complaining, though. It is tasty.

I have not watched much TV lately. Mostly I have been reading and listening to music. Hannah is crazy about Elvis, so I have been listening to her

56 When the authorities discovered that Junior had not died in the White Only Settlement
Massacre, a class action lawsuit was filed against the CFL by the players who had traded
or released Junior as a player after the Massacre. The lawsuit was eventually settled, with
the lawyers for the plaintiffs receiving $15 million in attorneys' fees and the class members
receiving coupons for discounts on CFL T-shirts and other merchandise.

57 According to Popularnames.com, Joshua is the third most popular male name in the
world. The top ten names are: (1) Quandre, (2) Jose, (3) Joshua, (4) Mohammed, (5) Messi,
(6) Lebron, (7) Larryarnold, (8) Christian, (9) Ali, and (10) Prince.

recordings of the King.[58] Somehow, she has access to recordings of live concerts that never made it to an album or CD. When I asked her how she got these, she just smiled and said Elvis was a Mossad agent back in the day. I'm pretty sure she is kidding.

Hannah could tell I was bummed out after Idaho, so to cheer me up, she allowed me to read a bunch of top secret/unauthorized reports prepared by the Mossad, the FBI, the CIA, and Interpol. They are all old, and are about to be declassified anyway, so there is no harm in letting me peek.

You would not believe what I have learned. For example, I know why Secretary of State Oprah Winfrey REALLY resigned after only two months in office. Hint: It was not because she was gaining too much weight, which was her stated reason at the time.

Bummer. Hannah says I need to turn off the computer for a while, because the Mossad geeks are going to run some sort of sweep for bugs. I will tell you more about Oprah later.[59]

Day 262

Today, ladies and gentlemen, is my birthday. I am thirty-one years old. Make sure you eat some cake. It's chocolate, my favorite. Hannah made it.

We are still in the bunker. The Mossad guys who ran the electronics check said we are bug free.

When I say bunker, don't get the wrong idea. It is very nice here. It is just underground, somewhere in Wisconsin.

I have been dead twenty-three days now, and it looks like maybe this death will stick. The MFM has produced a video of a guy looking like me walking into the turnstiles at the racetrack. I am accompanied by a woman who looks a lot like Mandy from the supermarket tabloids. The FBI has announced that it is putting its search for me "on the back burner, unless new evidence surfaces to warrant more intense investigation." Hannah says the FBI actually stopped looking for me the day after the racetrack massacre.

So, it looks like I have gone from being the most recognizable face in the world to Mr. Irrelevant. Huh. The question is: "What do I do now?"

---

58 See Day 13, footnote 11, regarding Junior's reference to Elvis as the King.

59 *Junior* does not reference Oprah Winfrey again. No declassified reports have suggested an alternative reason for Winfrey's resignation.

Day 265

Since I just celebrated my birthday, I got to thinking about my family. Although Senior is rich and semi-famous, he goes out of his way to keep his family out of the limelight. Senior is one of those guys who believes that his family is nobody else's business.[60]

So let me tell you a little bit more about our family. If you compare my birthday to my parents' wedding anniversary, you will note a short seven-month difference. Yes, despite all of my dad's rants about "sex-crazed zipper rippers" and "horny hormonals," it turns out I was the product of an unlicensed and unapproved backseat tryst.

Senior met my mom when he was a nobody—indeed, somewhat of a failure. Dad had shown up on the Chiricahua reservation with a bunch of seismic maps that he believed identified substantial natural gas deposits on the Apaches' land. He invested a great deal of money, most of it borrowed, in the project. Seven dry holes later, Senior was broke. Not only that, he had impregnated the chief's daughter.

I only learned about this part of my dad's life last year. Although I was old enough to connect the dots on the calendar, I had never broached the subject of the timing of my birth with either of my parents.

Dad mentioned it late one night as we were flying home on one of his private jets. After telling me the basics of the story, he said, "Junior, no matter what happens to me, I want you to always remember to take care of the Apaches. They are my people. They will always be my people. They are your people. Your mother's tribe saved my hide back when I was broke and totally without prospects. If it wasn't for the Apaches, you and I would be flying Greyhound. Get my drift?"

Hannah says there is something I should see on the television. More on the Apaches later.

---

60 This paragraph, known as the Day 265 "is paragraph," has engendered decades of controversy. Junior's use of the verb "is" suggests to some scholars that Senior was not killed in the New Mexico explosion. Other commentators, citing the Day 2 reference by Junior that he is not an accomplished writer, and noting the numerous grammatical errors in the book, consider the "is paragraph" to simply be a mistake by Junior, or possibly a consequence of Junior's confusion caused by receiving e-mail messages from Senior after his death.

Day 269

The Republican candidate for president was short and to the point: "Junior, we need you to come back from the dead again."

I was watching Eb Cohen on a big television screen. We were having a videoconference. I didn't know where he was. I was still in the bunker.

I explained to Eb that I kind of liked being dead—it was nice not having people chasing me. We talked for about thirty minutes on the subject of why my reappearance was necessary. Reluctantly, I agreed. Time to leave the bunker.

Day 275

Month number ten. And time for my funeral.

Unlike the funeral for my parents and sisters, my service was not covered by the national media. No CNN. No BBC. My fall from celebrity had relegated me to the Funeral Channel. The Joshua Jennings, Jr., funeral was broadcast just after the Herman Ringtone funeral in Boca Raton, Florida, and just before the Cynthia Mingfield ceremony in Inman, Kansas.

The ceremony took place on the reservation. Pete's mom was there. One of the elders of the tribe conducted the ceremony, which was a very minimalist affair. The elder read my obituary, which was brief, given my lack of accomplishments. The elder then spoke for a few moments in very general terms about life and death and fate. He seemed very uncomfortable. Finally, he concluded: "I did not know Junior, although I knew his father well. I can say with absolute certainty that Senior loved his son. My hope is that they are together now, in a better place, and that they are happy."

And that was it. My eulogy, such as it was, was about my father, not about me. Even in death, Senior overshadowed Junior. If I had not been alive, I would have really been ticked off. As it is, I am just happy to be alive and looking forward to whatever is going to happen next.

Day 276

Although my funeral did not rate national network attention, it did not go unnoticed by Samson Fairman. The Methodist Free Militia ran a two-hour special entitled *The Hunt for the Terrorist Criminal Joshua Jennings,*

Jr., which detailed how the MFM tracked me across the United States and Canada and how they planned the raid on White Only Settlement. Interestingly, the documentary did not mention Pete and me being in New Jerusalem, or my speech about Fairman's Arabian Nights fiasco. The show focused on following us from California up the coast and into Canada. Fairman, of course, was the hero of the whole deal. The Montreal convent disaster also was not mentioned.

The conclusion of the film featured Fairman raising a glass of liquor of some sort in a toast and saying:

True and loyal Americans. Drink with me to the freedoms we enjoy and to the death of Joshua Jennings, Jr., and all other criminal terrorists, both foreign and domestic, who prey on our people. The Methodist Free Militia is dedicated to defeating all terrorists and making our country safe for all true and loyal Americans who have a birth certificate proving they were born in America or on an American military installation abroad.

I'm guessing Fairman is not going to be pleased when he finds out that he has failed to kill me.

Day 280

Hannah brought home (pretty bizarre when I think of this bunker as my home) two supermarket tabloids today. The first, *Minor Celebrity Fitness*, had an article on "Junior's Super Ab Routine." The article did not talk about my death, so I guess I was still at least a minor celebrity before I died.

The second magazine, *Girlfriends of Minor Celebrities Monthly*, was more interesting. "Mandy," my blonde goddess girlfriend, went into great detail about our sex life ("the sex was moving—he was powerful, yet gentle"), our plans ("Junior wanted to settle down—we were going to have a bunch of kids and raise horses together"), and the status of my vital signs ("Junior was *not* killed in Idaho. I don't know where he is now, but we were in Bermuda when the massacre in Idaho took place."). According to Mandy, I had to leave her so she would not be killed by the MFM: "Someday, when all this is cleared up, we will be back together. I just know it."

Most of the pictures in Mandy's article were of her, but one picture of "us" supported her assertion that we were in Bermuda when the White Only Settlement massacre took place. Mandy and a trim guy with my face are standing in front of the Bermuda Standard Bank. The big electronic clock on the outside of the bank shows the date—and it is the date of the massacre.

I know it's not much, but it's the best we can do for now. At least it's a start.

Day 284

Well, we have finally left the bunker. So long, Wisconsin, and thanks for all the grilled cheese. If I never see another bunker again, it will be too soon. As we drove out of Wisconsin, I noticed how pretty it was. Maybe when this is all over I will come back and take in the OUTSIDE of Wisconsin.[61]

Day 290

Well, things have been happening. Since the new plan is for me to be seen, we had to figure out a way to make that happen. Plus, I wanted to see if we could make it profitable.

So, with Eb's blessing, I contacted Blue and she set up a website called "I See Junior." Blue and her friends Pink and Orange have resisted every offer to make money off of Pete and me, and I figured they would be willing to help. The deal I cut with the girls was that half of any money they made off the website (and I figured it would be a ton) would go to the Sisters of Mercy and Charity Convent in Montreal that Fairman blew up.

Eb knew I was not crazy about being undead again, so he gave me some latitude in where to go. I chose some places I thought it would be cool to be seen. First, I chose Abbey Road. For those of you who don't follow rock and roll, *Abbey Road* was the final album of the Beatles, the greatest group of all time. On the cover of the album, John, Paul, George, and Ringo are shown walking across the zebra crossing on Abbey Road in London, England. It is

61 Archaeologists have conducted numerous digs in Wisconsin and have located Junior bunkers in Humbird, Antigo, and Berlin, Wisconsin. It is unclear why *Junior* implies that Junior stayed in the same bunker for the entire thirty days in Wisconsin. Although archaeologists agree that only three Junior bunkers have been identified in Wisconsin, the Wisconsin Visitors Bureau lists twenty "Junior Bunker" tourist sites. For a more detailed analysis of Days 253–283, see *Bunker Mentality: Junior's 30 Days of Cheese*, by Steven Gunter.

one of the most famous album covers of all time. Because it is so famous, there is a twenty-four-hour web camera showing the Abbey Road zebra crossing that picks up anyone who walks across.

We got a little silly, I admit, but I haven't had much fun lately, and this was so cool. We imitated the famous album cover. Three Mossad guys walked across with me, dressed in clothes similar to the clothes the Beatles wore on the cover. I was the third guy from the right, which is where Paul McCartney was in the original photograph. Like McCartney, I was barefoot.

The reaction was immediate and universal. Ten minutes after we walked across, someone posted the following on Blue's website: "I see Junior on Abbey Road and he is barefoot!" The website received 150,000 hits in the next hour. Making some money for the good sisters.

We then scooted over to Stonehenge. I talked to a University of Alabama coed there who sent in a post that said: "I see Junior and he is standing next to the big rock thingy here in England. He is not quite as buff as the pictures I saw in *Formerly Famous People Magazine*, though."

The next stop was Florence, Italy, to be seen with Michelangelo's famous statue of David. Sure enough, a few minutes after I walked into the Accademia Galleria, a poster on Blue's website reported: "I see Junior. He is wearing a Boise State National Championship cap and he is standing next to a big white naked guy in Italy!"

We started in Europe because we were worried that if a local cop in the United States happened to see me, things could get ugly. We figured law enforcement in Europe did not care about me anymore, and we were right. We went to a bunch of other places, but there is no point in writing down all of them, because that would make this book longer, and I am concerned you may be losing interest. Just wanted you to get a feel for what we did, so you know it is the truth. Jehu says we need to chill for a while and let the buzz build. Be back later.[62]

---

62 Between Day 285 and Day 295, over 100 million hits occurred on I See Junior. According to these reports, Junior was seen, among other places, at (1) the Great Wall of China, (2) the Grand Canyon (3) the Grand Cayman Islands, (4) the Grand L station in Chicago, and (5) the Grand Hotel in Stockholm, Sweden.

Day 295

You will never believe where I am. I am here and I can hardly believe it myself. This entry requires a little background.

Remember when I told you that Senior hated paying taxes?[63] One day several years ago, Senior was reading the *Burger King New York Times* and he saw an article about the billions of dollars the United States spends each year to house prisoners. Senior thought this was an outrage, particularly since all the experts say that prison does not rehabilitate the guys in there, just makes them worse.

At about this same time, Senior learned on CNN that after decades of fighting in Afghanistan, all the United States had been able to accomplish was to create between ten and fifteen (depending upon the season) "secure areas" within the country. The U.S. Marines maintained these secure areas, but no civilians lived there, because they were afraid they would be killed if the marines left.

Senior told President Carrier that he could get a "threefer" if he would just send all the gang members in the federal prison system to the secured areas in Afghanistan. By sending the gang members to Afghanistan, the president could reduce the prison population by over two-thirds (and save billions of dollars), he could bring the marines home (saving lives and billions of dollars), and he could mess with the Muslim terrorists in Afghanistan by exporting some of our worst citizens to their hangout. "It's a win, win, win," Senior told the president, "and I get to pay less taxes."

The president liked the idea, but the Justice Department lawyers balked, citing rules of criminal procedure and the United States Constitution, and all that kind of stuff. The president told Senior that the lawyers concluded that even the president can't force prisoners to leave the United States.

This is where I come in, and I must admit I am all kinds of proud about this. I am one of those guys who loves to watch movies. I have seen lots of movies about gangs and criminals. And one of the things I have learned about criminals from these movies is that nothing is more important to a criminal than being feared. A criminal will do anything to be the baddest guy in town.

---

63 See Day 45.

So, I convinced Senior to propose a program in which the government offers a pardon to every gang member in the federal prison system who agrees to go to Afghanistan. I called the program: "Are You a Badass?" Basically, the government offers each recognized gang one of the secure areas in Afghanistan and agrees to provide food, liquor, drugs, money, weapons, video games, DVDs, CDs, and prostitutes to the secure area. The gang simply has to agree to protect the secure area from Muslim terrorists. Beyond that, the feds don't care what the gangs do. They can drink, drug, and whore to their hearts' content. In effect, the gang members get paid to be badasses.

Senior was skeptical. "Junior," he said, "this is a creative idea, but I don't know if the president will go for it." The president, however, loved the idea. In the end, the folks who fought hardest against my idea were the federal prison employees, because most of them knew "Are You a Badass?" would end up eliminating their jobs. The rest of America was so tired of gangs they did not care where the gangs went, as long as they were no longer in the land of the free and the home of the brave. Even the Democrats and the ACLU supported the program. And as a bonus that nobody anticipated (a "fourfer"?), with the gang leaders in Afghanistan, the young kids in the ghettos either (1) left for Afghanistan to join the gangs when they became old enough or (2) were able to grow up in a much safer environment and focus on their education.

In fact, "Are You a Badass?" was so successful the marines had to create a few more secure areas for the gangs. The gangs who moved to Afghanistan included the Big Circle Gang, the Bloods, the Crips, Joe Boys, Nuestra Familia, the Nazi Lowriders, MS-13, the Aryan Brotherhood, and the Tiny Rascal Gang. So far, all the gangs have maintained their secure areas, despite numerous attacks by Muslim terrorists. So, I guess all the gangs have maintained their "badass" status.

I realize that was a long lead-in, but it is a cool story and one of the few projects pushed by Senior in which I played an important role.

As you have probably guessed by now, I am in Afghanistan. I am in Secure Area 7, run by the Big Circle Gang. I have already been to Secure Area 5 (Nuestra Familia) and Secure Area 9 (Crips). I came to Afghanistan because (1) no law enforcement guys would dare come here, (2) each secure area has sophisticated video and computer equipment so my visit can be recorded and broadcast to the world, and (3) these guys like me. It turns out the gangs think I am cool because I have avoided the authorities all this time. In fact, each badass gang I have visited has offered to make me a badass member.

So, for all of you out there who have derided me as a faggy, overweight shlump, take notice. I am a badass. And I am alive.[64]

Day 299

Well, I think everyone agrees I am alive now. Even the MFM, which issued a terse statement on its website about how it will "continue to pursue the criminal terrorist Joshua Jennings, Jr."

I talked to Blue today. She confirmed that "I See Junior" has become a big hit, and the convent has made a ton of money. Blue went to the convent and came away very impressed with the nuns. "It's hard to explain," she told me, "but they have a certain calmness about them that I find remarkable. And they loved my hair."

Something happened in Afghanistan that I should mention. My last stop there was Secure Area 8, which was run by the Nazi Lowriders. The Lowriders call their town Secure Area 88, because H is the eighth letter of the alphabet, so 88 stands for Heil Hitler. It's amazing to me people still buy into this stuff, but that is a conversation for another day.

The chief honcho of the Nazi Lowriders is a guy named Clayton Singletary. Clayton does not fit the profile for your average Nazi Lowrider. Clayton is thin, pale, and wears wire-rimmed glasses. In short, he looks like an accountant.

Clayton looks like an accountant because he is one. Got his CPA and everything. He is in Afghanistan because he was busted for tax fraud and somehow wound up in a real prison instead of the prisons designed for white-collar criminals. He joined the Nazi Lowriders to avoid being gang-raped by all the other gangs. The Lowriders love him, Clayton told me, because he invested the gang's money in lucrative offshore investments that made each of the Lowriders a millionaire many times over.

Clayton told me that before he moved to Afghanistan, he was approached by a guy in jail about the best place to buy explosives. Said he needed enough to blow up a bunch of buildings. Clayton elaborated:

---

64 The "Are You a Badass?" program has since expanded to other countries semi-successfully invaded by the United States, including North Korea, Venezuela, and a number of African countries.

This guy was no terrorist. He was this chubby white guy who used to be a big-shot banker. I don't know why he was in our jail and not in a club fed. He must have made somebody really mad, because he shared a cell with this huge black guy named Big Rico. Everybody was scared of Big Rico. Even the hard-core Nazi types stepped aside when Big Rico walked down the hallway. The chubby guy did not explain why he needed the stuff, and I did not ask questions. I gave him the names of a few contacts on the outside who could handle what he needed. I am telling you this, Junior, because you don't seem like a criminal to me. I have been hanging out with criminals for years now, so I think I know one when I see one.

I am not exactly sure what to do with this information, but the way things have been going, it could be important. Over and out from your favorite badass.

Day 305

Welcome to month eleven of the Unfairly Accused Mass Murderer's World Tour. This is Tuesday, so it must be New York City. I am supposed to meet Veronica tomorrow.

Veronica is no longer with the Plumbing Fixtures Network. After her interview with Fairman in Canada, she quit PFN and signed on with the I Scream, You Scream Network at a substantial increase in salary. Her show *Screaming about Junior* got wonderful ratings for a while, but when it appeared I was dead for good, ratings for the show dropped and the network canceled her.

Although the television industry failed Veronica, the legal system did not. Remember when I told you that Veronica had filed a copyright lawsuit over the Let Him Be yellow bee?[65] Well, she won the lawsuit and came away with lots of money. So, she has started her own network. Not surprisingly, it is called the Veronica Network.

So far, the Veronica Network's most-watched programs are either about me or the election. Veronica interviewed Blue about the "I See Junior"

---

65 See Day 63.

website and then basically piggybacked onto Blue's website for stories related to Junior "sightings."

Plus, Veronica just made a lot of stuff up. For example, Veronica speculated "through informed sources" that:

(1) I am a descendant of Ringo Starr;
(2) I was once a promising sculptor until my hands were injured in a motorcycle accident;
(3) I was once a practicing Druid; and
(4) I have an illegitimate brother who is a Nazi Lowrider.

Amazingly, each of these speculations consumed several days of television airtime, with experts discussing how these "facts" affected my personality and could have led me to either blow up the president or not blow up the president, depending upon the expert.

Since her victory in the lawsuit, Veronica is also maxing out on the Let Him Be endorsement opportunities. You can buy a Granger Rectal Probe Let Him Be T-shirt in a variety of colors, an Ohio State Fair Tractor Pull Let Him Be cap, and even Let Him Be lip gloss.

The Cohen campaign has stayed in close contact with Veronica and has provided her with stories that help Eb's campaign. I think, but I am not sure, that Eb thinks he can use Veronica to help me, and I hope he is correct. Anyway, Eb asked me to meet Veronica in New York, and since Eb and his Mossad guys are the only reason I am still alive, I am not really in a position to disagree.

I guess we will find out tomorrow what Veronica wants. Good night.

Day 308

Finally met with Veronica today. She blew me off for a couple of days because a woman in Wyoming claimed that I had impregnated her daughter and Veronica had to fly out there to interview everyone involved. The interview did not last very long, because the daughter identified the guy in the Rio bathing suit pictures[66] as the father of her baby. When Veronica, in a great flourish, whipped out a picture of me, the daughter said, "Oh my, I

---

66 See Day 212.

would never have sex with that guy." Veronica gets a great television moment, I again get trashed.

We met in Veronica's office, which is across the street from the Yankee Stadium Solid Waste Disposal Station. I grew up hating the New York Yankees, because they had more money than all the other teams and bought all the good players, even the few good players that the Texas Rangers, my favorite team, developed. So when the Yankees went bankrupt because their owners invested in a hedge fund that turned out to be a Ponzi scheme, I was not sad in the least. In fact, the only time I ever talked politics with President Carrier was when the Yankees argued that they "were too big to fail" and should receive a federal bailout. I told President Carrier that the Yankees' argument was ridiculous. President Carrier, a New York Mets fan, agreed and instead offered federal funds to New York City to turn Yankee Stadium into a landfill. New York City, which was close to bankruptcy at the time, readily agreed.

When I asked Veronica why her office was across the street from a landfill, she responded, "I need to be in New York City because this is the media and style capital of the world. The rent across from the dump is cheap, and all that I really need to appear big-time is a New York City address. Nobody important actually comes to my office. Take one of those pine cone air freshener dealies off the desk and loop it around your neck." Noting to myself that Veronica did not think I was important, I took the pine cone and put it around my neck. It did not help much.

"Junior, you have a big problem," Veronica began, then she stopped talking and started rummaging around in her desk. This break in the discussion gave me a chance to think about my problems. There were so many, I was amazed Veronica could focus on only one.

Veronica continued. "Your problem is that you are not getting any support from your hometown. Are you aware that there has not been a single Let Him Be rally in Dallas County? Or that I have only sold one Granger Rectal Probe Let Him Be shirt in the entire Dallas–Fort Worth metroplex? Why don't they like you down there?"

Before I could respond, Veronica changed subjects. "What did you think about my screenplay? I can tell you several of the big studios are chomping at the bit to buy it. My agent says it could go for seven figures."

Note to self—I need to get an agent and try this screenwriting thing.

Veronica continued. "Your problem, Junior, is that the world does not really know the real Junior. There have been so many false stories and rumors about you that your real personality has not had a chance to shine through."

Now you, dear reader, and I both know that one of the main reasons the world "does not really know the real Junior" is that Veronica has made her living the last several months spreading false stories and rumors about me. Not knowing how to respond logically to Veronica without either laughing or screaming, I simply said, "What would you like me to do for you?"

So she told me.

Day 312

Hannah is a football fan. There is a pleasant melody to that phrase, isn't there? Are my male readers jealous? I am hanging out with a beautiful woman who can cook, kill bad guys, is crazy about Elvis and LIKES TO WATCH FOOTBALL ON TV. I know you may not be jealous about the whole wanted for mass murder and certain death penalty thing, but the beautiful woman/football combo is pretty good stuff, you gotta admit.

Anyway, we watched the Tier 4 Super Bowl today. The Dallas Cowboys, who moved up in the playoffs after their nineteenth-place finish, played the Denver Broncos. I am not sure I like the tiered Super Bowl system. Seems to me it was fine when there was just one Super Bowl. But now teams can get a trophy that says Super Bowl Tier 4 Champion, and I guess everyone likes a trophy.

Hannah is a Dallas Cowboys fan, like me. She says that when she lived in Israel, they always got the Cowboy games on television, so almost everyone from Israel is a Cowboys fan. I will have to ask Eb what team he roots for.

The Cowboys won, and Henry the Hammer was interviewed after the game. Henry said three times that the Cowboys' "back was up against the wall" and four times that he just "plays each game one at a time." He then concluded:

I know I can't talk the talk like the smart guys do on TV, but I just want to say that even though this Tier 4 trophy is very important, it's not as big a deal as real life. This trophy ain't real life. Living and dying is real life. I knew Joshua Jennings, Sr., and he was a good man. He got me a tutor so I could pass the tests to get into Stonewall Jackson Tech. Senior is dead now, and that's real life, man. Ain't nothing we can do about it. Junior, I know you are out there watching because you love the Cowboys, like all good Texans. I also know you loved your daddy and would never blow him to smithereens—that's real life too. Don't fret because of evil men, Junior. The bad guys are after you, Junior, so be real careful, and don't forget to take some chances. Real life means being real careful and taking some big chances.[67] Now if you will excuse me, pretty lady interviewer with really nice bosoms, I need to go tell Bubba Connolly that he is now a credit to his black Negro race again because he did not once try to illegally trip or chop block me today.

Like I have said on many occasions in my life, they teach 'em up good at Stonewall Jackson Tech, don't they?

Day 320

I sincerely hope the Hammer is right, because today I am taking a big chance and trying to be real careful at the same time. Veronica's big idea was for me to debate Samson Fairman on the Veronica Network. When I agreed, Veronica took out full-page ads in all the big newspapers and websites and bought commercials on a bunch of the big television networks. The commercials said, in essence: "Junior challenges Fairman to a debate. Fairman is a whipped pussycat if he does not agree."

Fairman, who loves publicity and carefully nurtures his "warrior" image, could not resist the challenge. I have never been in a debate before. I asked Veronica several times how the debate was going to work, but she was always too busy to respond.

Earlier this morning, Hannah cut my hair and told me to shave my stubble and lose my USS Obama cap. Then she gave me a long-sleeved blue dress shirt and told me to put it on and leave the top button unbuttoned. "You don't look great," she said, "but you don't look like a criminal, either."[68]

---

67 This statement is known as "The Hammer's Conundrum," the fourth of the Seven Conundrums in *Junior*.

68 Some commentators, noting that Hannah's statement is virtually identical to what the prime minister's wife said to Junior in Day 89, have speculated that Hannah was the prime minister's daughter.

The first thirty minutes of the program consisted of Veronica talking about how she arranged the debate and her history with "the accused mass murderer Joshua Jennings, Jr." Then there were twenty minutes of commercials. The Veronica Network made some serious money today, because these commercials were not for Granger Rectal Probe Let Him Be T-shirts. Google, Pepsi, Nose Jobs International, and Rader's Erectile Dysfunction Remedy, all huge companies, had purchased time for the debate.

Veronica then pushed a button and Fairman appeared on a big television screen. I did not know where he was, but I assumed he was far away in some safe MFM hideout. Fairman looked like a rich, successful banker or lawyer—silver hair, blue suit, red power tie. I knew right away I had lost the appearance battle.

After a few preliminaries, Veronica asked Fairman if he would like to make an opening statement. Fairman said he would, but "first, Veronica, could I say a prayer before we begin? I think that would be appropriate, don't you?"

Veronica looked at me as if she had just been administered a Granger Rectal Probe. She clearly did not know what to say. Fairman took her silence as consent and he began to speak, in a slow, soothing, deep bass voice:

Merciful father, who gave us this wonderful country, with its inalienable rights of life, liberty, and the pursuit of happiness, thank you for allowing us to live in a free country where those of us who put in the effort to get an advanced degree, work hard, and invest well can be happy and successful, or at least marry someone who is successful. Thank you for giving those of us who have high standards the knowledge and wisdom to avoid evil actions and nefarious company. And most of all, thank you for giving victory to those of us who have the courage to fight evil in every form, both foreign and domestic. Amen.

I admit I did not close my eyes and use my "praying hands," as I was taught years ago in Sunday School. I watched Fairman as he prayed. When he finished, he winked at me and said, "Good-bye, Junior. Say hello to Abu Abu Mohammed Mohammed for me."

And then the Yankee Stadium Solid Waste Disposal Station blew up, and everything smelled really bad.

Day 325

Well, the Hammer's advice worked. I took a big chance by sitting in Veronica's office to debate Fairman when I suspected he would try to blow me up again. I was real careful by having the Mossad guys use their superspy technology stuff to deflect the missiles from Veronica's office to the Yankee Stadium Dump across the street. Don't ask me how the technology worked—I am just glad it did.

Everybody says that Fairman will just slink away into oblivion and shame because of what he tried to do. I am less sure that will happen. Fairman is a truly horrible person, but the folks who like him will continue to like him no matter what. Fairman is sort of like the Hammer's nemesis, Bubba Connolly. Everybody knows Bubba is a dirty player, but the fans of the Denver Broncos love Bubba because he is THEIR dirty player. Broncos fans consider Bubba a "blue-collar scrapper" who "makes the most out of his ability." I promise you, though, if and when Bubba is ever traded to another team, the Denver fans will join the rest of the league in condemning Bubba's dirty play.

I am pretty sure that New Yorkers, be they Fairman fans or not, are not too happy with Fairman this morning. The MFM missiles made a direct hit on the landfill and there is trash all over New York City. The City That Never Sleeps is now the City That Really Stinks.

Samson will be happy to know, however, that he is now number one in the CFL standings. Property destruction is worth points in the CFL, and although the trash destruction does not provide Samson with any points, the Yankee Stadium Solid Waste Disposal Station infrastructure was very expensive and its destruction garnered Samson a bunch of CFL points.

I am no longer in stink range. Right after the explosion, Hannah and I and our Mossad bodyguards got into an armored car and drove to New Jersey, where we jumped on a helicopter and flew south. Don't want to say yet where I am.

Day 328

Hannah and Jehu had to leave. Apparently something important is going down in North Dakota. They did not explain. Said they would be back later.

I miss Hannah and Jehu (especially Hannah), but I am not lonely. It is difficult to feel lonely when you are surrounded by about 100 kids.

Hannah and Jehu left me in the safekeeping of the Sisters of the Holy Cross, who run a home for mentally and physically handicapped children near Seven Devils, North Carolina, in the Appalachian Mountains. When I asked why a bunch of nuns would live near a town named Seven Devils, I got one of those smiles that parents give their kids when they ask a stupid question.

The nun who has apparently been appointed as my "keeper" is named Sister Flannery, and to my pleasant surprise, she is young, vivacious, and pretty. My image of nuns has always been of women who could never get a date. Unfair, I know, but what are you gonna do?

Anyway, Sister Flannery, who says she is twenty-one but looks much closer to sixteen, makes sure I get enough to eat and she answers my questions to the best of her ability. If the MFM shows up, I doubt Sister Flannery or any of the other sisters will be able to protect me, but that is the way it goes. Hannah and Jehu said I would be safe here, so I guess I have to trust their judgment. Plus, I have no wheels, so it's not like I can just drive away.

The sisters have been very nice. They know who I am, and so far, at least, they have not asked any hard questions. Sister Flannery told me on my arrival that they knew I was in trouble, but that the prime minister in North Dakota had vouched for me. I wanted to ask about what seemed to me to be a strange connection, but I held my tongue.

I do, however, have chores. Everybody here has chores. I have to take out the trash and sweep floors, and I am the designated mover of heavy objects. "We don't have many uses for men around here," Sister Flannery told me, "but sometimes it is good to have a strong back in the house." So, I have gone from Joshua Jennings, Jr., mass murderer, to Joshua Jennings, Jr., Catholic beast of burden.

I have to go now. Sister Flannery says one of the kids has vomited in the cafeteria. Apparently my job description has just expanded. Cleanup on aisle 9.

Day 329

Sister Flannery is a runner. I am not. Sister Flannery is concerned about my health, however, so today we took a run on a beautiful mountain trail. After about half a mile or so I was totally pooped, so we sat on a scenic overlook and took in the view.

I was enjoying the silence, but Sister Flannery wanted to talk. "So," she said, "what is your next move?"

I told her the truth. "Sister Flannery, I have no idea. Right now, I am just living my life day to day, just getting by on the sly, if you know what I mean. Oh yeah, and trying to stay alive."

Sister Flannery did not let my response go by unchallenged. "The Father obviously has a purpose in all of this, Junior. You are destined for something important. You know that, right?"

I paused, not wanting to start an argument with this nice young lady. What possible good could come from me arguing with a nun? But when the sister persisted, I gave her my standard spiel on "God's will," and how none of us is really all that important in the grand scheme of things. I know I wrote about it earlier somewhere, so I won't repeat it here.[69]

Sister Flannery's response was direct and to the point. "What a load of poop! Are you saying that the events that have taken place are totally random and without meaning? Do you realize how ridiculous that sounds? Junior, you have been on the run for almost a year now from every law enforcement agency in the world, and you are still free. Don't you think there has been some divine intervention on your behalf?"

I replied in what I hoped was a pleasant but firm voice. "I don't know, sister. Why don't you ask the parents of those sweet kids who were blown up in White Only Settlement about the divine intervention expended on my behalf? Did the Father blow up those kids so I could escape? Did the Father, or the Mother, or the Great Spirit, or whoever is in charge, lead Fairman to Montreal to blow up the nuns because I needed time to get away? If that is divine intervention designed to help me, then I don't want it. Those innocent kids in White Only Settlement are dead because of me. So are the Canadian nuns. That burden is so heavy on me I can hardly stand up straight."

Sister Flannery quickly countered, "Are you saying you don't believe the Father is in control? That all of these events are just random?"

"Not necessarily," I said. "There probably is a higher power who is in control. I am just not convinced the higher power is organizing the world for my benefit."

Sister Flannery smiled, as if she believed she had won the argument, and continued, "You are right, Junior. He is not arranging things for your benefit. He is arranging things for His purpose."

---

69 See Day 248.

I wish I could tell you we reached a consensus, but we did not. We argued for a while longer, then Sister Flannery challenged me to a race back to the home. She even gave me a head start. Then she kicked my butt.

Day 332

We are now in month twelve of the I'm Still Not Blown Up Tour. Please check your weapons at the door.

Looks like Eb's Mossad investigators are still at it. Today, the Democrats announced that California Senator Arturo Salinas Ramirez Mendoza, the party's choice to replace Governor Moriah Moonsong Sunset Rodriguez as the vice presidential candidate, is no longer on the ticket. Turns out that Senator Mendoza had been using undocumented aliens from Egypt as maids and gardeners, and paying them about half the minimum wage. Senator Mendoza apologized to the American people and promised that in the future he would only employ Hispanic undocumented aliens.

Maybe the Democrats should try and find a nun to run as the vice presidential candidate. Based on the women I have met here at the home, a smart, no-nonsense nun would be a good choice to help run the country. Plus, I bet even the Mossad would have a hard time finding dirt on a nun.

Day 333

Speaking of smart, no-nonsense nuns, today I was called into the office of Mother Superior Marie Hookenstein. In addition to no-nonsense, she is also downright scary.

Remember the rabbi in the North Dakota synagogue?[70] That guy was Casper the Friendly Ghost compared to Mother Superior Hookenstein.

Anyway, the mother superior summoned me to fix her phone. "It is not working, Mr. Jennings. Please fix it and then you can return to your duties." She said the word "please," but somehow I did not take her statement as a request. Remember when I said that I always thought of nuns as girls who could not get a boyfriend?[71] The mother superior fits that mold, if you get my drift.

When I told the mother superior that I could not fix her phone, she was confused. "The phone is made by Apache Communications, is it not?"

---

70 See Day 78.
71 See Day 328.

"Yes, ma'am."

"And Apache Communications is one of your late father's companies, correct?"

"Yes, ma'am, it is."

She then looked at me incredulously, as if it was inconceivable that I could not fix a phone made by one of Senior's companies. I started to say that I could also not drill an oil well or butcher a cow, even though Senior owned oil companies and meatpacking plants, but I decided maybe I should refrain from my normal smart-aleck attitude. So I just said, "I am very sorry ma'am, but I never worked for Apache Communications."

"Well that figures, I suppose. You don't seem much like your father, after all."

I started to say that Senior could not have fixed the phone either, but before I could speak she said, "You know, young man, I knew your father. He was a great man."

I did not respond, since clearly this was going to be yet another morality tale explaining how Junior did not measure up to Senior. I wanted to stop her and walk out, since I was getting tired of these stories, but I was her guest, so I just stood there, waiting to take my medicine.

To my surprise, she smiled just a bit and invited me to have a seat. "It is not a long story, but you should sit down, young man.

"You remember, I assume, all the problems the Church experienced in America in the past. The pedophilia, the child abuse, the homosexuality, the drug abuse, the alcoholism, the lawsuits. The priests were out of control."

I nodded.

"Well, the Catholic Church in America was on its last legs. Basically every major diocese in the country was on the verge of bankruptcy because of the payments made to victims of the priests. And Rome had decided to pull back its support. The Vatican was worried the American priests would bankrupt the entire Catholic Church."

I did not know about the Vatican's threat to pull the plug, but again, I nodded.

"Because of the financial problems the Church was experiencing, our funding here at the home was shrinking dramatically. The situation was desperate. Do you know Mr. Samuel Lincoln Johnson?"

The change of topic caught me by surprise. I started to shake my head, then, it occurred to me who the mother superior was talking about. "You mean the Assassin?"

"Yes, Mr. Jennings, although I must say I find names like that totally inappropriate. There is already so much violence in this world, we don't need to glorify . . . I'm sorry. No need for my sermon on that issue at this point in time. Anyway, when it looked like we would have to close the home I contacted Mr. Johnson, who runs a similar type of home in El Paso, Texas, to see if he could take a few of our kids.

"And he put you in touch with Senior," I interrupted.

"You know this story?"

"No, but I have a hunch how it turns out. Please continue, ma'am. I apologize for interrupting."

"Well, long story short, I met with your father to explain our problem. He then organized a series of meetings with the plaintiffs' lawyers representing the abuse victims, representatives from the larger American dioceses, the highest-ranking American bishops, representatives of the nuns in America, and even high-ranking Vatican officials. When the negotiating was concluded, the end result was that every single priest in America was either let go or transferred somewhere else in the world. As you know, there are no longer any Catholic priests in America."

I figured I knew the answer, but I had to ask. "How did Dad do it?"

She smiled, and I realized that, back in her youth, the mother superior could have had a boyfriend after all. "He shamed and scared the Vatican, and then he money-whipped 'em. Your father told the Vatican's representative that his good friend Kirk McConn, an incredibly successful class action lawyer in Dallas, Texas, had already prepared a class action petition to sue the Vatican over the entire mess. Your father even brought a copy of the petition. Apparently, Mr. McConn had some amazing evidence that showed the Vatican knew about the problems and tried to cover them up.

"Your father said the only way to avoid the lawsuit, which even if unsuccessful would have been terribly embarrassing, was to kick out all the priests in America and let the nuns run the show." She smiled again. "He actually said 'let the nuns run the show.' I will never forget that moment as long as I live."

Mother Superior Hookenstein was silent for a moment, apparently just enjoying the memory. Then she continued. "The priests, of course, were indignant and raised all sorts of objections. The Vatican's primary envoy was silent as the priests rambled on. Then he said, 'Mr. Jennings, can we speak in private?'

"The Vatican's envoy and your father left the room. They returned thirty minutes later and announced that the deal was done."

"What went on in that meeting has never been disclosed, but I can tell you that the plaintiffs' lawyers and the abuse victims were paid and now the nuns in America have money to run their convents, all the churches, and innumerable charitable programs. Someone paid a lot of money to make that happen, and I'm sure it was your father. It was clear the Vatican had abandoned us."

I lobbed her a waist-high softball: "I confess that I have not paid close attention to the Catholic Church in recent years, Mother Superior. How have things worked out, without any priests?"

She swung and knocked it out of the park: "The nuns are running the show in America, Junior, and it is glorious. We are serving people and saving souls. We don't miss the men a bit."

For some reason, I decided to defend my gender: "But you needed at least one man to make it happen, correct?"

She smiled, delicately picked up the cross hanging on the chain around her neck, and kissed it. "I would say two."

Day 340

Senior, like all fathers, loved to tell his son how hard he had worked as a young man. Senior worked some tough jobs in his youth and never hesitated to remind me how the backbreaking exertion was good for a young man.

So, I got to dig postholes at one of Senior's cattle ranches, roughneck for one of Senior's oil companies, and load trucks at one of Senior's transportation companies. And I hated every minute of it.

For some reason, though, I am semi-enjoying the manual labor here at Seven Devils. The sisters are appreciative, and I feel like I am contributing to the success of the home.

Today, as I was raking leaves with Sister Flannery, I felt the need to verbalize my innermost thoughts. I should have known better.

"You know, Sister," I said, "I have enjoyed myself here. This manual labor thing ain't all that bad."

"This is a special place, Junior."

"So what inspired you to work with handicapped children, Sister?"

"What did you call them?"

"Who?"

"The children."

"Handicapped?"

"This is the twenty-first century, Junior. Sensible people consider that term to be inappropriate. Try again."

"Challenged?"

"Makes them sound inferior."

"Disabled?"

"They are perfectly able, within the limits God has given them."

"Developmentally impaired?"

"Impaired is worse than disabled. And if you say the "r" word, I will punch you in the shoulder. Hard."

I was glad she warned me, because the "r" word was all I could think of to try. I did not want to get punched by a nun.

"I give up. What do you call the children, sister?"

"I call each of them by their given name."

"That's cheating. You know what I mean."

"These children are God's Elect. He has chosen them."

That was an unfair answer. I was tempted to ask if she called them "GEs" for short, but I did not want to get punched. I decided to press the philosophical debate, however.

"So you are saying God chose these kids to be different?"

"Yes. Haven't you noticed that the name of this place is 'The Seven Devils' Home for God's Chosen'?"

"But why would God choose these children to have problems? Why would God choose to make a child deaf or blind from birth?"

"I don't know, Junior. I am not God. I do not know His reasoning."

"Well, Sister, I'm guessing that these kids, and their parents, may not be all that fired up about being chosen in this fashion."

"You need to get over yourself, Junior. The world does not revolve around what you or I want."

"I was talking about these kids, not me."

"Could have fooled me, Junior."

"Anyway, I do agree with you on one point, Sister. We are not that important in the grand scheme of things. That is really my point."

"And, again, you are wrong, Junior. We are all important to God. Even if we are not happy about our station in life. God has a purpose for these kids, Junior. And whether you like it or not, Junior, the Father has a purpose for you."

And then she punched me in the shoulder anyway. Hard.

Day 345

Sister Flannery and I were washing dishes today after the evening meal when Abby Laurel wandered into the kitchen. Abby is about seven years old, and she is blind and a little deaf. "Mr. Junior," she said in a too-loud voice, "I really need some help. Can you help me?"

"What do you want me to do for you?" I responded.

"Mr. Junior," she continued, "I really need some help with my ponytail." Abby was screaming a little bit, but she did not realize it because of her hearing problem.

I looked at Sister Flannery, who grinned and said, "I'm sure Mr. Junior would be glad to help, sweetie." I shot daggers at Sister Flannery with my eyes but proceeded to comb out Abby's thick dark hair and use one of those hair scrunchy things to tie up a ponytail. It took me about ten minutes. I worked hard at it, and I was proud of the result.

"Mr. Junior, are you blind?" Abby shouted. "Mercy me. This looks terrible! Sister Flannery, can you fix this?"

The sister spent thirty seconds on Abby's hair. "Thanks, Sister Flannery," Abby shouted. "I guess you are right about men not being able to do a lot of stuff." She then left the kitchen.

"You know, it's interesting," I began. "If I told the children that women were only good for having babies, you would go berserk. But you think it's OK to tell the children that men have no skills?"

"The Bible says we should not lie, Junior. And besides, I only say things like that to the girls. I would never tell the boys that."

"So, as far as you are concerned, men really don't have much of a purpose in this world, correct?"

"Not exactly, true," Sister Flannery responded. "Can I tell you a story to illustrate my point?"

"Can I prevent you?"

"Of course not. Anyway, back in the bad old days, when the priests were in charge, this place was under the jurisdiction of Father Lawrence Black. Father Black was lazy and not interested in the children. He ignored virtually all of our requests for improvements for the home and actually spent part of the money designated for the home to buy himself liquor. When he visited us, he was often drunk and rude.

"One day, after a particularly vile visit from Father Black, I asked Mother Superior Hookenstein why God would put such a disgusting man in charge of the home. She told me that God has a reason for everything and that God had a purpose for Father Black.

"When I asked her what possible purpose Father Black fulfilled, she said, 'Father Black is here to show all of us how to be a bad example. That is his special gift, and his purpose.'"

The sister smiled sweetly. "So, if nothing else, most of the men on this planet serve the purpose of showing the rest of us how *not* to act. They are not totally good for nothing."

Then she punched me in the shoulder again, although not very hard this time.

Day 350

As you can tell by my writing style, I was not a star in school. In fact, my favorite "courses" in elementary school were lunch and recess. Which puts me in good stead with most of the God's Elect here at the home.

Today I was digging up a flower bed next to the playground during recess when a football landed at my feet. I looked up and saw Sister Flannery and a bunch of the kids.

One of the kids yelled, "Sorry, Mr. Junior. Could you throw it back?"

I picked up the football, pointed to Justin Newton, one of the older boys, and said, "Go deep."

Justin knew exactly what to do and took off. I tossed the football high in the air and the kid caught it in stride. "Touchdown!" he exclaimed, spiked the ball into the ground, and did a pretty impressive shoulder shimmy. The children all screamed with delight: "Mr. Junior! Mr. Junior! Please come play with us. Please be our quarterback. You can throw it far! Sister Flannery throws like a girl."

Sister Flannery smiled and nodded, so I dropped my shovel and walked to the group of kids. Sister Flannery handed me the football and I punched her on the arm. But gently, and with affection.[72]

Day 355

Well, this is interesting. I am now officially on my own. Two nights ago Mother Superior Hookenstein came into my room and said I had to leave immediately. "I just received a call from the prime minister," she said. "There is a problem. You need to go."

She did not explain the problem. I had to leave without even saying good-bye to Sister Flannery.

Right now I am staying in a Red Rooster Motel in Pigeon Forge, Tennessee. I was lucky to find a room, according to the night clerk, because the Mountain Quiltfest started yesterday, and there is also a huge Cobra Mustang Club Rally in town. Maybe I should check out the quiltfest—could be a Tennessee quilting version of the snow globe girls there to tell me what I should do next.

It's weird being totally alone. Sister Flannery was a pain in the backside, but at least she was company. I wonder what the big problem is. I hope the MFM did not track me to the home. If Fairman hurts any of God's Elect, I will just kill myself. No, wait. I will kill Fairman first. Then I will kill myself.

Day 356

When I woke up this morning, I found a handwritten note that had been shoved under the front door of my room. It said: "Blue pony car—Dollywood IV parking lot, row G6. Be careful."

The Mustang is very cool. It's a four-speed, with a fine stereo system. The trunk of the pony contained a bunch of clothes in my size, including caps. There were also several small coolers, with drinks, sandwiches, and snacks. Right now I am at a rest stop overlooking the Newfound Gap in the Great

---

72 Junior's discussions with Sister Flannery have been the subject of numerous articles and books. See, for example: *Fate and Purpose Trade Punches: The Seven Devils' Dialogue*, by Eric R. Langenberg.

Smoky Mountains National Park, eating a ham and cheese sandwich and drinking a Dr. Pepper.

I found a handwritten note signed by Sister Flannery next to the pony's gearshift. It read: "Junior. Don't worry. We are all OK here. No collateral damage. The boys miss you, because I throw like a girl. The girls said you should wear the North Carolina Tarheel hat first. Don't forget who you are, Junior." The handwriting matched the writing on the note I found in my room this morning.

Before I can forget who I am, I need to figure out who I am. When I started this journal 355 days ago, I was hiding behind a rock in Texas with Pete and had no clue what was going on.

Now Pete is gone and I'm riding in a pony car in Tennessee. I've gone from Texas to Tennessee, but not a heck of a lot has changed. I have a few more clues than I did 355 days ago, but I am still clueless about who or what I am supposed to be, other than a falsely accused mass murderer being chased by the authorities and homicidal Methodists.

Oh well. Lunch is over. Time to put on my UNC cap, jam the pony in gear, and ride. Think I will go down the mountain.

Day 361

Month thirteen, and I am wandering aimlessly through the great state of Tennessee. If the MFM is still serious about hunting me down, I decided it would be harder for the Methodists to find me if I drove the pony car around the Volunteer State and stayed away from hotels and restaurants. So, I have been eating the food in the coolers and sleeping in the car.

To make it more interesting, I drove by a bunch of Tennessee tourist attractions. I did not go in. I just drove by and used my imagination about what might be inside. Here are a few of my favorites, along with my speculations:

(1) The Museum of Salt & Pepper Shakers in Gatlinburg—Probably have some Robert E. Lee shakers, Elvis shakers, and Peyton Manning shakers. The snow globe girls may want to visit this place. I think a snow globe museum would be a good idea.

(2) The International Towing and Recovery Museum in Chattanooga—I was confused a bit by this place because there was a big statue of some sort of Greek god–looking hero pulling a mother and daughter up from

a car sinking into a fountain. I have never thought of tow truck drivers as heroes. When I think of tow truck drivers, I think of the guys who tow your car when you are ten minutes over the limit on the meter in front of the dry cleaners.

(3) The End of the World Is Coming Museum in Crossville—I don't know what day these guys think the world is supposed to end, but I envision a big clock in this place counting down the hours and minutes. Do they have a snack bar? Is it okay to eat popcorn while you contemplate the end of the world? What about a gift shop? Do they sell End of the World gimme caps?

There were lots of other great places, but these were my top three.

To avoid getting stopped by the highway patrol, I have been driving at or just below the posted speed limits. This means lots of cars zoom past me. But to my surprise and concern, a number of the passengers in vehicles passing me wave at me or say "Rock on, dude!" or "You betcha!" or similarly upbeat but confusing things.

Today when I was putting gas in the pony car, I noticed the likely reason for my popularity. On the back bumper of the car is a red, white, and blue bumper sticker that reads: LONG LIVE THE KING. I can't tell which King the bumper sticker refers to. And given the diverse group of folks who have waved at me the past several days, I find it unlikely that everyone is thinking about the same King.

So tonight I decided to run "the King" through SCALP, the Apache Communications search engine, to see who would qualify. This is a small portion of what I got, in no particular order:

(1) Elvis
(2) We Three Kings of East Asian Heritage Are
(3) Richard Petty, King of NASCAR
(4) King Tut
(5) Jesus, King of the Jews
(6) Michael Jackson, King of Pop
(7) Nat King Cole
(8) George Jones, King of Country Music
(9) Martin Luther King, Jr.
(10) Bob Wills, King of Western Swing

There are a whole lot of Kings out there. The Kings all seem to be dead, though. Long live the King.[73]

Day 366

Welcome to year two of our world tour.

OK, here's the deal. I am not very good at this by myself. When Pete was around, we bounced ideas off each other about what to do next. Hannah and Jehu simply told me what to do, and that was OK too. Even when I was hanging out with God's Elect, I didn't have to decide what to do next. I just hung around and did whatever chores were handy.

Today I finally got some help. I think. I'm in Georgia now.

Earlier today I was still wandering around Tennessee, checking out tourist attractions from afar. As I drove down I-40, I noticed that people started yelling at me as they passed by. I won't repeat what they said, but I can tell you it wasn't very nice. I also got a bunch of middle-finger salutes, if you get my drift.

I pulled into a shopping center in Jackson, Tennessee, just to get off the main roads and collect myself. Why was everybody yelling at me? Did they know who I was? Would the feds be tracking me down in Tennessee now?

I decided to get a Dr. Pepper out of the cooler in the trunk to calm my nerves. And that is when I saw it. My LONG LIVE THE KING bumper sticker was gone. It had been replaced by a bumper sticker with the picture of a smiling alligator and the words: GATOR CHOMP: 98–2.

"Gator Chomp," for those of you who don't know, is what University of Florida sports fans do to support their team, which is nicknamed the Gators. The fans extend their arms, one over the other, in front of them and move them up and down to simulate an alligator's mouth. I think it is safe to say that all the other fans in the Southeastern Conference hate the gator chomp.

---

73 Junior's Day 361 Long Live the King Declaration has been construed in many different ways. Some scholars interpret the Declaration as a comment on the transitory nature of power and fame. Other scholars, noting the singular "King" in its conclusion, speculate that Junior is announcing or predicting the coming of a King that supersedes all other kings. Advertising executives have noted that SCALP was a relatively new search engine at this point in time and have speculated that Junior's comments are simply part of a marketing campaign.

The bumper sticker refers to a football game played earlier this year in which the Florida Gators beat the Tennessee Volunteers 98–2. It was the worst loss in Tennessee football history.

Remember earlier when I talked about the University of Nebraska football team not running up the score on United Presbyterian?[74] Well, Florida threw four long touchdown passes in the fourth quarter to run up the score on the Volunteers.

I tried to take the bumper sticker off the pony car, but it would not budge. My only choice, therefore, was to get out of Tennessee as quickly as I could.

So, I am guessing that the bumper sticker switcheroo was somebody's not-so-subtle way to get me out of Tennessee. I assume it was Senior, or one of his agents, but I don't know for sure.[75]

I am sitting in the pony car at a rest stop on Brasstown Bald, which is the tallest mountain in Georgia. I am wearing an Atlanta Falcons Super Bowl Tier 3 Champion hat, which I found in the trunk. It's raining tonight in Georgia. Also raining inside my head. Probably raining everywhere.

Day 370

I don't feel nearly as crummy now. It's amazing what a hot shower and a soft bed will do. Well, softer than the pony car, anyway. The Bulldog Inn in Ellijay, Georgia, is clean, but not particularly fancy.

Ellijay is the Apple Capital of Georgia, so I have had excellent apple cider, applesauce, and apple pie. I even used apple-scented soap in the shower.

Even though I feel better physically, I have to wonder what I am doing here in Ellijay, Georgia, consuming all sorts of apple products. I feel like I have done my best for the past 369 days, but it is just not enough. I feel pretty alone, like I am the only one left who is still pulling his weight on this deal, whatever this deal turns out to be. And I could be killed any day.

---

74 See Day 61.

75 After *Junior* was published, Ford Motor Company produced a blue Junior Special Edition Cobra Mustang. The entire production line sold out in one month. A University of Florida alumnus bought one of the cars, painted orange racing stripes on the car, and placed a GATOR CHOMP: 98–2 bumper sticker on it. The car is prominently featured as a part of the halftime ceremonies when the University of Tennessee football team plays at the University of Florida.

Big storm outside. Huge wind slamming against the door and windows in my little room. The noise is so loud I can just barely hear the voices of the announcers talking about the college basketball game on the very small television in my room. Sounds like they are whispering.

Looking back on this entry, it started out positive and kinda petered off into self-pity, didn't it? Sorry about that. Better tomorrow.

Day 372

Well, it took two days, but I feel better now. Today as I sat in my motel room and ate an apple fritter and drank apple juice, I saw a recognizable face appear on TV: Dr. Grayson Jaska. I met Dr. Jaska several years ago when Senior was trying to find a cure for AIDS. I need to explain the AIDS deal, and I will eventually. I promise.

Anyway, Dr. Jaska was standing next to Matthew Lopez, the FBI director, at a press conference. Director Lopez was talking:

> *For years, the FBI refused to admit to the public when an investigation was going poorly. Recent legislation, however, mandates that after a prescribed period of time the FBI must inform the public if it has no substantial leads in a case of national importance. So, today I am here to announce that the FBI has absolutely no idea where Joshua Jennings, Jr., is. Second, we have no clue as to who actually blew up President Carrier and others in New Mexico. We have ideas and thoughts on this issue, but no actual hard evidence.*
>
> *Because of our total failure to date in this investigation, a bipartisan commission has been established to work with law enforcement on the New Mexico explosion. This group is called the Blue Ribbon Commission to Figure Out Who Blew It All Up. Our first choice to head up the commission was Dr. Ravindra Svarup Gupta, the Indian physicist who most people consider the smartest guy in the world. Dr. Gupta, however, as you may know, is currently in the third year of his unbeaten streak on Triple Jeopardy and could not spare the time to head up the commission.*
>
> *Since Dr. Gupta was not available, Dr. Grayson Jaska has agreed to help us. As you may know, Dr. Jaska created the potion that cured*

AIDS. She is real smart. And quite a looker, if you know what I mean. Dr. Jaska, would you like to say anything?

Dr. Jaska looked at the FBI director like he had just belched the alphabet, and then she spoke:

Thank you, Director, for that very kind introduction. And for the record, the drug that cured AIDS is not a potion. The commission will work with law enforcement authorities to bring this investigation to a close as soon as possible. And let me add that although we consider Joshua Jennings, Jr., a suspect, we are keeping an open mind and will examine all the evidence to identify any and all individuals who may have had a motive to perpetrate this national tragedy. At my request, the FBI has rescinded the "shoot to kill" directive applicable to Joshua Jennings, Jr., and Peter Running Horse for the last year. These men should be arrested if they are located, but we do not consider them to be dangerous to the general public.

I did not know there was a "shoot to kill" order out there, but boy am I glad it's been rescinded. I think this Blue Ribbon Commission thing is a good idea. I think Dr. Jaska will be fair, because I know for a fact that she liked my dad, and because I'm pretty sure she knows I would not kill him.

Progress. Baby steps, but still progress.

Day 380

I am beginning to really like apples. Which is a good thing, because I am still in Ellijay.[76] I have decided to stay here at least a few more days, unless I find a new bumper sticker on the pony.

I know it doesn't make much sense, but now that the "shoot to kill" directive has been rescinded, I decided it was safe enough to move into a nicer place. So I am now at the Apple of My Eye Hotel. My room has a huge

---

76 Numerous paintings and mosaics depict Junior eating an apple. The most famous is *Junior in the New Eden*, which is located in the Religious Artifacts Museum in Stockholm, Sweden.

television and a king-sized bed with one of those really soft fuzzy quilt things. Earlier today, I had a massage in the spa.

When I returned from my massage, a maid was leaving my room. My room looked nice and clean, but it appeared to me that my computer had been moved from one side of the desk to another.

I realize I could just be paranoid, but frankly I think I have earned the right to be paranoid, thank you very much. My computer does not appear to have been turned on, but I am not exactly an expert in these matters.

My guess is that even if someone could have hacked into my computer and seen this timeless work of literature (I am kidding, Dr. Hoover), he or she would not have understood it. I mean, how many people out there can read Chiricahua Apache?

When I first started this effort, Pete suggested I write it in Chiricahua. He said that since only a few thousand people in the entire world could read Chiricahua, the odds were that if we got caught it would be days before it could be transcribed. The authorities could see that I had written something but would not have been able to understand it. I don't know why we thought that delay was important, but we did. Back then, we were pretty much just out of our minds anyway.

Something has been bugging me for some time now, so I guess I should get it off my chest. When I started this book, I was watching my mom and my two sisters get buried. I later learned from Senior that he knew the explosion was going to kill him. But Senior has not yet mentioned my mom and sisters. Didn't he know they would be killed in the explosion too? I mean, it's one thing to allow yourself to be blown up, but to allow your wife and two daughters to be killed as well is too much. He should not have done that. I realize Senior thinks he is coordinating destiny here, but family should not be sacrificed like that.

I miss Mom and the girls. I wish I could see them just one more time.

Day 383

Dr. Jaska didn't waste any time. Today she announced that the commission has issued arrest warrants for Pat Gilligan and Tim Lusty, the president and vice president of a group called Homicides for Homos, L.L.P. HFH is a group based in West Virginia that, as you might guess, does not approve of homosexuality.

Dr. Jaska released to the media the following prepared statement:

Homicides for Homos, L.L.P., has threatened the lives of a number of homosexuals in West Virginia and the surrounding states. According to its bylaws, the primary purpose of HFH is to kill homosexual men, although to date we are not aware of any people that HFH has killed.

Joshua Jennings, Sr., was instrumental in curing the AIDS virus. We suspect that Mr. Lusty and Mr. Gilligan may have planned the explosion in New Mexico because Senior saved the lives of many gays when he spearheaded the discovery of the cure for AIDS.

For example, the home page of the HFH website states, "Senior Sucks. Why didn't he just let all the queers die?"

The commission will continue to investigate and will provide the country with updates as necessary.

I suppose this is as good a time as any to tell you about Senior and AIDS. As I am sure you remember, the gays got into trouble big-time when an airborne strain of AIDS developed. Straight folks, including little kids, started dying by the thousands. There was hysteria in the streets. Every state legislature passed a law making homosexuality a felony, punishable by at least ten years in jail. Vigilante groups were rounding up every thin, well-dressed guy with a decent haircut.

The federal government was in a gridlock over the issue. The administration could not get Congress to come to a consensus on what to do.

Enter my father, again. For some reason (and I still don't know why), Senior had a lot of friends in the gay community. These folks asked Senior to negotiate on their behalf with the federal government, to try and get the feds to stop the lynching of gays. Senior did so, although this fact was never reported in the media. Senior also did something else very few people knew about at the time—he offered ten billion dollars to the pharmaceutical company that first came up with a cure for the airborne strain of AIDS. Not surprisingly, the antidote for the airborne strain was quickly discovered. Dad told me he knew the drug companies were already close to the cure, but were waiting for the government to offer them subsidies for "development." "Never underestimate the greed of the American businessman" was one of Senior's mantras.

Anyway, when Dad started negotiating with the drug companies, only a few people knew the cure was imminent. One of those people was Dr. Jaska, the scientist who was conducting trials with a new drug she had created. Senior and Dr. Jaska became good friends because Dad's money gave Dr. Jaska's bosses the incentive to rush the drug into the marketplace, where it was immediately and incredibly successful. Dr. Jaska was hailed as an American hero. Senior kept his mouth shut about his involvement.

I seriously doubt that Director Lopez knows that Senior and Dr. Jaska were friends, and that I met numerous times with Dr. Jaska during the airborne AIDS crisis when I was acting as a gofer for my dad. Although I would not classify Dr. Jaska as a good friend, I'm pretty sure she does not think I would blow up Senior.

Thank you, Dr. Jaska, for going after the HFH. I'm not sure Lusty and Gilligan blew everybody up, but at least there are other suspects out there now for the feds to bother.

Day 386

I am a sports enthusiast. I play sports, even though I am not very good. And like a lot of guys, I like to watch other guys play sports on television. I have watched football, baseball, basketball, rugby, lacrosse, and soccer on the boob tube. If there are really pretty girls involved, I will even watch Olympic figure skating. And if I need a nap, I will watch golf.

But when did board games become a television sport? The TV at the Apple of My Eye Hotel has a channel I have never heard of before: the Scrabble Channel.

Today's contest on the Scrabble Channel was between Frankie "Word Killer" Bergensteiner and Louie "Triple Threat" Mushpot. Before the game began, while the contestants were waiting offstage, there was a fight between Word Killer's entourage and Triple Threat's posse. I did not even know Scrabble guys had posses.

The color analyst for the contest said that Word Killer had been in a bit of a slump with blank tiles, while Triple Threat had been on a roll with the letter X lately. In his "Keys to Victory" segment, the color analyst predicted that if Triple Threat could control the X and Z tiles today, he would likely prevail. Turns out that in the last two games between these two guys, whoever had racked up the most points with the X and Z tiles had won the game.

When Word Killer and Triple Threat walked out to the table where the Scrabble board sat, the live audience went nuts. People were screaming, and the players were posing like pro wrestlers do—flexing their arms and scowling. I have never seen two skinny white guys with thick glasses pose like that. I have to say, it brightened my day.

I was also amazed to see that the players' shirts were covered with endorsements. Word Killer had a prominent advertisement for an online dictionary on his breast pocket and a patch advertising one-hour eyeglasses on his right sleeve. And then I saw something that made me laugh out loud—a small black bee on the collar of his shirt. Was Word Killer my newest messenger?

The game between Word Killer and Triple Threat was limited to the names of American cities. Word Killer took the lead when he was able to use the X tile to create both Toxey and Loxley. He crushed Triple Threat when he used the Z tile for a Boaz-Ozark combination.

As Word Killer jumped on the table and ripped off his shirt, showing Scrabble tile tattoos on his skinny chest, I plugged Toxey, Loxley, Boaz, and Ozark into the computer. All cities in Sweet Home Alabama, the Heart of Dixie. Thanks, Word Killer. Time to ride the pony.[77]

Day 391

Month fourteen, and a blast from the past. Got an e-mail from Hannah, who said she and Jehu were on special assignment protecting Ebenezer Cohen. The Mossad had intelligence reports that the Methodist Free Militia was planning an attack on Eb.

What is it about Methodists that makes them so violent? Were they always this way? I took a History of Religion class in college and I don't remember any violent Methodist stories. Of course, the textbook stopped in the late

---

77 Junior's sixteen days in Ellijay, Georgia, proved to be a marketing bonanza for the apple-growing industry. Parents all over the world have used Junior as an example to their children to encourage them to eat apples. Soon after *Junior* was published, agronomists cultivated the Junior Apple, which is the world's best-selling apple.

1900s, so maybe something happened in the early twenty-first century that ticked them off.[78]

Speaking of the MFM, why hasn't anyone discussed Fairman as a potential suspect in the New Mexico bombing? He certainly had motive—Fairman was the frontrunner to take the Republican nomination before my speech about his raping of the wives of Abu Abu Mohammed Mohammed. He would have benefited more than anyone from the death of virtually every competent candidate in the Republican Party.

And has it occurred to anyone other than me that Fairman likes to blow stuff up? So far, he has blown up the Catholic convent in Montreal, the White Power Rally in White Only Settlement, and the Yankee Stadium Solid Waste Disposal Station. Seems to me that Fairman is a very logical choice as the exploder of New Mexico.

So, Dr. Jaska, here is my telepathic message to you: check out Fairman![79]

Day 392

Looks like Hannah and her friends are still hard at work helping Eb by eliminating the competition. The Democrats' third vice presidential candidate has withdrawn from the race.

Carl Koehling, a gay rights activist and multi-Oscar award winner, was appointed to take Arturo Salinas Ramirez Mendoza's place when the Mossad uncovered Mendoza's penchant for hiring undocumented Egyptian workers. According to CNN, the polls showed that a Davis/Koehling ticket stood a very good chance of winning the election. Koehling was mesmerizing on

---

78 The Methodist Church was sued by ZG Scumhead, a Left Coast Rap musician, over an alleged copyright infringement by the church of Scumhead's song "The Jewboy Got Game." Scumhead claimed that the music used by the church in the hymn "The Saints on High" was a derivative of his song. Scumhead won a multibillion-dollar judgment against the Methodist Church. The Methodist Free Militia was formed soon after the judgment was affirmed on appeal, and the assets of the Methodist Church were sold to pay the judgment. It is unclear whether Junior was unaware of this lawsuit, or whether he was opining that this lawsuit was not enough of a provocation to radicalize the Methodists.

79 Although there are groups of Junior's followers who believe Junior had the power to communicate telepathically, most scholars view this statement as an attempt at humor by Junior.

television, and the Democrats had flooded the airwaves with campaign ads featuring the tall, rail-thin man with his trademark gray-blond ponytail.

Koehling's candidacy did not get off to a good start, however. Soon after he was appointed to take Mendoza's place, a film clip of Koehling surfaced in which he made fun of straight people, calling them "mouth-breathing breeders." I assumed at the time that the film clip was the Mossad's work, and I figured that would be the end of Koehling.

However, the Democrats obtained an injunction from a California federal judge that prohibited the showing of the video on the grounds that since Koehling was gay, the showing of the video constituted a "hate tort," specifically, "virtual hate battery." I guess even the Mossad did not want to violate a federal judge's order.

Looks like the breeders have prevailed after all. This morning a waitress in Las Vegas, Nevada, appeared on CNN to announce that she was carrying Koehling's child. Her attorney provided the press with the medical reports to confirm her claim.

Around noon, Koehling appeared at a press conference holding hands with his partner, a short Hispanic man who looked very angry. Koehling announced he was withdrawing from the race because he believed he could "make a more significant contribution to the country through my on-screen work and through my charitable foundation." He did not mention Las Vegas.

I wonder if the Democrats have figured out who is torpedoing their candidates. My guess is that anybody with a skeleton in their closet (and that would include all of us) is going to think twice about joining the ticket.

Day 395

Since I have written about the Democratic vice presidential candidates, I suppose I should say something about General Brooks Dozier, who is on the ticket with Eb. General Dozier is pretty much everything Eb is not. General Dozier has fought in wars, run the CIA, operated businesses, and raised a family. In other words, he is someone with a bunch of experience who, at least on paper, has the qualifications to run a superpower.

I have met the general a bunch of times, because he and Senior worked on a number of matters, both political and business, together. The general is actually a good guy and not as much of a hard-core tough guy as you might expect. I should also point out that the general helped Senior on the oil deal, which I promise I will explain later on.

The most interesting thing the general and Senior worked on was a bill that Senior wanted Congress to pass. Senior called the legislation the Big Johnson War Bill.

As I have mentioned numerous times, Senior hated paying taxes. And although Senior understood that war was sometimes necessary, he hated paying taxes for unnecessary wars. General Dozier also hated unnecessary wars, because he had fought in wars and knew the toll they took. General Dozier hated losing soldiers in unnecessary wars.

General Dozier and Senior both noticed that unnecessary wars were often started by presidents who had not fought in a war. In fact, most unnecessary wars were initiated by presidents who had never even served in the military. When a president had served in the military, he was much less likely to push for an unnecessary war.

Senior's theory, which the general supported, was that presidents who had not served in the military thought they could prove their manhood by sending the strongest military force in the world to conquer another country. The general and Senior thought war policy should not be made by a guy trying to convince everyone he had a big Johnson. Hence, the Big Johnson War Bill.

The premise of the bill was that, unless the United States had been attacked, the president could not sign a declaration of war unless (1) he had served in the military, (2) he had played major college or professional football (but not as a place kicker), or (3) he had a big Johnson. The bill only applied to men, not only for the obvious anatomical reason, but also because Senior and the general figured that women had no need to prove their worth or enhance their self-esteem by starting an unnecessary war.

The Big Johnson War Bill was enthusiastically supported by every women's group in the country, from the National Organization for Women to the Daughters of the American Revolution. "The women all know how stupid we are," was Senior's assessment on why his bill was supported by the women's groups.

The bill received a modicum of support in the House of Representatives but got bogged down in committee. The biggest issue concerned just how big the president's Johnson had to be. The debate on this issue, which I attended, was hilarious. After seeing Henry the Hammer's hot tub press conference way back when,[80] I can tell you with absolute certainty that the Hammer was qualified under any reasonable standard to be a wartime president under the Big Johnson War Bill, even if he had never played a down of big-time football.

I definitely think General Dozier will help the Republican ticket. Who knows, if the Democratic vice presidential candidates keep resigning, the Cohen/Dozier ticket might just take the election.

Day 400

Has anybody else ever survived a worldwide manhunt for 400 days? OK, maybe some Arab terrorist types, but how about just a plain old American half-white guy with no skills who can't hide out in the mountains in Pakistan or Afghanistan? Nobody comes to mind.

So, for what it's worth, congratulations to me.

I have learned that when you are running for your life, you pay attention to stuff more closely. As a consequence, you see stuff you might not otherwise see.

For example, last night around midnight I decided to take a walk. I pulled my Softee Tissue with Aloe, Vaseline and Antihistamines cap down low over my face and strolled leisurely around the town square.[81] As I approached a statue dedicated to a Confederate war hero, I saw out of my peripheral vision the headlights on a car flip on and off. Soon five men walked out of an alley and directly toward me. As I turned to run, I saw men coming from the other direction as well.

I decided not to run. I just walked up and hid as best I could behind the war hero's horse. Yep, the face of the infamous New Mexico Exploder was flush with a concrete horse's behind. And wearing a hat advertising soft tissues. This was going to make quite a headline.

To my relief, the men walked past me and into a wooded area across from the town square. I waited a few minutes and decided to follow. Stupid, I know.

---

80 See Day 95.

81 Day 386 references four towns in Alabama (Toxey, Loxley, Boaz, and Ozark) and implies that Junior is leaving Georgia for Alabama. Days 391 through 423, however, do not mention specific cities or towns in Alabama. Toxey, Loxley, Boaz, and Ozark each have a museum dedicated to Junior's alleged stay in the town.

After about a twenty-minute walk in the woods, I came to a clearing and stopped. The clearing was illuminated by a full moon, and I could see about thirty men who had formed a circle in the clearing. Each man was naked from the waist up and carried some sort of stick or small tree branch. They marched in a circle and chanted. Each man also hit himself in the back with his stick as he marched.

I have read about religions in which believers hit themselves with sticks or whips to prove their faith, but I thought that mostly happened overseas. I could not imagine a bunch of Alabama good old boys hitting themselves for religious purposes.

As I watched and listened, I noticed a pattern. The men would all speak a few words in unison and then slap their backs. Then a few more words, and another tree branch application. Finally, I figured out what they were saying.

"Beat the hell out of Auburn!" Whack! "Roll Tide!" Whack! "Save us Saban!" Whack! "The Bear Lives!" Whack!

Then I understood. The flagellants were University of Alabama football supporters. This was an Alabama tailgate party!

I knew that Auburn had beaten Alabama the last few years, but wow, this was a bit over the top. I guess the pundits were right when they said college football was a religion in the South.

I just turned on ESPN. Auburn is winning 42–0 in the third quarter. Guess those guys should have beat themselves harder and yelled louder. Obviously Bear Bryant and Nick Saban did not hear them from football eternity.

Day 405

In case you have never been to Alabama, let me say that you could probably spend a month here just looking at Civil War statues and memorials and stuff like that. These guys have obviously never gotten over the War of Northern Aggression.

Today I decided to take a break from the Civil War tourist attractions and watch television. I watched the Veronica Channel for a while, but frankly, it was kind of boring. Now that I am out of the news, Veronica appears to be struggling for content. Her feature today was an investigation into whether jock itch cream really worked or whether it was a scam. Not really scintillating stuff.

When I left the Veronica Channel, I came across the Hate Channel, which I had never seen before. I could not tell if it was a local Alabama cable channel or a nationally syndicated channel I had just overlooked.

The Hate Channel, like its name suggests, gives people a chance to rant about what or who they hate. Although there are regularly scheduled programs regarding specific subjects of hate, like "I hate Yankees" or "I hate Republicans," I was most fascinated by an open mike slot where anyone could go on camera and talk for ten minutes about who they hate.

I have gotten used to the professional haters, the guys who go on TV or radio or the Internet and rag on folks they don't like. These guys (and I am including females here) are so predictable and so one-sided in their arguments that it is pretty clear to me they don't believe half of what they say—they have just figured out they can make a lot of money by being hatemongers.

The open mike haters, however, just flat-out depressed me. These are normal folks, people whom I assume raise kids and go to work every day. And they apparently hate everyone who is not just exactly like them, with a vehemence that is troubling. I saw one grandmotherly type scream that "all queers should be castrated." The next segment featured a cattle rancher who said that vegetarians were ruining our country and should be force-fed beef until they "converted."

The primary commercial sponsors for the open mike segment sold toilet paper and heartburn remedies. Guess that makes some sense.

When did we get so angry in this country? Were we always angry and just kept it inside until it became OK to go on TV and scream about who we hated? Or is this some new problem?

Note to self—check with the snow globe girls and see if the Love Channel is a possibility.

Day 408

The last few days have been interesting. Remember when I talked about how much I liked to drive fast, eat french fries, and drink Dr. Pepper?[82] Well, the other day I left my motel room and decided to do exactly that. I gunned the

---

82 See Day 15. Some scholars contend that since Junior did not add "making fun of fat people" in this entry, Junior was not serious in his Day 15 entry when he said he really liked making fun of the calorically challenged.

pony car down the road until I came to one of those burger joints where you can smell the grease from the road and the waitresses roller-skate to your car. I heartily enjoyed my double bacon cheeseburger and cheese fries, and I drank two large Dr. Peppers.

I was savoring my grease-and-carbonation-induced high when the waitress brought me my change. Along with the change, she left a handwritten note that read: "Junior. I need your help. Please meet me at 11:30 tonight in the Peaches parking lot. I will come to your car. You won't need to get out."

By the time I read the note, my waitress was already waiting on another car. I pulled out quickly, in case she changed her mind and alerted the authorities. Note to self—buy another hat and never go out in public again without one firmly planted on your stupid, brainless head.

I had a few hours to kill, so I drove around until I found Peaches. Sure enough, it was a strip joint. I had hoped that maybe it was a farmer's market or something like that.

I considered blowing out of town, but the way things have been going, I figured that maybe the waitress had some important information for me. I mean, if I'm relying on television Scrabble players for clues, who am I to turn away a waitress in trouble who may also be a stripper?

As I write this, Suzanne (the waitress/stripper) is in the shower. I have driven to a different town and checked into a motel room. Suzanne and I are registered as husband and wife. Before you get any ideas, absolutely nothing untoward has occurred. I can't write down all of what happened, but suffice it to say that I felt like I had to step in and help Suzanne get away from certain people. I will tell you more later. And, I repeat, NOTHING has happened. I mean it. Get your mind out of the gutter.

Day 412

I have a confession to make. I am a spoiled, selfish son of a gun. You may have already reached that conclusion, but honestly, until recently it never occurred to me. I guess I started thinking about this issue when I was in North Dakota, talking to the prime minister about Israel's problems. Then, I talked to Eb, a guy with virtually no skills who went to bat for the Standing Rock Sioux tribe in North Dakota. I mean, I have never done anything like that. Next, I meet Sister Flannery and Mother Superior Hookenstein, who are working with those poor handicapped kids (or God's Elect, depending on your perspective). And two days ago, I met Suzanne.

Suzanne is, as she puts it, "white Alabama trailer trash through and through." Born to a teenage mom living in a trailer park. Left home at the age of sixteen to escape the advances of her drunken stepfather. Supports her lazy, part-time drug-dealer boyfriend by waitressing and stripping. A tattoo on each butt cheek. (I took the last fact on faith. Not an eyewitness.)

So, I have finally realized that I have led a charmed life compared to 99.9 percent of the world. AND, I have not done a dadgummed thing to help anybody else.

I think this realization is why I decided to help Suzanne. Then again, it could also be because she is really pretty and I have always had a hard time not doing what pretty women ask me to do.

The bottom line, at least for now, is that I picked up Suzanne in the Peaches parking lot and we drove the pony car out of town. My guess is that her boyfriend, Robert Earl Bankes, is unhappy and is looking for her.

So, in conclusion, I am now being hunted by all the major law enforcement agencies in the world, a blue ribbon commission, angry Methodists, and an Alabama meth head named Robert Earl. If this was a novel, nobody would believe it.

Day 423

Month fifteen, and Alabama hates me. Suzanne and I were driving the pony car down some two-lane highway today and we saw a billboard that had a yellow bee in the middle of a circle with a line drawn through it. Like a no-smoking or no-dumping warning. Ouch.

Beneath the circle was the following notation: Galatians 1:8. I asked Suzanne if she knew what that meant, and she said, sure, it was a Bible verse. When I asked her if she knew what the verse said, Suzanne hesitated, but I finally got her to recite it.

"Galatians one, verse eight," she said in a sort of singsong voice. "But even if we or an angel from heaven should preach a gospel other than the one we preached to you, let him be eternally condemned."

I looked at her with my mouth open, amazed that she knew the verse by heart.

"So," she continued in a voice that seemed way too happy for the circumstances, "do you get it? Some folks like you, so they say 'Let Him Be.' Other folks think you are a bad guy, so they say 'Let Him Be Condemned.'"

I told Suzanne that yes, I got it. Then I asked her how far we were from Florida.

Day 427

Ever heard of Britton Hill, Florida? Me neither. Let me enlighten you. Britton Hill, Florida, is 345 feet above sea level, which makes it the HIGHEST point in the state of Florida. According to the brochure I am reading, Britton Hill is the lowest state high point in America. Make sense? Didn't think so.

Suzanne and I have been hanging out in Florida for a few days now. I have to say that so far, Britton Hill has been the low point of our sightseeing activities. Low point, get it? Thanks. I'll be here all week.

Believe it or not, one of the problems of being on the run chased by every law enforcement agency in the world is that sometimes it is actually . . . boring. Think about it. Every morning, most folks wake up and go to work or school, or help get people ready to go to work or school. When I wake up, I technically have nothing to do or nowhere to go. Sure, I worry that a law officer will identify me and then shoot me and/or arrest me, but there is nothing special I can "do" to avoid that.

Suzanne just asked what I was writing, since she can't read Chiricahua Apache. When I told her, she said, "Having a pity party, are we? Let's go. I can find us something fun to do."

This should be interesting.

Day 429

I am still feeling the effects of Suzanne's attempt to make me happier. It was fun, but I am still in pain. More later.[83]

---

83 Day 429 has been the subject of much speculation, since nowhere in his book does Junior explain what he and Suzanne did between Days 427 and 429.

Day 434

Today, Suzanne and I took the pony car for a drive down Highway 98 to check out the Gulf of Mexico. Suzanne had the satellite computer tuned in to one of those stations that plays country music without commercials. We were singing along with a poor guy whose drunk father had run over his best hunting dog with a tractor (I think it was the third or fourth song of the day about dogs) when a CNN news bulletin broke in.

The computer screen showed a guy whose forehead was about two inches longer than it should have been, plus it was covered with some horrible-looking scars. A classic meth-head face. The face spoke:

My name is . . . (the face paused, as if contemplating a difficult problem) Robert Earl Bankes. I live in Alabama. My girlfriend's name is Suzanne. She's not with me anymore 'cause she has run off with the Joshua guy who killed the president. I don't think this is right. Suzanne was paying some of our bills with her strip dancing over to the Peaches Club and it was mean of the Joshua guy to take her away. I know Suzanne is with the Joshua guy because she called me on the phone and told me and I can't find her nowhere.

At this point I looked at Suzanne with what I assume were eyes the size of those round chocolate ice cream things you get "over to" the Dairy Queen. How could she possibly think telling Robert Earl that she was with me was a good idea? Suzanne was looking at the screen, but she knew I was staring at her because she raised her hand as if to say, "Wait for it, Joshua . . ."

Then the meth head spoke again:

Suzanne said she and this guy were in North Dakota where all them Jews live. I was gonna go there but my truck is outta gas and I ain't got no money. So I am asking the FBI to go to North Dakota and bring Suzanne back. And please hurry—we are almost out of beer in the fridge. I know everything happens for a reason, but I can't last too long without beer. Thank you.

OK. Now not only does the world think I exploded the president, everybody also now knows I stole an Alabama meth head's girlfriend. And she is a stripper.

Day 437

It occurred to me today as I used SCALP to find a Florida restaurant with good chicken fried steak that you may not know the story of Apache Communications. Granted, you may not care, but I have time on my hands, so here goes.

It all started when Senior tried to buy a cell phone. Senior, like a lot of rich guys, didn't pay too much attention to things like cell phones, personal computers, and stuff like that. All he cared about was that he had the device when he needed it, it was programmed so that he could just push a button and get what he wanted, and that it ALWAYS worked.

Senior was working late in his El Paso office one night when his cell phone stopped working. The most likely reason for the phone's failure to perform is that Senior did not charge it up. I was the guy "in charge" of things like that for Senior, but Senior had sent me to what was then known as Mexico to meet with two Mexican bank presidents, two Mexican generals, and three Mexican drug lords. (I will talk more about the Mexico deal later.)

Although Senior never admitted this to me, his chauffeur, Casey Sileo, told me than when Senior came down to his car that night, the phone was broken into about five pieces. Senior was not a guy known for his patience with tools like cell phones.

Senior instructed Casey to drive him somewhere "where he could get a damned phone that did its job." Casey drove Senior to one of those retail phone stores (I don't remember which one) and that is when the real fun began. According to Casey, Senior told the clerk, a young man with a shaved head, a pierced nose, and three earrings in each ear: "Mr. Clean, I need a new phone pdq. I have ten minutes."

Casey swears that Mr. Clean was very gracious and accommodating to Senior, but the transaction took about one and a half hours, primarily because Senior questioned every charge on the bill. Senior's biggest complaints:

(1) a $300 charge because Senior was buying a new phone with fewer options than his current phone within the first six months of his contract;

(2) a $100 charge because he was deleting Internet service from his new phone;

(3) a $30 charge because Senior's new phone was not connected to a family plan like his old phone;

(4) a $100 charge for unlimited minutes;

(5) a $20 charge because Senior was deleting international coverage from his contract;

(6) a $30 charge for deleting the phone's capability to play games and music videos; and

(7) a $75 charge for agreeing to a new two-year contract.

Casey said Senior was particularly incensed about being charged to *extend* his contract. "Mr. Clean," he roared, "you mean I am paying you extra money for agreeing to pay you extra money? Son, that just don't make any sense! This is America, for goodness' sakes!"

Senior's first call on his new phone was to yours truly. "Junior," he said, "when you get back from talking to the Mexicans, we need to talk about these damned cell phones. I sense a business opportunity." And thus was Apache Communications born. As an aside, let me add here that Senior was not a foul-mouthed man. He knew all the bad words and how to use them, but he was not one of those guys who cursed all the time. I am pretty sure, however, that Senior never said the words "cell phone" without the word "damned" as a condition precedent. "Damned cell phone" was a proper name for Senior, like Dallas Cowboys or Texas Longhorns.

After I returned from Mexico and met with Senior about the "damned cell phone" business opportunity, I did some research and found a Belgian entrepreneur who knew everything there was to know about satellites and international telephone technology. Within a year, Apache had a couple of satellites in the air and offered free cell phones with worldwide unlimited minutes and all the other bells and whistles to customers who would agree to pay twenty dollars per month, which was deducted automatically from their bank account or credit card. No contract. No Friends & Family. No Calling Circle. No Matrix Plan. The customer could cancel the deal simply by calling the company.

Virtually overnight, Apache Communications became the biggest telephone company in the world. All the other phone companies either folded or adapted. As you may know, only Manchester United Phone Company and

Saudi Arabian Kingdom Phone Company currently compete with Apache on a global basis, and I can tell you for a fact that the Saudi Arabian Kingdom Phone Company is hemorrhaging money.

As you might expect, the American phone companies did not go down easily. They lobbied Congress and the FCC hard to pass laws or regulations that made it impossible for Apache to offer such cheap service. Senior's lawyers and lobbyists, however, prevailed. Plus, Senior hired a public relations firm that highlighted the phone companies' attempts to convince Congress to raise everyone's phone bills. Although the telephone companies threw millions of dollars into the Congressional fight, there weren't any members of Congress willing to come out in favor of higher phone bills. Plus, several members of Congress told me they enjoyed watching the telephone trillionaires take it in the shorts, since NOBODY liked the way they had been screwing over folks for years.

The fallout from the collapse of the phone companies was significant. The folks who did not sell their telecommunications company stock in time lost a ton of money, and literally thousands of people lost their jobs when the telephone companies shut down. Although a lot of the retail-level employees were scooped up by Apache, almost all the managerial types wound up on the streets. Senior made a bunch of enemies when he took over the phone business.

In case you were wondering, Senior made sure that Mr. Clean was put in charge of Apache's first retail store in El Paso. Senior did not even make him lose the nose ring. "If not for Mr. Clean," Senior told me, "I would never have come across this incredible business opportunity."

That may be more information than you wanted, but I think it's a great story. One of the most successful businesses in the world came about because a big dog forgot to charge his cell phone and had to do a menial chore on his own instead of delegating it to his idiot son. Surely somebody can take this example and transform it into some sort of management theory that business students have to memorize to pass Business Management 101.[84]

SCALP has come through for me again. If you are ever in Bagdad, Florida, stop by Omar's and order the chicken fried steak with fried okra and mashed potatoes. Good stuff.

---

84 "Make the Big Dog Do It" is now an established management theory and is taught in virtually all universities.

Day 440

Did I mention that Suzanne is really pretty? She has that Southern Girl thing going on where her eyes get big when she's talking to you, and she could be flirting with you but you're not sure, and she knows more about college football than half of the guys you know. Plus, sometimes when she talks to you, she puts her hand on your arm. And somewhere, deep in your reptile brain, you understand that if she had to, she could gut you like a fish. Is that too harsh?

Anyway, I say all of that as a compliment. I am grateful for Suzanne's Alabaman girl qualities, because they have scored us a very nice ground-floor condominium on the beach here in Florida. I am not sure exactly what she said, because I was in the pony car, but I watched her through the window as she cajoled the chubby hotel manager into giving us the most isolated condo on the beach, with an enclosed garage for the pony car, for cash up front, no ID check, and no written agreement. I knew she had him when she leaned forward across the desk and put her hand on his arm. Chubby bald guys fall for that one every time.

So right now, I am sitting on a beach chair watching the sunset and drinking a margarita. Yes, Southern Girls also make great margaritas.

Day 446

Sometime before the New Mexico explosion, back when life was a little more normal, I went over to Senior's house on a Sunday morning. I don't remember the reason, although I'm sure he told me to come over to discuss some business thing he wanted me to help him with. Mom and the girls were at church—Senior stopped going to church when I was in about the seventh grade.

Anyway, I found Senior watching television and laughing. His face was so red, I feared he was about to have a heart attack.

Senior was watching two televisions. On one screen, four people on one of those Sunday morning shows where Washington political figures strut, lie, and debate were talking about a bill pending before Congress. On the second screen, a man in a bright red robe was speaking from behind a pulpit to a church congregation. I am not sure what he was saying.

"Junior," Senior said between fits of laughter, "I have not had this much fun in weeks. I should really do this more often. These guys crack me up, they are such idiots."

Then Senior paused and he got that look on his face that said: "Listen well, son, as the old man imparts some important wisdom."

"Junior, there are two things you need to remember when someone wants to talk religion or politics with you. First, 98 percent of what they tell you is a lie. Second, never forget that, outside of maybe the topic of sex, people are never stupider than when they are promoting, defending, explaining, or criticizing politics or religion. Politics and religion make all of us stupid liars."

I know you probably think this is kind of a random conversation to bring up as I run from the law, but today the advice Senior gave me is rattling around in my brain like a pinball. Read on and you will see why.

This morning I was sitting in a comfortable chair on the beach watching the waves of the Gulf of Mexico and listening to Bruce Springsteen on my headphones when Suzanne tapped me on the shoulder and said I needed to see what was happening on the television.

The condo has one of those big televisions with incredibly clear crystalline pictures created by uranium-enriched plutonium or Kryptonite, or whatever special cool stuff they are using now. Anyway, on the screen there were three guys standing in front of a microphone holding a press conference. They had black hoods covering their heads. At the bottom of the TV screen a moving script read: "Methodist Free Militia Press Conference."

The man in the middle of the threesome cleared his throat into the microphone and then spoke. His voice was that of a man with a naturally high tenor voice who was trying to lower his voice to sound more dramatic:

The Methodist Free Militia is tired of waiting for the United States government to capture the criminal terrorist Joshua Jennings, Jr. Not only is he a criminal terrorist, he's consorting with a stripper who has a drugged-up boyfriend. Therefore, we're issuing a fartwa that authorizes every true Christian, as long as he is a legal American citizen actually born in America or on an American military installation in a foreign country, to kill Joshua Jennings, Jr. The man who kills Joshua Jennings, Jr., will be richly rewarded, both in this world and the next.

The speaker paused, turning to the next page of his notes, when a female voice in the front row spoke up: "Veronica Wells, Veronica Network. Did you say *fartwa*? That sounds kinda gross. What is that?"

The hooded speaker looked at his notes, decided the answer was not there, and replied in a soft, higher-pitched voice: "A fartwa is a death sentence issued by a religion to kill a bad guy because . . ."

Someone else spoke up: "Don Kuhn, Retired Naval Officers Network. Do you mean *fatwa*, like what the Islamic terrorists do? I don't think it has an 'r' in it, bud."

Another voice off camera: "Susan Horn, Religious History Channel. I have never heard of Methodists issuing fartwas. What branch of Methodist are you? Armenian or Calvinistic? Did either John Wesley or George White-field authorize fartwas?"

The three hooded men each raised their rifles and the questions stopped. The leader spoke, his deep voice back: "No more questions. The fartwa is officially announced. Junior is fair game. Go get him, America."

Somewhere, Senior is laughing his butt off. And I'm facing a fartwa.

Day 453

Month sixteen. Still on the beach in Florida. Still drinking margs. Still hanging out with a lovely Southern Girl. Still under a fartwa.

I was surfing the Net today and came across a website I had never seen before, called "My God Is Better than Your God." Believers in one deity challenge the believers of another deity to a contest of who has the best god. Each proponent lists the good qualities of their god and the bad points of the opposing god. Then, anybody who is signed up as a member on the website (which costs a few bucks) can vote.

The contestants today were Elvis and Baal. Elvis won in a landslide because he invented rock and roll, taught the world how to wiggle its hips, and had cool hair. The best the proponents of Baal could come up with was he was a god of fertility who helped crops grow. The Baal guys, of course, criticized Elvis for getting fat and dying on the toilet. However, I'm guessing most folks figured the bloated, potty critiques were not nearly as much of a drawback as Baal's requirement that children be sacrificed to him.

Next week, Elvis takes on Peyton Manning. Manning beat Quetzalcoatl, although it took two overtime periods to finish him off. Manning was always money in overtime.

Day 459

Today was the first episode of the *Junior Virtual Reality Show* on the Veronica Network. I'm actually surprised it took Veronica this long.

The actor playing me is about five feet eight inches tall and weighs about 300 pounds. Suzanne is played by an actress who looks like an anorexic coke whore who hasn't showered in a week.

The virtual Junior and Suzanne are hiding out from the law in a seedy hotel in North Dakota. After having sex, the couple argue about whose turn it is to buy drugs. Junior hits Suzanne in the face, which apparently turns her on, so they have sex again.

I don't think this show is going to help my image much. I think anybody who watches the show will be glad to take the MFM up on their fartwa offer and put me out of my misery.

Day 465

One of the consequences of the New Mexico explosion is that, for the first time ever, the secretary of agriculture was directly promoted to the job of president. That's what happens when you have the president, vice president, speaker of the house, president pro tempore of the Senate, secretary of state, secretary of the treasury, secretary of defense, attorney general, and secretary of the interior all in attendance at a rally when a bunch of bombs go off. Ken Strickland, the secretary of agriculture, was supposed to be in New Mexico, but he missed his flight from San Angelo, Texas, to Albuquerque. Yes, Ken Strickland is the most powerful man in the world today because the pig-judging contest at the Tom Green County Fair ran long.

Given the way things have turned out, it should be no surprise that President Strickland is one of Senior's best friends. In fact, President Strickland was Senior's best man when my parents married. The current president has just been "Uncle Ken" to me for my entire existence.

Uncle Ken is one of those slow-talking Texans who also happens to be very intelligent. So even though he spent most of his life running a cattle ranch in South Texas, he is no schmo. It has been a lot of fun watching Uncle Ken run the country while we await the election.

The media types, of course, know about the new president's connection to Senior, and Uncle Ken is constantly being asked questions about the explosion and about the manhunt for me. Today, during a press conference concerning the latest economic indicators released by whatever government agency does that sort of thing, President Strickland was asked about the search for the "terrorist Joshua Jennings, Jr."

As CNN provided a close-up of Uncle Ken's face, he frowned. Then, pausing as if to make up his mind, he said:

Y'all know I'm just a country boy who spent most of his life raising cattle. I'm truly not smart enough to be the president and I'm only here to hold down the fort till the country elects a new president. But you do realize, don't you, that you are accusing a young man of blowing up his own parents and sisters? We are talking about Joshua, the son of Rebecca Jennings. I can't imagine, under any set of circumstances, Joshua blowing up his own family. Plus, where would he obtain the materials to do such a thing? Joshua has a history degree—he has absolutely no qualifications, experience, or background in this sort of thing.

Don't get me wrong, now. If Junior did this, he should be punished. But I just don't think he has it in him. Joshua is simply not that ambitious.

Thanks, Uncle Ken. I think.

Day 467

Well, it looks like Robert Earl's declaration that we are in North Dakota has borne some fruit. According to CNN, fifty different people—forty-five men and five women—have been arrested in North Dakota in the last month. Each of them had in their possession a pamphlet entitled "The Junior Fartwa Rules" and the picture from *We Are You and You Are Us!* magazine showing Joshua and Mandy jogging on the beach in Rio.

The Veronica Network has created a daily one-hour program called *The Junior Fartwa Show*, with Veronica as its host. Today, Veronica reported that the MFM has confirmed that over 5,000 individuals have contacted MFM headquarters on how to collect on the fartwa. Veronica seems rejuvenated by the fartwa story—she has obviously lost some weight and her on-air reporting is crisper and more professional than it has been in quite a while. I watched the entire program today to see if she would repeat her "Let Him Be" mantra or try to sell any "Let Him Be" products, but she did not.

Instead, there were several commercials for "Junior Fartwa" products, including a T-shirt with "Junior" printed in the bull's-eye of a target. I am not totally surprised by the promotion, but to be honest, the T-shirt hurt my feelings a bit.

Day 471

Took the pony car out for a run today. Low on gas, so we stopped in Red Head, Florida. Great name for a town.

As I was putting gas in the car, Suzanne said, "Your computer is beeping. Should I turn it on?"

I told her yes and she said, "Ask the gas station guy where the Red Head Veterans' Hospital is." So I did.

When I returned to the car, Suzanne showed me the computer. On the screen was a message in bright red letters: "Junior, go to the VA hospital in Red Head. GATOR CHOMP!"

I couldn't tell from Suzanne's expression whether she was surprised that someone knew where we were, or disgusted that our messenger was a Florida Gators fan. Suzanne is a Crimson Tide girl, through and through.

I briefly explained to Suzanne that sometimes I got messages on my computer and that so far, it has been a good idea to follow the instructions received. That explanation seemed to satisfy her, so we drove the pony car to the hospital.

Turns out the Red Head facility is one of those hospitals where veterans of one particular war are housed—in this case, Vietnam V. A smart guy had figured out that certain wars can wreak body-part or weapon-specific injuries on soldiers, and it made sense to treat similarly situated soldiers in one location with equipment and treatment regimens designed to rehabilitate similar injuries.

Vietnam V, as you may or may not remember, was fought almost entirely in the dense jungles of Vietnam and Cambodia. A bunch of the American soldiers who fought in the war were infected with some kind of strange virus that messed up their vision. Our doctors are still trying to figure out how to fight the virus, which means that the Red Head VA hospital is populated almost exclusively with guys who can't see very well.

I parked the pony car outside the hospital and Suzanne and I just sat in the car and watched. What we saw was a bunch of guys in their forties and fifties sitting in chairs outside a slightly shabby-looking brick building. The men were all wearing sunglasses. Some were talking, some had headphones on and were bobbing their heads in time with music. Some just sat there and stared off into the distance.

Suzanne looked at me—she had tears in her eyes. "These guys fought for our country, Junior," she said. "Now look at them! They look so lonely. You have to do something for them. Right now, Junior."

I started to give my "I'm just a guy running from the law" speech, but she put her hands on her hips and stared at me. Why do women put their hands on their hips when they are angry or are determined to make you do something? And more important, why does it scare me so much when they do it?

Suzanne and I got out of the pony car. I had no idea what I was going to do. I thought that at least nobody would recognize me, since they couldn't see very well, when one of the soldiers, skinny as a nail with ghost-white skin and a wispy black mustache, turned in my direction and said, "Yo, Junior. Over here, dude!" So much for flying under the radar.

I hesitated and he yelled again, even louder: "Junior, dude! I know it's you, man. Come on over here. And bring the pretty chick. I won't bite."

So we went over to talk to him. Mostly, we listened, as he and his buddies told war stories about Vietnam V. After about an hour, I went back to the pony car and brought some Clinton Gold over—none of them had any extra money for smokes. After a few minutes of the Gold, the stories became more colorful and exaggerated. I listened to them all, even though it was clear that not even the soldiers believed half of what they were saying.

As evening approached, we all got the munchies. I had a bunch of cash in the pony car, so Suzanne drove over to the local pizza joint and brought back pizza and beer for everyone. I'm guessing we made the pizza joint's nut for the entire month.

The guys all ate until they were stuffed. We had a bunch of pizza left over so they rounded it up and gave it to one of the hospital's nurses so she could save it for later in the week.

As you may remember, dear reader, Vietnam V was probably the stupidest Vietnam war we fought, although some folks say Vietnam III was stupider. (Is "stupider" a word, Dr. Hoover?)

Anyway, Vietnam V lasted about eighteen months, and absolutely no ground was gained or lost by either side. Many well-respected historians have theorized that Vietnam V was really just an exercise by the United States government designed to try out new jungle fighting techniques and weapons.

After we stopped eating, we sat in the gathering twilight and drank our beer. The war stories petered out and the guys talked about what they had lost fighting in the war—their sight, good jobs, girlfriends, even wives. Although their stories were sad, I did not detect a whiff of self-pity. These guys just accepted their fate as soldiers.

Finally (probably spurred on by too much Clinton Gold and beer) I blurted out: "This sucks! Vietnam V was a ridiculous war that never should have been fought. Doesn't that make you angry?"

There was a silence for a full minute—no noise except the chirping of the crickets. "You know," a big Hispanic guy with an East Coast accent said, "sometimes you do what you are supposed to do, even if the result turns out to be stupid. My job was to fight, so I fought. I did my job and I'm proud of what I did. Being practically blind sucks, no doubt about that—but I sleep good at night because I did my job to the best of my ability. I defended my country. All of us have a job to do, a destiny to fulfill."

Somebody decided the mood was too serious and started singing "Louie Louie." We all joined in, even Suzanne, for about twenty minutes, the lyrics growing raunchier and raunchier. It's a scene I will never forget: a bunch of stoned, semi-blind war vets singing "Louie Louie" at the top of their lungs and dancing crazily in the humid Florida night.

As we were shaking hands and preparing to leave, Suzanne said in her sexiest Southern Girl voice: "Now boys, you all know it's best if you don't tell folks that Junior was here. Can you all help us with that little situation?"

One of the soldiers smiled and responded in a similar accent: "Honey child, you are the absolutest best-looking woman I have seen in years. But don't you worry your pretty little head, because as you can plainly see, we be BLIND! We ain't seen NOBODY!"

As I write this, I am struck once again by my good fortune. I never had to fight in a war, stupid or otherwise. I wonder if the soldier was right—if everyone has a predestined duty, a specific destiny to fulfill. And if so, I wonder what mine is?

Day 473

When we arrived back at the condo from our Red Head VA Hospital experience, Hannah was waiting for us. With very little explanation (she was quite brusque, actually), Hannah said we were flying to an undisclosed location in the western United States. When I pressed for details, all Hannah would say was that we were going to Colorado.

Suzanne said, "Oh, Junior, I have always wanted to go to Colorado in the summer. I hear the weather is so wonderful. Don't you want to get out of the heat and humidity for a while?"

I confess that up to that point I thought Hannah just wanted me, and not Suzanne, to leave for Colorado—I figured Hannah would not want anyone else to watch over. To my surprise, Hannah said to me, "I think you and Suzanne would really like it in Colorado, Junior. We will put the Mustang in a safe place. We've already packed your belongings. Can we go now?"

Hannah and Suzanne seem to be on the same page here, which makes me a little curious. Note to self—pay attention to these two women. It seems unlikely that a Mossad agent could be undercover posing as the white trash stripper/waitress girlfriend of an Alabama meth head, but you never know.

My hair has now been dyed a different color and I have to wear some sort of full-body man-girdle thing that makes me look about twenty-five pounds thinner. When I go out, I am also supposed to wear shades and a baseball cap.

Since the world also knows what Suzanne looks like, she is also in disguise. Her hair has been cut short and dyed an outrageous purple color. She also has fake tattoos on one arm and numerous piercings. Suzanne did not complain about any of these changes, which makes me wonder even more about who she really is.

I am sitting on a redwood deck attached to a huge house that, at least to me, seems too precariously stuck on the side of Red Mountain in Aspen, Colorado. Yes, that Aspen, where all the beautiful and incredibly rich people hang out. I am watching the sunset as I drink some really good sangria. The temperature is about forty-five degrees lower than it was in Florida.

I am tempted to say that life is really good, but then I remember that I am a wanted mass murderer and I am hanging out with people I don't really know. Two of those people, the beautiful Hannah and the beautiful and newly tattooed Suzanne, are inside the house fixing dinner.

The sun has set, so I guess it is time to go inside. Hannah said that I will be meeting with Eb tomorrow. I guess then I will learn why I am in Aspen.

Day 474

Back on my deck watching the sunset. More sangria. Still two beautiful women in the kitchen cooking dinner. Totally, unbelievably exhausted. And kinda scared.

This morning I was rousted out of bed at 6:00 a.m. and told to put on my man girdle and the clothes laid out for me. We then drove to the Maroon Bells–Snowmass Wilderness Area, a few miles outside of Aspen. Spectacular views. Despite the fact that I was barely awake I was actually happy to see such a wonderful sight. Until the hike.

Hannah said that for security reasons, we were going to meet Eb at Crater Lake. To get to Crater Lake, we had to hike approximately 1.8 miles through the wilderness area. She said the trail was rated as "moderate," so it should not be a problem.

When I got back to the house on Red Mountain, I looked up the word "moderate" on the electronic dictionary just to make sure the definition had not changed. Sure enough, one of the definitions provided is "mild or calm." How anybody can honestly describe the trail we took as "mild or calm" is beyond me.

Anyway, by the time we reached Crater Lake I had sweated through my man girdle, my faded Chevron Shell designer jeans, my Denver Broncos

T-shirt, and my denim long-sleeved shirt with the Eat Colorado Organic insignia on the breast pocket. Suzanne looked like she was ready to go to the prom—not a hair out of place, not a bead of sweat anywhere. Again, would a self-proclaimed Alabama white trash girl who had never been to Colorado look this good after a hike up a mountain? Even a "moderate" hike?

Eb was waiting for us when we arrived. He looked a little red in the face, but was in much better shape than I was. Eb tactfully refrained from mentioning that I was wet from head to foot, introduced himself to Suzanne, and then we all sat down on some boulders by the lake. A bunch of Secret Service guys circled us and looked into the mountains, as if a band of marauding Indians might appear at any minute.

"Did you know," Eb began, "that 'Louie Louie' is ranked number fifty-five on *Rolling Stone*'s list of the 500 Greatest Songs of All Time? I had one of my researchers check it out for me. Being a presidential candidate has its perks— I just get people to look stuff up for me."

"So you know about the Red Head trip," I said, glancing at Suzanne.

"We've been keeping tabs, although from a distance. Have to admit you surprised us by hooking up with Suzanne, here." Suzanne beamed at the mention of her name.

I stifled a laugh at Eb's "hooking up" remark. I don't think the Eb I met on the New Sea of Galilee would have used the phrase, at least without stuttering.

Eb continued. "Junior, my advisers tell me that my election campaign is losing steam. Despite the resignations of three Democrat vice presidential candidates, we just can't seem to gain sufficient traction with the American public. We are not far behind in the polls, but if we don't get a bump soon we may never be able to catch up."

I have unhappily followed Eb's difficulty relating to the average American Joe. One of Eb's biggest problems is that he is not a sports fan. He never played or followed football, basketball, baseball, or even soccer as a kid, so it is difficult for him to fake it when sports-related issues come up during the campaign. Eb is pretty smart, and his handlers are stuffing his head with sports information to make him seem more like a regular guy, but they simply can't anticipate every situation that may come up.

The most recent boo-boo took place at the College Baseball World Series in Omaha, Nebraska. Both presidential candidates made an appearance at a banquet honoring the teams participating in the College World Series.

Dr. Kevin Davis, the Democratic candidate, grew up a Boston Red Sox fan and regaled the crowd with wonderful stories about following the Red Sox as a child. He concluded his remarks with what I thought was an incredibly great analogy:

You know, I have talked to a bunch of good baseball players, both college and pro. And I have asked them: "What is the mark of a truly great clutch hitter? What distinguishes the superstars who get timely hits in big situations from the guys who are solid but not great clutch hitters?" Almost to a man, the answer I got was: "Kevin, the great ones can hit the 2-2 curveball."

I see a bunch of you guys smiling and nodding your head right now, so it looks like you agree. I know sports analogies don't always work, but here's the deal, guys. You want your president to be a guy who can stand in there with a two-ball-and-two-strike count and hit the curveball with the game on the line. Hitting Uncle Charlie at 2-2 under pressure takes concentration and requires supreme confidence. I am confident I can lead this country through the difficult times we will face, just like the great ones are confident they can hit a nasty yakker at 2-2.

Davis got a standing ovation.

Eb did not have any sports memories to relate, so he gave an accurate but boring speech about the history of the College World Series and its importance to American sports. He also talked about the schools in the tournament and commented specifically on each school's fine academic reputation.

Eb tried to ad-lib and counter Davis's 2-2 curveball analogy, but he clearly had no idea what he was talking about. He made a reference to "driving in points" as president, not realizing that in baseball you drive in "runs," not "points." He also talked about "putting on a full-court press" against America's enemies, not understanding that a "full-court press" is a basketball, not a baseball, term. Eb was clearly embarrassed when he left the lectern to tepid applause.

Sorry for the long digression, but stuff like this was running through my mind as Eb went into more detail about his poll numbers and his difficulty raising funds in the face of those numbers.

"Junior," Eb continued, "you know who I really am, and you know that I would not be the Republican candidate for president without some amazingly serendipitous and tragic events, most of which were likely orchestrated by your late father, may he rest in peace.

"I am not a great warrior, like General Dozier. We had hoped that General Dozier's reputation as a man's man would make up for my limited reputation in that arena, but that has not been the case. My advisers have told me I need to do something dramatic that shows the country I can be a bold leader. As General Dozier put it rather crudely last night, 'Eb, the American people need to know their president has stones in his britches. Can't say it any plainer than that, son.'"

Then Eb explained to me the plan his advisers had concocted that would show America he had stones the size of a Ford F-150. "Junior," he said, "I could really use some assistance here. If you are willing to help me, I would stand a much better chance of getting elected." I told Eb I was willing to help cleanse his mama's boy reputation (although I didn't use those words, of course). Frankly, I was too embarrassed, after all the "big stones" talk, to refuse. But as I sit here on the deck sipping my sangria, I don't know if I can go through with it. The reason I never made the varsity baseball team in high school was that, although I was a decent glove man, I could never hit the curveball. On any count.

Day 481

Month seventeen. Still in Aspen. Hard to complain about being in Aspen in the summer. Suzanne said the temperature in Florida today was over 105 degrees.

Today, as part of the plan to show the American people that Eb would satisfy the Big Johnson War Bill requirements, Suzanne and I met with two agents: Morty Rubenstein and Clarence "Big Foot" Sims. We met in a big office in the cool house on Red Mountain. I was a bit nervous, so I did not wear my man girdle. Did not want to sweat through it again.

I had heard of Morty, but never met him. Morty is well known for representing famous movie stars in Hollywood and getting them big movie deals. Big Foot is the premier sports agent in the NFL. His biggest client is Sammy Assassin.

I know this may seem hard to believe, but part of the master plan created by Eb's team is for me to become more "accessible" to the American public, while still maintaining a relatively low personal profile. Or, as Big Foot Sims put it: "Junior, you are going to be everywhere and nowhere at the same time.[85]

Morty told me that he was a close personal friend of the prime minister of Israel and that the prime minister had asked Morty to represent me as a special favor. "Consequently, Mr. Junior," Morty said in a gravelly monotone, "my fee will only be 25 percent. The prime minister Jewed me down from my usual 30 percent. He is one tough negotiator, let me tell you. I normally don't represent people who are not in the business, particularly goyim, but we all know what your father did to help my people, so there you go.

"I've had my people working on this day and night, Mr. Junior. We decided the most important thing to do was to create a symbol for you. A brand, so to speak. Here's what we came up with."

Morty placed five eight-by-ten-inch laminated cards on the table. On each card was the drawing of a bee and the circular peace sign made famous in the 1960s. Each drawing had a different configuration of the bee and the peace sign. The drawings were all red, white, and blue.

Morty continued. "We checked Veronica Wells's copyright information, Mr. Junior. My attorneys assure me that none of these symbols violate the copyright laws. The bee drawing is not the same as Veronica's, and you'll notice there is no yellow or black in our drawings. Also, Veronica's bee has not, to date, been associated with a peace sign."

Morty then placed a sheet of paper on the table. Written on the paper, in various fonts, were the following words:

(1) Beelieve
(2) Bee Strong
(3) Bee Kind
(4) Just Bee
(5) Peace Bee With You

"The way I see this, Mr. Junior, is that, thanks to Veronica Wells, you are already associated with the bee. The bee is industrious. The bee is productive. The bee is cute, but it can also sting you. All good images for you.

"Because of your legal predicament, we thought it also would be good to associate you with nonviolence, hence the peace symbol.

---

85 This statement is the fifth of the Seven Conundrums in *Junior*. It is known as "Big Foot's Conundrum."

"Finally, the red, white, and blue works with everyone, because of the patriotic theme. It is also practically impossible for the American public to dislike a product wrapped in the colors of the American flag. Plus, by not using black or yellow for the bee, we avoid a potential copyright violation. What do you think?"

I did not know what to say. I'm not sure what I expected from this meeting, but I did not expect symbols and slogans. I picked up the piece of paper Morty had placed on the table and absently said to myself, "Peace be with you." Suzanne immediately and automatically responded, "And also with you."

When everyone in the room looked at her, Suzanne said sheepishly, "Sorry, it's what we say in church. You know, the preacher says 'peace be with you' and everyone in the congregation responds 'and also with you.'"

Morty smiled and spoke. "Thank you, miss. You have done us a great favor. You are better than an expensive focus group. 'Peace Bee With You' is now officially off the table. We don't want to project rural, backwater religiosity. No offense, of course."

Suzanne reddened a bit, then recovered, and said in her best Southern Girl accent: "None taken, Mr. Goldberg."

"It's Rubenstein, dear, but you can call me Morty."

Suzanne lightly touched Morty's arm and put her face right up next to his. "So sorry, Mort, all those Hebrew-type names kind of sound the same to a backwater Alabama goyim like me, I'm afraid."

It was then I decided that Suzanne was likely not a Mossad agent, unless she was also an Academy Award–winning actress.

Clarence Sims spoke up to break the tension. "Junior, the Assassin says to say hey. He wants you to know he is praying for you." I had met Clarence on several occasions, mostly at charity events to raise money for the Assassin's home for retarded kids in El Paso. (Don't tell Sister Flannery I used the "r" word. She will punch me.) We talked for a few minutes about the Assassin, then Clarence got down to business.

"Junior," Clarence said, "as you know, I have a bunch of contacts in the athletic apparel industry and I have thought a bunch about how you might be marketed in that arena. This may surprise you, Junior, but our market research indicates a lot of people admire you for remaining a free man, despite the fact that the law is trying to apprehend you. You are, in effect, running for your life.

"So, like Morty here, we created a few symbols for you to look at. Each shows the outline of a man who is running. And the slogan we have come up with is 'Man on the Run.'

"We have run this concept by Nike, Adidas, Taco Bell Athletics, and others. Everybody loves it. You see, each of us, in one way or another, is running for his life. We see Man on the Run running shoes, running shorts, T-shirts, and caps as blockbuster best sellers."

The "Man on the Run" idea was about the coolest thing I had ever heard, particularly since I could barely run around the block twice. Like most overweight nonathletic guys, I have always wanted to be a world-famous athlete.

Trying to hide my excitement, I said calmly, "Should I have two symbols, then? Or is that too many?"

Morty and Clarence explained that the bee and the running man were aimed at two different markets, so having two "brands" associated with my name would not be a problem. Morty was very upbeat and excited as he jumped back into the conversation: "These things happen for a reason, as we all know. This venture will be huge, Mr. Junior. Absolutely huge. Undoubtedly the biggest marketing campaign of my career. And I have been involved in some big ones, let me tell you."

Not knowing what else to say, I lamely offered, "OK. What happens next?"

Before Morty or Clarence could answer, Suzanne said in her best sweeter-than-sugar voice: "Just wondering, fellas. How much money are we talking about here? And what is Junior's share?"

Clarence spoke first. "Based upon my initial calculations, we could be talking over a billion dollars a year on the athletic side. If we can get the Chinese and Indian markets interested, maybe double that. Junior's share, after you consider the manufacturing and marketing costs, would be about 52 percent of the total, depending upon how we structure the final contracts."

"And your cut of Junior's share?" Suzanne countered.

"Not a penny, ma'am," responded Clarence quickly. "Mr. Jennings, Senior, did me an absolutely huge favor many years ago. This here's my payback for that favor."

Morty frowned at this revelation. Suzanne turned to him. Her voice lost some of its sweetness. "Mr. Goldberg, I don't expect you to do this for free, but since you have admitted that this is the biggest marketing campaign of your career, could you drop your commission to 10 percent? If not, my guess is that the prime minister could give us another reference."

Morty did not even correct Suzanne's apparently intentional failure to get his name right. After a few minutes of negotiations, Suzanne (who I guess is now my agent to deal with my agents) and Morty agreed on 12½ percent for Morty's share.

We talked a few more minutes and when the subject arose of how my money would be distributed, I said that Suzanne would get 10 percent and the rest would go to charities. I told Morty and Clarence that Suzanne or I would get them the names of the charities.

Suzanne protested vociferously about me giving her 10 percent. "Junior, you don't have to do that. You may need this money." I responded: "Don't I have the right to do what I want with my own money?" Suzanne did not push it, but it's clear I will hear more from her on this issue.

Eventually Morty and Clarence left, promising to bring back contracts for us to sign. I am back on the deck, sipping sangria and watching the sun set. I wish I could be there to see Sister Flannery's face when the first check arrives. Maybe she will concede that some men are worth something after all.

Day 484

Went for a bike ride today. Suzanne suggested it, probably so I can lose weight and stop wearing the man girdle. Worked up a good sweat.

When we made it back to the house, the contracts sent by Morty and Clarence had arrived. Suzanne went over them with a fine-tooth comb and pronounced them acceptable. It crossed my mind to ask Suzanne how her waitress/stripper career qualified her to perform a review of sophisticated endorsement contracts, but decided that would be cruel. I trust Clarence not to screw me. I don't trust Morty quite as much, but it's clear to me that I am riding on a train with a predetermined destination and a motivated conductor. Might as well settle back and enjoy the ride.

News of my impending endorsement opportunities has leaked. According to CNN, the CFL is rewriting its rules to account for the money I will receive as a result of the endorsements. Although my endorsement money technically did not result from a theft or robbery, since I am capitalizing on my fame as a criminal, the dollars count toward my point total.

On the deck later tonight than usual. Suzanne has gone to bed. Before she left, she was kind enough to leave me a pitcher of sangria. Smells like rain. Hope I can finish the pitcher before it falls.

Day 490

Aspen is one of those places where famous and smart people (and in my humble opinion, those are two distinct categories, for the most part) come to talk about Big Ideas. Since everybody enjoys Aspen, particularly in the summer, I guess the people who organize these Big Idea conferences don't have to pay famous and smart people to attend.

The current Aspen Big Idea conference, the Aspen Summer Caucus, has been in town for several weeks now. When I met Eb earlier up in Maroon Bells, he was in town to address the caucus on the issue of global rain.

Reading the Aspen paper this morning, I noticed that the Aspen Summer Caucus topic for the week was "The Banking Crisis—Are There Solutions?" Since I have been out of the loop on financial matters, I'm not exactly sure what the current banking crisis is all about. But since I know something about a previous banking crisis that you, dear reader, might find interesting, and since dinner is not ready yet, I thought I would fill you in.

Plus, this story also involves Senior, and since this opus I am writing seems to be more and more about Senior, it seems appropriate to include it here. And besides, I'm sitting on the deck with a pitcher of sangria, and for some reason this view of the mountains makes me feel expansive.

For those of you who are tired of reading about banking crises, I certainly understand. You can skip on ahead to the next entry, assuming, of course, that the MFM does not blow up this cool house tonight while I am drinking sangria.

To be honest, I'm not sure if it was Bank Crisis #24 or Bank Crisis #25 when Senior got involved. The problem had something to do with reverse air power and solar power credit development derivatives. The major banks and brokerage houses had first created, then invested heavily in, these derivatives and then insured them, and then sold them, and then, I think, bought them back and canceled the insurance. Something like that. Anyway, they made a bunch of money and then lost even more money. Then these guys went to Congress for help, arguing that the country's financial system would collapse if the government did not intervene and save their bacon.

Senior, like everyone else, was tired of bailing the money guys out. He did not like big banks much and he really didn't like Yankees, so the prospect of using his hard-earned money to fix a problem caused by a bunch of New York bankers AGAIN was too much for him to stomach.

Senior kept a guy named Michael MacDowall on staff for what Senior called "Special Projects." Mac, as he was known to everyone, was a former FBI agent who seemed to know everybody and who could work low-profile, behind-the-scenes miracles. Senior loved the guy. In fact, Mac was the only man I knew who could tell Senior he was "full of blue mud" (Mac didn't curse) and get away with it. Note that I said "man"—for all of his bluster, Senior was still second banana to my mom in the family hierarchy, a role he accepted with relative good humor.

When it was clear that the power derivative problem was about to blossom into a new banking crisis, Senior told me to tell Mac to investigate and see what he could come up with: "Tell Mac to investigate all of these slimy dogs. The appetite these guys have for money is never satisfied. They just never have enough. I want to take everything they have and give it back to the taxpayers."

Mac made a show in front of strangers of being a bit slow, but in addition to being a former FBI agent, he also had a CPA license and a law degree. He was no dummy.

Despite Mac's talents and contacts, however, he initially came up dry. He found some interesting stuff, but the banks had covered their tracks well. When I reported this to Senior, he said, "Tell Mac to find the bimbos! Find the gold diggers! These guys aren't going to be spending this money on their wives."

While he was looking for bimbos, Mac found someone even better: an angry wife. Mrs. Virginia Timmons, mother of four and grandmother of ten, was royally peeved that Mr. Randall Timmons, the chairman of the board of Timmons Securities, was off the reservation with a young thing less than half his age. Without her husband's knowledge, Mrs. Timmons had hired New York City divorce lawyer Carroll "the Hatchet" Martin. The Hatchet, by happy coincidence, had dated Mac when they both attended the University of Texas Law School. Mac and the Hatchet had remained friends, and met for a friendly drink in New York City when Mac was doing some research into the power derivatives issue. They started talking about their work and one thing led to another, and they realized they could help each other out and help their respective clients out at the same time.

Mrs. Timmons, a Smith College graduate, had paid close attention while her husband's company made billions off the power derivatives. She had copies of incriminating e-mails and offshore bank statements. Senior used his contacts and set up a meeting between Mrs. Timmons, the Hatchet, and Steve Britt, the United States attorney general. I attended the meeting as Senior's representative. Don't ask why Senior was entitled to have a representative at the meeting. That's just the way things worked with Senior.

When the Hatchet presented Mrs. Timmons's documents to General Britt, he was at first very aggravated because his subpoena to Timmons Securities had obviously been ignored. When General Britt got over his initial irritation and reviewed the documents, he laughed for at least five minutes. The rest of us did not know what to do, so we just sat silently and uncomfortably at the conference table and watched the attorney general of the United States laugh so hard there were tears running down his cheeks.

When General Britt calmed down, he apologized to Mrs. Timmons: "I am very sorry, Mrs. Timmons. My laughter was inappropriate. I realize this is not funny to you. This will not go well for your husband. He is probably going to jail for a long time."

"Actually," replied Mrs. Timmons, "I insist on it. I'm not going to allow you to keep these documents unless you promise to do your best to put my slimy husband in a cell with a guy named something like Big Harry, who is partial to chubby, white, middle-aged men who cheat on their wives." The white-hot glow in Mrs. Timmons's eyes was matched in intensity only by the sadistic smile on the Hatchet's face. Reflexively, I reached below the table to protect my manhood.

The negotiations between the Hatchet and General Britt were civil, but intense. General Britt wanted to take all of Mr. Timmons's money, but that would not have been a good thing for Mrs. Timmons, who wanted all of Mr. Timmons's money in a divorce settlement. When it looked as if they were at an impasse, I blurted, "How about a finder's fee?"

Both sides were surprised, since I had not said boo throughout the meeting, but the Hatchet said, "The kid has a decent idea. Without Mrs. Timmons's help, you will get zippo from these guys. With the documents she has, however, the government is going to get a bunch of convictions and a bunch of money in fines and reparations. Let's give her 33 percent of everything the government gets. Like a contingency fee."

General Britt was not happy, but he wanted the convictions, so he agreed to a finder's fee of 10 percent. And that, dear reader, is how the now famous Timmons Fee was created. As everyone who follows governmental investigations knows, the Timmons Fee is now an integral factor in every investigation. A lot of ex-wives, ex-girlfriends, and ex-mistresses have become Timmons Fee millionaires.

The Hatchet took credit for the Timmons Fee idea (which was OK with me), and I believe she is the most famous and successful Timmons Fee lawyer in the country, although I have seen several billboards on my post-explosion travels touting the exploits of other Timmons Fee attorneys.

I don't remember how much jail time Mr. Timmons got, but I do remember he was one of the few power derivative bankers who was not sent to a country club jail. I don't know if he had to room with a guy named Big Harry, but . . .

Excuse me, but a lightbulb just went off in my pea-sized brain. Goodness gracious me. Oh my stars and garters. Remember when I told you about Clayton Singletary, the accountant who wound up in Afghanistan with the Nazi Lowriders, and how some chubby white guy who shared a cell with Big Rico asked him about explosives?[86] That must have been Randall Timmons! Maybe the bankers blew up Senior!

It makes some sense when you think about it. The bankers who got busted in the power derivative banking crisis (and there were a bunch of them) took it totally in the shorts. They lost all their money, lost their professional licenses, and were forever banned from working in the banking or securities industries. These guys certainly had the motive to blow up Senior. And Randall Timmons may have had the biggest motivation of them all: Big Rico.

Since dinner is still not ready, maybe we should identify all the people we know about so far who may have killed Senior:

---

86 See Day 299.

(1) The Bad Jews, who are angry that Senior convinced the prime minister to leave Israel for North Dakota

(2) Drug dealers, who lost trillions of dollars when Senior got drugs legalized

(3) Mexico is for Mexicans—I have not talked about the Baja, Texas, deal that made these guys mad. More on that later.

(4) People who don't like homosexuals, including, but not limited to, Homicides for Homos, L.L.P.

(5) The Sister Golden Surprise–type folks who are angry that the New Jerusalem is in North Dakota, and worse, is full of Jews

(6) Federal prison employees who lost their jobs because of "Are You a Badass?"

(7) The Catholic priests who were kicked out of America

(8) Samson Fairman and the Methodist Free Militia

(9) Folks who lost money and/or their jobs when Senior took over the telephone industry

(10) Power derivative bankers

Quite a list, huh? I am sure there are others, but these are the ones who come to mind tonight as I sit on the deck and drink my sangria.

Looks like Suzanne finally has dinner ready. Later.

Day 495

Sometimes when I write this stuff, I wonder about the people who will eventually read it. I realize there is a better-than-even chance nobody will ever see this, since if I am ever caught and/or killed, my captors/killers could simply destroy this computer. Plus, for anybody other than an Apache to read this, somebody is going to have to translate it into English. And who would go to that trouble?[87]

Anyway, if someone IS actually reading this, are you bored with my Aspen entries? I mean, nothing exciting has really happened in a few days. Nobody has tried to shoot me or blow me up. I haven't received any

---

87 *Junior* has been translated into more than 200 languages.

beyond-the-grave messages on my computer. If this were an action movie or a made-for-television special, this would be the place where we would have a musical interlude or a steamy sex scene, while the producers and writers figured out what cool thing to have happen next.

So, for you excitement junkies, I apologize for my relatively peaceful existence the last few days. I admit, however, I have really enjoyed my evenings sitting here on the deck with my pitcher of sangria.

Wait a minute. The peaceful chatter in the background between Hannah and Suzanne as they make dinner has gone up a notch. Voices have been raised. Now they are standing toe to toe and yelling at each other. Suzanne is pointing at me. Now Hannah is pointing at me.

Should I get up to see what is happening? No. Although the women are both still facing each other, they both point their palms at me to stay seated. I can't make out what they are saying, but there is definitely an argument going on here. Oh well. So much for peace and quiet.

I have decided to go inside and intervene. You can insert a musical interlude here if you wish. I don't think a steamy sex scene is about to take place.

OK. I'm back. In case this book ever gets made into a movie (and remember, I own the rights), here is my crack at writing the screenplay version for what just happened. I am using the format that Veronica used in the screenplay she gave me to read, so if this is not the way it is supposed to look, blame her.

INT. KITCHEN IN HOUSE ON ASPEN RED MOUNTAIN. NIGHT

Hannah and Suzanne are standing next to the stove, which has several pots on it. Steam is rising from the pots. Hannah is holding a rubber spatula-looking thing. Suzanne has a big wooden spoon in her hand. Both women are wearing aprons. Junior tentatively enters the room, closing the sliding glass door that leads to the deck.

Suzanne: You can go back outside, Junior. I will call you when dinner is ready.

Junior: I am out of sangria. Came in to get another pitcher. What are you guys arguing about?

Suzanne: Nothing important, Junior. You know how women are. Just a silly catfight over nothing important. Go on back outside now, and I will bring you some more sangria in a Georgia jiffy.

Hannah: Catfight? That's the best you can do? We are talking about the future of our country and you tell Junior we are having a catfight? That is so insulting! Junior, this is an important discussion and we need your input. Can you help me talk some sense into this lady?

Junior: Uh . . .

Suzanne: Future of this country my left . . . (pausing and looking at Junior) eyebrow! You mean the future of your employer. That's all you care about. You don't care what happens to Junior. You realize that, don't you, Junior?

Junior: Well . . .

Hannah: How can you stand there and say I don't care about Junior? We are the only reason he is alive. Junior, here's the deal. We need you and Suzanne to work with us to implement the plan you and Ebenezer discussed up on Maroon Bells. Suzanne is absolutely not being cooperative. I can't do this all by myself. I need her help.

Suzanne: Junior, all I care about is you. I don't want you to get hurt. I don't want to lose you. My job is to take care of you and make sure you are OK. Hannah doesn't need my help. She has other Mossad people to help her. She is just angry because I won't agree to some of the things she wants you to do.

Hannah: So you are his agent now? I thought you were just a damsel in distress that Junior saved from a drug-crazed boyfriend in Hicksville, Alabama. So what's the deal, Junior? Does this woman speak for you now?

Junior: Well, Hannah, you know, Suzanne did help me on the one thing we did with Morty and Big Foot, so . . .

Hannah: OK, fine, whatever. Now at least I know where we stand. You guys have chosen each other on this deal, which puts you fundamentally at odds with Eb. I think you could have chosen better, but I will do my best to avoid the distractions this will inevitably create.

Suzanne: Thank you, Junior. Now you go on back outside and let us girls finish up dinner. And here's a new pitcher of my special sangria to tide you over till we are done.

END SCENE

Did you follow what just happened? I am not totally sure I did. I think Suzanne just risked her neck for me. And Hannah, for all her bluster and anger, seemed to accept Suzanne as my "agent" without much of a fight. I guess this means I'm a big deal. I mean, is there anybody else you can think of who has an agent to negotiate with the Mossad? Not bad for a guy with a history degree and limited work experience.

I hope dinner is ready soon. Kinda hungry. I'll close now and sit here with my pitcher of sangria and enjoy the view.

Day 498

Well, I am on the deck again, but it is early morning. I am checking out the sunrise. Downright chilly up here before the sun comes up, even in the summer.

I was going to write an entry last night about the revised plan that Suzanne, my Alabama white trash waitress/stripper/agent, has negotiated with Hannah and Eb's group, but I got sidetracked by a visitor. As I sat on the deck with my postdinner sangria, this big guy just hopped over the railing of the deck. He did it very quietly. If I had not been looking up when he appeared, I never would have known he was there.

I was about to run inside, or throw up, or both, because I figured this was one of the fartwa guys and I was about to be killed. Then I noticed that the black T-shirt the guy was wearing had a little white symbol on it that looked like a guy running. He noticed me looking at his T-shirt.

"Pretty cool, huh? Big Foot does good work, don't he? This is just a proto-type, though. My name is Dale Piper. How you doing, Junior?"

"Since you are wearing one of my T-shirts, does this mean you are on my side and did not come here to kill me?"

"I am definitely not here to kill you, Junior. If I were, you would already be dead."

I noticed he did not say he was on my side, but I let it pass. So I asked Dale how he found me.

"Not too hard, dude. It's the lamp you have on your table. It's the only light shining in the darkness up here this time of night. All the other rich folks on the mountain are asleep or dead drunk."

Dale pulled a chair up to the table. I offered him a glass of sangria, but he declined. "I try not to imbibe while I work."

"OK," I said, "so what do you want, Dale, if you are not here on a fartwa?"

Dale smiled, showing perfectly white and straight teeth. This guy's parents had definitely spent some money at the tooth doctor. "You know, when I get through with this gig, I may have to call those MFM boys up and offer them my services as a grammarian and speller."

I was confused. "So are you a teacher, Dale? Did you somehow scale this mountain and leap onto my deck in the middle of the night to help me with my homework?"

Dale smiled, showing his pretty teeth again. "I am a consultant, Junior. I know a lot of people and I get hired to help folks get stuff done. And sometimes to get stuff undone, if you get my drift. For example, I know Big Foot Sims. And as you can plainly see, I help road test products for Big Foot. When I finish our business here today, I am going to send an e-mail to Big Foot and tell him this particular brand of T-shirt is a little too tight in the arms. Almost ripped open when I jumped over the railing here."

I did not respond, so Dale continued. "Junior, I am here tonight on behalf of the United States Department of Defense."

I did not know what to say, so I just blurted out, "You mean the guys in the Pentagon? Are you in the Army?"

"Used to be, but not for the last decade or so. I still have a lot of contacts there, and I do contracting jobs for them from time to time. Anyway, I have a message for you from the DOD. The message is: 'We did not do it.'"

I was still confused, although my confusion could have been exaggerated by the sangria. "Didn't do what, Dale?"

"Didn't blow up Senior, Junior."

"I have been giving this issue a lot of thought, Dale, and I never once considered the possibility that the Department of Defense blew up my dad."

"Well, the fact of the matter, Junior, is that your dad had already talked his good buddy President Carrier into a bunch of budget cuts for the military and your dad was clamoring for even more. There is a rumor floating around out there that President Carrier was going to announce even more drastic military spending cuts in his speech at the reservation. And word on the street is that the FBI has recently discovered that some of the ordnance that blew everyone up in New Mexico was cutting-edge-type munitions that only the military would have access to. So the media is going to jump all over this in a day or two."

"Why tell me?" I asked. "There is really nothing I can do about this one way or the other. I am just the son of a famous man who is on the run from the law."

"I think we both know you are more than that, Junior. The military sent me to talk to you for three reasons. First, to let you know they didn't do it. Second, to give you a heads-up on the story so you won't be ambushed, and to ask you to keep an open mind as the evidence plays out in the court of public opinion. Third, to let you know they want to help you." With that, Dale quickly leapt back over the deck's railing and into the darkness.

I was confused why Dale left so quickly, until the sliding glass door to the deck opened and Hannah walked out onto the deck and spoke to me: "I heard voices. Who were you talking to, Junior?"

"Sorry to bother you, Hannah," I said, with what I hoped was a touch of nonchalance. "I was actually just talking to myself. I do that sometimes to help clarify my thoughts and relieve stress."

I am not a good liar. Hannah clearly didn't believe me, and she looked over the deck railing. "You are a little old for an imaginary friend, aren't you, Junior?"

"Hannah, I can use all the friends I can get, imaginary or otherwise. You know that better than almost anyone in the world."

So that was the way last night ended. I had hoped that when I woke up this morning I would have a better handle on what happened last night, but I don't. I am inclined to believe that the DOD did not blow up Senior. Senior had a lot of friends in the military, even if he did complain sometimes about how much of his tax dollars the military spent.

The more interesting question is why the army guys want to help me. That makes me a bit nervous.

I smell bacon. The ladies must be making breakfast. I really like bacon. Later.

Day 500

Well, it looks like I have some new competition in the CFL, or as it is now known, the WCFL. According to CNN, the CFL, a Canadian/American league, was sued by the World Criminal Fantasy League for antitrust violations, and as part of the settlement, the leagues merged. In the new WCFL, you no longer get extra points for killing Islamic terrorists, since there are a lot of Muslim guys playing in the league.

Now I am competing with a bunch of foreign criminals and terrorists, and that means my new main competition is Alberto Gonga Mutsapi, a Swaziland terrorist. Since I am a lazy typist, I am going to call him "Al" and his country "Swazi." I hope that does not offend anyone.

Al is, as far as I know, the world's only seven-foot-tall black African Quaker terrorist. Several years ago, when huge deposits of gold, oil, and natural gas were discovered in Swazi, the United States entered into development agreements with Al's father, Jagger Mutsapi, the king of Swazi. When the king became disenchanted with the arrangement and sought to renegotiate, he was killed when his helicopter mysteriously crashed in the Burppot Jungle in southern Swazi.

Al was studying at the University of Pennsylvania when his father was killed. After returning to Swazi to bury his dad, Al renounced his right to the Swazi throne, put his significant inheritance in several Swiss bank accounts, and publicly vowed to destroy America for raping his country and killing his father.

Because he became a Quaker while studying at Penn, however, Al declared he would not directly kill people. Al, therefore, has become one of the most creative terrorists in history.

The first terrorist act Al took credit for was the disruption of the satellite signal for five minutes during sudden death overtime in the Super Bowl Tier 1 game between the Dallas Cowboys and the Houston Texans. The resulting death toll was not insignificant. Twenty men were killed when they fell off their roofs trying to adjust their satellite antennas, fifteen men died of heart attacks, and ten men killed their wives during this five-minute period. And that was just in Houston and Dallas.

Several years ago, Al incited a riot in Boston, Massachusetts, when he started an Internet rumor that the Boston Animal Shelter, because of a lack of funding, was going to secretly gas hundreds of puppies and kittens on Christmas Day. More than 5,000 people stormed the unsuspecting skeleton crew working at the shelter on Christmas Day. Two shelter workers and thirty rioters were killed in the confusion. No puppies or kittens were injured.

I don't know if this is just a bizarre coincidence, but Al has chosen today, the date of the Criminal Fantasy League merger, to announce his latest "nonviolent" act of terror. And it is a doozy.

You need a little background to follow this one. Those of you who pay attention to such things may remember that about five years ago a male enhancement drug named Big Boy was introduced to the American market with much fanfare. Mitzi Hyatt, a voluptuous actress, was featured in a series of scintillating ads for the drug. Her catchphrase, "Come on in, big boy," won several advertising awards.

Approximately three years after Big Boy's debut, the Sexual Dysfunction Network reported a significant increase in the rate of sexual dysfunction symptoms in American men over the age of forty. Last year, the Centers for Disease Control in Atlanta announced that sexual dysfunction in American men over the age of forty had become a pandemic. The *Burger King New York Times* reported that urologists were overwhelmed with patients, as tens of thousands of men sought medical help. *Big Vacation Homes Quarterly* published a special issue highlighting the vacation homes purchased and/or built by urologists with their newfound wealth.

Today, we now know what caused the pandemic. In an exclusive interview on the Veronica Network, Al revealed that he created Big Boy as a nonviolent terroristic weapon. Al told Veronica:

*I created **Big Boy** to punish the fat American pigs who pillaged my country and murdered my father. The men in America are fat, lazy, and weak. They also apparently believe their maleness is not sufficient* *enough to satisfy their fat, lazy women. This means that the fat, lazy, and weak American men are also stupid, since women do not need to be satisfied and do not deserve to be satisfied.*

Because I knew that American men were fat, lazy, weak, stupid, and had small wee-wees, I created and developed Big Boy specifically for Americans. I hired expensive Washington, D.C., lawyers to bribe the Federal Drug Administration to approve Big Boy without the testing required for these types of drugs.

The primary ingredient in Big Boy is mishtang, which is found in the sap of the Mnnortingal tree. The Mnnortingal tree is found only in the Burppot Jungle, where my father's helicopter crashed after it was sabotaged by the American secret service spies. A little poetic justice, don't you think?

Veronica, apparently not realizing this was a rhetorical question, began to speak, but Al continued:

Mishtang does, in fact, initially make a man's wee-wee bigger. However, over time, mishtang negatively affects a man's nervous system, eventually rendering a man's wee-wee permanently flaccid. This side effect will occur in every man who took more than three Big Boy pills.

America, you should not have messed with my beautiful country. I cannot defeat you militarily, but I can humiliate you and make you suffer. America is now a country full of limp and small wee-wees.

Veronica, like she was interviewing a movie star promoting a new movie, asked, "So, Alberto, what is your next project?"

Ignoring Veronica, Al said:

And one more thing. "I did not kill the president or Joshua Jennings, Sr. I am glad they are dead, because they ignored my pleas to give my country back to its citizens and restore Swaziland's mineral rights.

However, because I am a devoted Quaker and I abhor violence, I did not blow them up.

Al then flashed the two-fingered peace sign and walked off camera.

Veronica, looking a little peeved at Al's rudeness toward her, put her hand to her ear as if she was listening to a message from her director. She nodded and then said, "Mr. Mutsapi has left the building, thereby evading my many insightful questions about his horrific actions relating to Big Boy. We can only wonder what this horrible crime will do to America's psyche.

"And," she continued, putting her hand to her ear again, "you also have to wonder about Mr. Mutsapi's statement that he had nothing to do with the New Mexico explosion. I did not ask him about the explosion, so it strikes me as odd that he volunteered this information. We will definitely follow up on this potential new suspect in the murder of the president. We will return after the following commercial message from Urologists R Us."

After a truly graphic and disgusting commercial that I can't even begin to describe here, Veronica returned to the screen and with a smile and a lilt in her voice said:

We have breaking news on the Big Boy story. My sources in the legal community tell me that five nationwide class action lawsuits have been filed against Mr. Mutsapi, his Washington, D.C., law firm, the Federal Drug Administration, the advertising agency that created the popular Big Boy television commercials, and Mitzi Hyatt. We will give you more details as this story develops.

According to CNN, after Al's appearance on the Veronica Network, the WCFL board of directors called an emergency meeting to determine how to count Al's Big Boy victims for purposes of the WCFL standings. The directors determined that once the research had been finalized on how many men had taken more than three Big Boy pills, these men would be considered "maimed" under league rules, and Al would receive one-half point for each victim. Given the commercial success of Big Boy, the fantasy league experts are predicting that Al will soon be atop the standings.

As you know, I could care less about the WCFL standings. In fact, once the real exploder of New Mexico is discovered, it is my hope that (if I am still alive) nobody ever hears about me again. For what it's worth, I hope Al can find some peace and stop his reign of terror.[88]

I guess this concludes my report for Day 500. Good night from the deck. And be wary of artificial enhancement.

Day 508

Still in Aspen, but not on the deck tonight. There is a decent chance a sniper is out there looking to snipe (is that a word, Dr. Hoover?) me, so I have been moved to the basement. But since this is Aspen, it's a heck of a basement. Pool table and indoor swimming pool, along with five huge flat-screen televisions. Hannah says the guy who owns the house is a gambler affiliated with the Israeli mafia who makes his living betting on sporting events, so he likes to watch multiple games at once. I did not even know there was an Israeli mafia. Does every country have a mafia?

Believe it or not, being hunted by a sniper is part of the plan, so hunkering down in the basement is a good thing. Let me explain.

Part of Eb's plan, as refined and negotiated by my superagent Suzanne, is for me to become just a tad more visible than I was under the "everywhere and nowhere at the same time" plan I mentioned earlier.[89] The hope is that my increased visibility will lure Samson Fairman out from whatever rock he is currently under, so Fairman will try (hopefully just try) and kill me. In other words, I am bait for a Methodist megalomaniac. Sounds great, huh?

To be honest, I am not really sure why I am helping the Israelis. I like Eb and all, and the Jews have certainly helped me, but I am not sure that risking my life is an equivalent consideration for their assistance. ("Consideration" is a word I learned while listening to Carroll "the Hatchet" Martin negotiate the first-ever Timmons Fee with the United States attorney general.) Plus, I seem

---

88 Several months after *Junior* was published, the World Health Organization reported that thousands of bottles of Big Boy had been sold over the Internet in Swaziland and that men over forty in Swaziland were suffering the same symptoms described in Day 500. Alberto Gonga Mutsapi flew to Swaziland to set up medical clinics for the victims. He was killed when his helicopter mysteriously crashed in the Burppot Jungle in southern Swaziland.

89 See Day 481.

to recall that Senior wanted Eb to LOSE this election. Plus, plus, as Suzanne put it: "Junior, this just ain't your cross to bear." Gotta love it when a Southern Girl riffs on The Allman Brothers.

Anyway, my working theory at this point is that since I have not received any e-mail or bumper sticker or snow globe or Scrabble messages to the contrary, Eb's plan fits within whatever grand scheme Senior has in mind. Since Eb's plan is a bit frightening, it won't take much of a sign for me to bail, trust me.

Pursuant (I also learned this word from the Hatchet) to the revised plan, I attended today's session of the Aspen Summer Caucus. The main event today was a panel discussion between four of the country's most eminent life critics. The topic: "Rating the Lives of President Carrier and Joshua Jennings, Sr."

I wore my man girdle, but I did not wear a baseball cap over my still-dyed hair. Suzanne accompanied me to the conference, still sporting her purple hair, tattoos, and piercings.

I was not given any specific instructions on what to do at the conference, but I think it is safe to say that Eb and his entourage knew I would not be able to keep my mouth shut, given the topic of discussion.

The ratings for President Carrier were all over the board, which is typical for a president. Norris Gillespie, a life critic with very conservative political views, gave President Carrier's life three and three-quarters stars, stating it was "a marvelous coming-of-age life with a thrilling, unexpected ending" and that "the chemistry between the president and his wife was off-the-charts believable."

Jana Mars, a life critic for the Donut Network, gave President Carrier's life only one star, finding it "remarkably unimaginative and wholly derivative. Predictable in the extreme." I wondered how getting blown up on an Apache reservation during a campaign rally could be extremely predictable, but I held my tongue.

Pursuant (my new favorite word) to my instructions, Suzanne and I sat in the back row of the auditorium. We had a few Mossad guys sitting in front of us in case things got hairy. When the life critics began to discuss Dad's life, the Mossad guys sat up a little bit straighter and started looking around a lot more.

Ms. Mars was first. As I mentioned earlier, she works for the Donut Net-work, and unfortunately, it shows. She is 400 pounds on a good day after fasting, running a marathon, and sitting in a sauna. Ms. Mars adjusted her thick horn-rimmed glasses on her flabby black face before she spoke:

You know, this man's life is one of the most difficult to rate in my entire career. It was so uneven. It had absolutely brilliant moments followed by stretches of incompetence and downright tedium. Senior was a capitalist pig who took advantage of every possible legal loophole to amass a personal fortune. However, he was also instrumental in creating the Queer Cities of Refuge and finding a cure for AIDS.

Ms. Mars took a tissue and wiped tears from her eyes before she continued.

Senior literally saved the lives of hundreds of thousands of people. He saved many of my close, personal friends from certain death. Therefore, I view Senior's life as a flawed, tragic masterpiece. I give Senior's life four and one-quarter stars. It was easily the best life I have reviewed this quarter, and possibly the life of the entire year.

Mr. Gillespie loved Senior's life. Gillespie listed a number of Senior's achievements and then concluded:

This life was a work of genius, magisterial in proportion. Senior's life is the best life I have ever reviewed. For me, this is a top-ten life for the ages. I wholeheartedly give it five stars!

The next speaker on the panel was Dr. Robert Van Jones, a professor in the Life Criticism Department at the University of Southern California. As Dr. Van Jones approached the microphone, I noticed one of the Mossad guys sitting in front of me get up and walk over to the back door of the auditorium right behind me, so I figured the fun was about to begin.

Dr. Van Jones spoke in a nasally tinged voice:

You know, a life critic applying classical life theory could, although incorrectly in my view, conclude that the life of Joshua Jennings, Sr., merits five stars. However, as I explained in my recent bestseller, A Life Critic Critiques Life Theories, the classicist approach to life evaluation is now hopelessly outdated. The modern life critic should look not at what a person has done, but why he did it. In other words, internal motive trumps actions, and ultimately, even results.

I figured what the guy said was somehow important, but it was so boring I was having a hard time staying awake. What the weasel said next got my attention, however.

My in-depth research indicates that while Senior did many wonderful things, there was always a selfish motive behind these actions. For example, while it is true that Senior revolutionized the telecommunications industry and made it possible for virtually everyone to afford a cell phone, the fact of the matter is that he also made a ton of money doing so. This greedy search for monopolistic power does not justify a high life rating under the new modern theory of life criticism that I have created.

Likewise, I have it on good authority that although Senior was instrumental in developing the AIDS vaccine, he also negotiated a royalty on the product, for which he received literally billions of dollars.

Turning to Ms. Mars, Dr. Van Jones said, "I'm sorry, Jana darling, but Senior made a financial killing saving you and all the other homosexuals in the world." The tone in Dr. Van Jones's voice and the sneer on his face made it clear he was not sorry at all.

Since I knew for a fact that Senior *paid* ten billion dollars to develop the AIDS vaccine and had not received a dime back, I stood up and shouted: "Who is your source, Professor?" Each Mossad guy sitting in front of us touched a finger to his ear and unbuttoned his jacket. This is what they had come for.

"I would be happy to take questions later, young man," the professor began.

"I am not one of your students, Doc. You have just slandered one of the greatest men of this century. I know for a fact that you have absolutely no proof that Senior got a royalty on the AIDS vaccine. So back it up, big boy, if you can. Give me the name of one person who can say Senior made money on the AIDS cure. As we say where I'm from, fish or cut bait."

Jana Mars, clearly enjoying Dr. Van Jones's discomfort, spoke up:

> *Robert, darling, I don't understand the fishing reference, but I think we are all interested in the factual support for your review. If what you say about the AIDS vaccine is true, I will certainly have to reevaluate my four-and-one-quarter-star rating. I know, given your outstanding reputation in the academic community, that you would never make a statement like this about a life you have reviewed without considerable substantive proof.*

The auditorium was silent as Dr. Van Jones rummaged through a sheaf of papers as if he was looking for an answer to my question. After about thirty seconds of this, Suzanne yelled, "Prove it!" Then someone else yelled, "Come on, Doc!" Soon half the auditorium was yelling "Prove it! Prove it!" as Dr. Van Jones left the stage in a red-faced huff.

Suzanne and I were immediately surrounded by photographers and television cameras. Reporters covering the conference started yelling questions: "Who are you? Are you a professional fisherman? Are you gay? Are you wearing a man girdle?" As the Mossad guys cleared a path for us I yelled, "Senior was a five-star!"[90]

So, as planned, I brought attention to myself as I defended Senior in a very public forum. We all hope that Fairman will see the footage from the conference and figure out that the "as yet unnamed and unknown demonstrator," as I am being referred to in the media, is his old buddy. I am going to sign off

---

90 Many scholars have noticed and debated the significance of the contrast between this statement and Junior's remark in Day 39 that his father "was no saint, and I don't understand why everyone is making such a big fuss about him now that he is dead."

now, drink my sangria, and see if I can find five ball games to watch on the television sets down here. Stay tuned.

Day 512

ℭelcome to month eighteen. Still in Aspen. Still in the cool basement. Still alive. Still drinking sangria.

Dr. Van Jones showed up on the Veronica Network today. I knew from news reports that the University of Southern California had fired Dr. Van Jones when he could not produce a source to confirm that Senior had profited from the AIDS drug. The interview went something like this:

Veronica: I'm here today with Dr. Robert Van Jones, disgraced former professor of Life Criticism at the University of Southern California. So Dr. Van Jones, what are you up to these days, now that you've been publicly humiliated and lost your job?

Dr. Van Jones: Veronica, first let me say how pleased I am to be here today. I have always been a big fan. Tomorrow I start my nationwide "I'm Sorry" tour to promote my new book, I Should Not Have Said That. *My first appearance will be at the Toilet Paper Warehouse in Cedar Rapids, Iowa.*

Veronica: I've been to that store. Did several live remotes from there when I worked for the Plumbing Fixtures Network. Such a wonderful selection of toilet paper. Anyway, I understand that the University of Southern California replaced you on the faculty with Jana Mars, formerly of the Donut Network.

Dr. Van Jones: Yes, the university is fully committed to diversity, and the Life Criticism Department did not have a black female calorically challenged lesbian faculty member, particularly one whose highest degree is a correspondence-course GED.

Veronica: And we applaud the university's diversity efforts. So what's your message, Dr. Van Jones?

Dr. Van Jones: I want to reach the nation's children, Veronica. I have learned a valuable lesson—that you should not lie, particularly about a beloved public figure who has been killed in a terrorist bombing. It's important not to lie in public, because your lie can be challenged by smart people who can prove you're lying. Everything happens for a reason, Veronica. And maybe the reason I have been publicly disgraced is so our children can learn the importance of not lying in public when you can easily be proven wrong. I think our children need to know that, and I hope they can learn from my mistakes.

Veronica: I'm sure they will, Dr. Van Jones. You have become a public laughingstock and I think the nation's children will think twice now before slandering a beloved public figure, be they living or dead. We at the Veronica Network applaud your initiative and hope our children learn from your public humiliation.

Veronica (turning away from Dr. Van Jones and toward the camera for a close-up): Next up, we explore the vicious rumors circulating about Shane Silvers of the Abdomen Exercise Network. Did she get her six-pack from diet pills and surgery instead of doing her patented belly exercises? More after this commercial.

Dr. Van Jones is an idiotic poophead. Wait. Did I actually write that? I'm sorry. I should be the bigger man. I had no idea I would get so riled up about Van Jones's criticism of Dad. I mean, I know that I have criticized Senior in this book, but it's OK for me to do that because I'm his son, right? And you've got to admit Senior has put me in one weird, dangerous situation. Dr. Van Jones has no business criticizing Senior, particularly with a vicious lie.

OK. I am over it now. Good luck with your tour, Dr. Van Jones. You idiotic poophead.[91]

---

91 Dr. Robert Van Jones died several years after *Junior* was published from an overdose of Hardball, an over-the-counter drug he took to combat the side effects of Big Boy, the male enhancement drug unleashed on unsuspecting American males by the black African Quaker terrorist Alberto Gonga Mutsapi. The University of Southern California Life Criticism faculty held a seminar to rate Dr. Van Jones's life. It received one and one-half stars. Jana Mars, the keynote speaker for the seminar, described Dr. Van Jones's life as "a morality play without a moral, burdened by weak plot lines. Wholly derivative and remarkably unimaginative."

Day 520

So I have been on the run for 520 days now, and tonight I can safely say this is the scaredest I have been. I know scaredest is probably not a word, Dr. Hoover, but it perfectly describes my feelings at this very moment. I am wearing some sort of body armor over my man girdle, and the Israelis say they have turned on an experimental, not yet perfected, invisible electronic force field that will cover the deck. I am about to go outside and sit on the deck of the cool Aspen house owned by a member of the Israeli mafia and drink sangria like I used to do before the Life Criticism Incident.

I am not supposed to take my computer and write like I normally do, however, because the Israeli geeks are concerned it might affect the force field. We don't want to mess with the force field. We want the force field to be with us. We want the force field to stop any sniper bullets shot by Samson Fairman, the fartwa guys, or maybe even Suzanne's meth-head boyfriend, who is probably some sort of crack Davy Crockett–type hunter.

To make me feel more comfortable about all this, my old Mossad buddy Jehu has taken a short leave of absence from guarding Eb and has come to Aspen. Jehu says he has personally supervised all the preparations for tonight. I told him I appreciated his help and it is time to get all this over with. I asked him to give me five minutes to finish this entry, and then he can do what he came here to do.

So, dear reader, this may be it. The hour is near. If something goes wrong, this could be my last entry. The end. Finito. Wish me luck.[92]

I am probably being overdramatic here, but I have never felt this close to death before. I am a bit overwhelmed. Having a moment of serious doubt that is actually physically painful. So, before I walk outside, let me say that if it all goes south, I don't blame the Israelis. They are doing what they think is best, and I respect that about them. Also to Suzanne, I'm sorry. I know you didn't want me to do this. I'm sorry I made you cry.

Finally, here's to you, Dad. It looks like there is a decent chance I may see you sooner rather than later. I haven't heard from you lately, which, truth be told, is more than a little disappointing. I look forward to seeing you again. I hope this is what you wanted.

---

92 As noted earlier (see footnote 12), the Chiricahua Apaches consider the number thirteen to be a lucky number. Numerous commentators have found significance in the Day 520 "wish me luck" reference, since 520 is a multiple of 13 (40 x 13 = 520).

Day 523

Hello again. Still here. Not dead yet. Sorry for the drama in the last entry. Never been that scared before.

What happened after I went out on the deck was kinda funny, at least for my nemesis Samson Fairman. I sat on the deck and drank sangria like all the sangria trees had died and there would never be any more sangria in the world to drink. In about two hours I went through four pitchers and I was so drunk I started singing show tunes. While I was singing, very loudly, "Don't Rain on My Parade" from the movie *Funny Girl* (remember, I am not gay) I heard a screaming sound like a bottle rocket had been shot off and I looked up to see a small parachute floating down from the sky.

For some reason none of my protectors saw the parachute and it landed right next to my pitcher of sangria. Then the parachute started to laugh. Then three really big guys rushed onto the deck, knocked me down, and fell on top of me. Suzanne tells me I passed out, but not before I finished the song with a flourish, screaming that nobody was going to rain on my . . . paraaade.

It turns out that the MFM geeks were one step ahead of the Mossad geeks. The parachute had some special kind of force field killer on it that allowed it to float right in. I know I am not saying that right, but suffice it to say that the Mossad geeks' force field was bupkes.

The note attached to the parachute was short and to the point: "Junior, killing you today would have been too easy. I'll be in touch."

So now I am riding in a really cool recreational vehicle while all the smart people figure out what to do next. I can't tell you where I am just yet.

I am sorry I had to leave Aspen. I really loved it there. I hope I can go back someday.[93]

---

93 There is no verifiable evidence confirming that Junior ever went back to Aspen. Numerous books have been written about Junior's stay in Aspen. The most famous is *Junior's Discourses from the Deck*, by Galileo Penny, which won a Pulitzer Prize. Aspen is the location for one of the largest Junior colonies in the world, and undoubtedly the most controversial. Soon after *Junior* was published, over half of Aspen was purchased by the JJ2 Trust, a private trust registered in Lithuania, which then created the Aspen Junior Colony. The JJ2 Trust created private subdivision restrictions that allowed only Junior followers with more than $500 million in assets to live in the colony. The house where Junior stayed while in Aspen is located within the confines of the colony. Nonresidents of the Aspen Junior Colony are allowed to tour the house every other Monday, and on Junior's birthday.

Day 527

We have gone north. We are in Wyoming. Somewhere near Big Horn. Some really big moose up here.

I was sitting in the RV today listening to some music and looking at wild-life when Suzanne yelled that I should turn on the satellite television. So I did. And there, big as Dallas, was my old buddy Pete being interviewed by Veronica Wells:

Veronica: Well, I don't know where I am, but wherever I am, I am here with Peter Running Horse, the best friend of Joshua Jennings, Jr.

Pete: Sorry about the secrecy, Veronica, but as you know, I am a wanted man.

Veronica: I see you are wearing a shirt with a bee logo and the word "Beelieve" on it. My attorneys, by the way, have so far failed to obtain an injunction against the mass production of this shirt. Can you tell me why you are wearing it?

Pete: Veronica, I had to leave Joshua for a while to take care of some personal business. I don't know where he is, but I am wearing this shirt to support him. I encourage others to do the same. Joshua is a really good guy and he didn't kill his dad. Joshua loved his dad.

Veronica: Then why is he running?

Pete: You know better than anyone how the media can prejudge people, Veronica. Most people think Junior is guilty. He'll probably stay hidden until the truth behind the bombing comes out. And by the way, thanks for reminding me that Junior is running. For those of you who want to support Junior, or who just like cool running gear, check out Manontherun.com to see Junior's exclusive line of running accessories.

Veronica: Samson Fairman has been publicly saying some bad stuff about Junior, and Junior has not responded. Care to stick up for your friend?

Pete: Fairman is a bold and arrogant man who is obviously not afraid to slander the good name of a wonderful human being. Fairman is as dumb as an ox, and like a dumb animal, he will eventually be captured and destroyed. Fairman's boastful words will eventually lead to his downfall. And oh, by the way, Fairman is a coward. He raped those defenseless women in Pakistan and he blew up innocents in Montreal and White Only Settlement. A man with a real backbone doesn't harm weak and innocent people. I think Fairman is afraid of taking on Junior man to man, because he is afraid he will lose.

Veronica: Strong words for sure, Pete. Mr. Fairman, do you have a response? The world is waiting. This is Veronica Wells, live from somewhere, signing off.

Thanks, Pete, for saying all of that. You rock, dude.

Day 530

Well, since we are just kind of wandering around out here, I convinced Hannah to drive the cool RV over to Montana so we could see the Little Bighorn National Monument. For those of you not up to speed on famous American massacres, this is where General George Custer and more than 200 American soldiers were killed by somewhere between 2,500 and 4,000 Lakota–Northern Cheyenne and Arapaho Indians led by Crazy Horse and Sitting Bull. I don't know what the victorious Indians call the massacre, but the paleface call it Custer's Last Stand.

As an aside, it just occurred to me that I will forever be associated with a famous American massacre. I wonder what historians will call what happened down in New Mexico?[94]

Sorry for the tangent. As I was saying, the Indians slaughtered the white guys here, and despite the fact that this is a United States national park, the Indians get a pretty fair shake. There are grave markers for both 7th Cavalry troopers and Indian warriors, which I found rather interesting. One of the

---

94 The New Mexico tragedy is generally referred to in the historical literature as the Assassination on the Reservation.

Indian grave markers is for a Cheyenne warrior who died "while defending the Cheyenne way of life." I could be wrong, but I doubt that the Smithsonian's Islamic Terrorist Severed and/or Mutilated Body Parts Exhibit praises any of the guys whose body parts reside there as men who died "while defending the Islamic way of life."[95]

I bring this up because generally the Indians in America have been treated like pig poop. Not an insightful or original revelation, but I feel like saying it anyway. And to the Apaches, I apologize in advance that history may very well blame the New Mexico explosion on someone who is half Apache.

I did learn one thing today that most of you probably don't know. There is a grave marker on the Little Bighorn battlefield for a Cheyenne chief named Lame White Man. During the battle, he wore a captured U.S. cavalry jacket and was shot by another Indian who mistook Lame White Man for an Indian scout helping out the U.S. cavalry.

That's it for today. Sorry this was not an exciting entry, but you learned something, so it hasn't been a total loss. As for me, I am considering calling up Big Foot Sims to see if maybe Lame White Man would be a more appropriate symbol for me.

Day 536

Still in Montana. Still attempting to implement the "Eb Cohen should be president because he has stones in his britches" plan. As Suzanne has pointed out to me, however, Eb's plan would still be successful even if Eb captures Fairman AFTER Fairman kills me. Suzanne does not like the plan and has made her displeasure known loudly, proudly, and continually.

Today we held a videoconference on the big television here in the cool RV. We could see Eb on the screen, although we did not know where he was. When Suzanne pointed out that Eb would be a hero even if I was dead, Eb

---

95 In a remarkable instance of life imitating art, the site of the New Mexico explosion has been turned into a national memorial very similar to the Little Bighorn National Monument. The Assassination on the Reservation National Park by Firestone Tire Company covers over 500 acres and contains a cemetery that includes a grave marker for every person killed in the explosion. The memorial for President Carrier in the park states in part that he was killed while "defending the principles of democracy that have made America a free and prosperous nation." The symphony "Senior's Last Stand," written by Academy Award–winning composer Jeff Moore, was commissioned by the United States National Park Service and is played by the Los Angeles Symphony every July Fourth at the park.

admitted that was true. "You are correct, Suzanne. But I don't want Junior to die and we will do everything in our power to prevent that from happening." Suzanne started to respond, but I put my hand on her arm to stop her. Eb's face said it all. Eb did not want me to be hurt and he was embarrassed that he was putting me in this position. Eb is a good and true Jew—there is no falsity in him. In fact, he may actually make a good president if he can get elected. My guess is he won't, at least not in this election. I think Senior already has that taken care of.

Speaking of Senior, a weird thing happened today. Our family home in Dallas blew up. As you might expect, the house was big and had a lot of rooms. It took the Dallas Fire Department several hours to put out the fire. I am assuming Fairman is behind the explosion, but there's no word on anyone claiming responsibility for the destruction.

Day 539

Montana is a really beautiful place. Although riding around in an RV while waiting to be attacked by a homicidal Methodist is not a ton of fun, at least the scenery is gorgeous.

Montana is in the midst of a statewide election on a bunch of special initiatives. The landscape is dotted with both billboards and hand-painted signs urging us to vote for or against these initiatives. Since I spend a lot of my time looking out the window, I have read a bunch of these billboards and signs.

My favorite initiative is Proposition 14, which deals with personal body fat. The voters of Montana are being asked to pass a law that makes it illegal for a citizen of Montana to have more than 29.5 percent body fat. The justification for the law is that people who are fat cost the state more in tax dollars for health care and other state-funded services. The 29.5 percent figure is based on a University of Chicago study that concludes that 29.5 percent body fat is the maximum "body fat footprint" that should be permissible in the United States. The percentage differs by country. For example, people who live in India are only allowed 18 percent body fat. Not sure why that is.

Proposition 14 is the first proposed body fat footprint law in the country and it has garnered a ton of attention. Body fat footprint proponents and opponents are spending hundreds of thousands of dollars in political advertising. Body fat issue activists have also arrived in Montana in droves.

Today as we drove through Missoula, Montana, we had to pull the RV over and park it because of a Fatty Pride Parade. The Mossad security guys on the RV were going bonkers because this was not planned and they thought it was dangerous, but what could they do? The parade took forever, because, well, fat people tend to walk slowly. So, we just sat in the RV and watched the parade.

Have you ever watched a few thousand fat people walk down a street? I don't mean slightly overweight or chubby people. I mean FAT people. It was like the organizers of the parade found the most obese people in the western half of the United States and brought them to Missoula. There were lots of Fat Pride and Fat Is Beautiful signs. I saw a really fat guy being pulled down the street in a blue bathtub on wheels. He looked a little depressed, though. I even saw a fat guy carrying a Let Him Bee Fat sign. I hope for the fat guy's sake that Veronica Wells's lawyers did not see that sign.

I have to say that even though I am a bit chubby, the parade did not endear me to the participants' position because quite frankly, fat is NOT beautiful, and not healthy. Several of the parade walkers had to be given oxygen by medical personnel and could not even finish the walk.

Hannah says that from a law enforcement perspective, the body fat footprint law would be a nightmare. "Think about it, Junior. Are you going to have special body fat police? Do they carry special calipers to measure body fat?" I guess she has a point.

I have asked one of the Mossad security guys if we could find a running trail somewhere. If this body fat footprint idea catches on, I don't want to get a citation.

Day 544

Welcome to month nineteen. Today was photo op day in the Eb Cohen I Want Everyone To Know I Am Not A Coward So I Can Be Elected President Campaign. We drove to Scapegoat Mountain, which is one of the tallest mountains in Montana. Nobody in the RV commented on the irony of the mountain's name, so I kept my smart-aleck thoughts to myself. But seriously, could you have made up a more appropriate name for this situation?

When we arrived at Scapegoat Mountain, Big Foot Sims was there. Big Foot handed me a white sweat suit with a black Man on the Run logo stitched on it. "I was told to bring you the whitest outfit we had," Big Foot said with a touch of apology in his voice. "You're already pretty doggoned white, Junior, but with this suit I'm afraid you're going to look like you've been bleached from head to toe."

I followed Hannah's instructions and put on my man girdle, the white sweat suit, white tennis shoes, and a white Man on the Run baseball cap. I stood on top of Scapegoat Mountain and let a freelance photographer shoot a bunch of pictures of me until a big storm cloud settled on top of the mountain and everyone got scared of a lightning strike.

The pictures appeared on the Internet and on all the television news stations. The Diet Channel reported that I had lost weight on the Grapefruit and Tequila Diet. The Sports Fashion Network opined that the Man on the Run suit was a classic. The Mountain Man channel claimed that I had run up Scapegoat Mountain. And the supporters of Proposition 14 claimed that I supported the body fat footprint concept. No word yet from the MFM, but I am guessing Fairman is licking his chops.

Thankfully, we are miles away from Scapegoat Mountain now. Just got an e-mail from Sister Flannery. She wrote:

The kids saw you decked out in your all-white outfit on the mountain. They think you look really cool. I think, however, that you are wearing a man girdle.

Thanks for the money. We were in a real bind here because of the economy—the cash came just in the nick of time. You were the answer to our prayers, Junior. How does that make you feel? Like there is some kind of greater purpose here? Huh? Huh? How about it?

Mother Superior Hookenstein says to tell you that the number just went up from two to three. Not sure what that means, but she made me repeat it three times so I could write it down word for word. Take care and watch out for the meth-head boyfriend.

Day 550

Looks like Veronica is the first reporter to break the Department of Defense story. Not to be ugly, but I suspect Dale Piper may have given

Veronica some help. Better Veronica than a legitimate reporter who knows what she is doing.

A Mossad security guy told me that there was a breaking news story about the explosion on the Veronica Network, so I turned on the television. Veronica did not appear to be in her studio. She was dressed very casually, which is unusual for Veronica. Veronica was wearing a USA World Cup championship sweatshirt, to which was attached a rather large black-and-yellow pin in the shape of a bee. She spoke in a semi-whisper:

> *This is Veronica Wells. I am undercover. I can't tell you where I am, and I apologize for whispering, but you never know who might be listening. Using my contacts inside the FBI and the Pentagon, I have uncovered an amazing story. It seems that Joshua Jennings, Sr., who was known far and wide as a busybody who could not keep his nose out of the government's business, was upset with the size of the nation's military budget and was lobbying the late President Carrier to take money away from the army guys. President Carrier was allegedly about to announce these budget cuts in his speech at the Apache reservation, but then, you know, everyone got blown up.*
>
> *But that's not the most amazing part of the story. I have in my hand a Department of Defense report. The title of this report is "Plan to Blow Up Public Officials at an Indian Reservation during a Presidential Election Campaign." I quite frankly don't understand a lot of the lingo in this thing, but military types have told me off the record that the plan in this report is remarkably similar to what happened in New Mexico. Which leads to an obvious question. But before we get to that question, a word from our sponsor.*

After a disgustingly graphic commercial for a feminine hygiene product, Veronica returned, still speaking in a whisper:

> *The obvious question, of course, is, Did the Department of Defense blow up President Carrier and Joshua Jennings, Sr., to prevent them from cutting the department's budget? I mean, come on, they had a*

written plan for it and everything! Who better to blow stuff up than the army guys? They have been doing it for centuries, right?

I called the Pentagon and asked these insightful questions and the army guys e-mailed me a response. The e-mail reads: "Veronica. We love your show and your thought-provoking reporting, although we think you probably committed at least three felonies by obtaining the contingency plan regarding the reservation explosion. One of our federal prosecutors will be in touch with you in the near future. As you know, we here at the defense department are charged with planning ahead and thinking of every possible contingency that our country might possibly face. You never know when you might need to blow up public officials at an Indian reservation during a presidential election campaign. It is unlikely that we will ever need to do so, but we need to be prepared. The contingency plan you stole is simply that—a plan. We did not execute this plan in New Mexico and any similarity between this plan and the New Mexico explosion is simply a coincidence."

Veronica looked up from her notes with a smile. She spoke a little louder:

I would like to thank the Pentagon for admitting that they enjoy my reporting. It's so refreshing to hear from a government agency that supports a free press. We'll bring you updates on this story as it develops. Over and out.

Huh. I still doubt that the military blew everybody up, but the "contingency plan" certainly looks incriminating. Mr. Piper was right—this does not look good at all. I wonder if Dr. Jaska will investigate the military now.

Day 553

I don't want to violate any election laws regarding equal time, so today we visited a pro–Proposition 14 rally. Actually, we happened upon the rally by chance as we drove through Great Falls. So we stopped at a Microsoft Fajita and Taco Bar, ordered a bunch of Mexican food (mediocre) and some margaritas (surprisingly good), sat in lawn chairs and watched people with a body fat percentage of less than 29.5 percent march by.

Several of the beautiful people gave us the finger as they marched by. I don't know if they were upset because I blew everybody up, because I would not qualify under the proposed proposition (I was not wearing my man girdle), or because we were eating and drinking and they thought we were hedonist gluttons. I have to admit I generally don't like people who parade their health food bodies around in skintight workout clothes, but there is a half-decent chance I am just jealous. If I looked that good in free-range spandex, I would probably wear it too.

I saw a bunch of folks wearing Man on the Run gear and I raised my margarita glass to them and shouted something inane about supporting God's Elect. I think a few of the buff guys thought I had insulted them and moved toward our group. When my Mossad guards stood up, however, the pretty boys retreated.

This parade was a lot bigger than the fatty rally, and much easier on the eyes. Lots of pretty girls. I am not sure why, but there were also a lot more signs. I saw signs that said Gym Teachers for Prop 14, Hot Nurses for Prop 14, Buddhists for Prop 14, Illegal Aliens for Prop 14, and a host of other signs proclaiming various groups' support for the body fat footprint ordinance. There were also some disturbing signs, like Fat People Are Dirty, Fatties Stink, Deport the Chubsters, Send Them to Fatty Concentration Camps, and Mandatory Birth Control for Fatsos.

Suzanne sat in the lawn chair next to me. She leaned over and said, "These skinny people seem kind of mean to me, Junior. I don't think it is nice to make fun of people who are overweight. Do you think fat people are dirty and yucky?"

Now, dear reader, if you were paying attention earlier in what is becoming a rather long semi-diary, I may have said that one of the things I really like to do is make fun of fat people.[96] So I paused while I considered my response.

Then Hannah joined in: "Well, Junior? Are fat people dirty and yucky? Should we punish them for their fatness?" Hannah had a slight grin on her face and I wondered if somehow she knew that one of my allegedly favorite things to do was to make fun of fat people.

"Why are you trying to trap me?" I asked as I pondered my answer.

96 See Day 15.

"I would never try to trap you," Suzanne replied. "I am just curious what you think."

I looked out at the beautiful people with their mean signs and came to a slightly revised conclusion. "I don't think eating too much is very healthy, but I don't think that fat people stink or are yucky just because they stuff too many tacos and cheeseburgers down their gullets. After watching this parade, I am inclined to think that the fantastic-looking people with the mean signs are the stinky and yucky ones. Even if the body fat footprint is a good idea, there is no need for the pretty people to be mean-spirited."

Hannah and Suzanne (who, by the way, are both pretty enough to fit right in with the free-range spandex crowd) nodded in agreement as the parade passed us by. I stuffed another mediocre taco down my gullet.

Day 557

Did you know that Flathead Lake, located in the northwest corner of Montana, is the largest natural freshwater lake in the western United States? Well now you do. Maybe if this book ever gets read, even if a jury decides I did what I DID NOT do, you folks will learn a little bit about American geography.

We rented a few cabins by the lake. This morning when I woke up I went down and sat by the lake. Quite beautiful. Suzanne came over from her cabin and suggested we get a boat and motor around on the lake. The Mossad guys said it was OK, as long as they got a boat too and hovered nearby.

After twenty minutes or so of driving the boat, Suzanne and I cut the engine, floated, and enjoyed the silence. At least I did. Then Suzanne decided we needed to talk.

"Junior, can I ask you a question?" I did not respond, hoping she would give up on the conversation. For some reason, and I can't tell you why, I knew this was a discussion I did not want to have. She was not deterred, however.

"How do you see all of this playing out?"

"Suzanne, I would think you of all people should know by now that I am not necessarily a long-range thinker or planner. I guess I hope that somehow the real exploders are arrested and everyone will leave me alone."

"Junior, I'm pretty sure that even if the true criminals are tried, convicted, and executed tomorrow, you will never ever be left alone. People all over the world know your name and your face."

"That's probably true. Maybe if my book is published, I can live off the royalties in some remote location where people won't bother me."

"Junior, do you know why I left that note for you with your change for the double bacon cheeseburger back in Alabama?"

I confess that just thinking about a double bacon cheeseburger at that moment froze my brain for a few seconds before I could respond. "Not really. I mean, I think you said you were in trouble and needed my help, or something like that."

"When I brought your double bacon cheeseburger and cheese fries to you, I could feel a power coming from inside the Mustang. I can't explain it, but somehow a tangible force touched me and I knew you were the guy everyone was looking for. And I thought that if I could just meet you and talk to you, this power you radiated would help me with Robert Earl. Robert Earl had been using me and bleeding me dry for years, but I just could not break his hold on me.

"And you saved me from Robert Earl, Junior. I haven't felt this good in years. I have peace. It's like I am a new person."

"That's very sweet of you to say, Suzanne, but I don't feel very powerful."

"I know! That's why I decided to tell you what happened in Alabama. You need to recognize what's going on here. You're an important guy, Junior. I'm not sure exactly why or how you are important, but I sense it in every fiber of my body. And that means you can't always just let Eb or Hannah or anyone else tell you what to do. You need to be more selfish."

I did not respond, because frankly I did not know what to say. We sat in silence and listened to the waves lap up against the boat.

After a few minutes, Suzanne broke the silence. "I don't know what is going to happen, Junior, but I will stay by your side no matter what. I'm not sure Eb and the Israeli guys will do that for you. I think they will turn you over to the authorities when it suits their purpose."

I'm back in the cabin now. Still don't feel all that powerful. I hope Suzanne is wrong about the Jews.

Day 560

Still hanging out at Flathead Lake. Quiet here and the Mossad guys say that, at least for now, staying at the lake is safer than driving around in the RV. So, I'm sitting on a chair by the lake and enjoying the view.

Today is Vietnam Wars Veterans Day, where the nation honors the veterans of Vietnam Wars I–VI. I don't remember who decided that we should have separate Veterans Day celebrations for different serial wars, but I think it is a great idea. That way we can give special recognition to more soldiers.

Let me say that I am not really a gung-ho patriotic guy who gets all goose-bumped about flag and country. In fact, I think most of the wars and police actions we have fought in my lifetime were just plain stupid. However, that is not the soldiers' fault. Got a lot of respect for those guys.

Suzanne says I should come inside for a minute. Be back soon.

I'm back. That was fun. Since today is Vietnam Wars Veterans Day, there are a bunch of reports on television about Vietnam veterans. Suzanne found a reporter who was interviewing vets at the Red Head VA Hospital in Florida. Unbeknownst to me, Suzanne, as my agent, had authorized the distribution of some of my endorsement royalties to the hospital. The hospital buildings have been renovated, and a state-of-the-art eye surgery facility has been constructed. A hand-painted Thank You Junior! sign was hung on the front door of the hospital.

Buster Bitting, one of the guys Suzanne and I ate pizza and smoked dope with at Red Head, was interviewed by the reporter. He was obviously high:

The Junior dude, he be alright by us. Not only did he pay for the new building stuff, he also paid the pizza joint so we get to have a pizza and beer party every Friday night. Is that cool or what? Junior supports us veterans, so we support him, too. You tell Junior if he needs any help, just say the word. We still be soldiers and we know how to follow orders and kick butt. After the Vietnam gig, I believe we can handle a bunch of lame-ass Methodists.

Thanks, guys.

Day 565

Well, it's time to let you in on a little secret—I'm a rock star. Back when we were in Aspen, Morty and Big Foot took me to a recording studio to record a music video for the clothing line. Part of the plan to make me more visible.

The music video was released today and we all watched it in Hannah's cabin on Flathead Lake. From my perspective, it is a marvel of technology.

The producers and engineers took a chubby guy with a terrible singing voice and turned him into a relatively hot rock-and-roller who belts out lyrics with considerable soul. I am not sure whose voice they used, but I sound great.

The other amazing thing is that I'm the only one who went to the studio in Aspen. They filmed and recorded me in Aspen and then added the band and girl dancers later. It looks like I'm jamming with this tight band, but in reality it was just me being silly in the studio.

Even though the body is not really me and the voice is not really me, I'm proud to say I came up with one verse and the chorus of the song. The verse goes like this: "You heard I blew them up, my father and the pres, But I'm telling you the truth, I wasn't at the res." Pretty cool, huh?

The chorus is even better: "Come and see, the Man on the Run. Let him be, the Man on the Run."

There is no need for me to describe the video in detail since I'm sure you will see it. I will say, though, that I really enjoyed the pretty girl dancers with their red, white, and blue Peace Bee With You shirts, and the picture of Fairman with a line drawn through his face floating behind us on a big screen as I performed my magical guitar solo.

I am guessing that the "lame-ass Methodists" comment by the Red Head vet and the music video are designed to bring Fairman out of seclusion. Maybe if Fairman gets me soon, the people will remember me as a cool rock star instead of a chubby exploder.

Day 568

Woke up this morning feeling fine. Still at Flathead Lake, which is still beautiful and serene. Nobody has tried to kill me in several weeks, I am a rock star, and the vets at Red Head have got my back, even though they would probably need seeing-eye dogs to find me.

The big news today is that Proposition 14 passed in Montana by a vote of 51 percent to 49 percent. The People for a Prettier America, a Washington, D.C.-based organization that got the proposition placed on the ballot in Montana, issued a press release proclaiming that the voters of Montana had "issued a mandate that the American people are tired of fat, ugly people walking the streets and making a mockery of the America the Beautiful concept we have all grown to love." The press release also announced plans to put similar body fat footprint propositions on the ballot in other states, as well as voter initiatives to impose red meat footprints, sugar footprints, and corn syrup footprints.

The not-so-big news today is that I learned how to fish, sort of. Some of the Mossad bodyguards wanted to go fishing in the lake and I had to go because they could not leave me alone and unguarded. Would probably look bad if Fairman killed me while my guards were out fishing. They showed me how to bait a hook and I caught a few fish. Really, though, I found the whole experience boring after a while and I fell asleep. Fortunately for me, a thunderstorm appeared out of nowhere and the excursion had to be cut short.

Before any fishermen who read this book get mad, let me say that I respect guys who catch fish and I realize they are important. We need guys who are willing to fish. Let me also add that I really enjoyed the grilled fish we ate when we returned to the cabins. Let's hope there are no proposed grilled fish footprint laws out there.

Day 573

Welcome to month twenty. Time flies when you're having fun. We are no longer in Montana. Today we crossed the border into the great state of South Dakota. You probably are not aware of this (I only know because I helped Senior on the deal) but South Dakota was Senior's first choice for the new Israeli homeland. The deal fell through when, at Senior's request, I checked the voting records of the state's senior senator and discovered that he voted against every proposed bill to provide financial aid to Israel.

I was informed today that South Dakota is not very fond of the Jennings clan. The Mossad guys were checking out information on the state before we crossed the border, and it seems that the South Dakota legislature was really mad at Senior when the North Dakota Jewish homeland deal went through. Some of the lawmakers were upset that North Dakota was chosen instead of South Dakota, and others did not like being that close to God's chosen people.

The anger of the state's leaders became a big practical problem when the South Dakota Highway Department refused to allow the moving vans with the Jews' possessions to pass through South Dakota on the way to North Dakota. The caravan of vehicles was stuck in a snowstorm on the northern Nebraska border for over twelve hours while the federal government tried to convince the South Dakota officials that the Jews' vehicles would drive straight through the state, would not stop, and would not bother anyone. The South Dakotans held firm, however, and the Jews had to detour through Iowa and Minnesota to get to their new home.

The state's dislike for the father also extends to the son. Two days after the New Mexico explosion, the South Dakota legislature issued a proclamation declaring Joshua Jennings, Jr., "a despicable criminal in league with satanic forces." Although a lot of people are mad because they think I blew everybody up, South Dakota is the only state I am aware of that issued a proclamation linking me up with the devil.

All of which leads to the obvious question: Why am I in South Dakota, even for one minute? These folks hate me and they hated my dad. I asked Hannah this obvious question. She just shrugged and said they received instructions to drive into the state and await further orders. She seems a bit on edge as well.

To top it all off, I think I am coming down with a cold. Coughing, sneezing, all that stuff. I should probably stop now. I am getting depressed and I am sure, dear reader, you are not enjoying this entry very much. We shall resume when times are better.

Day 577

Well, I can't say that times are a bunch better, since I am still in South Dakota, where people hate me even more than they do in other states, but I did get a bunch of "thank-yous" today from folks who have received money from my endorsement royalties. The Assassin sent me an e-mail saying he had used the money to take in fifty more kids in his home for the retarded, I mean God's Elect. And I got e-mails and text messages from a bunch of Indian reservations thanking me for the money and inviting me to come visit. I would like to visit a couple of reservations if I can do so without getting the Indians in trouble for harboring a fugitive.

Another positive note, if you are a sports fan, is that Major League Baseball has implemented new rules to make baseball games faster. MLB issued a report today that identified rules designed to bring games to a conclusion in less than the six-hour average that it takes to play a nine-inning game. I haven't read the report yet, but I hope it reduces the maximum time for video replay on ball/strike calls to two minutes instead of the current ten minutes.

Seems to me the baseball rule makers should also restrict how many times a batter can scratch his crotch, but there may be health or First Amendment considerations to consider in this type of limitation.

Speaking of baseball, I don't think I have written anything about the latest Democratic vice presidential candidate, the Reverend Bobby "Big Fly" Washington. Big Fly led the majors in home runs for ten straight seasons before he retired to preach the gospel and use his considerable baseball wealth to create organic farms that would produce food for the poor. Big Fly reluctantly agreed to join the Democratic ticket after Carl Koehling resigned in disgrace over the Las Vegas waitress fiasco.

I have to say I am a solid Big Fly fan. He and the Assassin are big buds and I met Big Fly several times when he came to El Paso to sign autographs at the Assassin's home for God's Elect and to play in a golf tournament to raise funds for the home. Smart, talented, sincere, and bristling with integrity—Big Fly would be a great choice for any elected office. Usually, people like that don't get elected in our country, but I think Big Fly may have a chance, in large part because Senior apparently wants the Democrats to win this election. I can't say for certain that Senior rigged it so Big Fly would be added to the ticket, but I know Senior contributed heavily to Big Fly's organic farming project and really admired what Big Fly was doing.

I just asked Hannah if they had found any dirt on Big Fly and she told me to mind my own business. I will take that as a no.

I smell fried okra, which means Suzanne the Southern Girl is cooking supper. I predict the day will improve in just a few minutes.

Day 580

Day 580 and South Dakota still sucks. I learned today that Clarke Steinbach, one of the most rabid radio hatemongers in the world, lives in and broadcasts his radio show from Rapid City, South Dakota. I learned this because we passed by a huge billboard with his face plastered all over it. "Face absolutely made for radio," Hannah muttered as we drove by.

I did not know much about Steinbach, so I looked him up on the Internet. He is both rich (number two on the Forbes Hate Millionaire List) and powerful (arguably controls a voting block of over two million listeners). His show is syndicated in fifteen countries. He has made so much money he has gone public and his company is traded on the New York Stock Exchange.

And, he really hates me. The introduction to his show today began with the following words: "This is the Clarke Steinbach Program. Today is Day 580 of the Junior Should Be Dead By Now Watch." Catchy. Hannah and Suzanne suggested I turn the show off, but really, could you have turned it off if he was talking about you that way?

Steinbach continued in a deep melodic voice that was definitely made for radio:

Almost two years ago this country was brought to its knees by a mama's boy with a history degree and no real job experience. Junior Jennings brutally murdered both the president and vice president and our country has done absolutely nothing to bring him to justice. Instead, we see Junior clothing lines and Junior music videos. Junior is stirring up the riffraff in this country and basically sticking his tongue out at us. Since when does America put up with that kind of foolishness? Where is the country I love, the country that defeated Grenada, Tunisia, and Peru? Why can't our law enforcement officials bring this terrorist to justice? More importantly, why is the great American hero Samson Fairman the only one who is trying to capture Junior Jennings?

The problem, as I have said on many occasions, is that our country is now run by . . .

Steinbach stopped talking and the sound of a cat meowing came over the airwaves. Steinbach continued:

Until we get rid of the (meow) in charge and replace them with men of courage and integrity who are not (meow), our country will never recover its greatness. Joshua Jennings, Jr., needs to be killed or captured immediately and anyone who disagrees with me is a (meow).

Let's examine the kind of person Junior is. First, he's a rich man's son who has had everything handed to him on a silver platter. Never held a real job. His only real accomplishment is to be the son of a powerful, accomplished man who impregnated an Apache squaw out of wedlock and had the honor and integrity to marry her even though she was far below his station in life.

Second, what has this slacker accomplished, other than mass murder? He struggled to get a history degree and did not even attempt to go to graduate school. Then he worked for his dad as an errand boy. He did not get married and have children, like a normal guy. Instead, he hangs out with his Apache friend Peter Running Horse, who also has accomplished little, if anything.

As I've said on many occasions on this show, America is a can-do nation. You can do great things in this country if you put your mind to it. Junior Jennings is a prime example of someone who has chosen to be a can't-do person in a can-do nation.

Third, look at who the man hangs out with: an Alabama stripper with a meth-head boyfriend; Idaho racists; slutty Iowa snow globe teenagers with weird hair; a blonde bombshell named Mandy; Veronica Wells, the nation's foremost media whore; and drug-addled Vietnam war vets. What kind of person hangs out with these types of characters? Not an innocent man, that is plain.

So, to all the (meow) in charge, I ask, for the 580th straight day, please get this slimeball.

As Steinbach went to a commercial, I looked around the RV for some reaction. Hannah grinned and said, "Could be worse. Imagine what the loudmouth would say if he knew you were hanging out with a bunch of Jews?" Everybody laughed, and the tension dissolved.

After a series of commercials, Steinbach returned to the air:

As you know, listeners, I have for weeks now promised you my endorsement for the presidency. When you go to the polls, you will have a choice between (a) Cohen and Dozier or (b) Davis and Washington. I have given this a lot of thought and my strong suggestion is that you choose . . . (c). What does that mean, you ask? I will let you know after this commercial break.

We, and the rest of Steinbach's multimillion-person audience, then waited through eight minutes of commercials. When he returned, the national anthem played in the background while Steinbach spoke:

OK, America, listen up. The Israeli candidate is a joke. This country does not need a president who wears one of those silly Jew hats and refuses to work on Saturdays. What happens if one of our sworn enemies, like the Tunisians, decides to attack on a Saturday? Do we have to wait until Sunday for our president to respond? I have tremendous respect for General Dozier, but my admiration for what he has done for this country simply cannot overcome the glaring deficiencies of the Jew.

The Democrats, as usual, are a joke. Once again they have nominated for president an Ivy League liberal who has absolutely no connection with or empathy for the common man, although at least he is a heterosexual. And who knows who the Democrats' vice presidential candidate will eventually be? How many have they had so far? Four? Five? Do we really want a former professional baseball player to be a heartbeat away from the presidency?

So listeners, since A and B are simply horrible choices, I recommend that you write in Samson Fairman as your choice for president of this country. Choose C, Samson Fairman. We will all be better off.

South Dakota just keeps getting better and better, doesn't it?

Day 585

OK, so maybe ALL of South Dakota doesn't suck. I am sitting on a cliff in Badlands National Park watching the sunset. Wowee zowee. I sure am glad a bunch of protons and electrons and all that stuff randomly combined to create this scene. Are we lucky or what?

Speaking of random, Dr. Jaska appeared on the airwaves today. It has been so long since she made a public appearance, I figured her Blue Ribbon Commission to Figure Out Who Blew It Up had been disbanded. Dr.

Jaska announced today that a group calling itself Crankens Sooner Troopers is being investigated as the potential exploder.

I'm pretty sure I mentioned Trooper Bobby Joe Crankens and the University of Oklahoma football scandal earlier.[97] Since Bobby Joe apparently now has dedicated followers, I guess I need to fill in the gaps for you. Wait a minute . . . just saw an American eagle fly across the expanse of rocks beneath me. Wowee zowee.

OK. Back to Crankens. I am not sure if I have mentioned this or not, but both Dad and I graduated from the University of Texas at Austin. Dad was a dedicated supporter of UT and gave millions of dollars to the university. In fact, I think there are several buildings on campus with his name on them.

Anyway, the University of Oklahoma and UT were big football rivals back in the day. Senior hated the Sooners and was depressed for days when the Okies beat the Longhorns in their annual October football game in Dallas. After the Sooners beat UT five years in a row, Senior became convinced the Okies were cheating, so he commissioned Mac to investigate. Senior brought Mac and me into his office and said, "Mac, those Okies are recruiting all the best high school players in Texas. They have to be paying those studs. No Texas kid who is any good would go to that school just for a scholarship. Figure out what is going on. The Okies aren't smart enough to hide their tracks from you."

Senior, as usual, was right on both counts. The University of Oklahoma was paying its players, and the Okies could not hide that fact from Mac. Senior took Mac's findings and published a report called "Sooner Football: Whores for Scores." The report confirmed that Oklahoma football players had twenty-four-hour access to a brothel on campus and were paid thousands of dollars a month from the state's oil royalty fund. Senior held a press conference in which he distributed the report to the media. He also provided pictures of Sooner players cashing checks, as well as video interviews with some of the ladies of the evening.

Senior claimed he did the investigation and report on his own, without any help from the University of Texas, because he did not want anyone to think the report was biased. Everyone who saw the press conference, however, knew

---

97 See Day 151.

that Senior was not an impartial observer or investigator. Senior made several cracks about how ugly the hookers were ("You would think a Heisman Trophy winner would warrant better than this chubster") and OU's general reputation for running an outlaw athletic program ("Question: Four Sooner football players are riding in a car. Who's driving? Answer: A policeman.").

"Whores for Scores" forced the NCAA to investigate, and the Sooners got blasted. The entire athletic department was forced to resign, the football team had to forfeit every victory in the last four years (which also meant forfeiting one national championship and two Heisman Trophy awards), and the football team's scholarship limit was reduced from twenty-five scholarships a year to two scholarships a year for four years. The Sooners were also forbidden from playing on television or in a postseason bowl game for five years.

Senior was pleased with the NCAA sanctions, but he wanted the Sooners to feel even more pain. So he called up his buddy Kirk McConn, a jugular-slashing Dallas lawyer who I think I have talked about earlier,[98] and hired him to take "Whores for Scores" and wreak whatever legal havoc he could conjure up. McConn, who hated the Sooners because they regularly trounced his alma mater, Oklahoma State, filed three separate class actions. The first class action was on behalf of the citizens of Oklahoma, who were damaged when the state of Oklahoma allowed its oil well revenue to be siphoned off to pay football players. McConn's mother, who lived in Ada, Oklahoma, was the lead class representative.

The second class action was on behalf of the Sooner football players, who were damaged when they were placed in an environment that encouraged criminal behavior and where they were repeatedly exposed to potentially disease-ridden prostitutes. McConn found a mom in Plano, Texas, whose son was a freshman running back at OU to be the lead class representative for this case. The third class action was on behalf of all current OU students, who were damaged because they were paying tuition for what they believed was a first-class education, but in reality their education took second place to the promotion of the football team. The lead class representative was the president of OU's senior class.

I don't remember how much money was eventually paid out on these lawsuits, but I know McConn was able to buy a hotel on a beach in Maui with

98 See Day 333.

just a fraction of the attorneys' fees he was awarded. The lawsuits also forced the governor of Oklahoma and the president of the University of Oklahoma to resign.

The OU football team continued to play, but without scholarships it was impossible for the Sooners to compete with the more established football programs. Plus, what mother wants to send her son to a school that hired whores for the players? The Sooners hit rock bottom when they lost to Abilene Christian University, a small Division 4 school from West Texas, by a score of 69–0. Bobby Joe blew up OU's football stadium the very next week.

Dr. Jaska reported in her press conference that the commission has uncovered evidence that the Crankens Sooner Troopers purchased large amounts of explosives just a few weeks before the New Mexico bombing. Based upon this discovery, the FBI raided a warehouse in Norman, Oklahoma, and found, among other things:

(1) a poster-sized picture of Senior with an X drawn through it;
(2) a map of the area in New Mexico where the explosion took place;
(3) thousands of counterfeit University of Texas football tickets;
(4) Photoshopped pictures of UT football coaches in amorous poses with famous actors and actresses; and
(5) a draft report on how to sabotage the University of Texas football program, entitled "Turning Steers Back into Queers."

Dr. Jaska concluded, "We are still in the preliminary stages of this investigation, but we wanted to keep the country apprised of where we are. Arrest warrants have been issued and we will let you know when we have more information."

One of the members of the press asked Dr. Jaska, "Dr. Jaska, are you aware that radio personality Clarke Steinbach has accused you of dereliction of duty because you have not arrested Junior Jennings for the explosion?"

Dr. Jaska smiled and said politely, "I do not listen to Mr. Steinbach's program, but I have been informed of his opinion."

The reporter pressed: "Do you have a response to Mr. Steinbach?"

Dr. Jaska conferred with someone standing next to her and continued:

I really don't wish to respond, but I have been advised that it is best for the country if I just say what is on my mind. So here goes.

I have three PhD degrees. I helped cure AIDS. I have written three books. I have access to information collected by the FBI, the CIA, and every state and local law enforcement agency in this country. We are conducting a massive investigation and we have not seen any hard evidence that directly links Joshua Jennings, Jr., to the explosion. Mr. Jennings is still a suspect, however, in large part because he has disappeared, and we would still like to talk to him.

My understanding is that Clarke Steinbach, whose real name, by the way, is Pierre Smoot, flunked out of South Dakota Tech Junior College. He has been in and out of several drug rehabilitation programs. Mr. Steinbach Smoot has no connections with law enforcement and no resources to conduct an investigation. Mr. Steinbach Smoot apparently sits in an office in South Dakota and says whatever he feels like, with absolutely no concern for the truth, national security, or what is best for this nation.

So, America. You can believe me, a person with sterling academic credentials who is using all the resources this country has to offer to apprehend the perpetrator of the New Mexico explosion, or you can believe a junior college dropout with a drug problem, a fake name, and a big mouth who will say anything to increase his ratings. Your choice. Have a good evening. This press conference is over.

Wowee zowee.[99] What a woman. The sun has officially set over the Badlands for the evening. More later.

---

99 The phrase "wowee zowee" appears only three times in *Junior*, all in Day 585. The phrase has been the subject of much speculation. Some commentators opine that the phrase is simply one of exclamation, similar to "that's amazing!" or "whoa, dude!" Others, noting that the phrase first appears in the context of what appears to be a vague description of how the world was created, contend that Junior was commenting on the various theories for the creation of the universe. Several decades after *Junior* was written, astrophysicist Dr. Aleksander Reisling paid homage to *Junior* in his Nobel Prize acceptance speech, stating: "I am very proud of my research and my profession, and I encourage others to continue the investigation into how the universe was created. In my heart of hearts, however, I have become convinced that we are simply not smart enough to figure it out. Maybe it's because I am an old man now, but at this point in my life I am content just to sit back and marvel at the universe and say, with gratitude and admiration: Wowee Zowee."

Day 589

Still in the Badlands. Still very cool. As you might have expected, Steinbach has been going crazy making up stuff about Dr. Jaska. The other top hate jocks throughout the country have joined in, both to bash Dr. Jaska and to encourage a write-in vote for Fairman. Hannah tells me that all the top ten Hate Millionaires on the Forbes Hate Millionaire List have joined forces with Steinbach on the write-in vote issue.

Hannah also says the timing of all of this is seriously bad for Eb, because he is still having difficulty raising money for the campaign. Eb's campaign team had hoped that Eb would capture Fairman trying to kill me by now, and that would boost fund-raising and help get Eb elected. Unfortunately, Fairman is now unlikely to try and kill me any time soon since he is receiving so much support in the media.

I have to admit I am not all that sorry that Fairman has lost some of his incentive to kill me. I did not mention that to Hannah, however.

Dale Piper showed up today. Instead of appearing out of nowhere and scaring me to death, he called Hannah and made an appointment. I guess it is a reflection of Piper's reputation and contacts that (1) he knew Hannah's number and (2) Hannah readily agreed to the meeting. Suzanne joined me at the meeting as my representative.

Dale was anxious to please. He said he was still representing the Defense Department and that the DOD was still ready to assist in any way possible. Dale listed the following six options:

(1) kill Fairman;
(2) kill Steinbach;
(3) kill Fairman and Steinbach;
(4) kill Fairman and all the Hate Millionaires;
(5) frame Fairman for the New Mexico explosion; and
(6) frame Steinbach and the Hate Millionaires for any crime we could think of.

Suzanne asked if there was a DOD option that did not involve murder or illegality. Dale said he had one idea that was mostly legal and did not involve death. After he explained the mostly legal idea, I called Hannah in to listen to it. She liked it and called Eb. Eb's advisers said they could see some flaws, but they were desperate and bought in. Stay tuned and see if Dale's mostly legal but nonfatal idea works.

Day 593

Eb did something today that took a lot of guts. I hope it works. Even if it doesn't work, though, I'm really proud of him.

Both Eb and General Dozier were asked to attend a rally in Athens, Alabama, at the Tomb of the Unknown NASCAR Soldier to commemorate and honor the soldiers who died during the NASCAR Wars. Eb and General Dozier placed a wreath on the tomb while thousands cheered.

General Dozier then spoke to the crowd:

> *Thank you for inviting us here. Before I turn the microphone over to Ebenezer, I would like to say just a few words. We live in a great country. Some folks believe we live in a great country because we fight and win wars.*

Applause erupted and the general paused before he spoke again:

> *As you know, I have fought in wars and led fighting men and women in wars. I am no stranger to war and I have never been afraid of a fight.*

More applause.

> *But I can tell you that America is a great county despite the fact that we have fought and won wars. We Americans fight too many wars. You are probably not going to like what Ebenezer is about to say, but I agree with him 100 percent.*

Eb took the microphone to absolute silence. He smiled and spoke. "Thanks, General for warming up the crowd for me." General Dozier and a few people on stage laughed, but the audience remained quiet. Eb took a breath and began to speak:

We are here today to honor those who died in the NASCAR Wars. Obviously I'm not from NASCAR country. I did not grow up rooting for a particular driver or team, but I know that NASCAR loyalties are very important in this part of our great country and I respect the fervor and pride that the folks down here have for the sport.

The NASCAR Wars were before my time, so I had to do some research on them to prepare for this speech. NASCAR I and III were fought between the supporters of the 54 car and the 99 car.

A cheer rose up from the crowd and the cameras showed people waving 54 and 99 flags. Eb continued:

NASCAR I started when the 54 car caused the 99 car to crash on the final lap at Talladega. The war was fought in Alabama and Mississippi and lasted twenty-eight days before the federal government stopped it. Over 2,000 people were killed, eighty-five of whom were women and children.

NASCAR III began after the 99 car caused the 54 car to crash on the first lap at Talladega. The war was fought in Alabama, Mississippi, and Georgia, and lasted nineteen days. Over 3,000 people lost their lives in NASCAR III, seventy-five of whom were women and children.

The cameras panned the crowd. No flags were flying now. Eb flipped through the pages of his speech, held it up for the audience to see, and continued:

I could go on, war by war, but the description of each NASCAR War is depressingly similar. One driver gets mad at another driver, a small regional war erupts between the drivers' fans, innocent people are killed, property is destroyed, and absolutely nothing is gained. All eight NASCAR wars follow this same pattern.

Now I am here to honor the unknown NASCAR soldier and I do that proudly. I do not denigrate dying for one's beliefs or convictions. But I think we need to ask ourselves if we really need to fight wars and kill each other over race car drivers.

The crowd did not boo at this point, which surprised me. Eb pressed on:

> *Let me expand this idea to wars that previous leaders of our nation have committed us to. Was there really any need to attack Tunisia because it refused to allow Christian missionaries to enter the country? I would say no. Yet because of America's invasion of Tunisia, we have now fought three Tunisian wars. Do you remember why we invaded Peru? We invaded Peru because the president of Peru called America a bunch of weaklings because it took us over a year to defeat Tunisia in Tunisia I. To show Peru we were tough, we invaded Peru.*

Eb held up the pages of his speech again. He spoke a little louder, as if gaining momentum:

> *I could go on but what's the point? Grenada I and II. Greenland. Vietnam II, III, IV, V, and VI. Portugal I, II, and III. Why did we fight these wars? The truth is, there was no good reason for these wars. Our leaders pushed us into these wars for their own glory, not for the good of our great country.*
>
> *So today I propose a rather simple rule for our country, a rule that General Dozier and I will follow if elected. That rule is: "No more stupid wars." Let's only fight wars that are absolutely necessary to the defense of our country. Let's not waste our young people on stupid wars. We are better than that. Thank you for your attention.*

Eb and General Dozier left the podium to silence. At least there were no boos, and nobody threw any tomatoes. Be interesting to see how this plays out.

Day 600

Welcome to day 600, a nice round number. And, as it happens, Thanksgiving Day. When Suzanne and Hannah asked me a few days ago what I wanted to eat on Thanksgiving, I told them I wasn't all that excited about celebrating the holiday. They both took my response as a sign of ungrateful-ness and proceeded to tell me all the things I have to be thankful for. I took both lectures like a good soldier, but my real reason for not wanting to cel-ebrate Thanksgiving is that the holiday reminds me of how much I miss my family. My mom always cooked up a storm for Thanksgiving, and we always had extended family and lots of friends over for dinner. Most years we even had a few of God's Elect from the Assassin's home over for dinner.

Plus, Senior never missed Thanksgiving. Senior worked hard and traveled a lot, but he was never gone over Thanksgiving. After we stuffed ourselves with Mom's cooking, Senior and I would plant ourselves in front of the tele-vision and watch the Cowboys play football in the afternoon and the Horns and the Texas A&M Aggies tee it up in the evening. Those Thanksgiving days were some of the best days of my life. And we will never have them again because Senior decided to blow himself and the president up.

Despite the strangeness of that last sentence, I stand before you, dear reader, as a thankful man. One of the stranger consequences of the last 600 days is that (1) running from the law, (2) being falsely accused, (3) losing my family, and (4) being hunted by crazy killers of virtually every creed and race has made me more thankful than back when I had a "normal" life and my toughest decision was whether to eat peach cobbler or dewberry cob-bler for dessert after finishing the brisket and sausage platter at Joe Willie's BBQ in El Paso. I have no explanation for this phenomenon. If Pete was here, maybe he could explain. I always relied on Pete for the heavy lifting in the philosophy department. I miss Pete. Wherever you are Pete—Happy Thanksgiving, dude.

Suzanne and Hannah worked really hard today and came up with a great meal. All of us, including the Mossad guys, ate way too much food and lay around like bums. It was great. Just so there is no mistake, dear reader, I am very thankful for my life. And while I am at it, since I have dissed South Dakota in these pages, let me say that I am also thankful for South Dakota, especially Badlands National Park.

Since Hannah and Suzanne did most of the cooking, the Mossad guys and I did the dishes. Never pictured Mossad guys as the domestic type. I con-sidered making a smart comment, but then I remembered these guys were protecting me from the bad guys, so I swallowed my sarcasm.

When we finished the dishes I sat down beside Hannah, who was going over some papers and frowning. When I asked her what the problem was, she said, "I know you don't keep track of how much money you have contributed to charities from your endorsement royalties, but it is a ton of money, Junior."

When I asked her why that fact made her frown, she said, "Suzanne delegated to me the job of finding Jewish charities to receive funds. It was very kind of her to do so, and I was honored to help. But I am embarrassed to say that most of the Jewish charities that received money from you have never once sent you any sort of thank-you card or note. They took the money, but unlike all the other charities, they never exercised the simple human courtesy to say thank-you. All the goyim were grateful, but God's chosen people have taken your gift for granted. Why would they ignore you like that? You deserve better, Junior."

Since I did not really have an appropriate response, I suggested we leave the papers on the desk and have another piece of pecan pie with whipped cream. Hannah agreed and we ate pie and talked about happier subjects.

Happy Thanksgiving, everyone.

Day 604

Welcome to month twenty-one of the I'm Still On The Lam But I'm Thankful Tour. And today I'm thankful for . . . an unexpected offer of asylum . . . from the king of Rabonia. Remember the story about how Senior got miffed at his cell phone so he started his own telephone company?[100] Well, one of the first guys we talked to before we got into the phone business was Rayfield Ashmont Griffin. Rayfield is my age, but he was incredibly rich even back then because his incredibly rich father had died way too young but had the incredible foresight to have an incredibly ironclad prenuptial agreement to keep his money away from incredibly beautiful and incredibly greedy wife number four. Senior and Rayfield's dad were buddies, but I don't remember what the connection was between them.

Rayfield is a Princeton grad who, when he wasn't having fun being rich, invested his incredible fortune. Somehow Senior knew that Rayfield

---

100 See Day 437.

had a bunch of expertise in evaluating businesses in the telecommunications industry.

We told Rayfield what we were planning to do and he made some very helpful suggestions. Rayfield then sold all of his telecommunications company stock (when the price was still sky high), combined that with half of his incredible fortune, and put all the money in Apache Communications. In eighteen months or so, Rayfield went from being incredibly rich to being "I am richer than a small country" rich.

To prove this point, Rayfield purchased a small country. I can't remember which global economic crisis precipitated the island country's financial demise, but Rayfield was able to buy the country in a bankruptcy court auction. He then renamed the country Rabonia and declared himself king.

I realize that was kind of a long introduction, but if you have hung with me for twenty-one months, what's a few more paragraphs?

The e-mail I received from Rayfield today was short and to the point:

Dude, I'm a king now. My country doesn't have an extradition treaty with the dear old US of A. I'm pretty sure I could tell my royal legal adviser to write up some sort of kingly proclamation granting you asylum or citizenship or whatever else you want. Everybody knows you're a good dude and would not hurt your dad or anyone else. We could hang out. Island chicks, man. Know what I'm saying?

My response: Ray, thanks for the offer. Sounds great, and I REALLY appreciate it, but I need to stay over here and take care of some stuff. What's it like being a king?

King Rayfield: Oh, you know, the usual. People bowing to me, paying me taxes, naming their kids after me, having parades in my honor. And did I mention island chicks?

My response: Yes, you did. Sounds tempting. I think I should stay here, though, and see this deal through. Would you like to come over and hang out with me? Running from the law can be exhilarating. And why is there a camel on Rabonia's flag? Are there camels on the island?

King Rayfield: Sadly, I can't come over. I kind of need to be here and make sure the kingdom runs smoothly. It's a pretty big investment and I can't afford to let it depreciate. Good luck with the whole explosion investigation deal. Re the camel, I just thought it looked cool on the flag. No camels here. Don't forget, you are always welcome here. Oh yeah, if your clothing line company is looking for cheap labor, I've got several thousand Rabonians who can flat-out thread a sewing needle. Later.

Wasn't that a nice gesture? You never know, it could be good to have a king for a friend down the road, even a king with a rather bizarre taste in flags. Long live King Rayfield!

Day 610

I'm told Dale Piper's plan to salvage Eb's campaign is in full swing. Suzanne is talking to a bunch of people on the phone and revising spreadsheets. Don't tell anybody. Don't want to spoil the surprise.

Speaking of surprises, I got a very nice thank-you today from Ricky "Chuck" Norris, the founder and leader of the Adamic White Power group. As you may recall, Hannah and I spent some quality time in White Only Settlement, Idaho, the headquarters for the AWP, before Fairman blew up a bunch of innocent people there trying to kill me. I had specifically instructed Suzanne to send some of my endorsement money to the AWP to help out the folks who lived there. There is no way I could fix what happened, but I had to do something.

Norris wrote:

Junior—Thank you for the money. I have done some research on you, and I am pretty sure you're not a fan of the AWP's policies and politics. I know Senior was not. To be honest, if I had known you and the Mossad chick were here, I would have had you arrested and horsewhipped. I'm glad I didn't know, because that would have been wrong. It's pretty clear to me you are being persecuted because of who you are, not because of what you have done.

The money you sent will be put to good use. We will invest the money in our children's health programs. And Junior, listen to me. I say the following with my heart—you are NOT to blame for what happened here. The massacre is all on Fairman. Fairman is a murderer and I hope he eventually pays for what he did here. Trust me, if we catch him before the feds do, there will be no constitutional due process for Fairman. I wish you the best, Junior—you are a good guy. And tell that Mossad chick that if she ever wants to cross over to the AWP to personally give me a call. She is a looker.

I won't repeat what Hannah said about being called "the Mossad chick." Children may be listening.

Some interesting election news today. Dr. Davis and Big Fly Washington, the Democratic candidates, held a rally today at the University of Wisconsin in Madison, Wisconsin. Dr. Davis told the crowd: "I am going to say something very unusual, so you should probably pay attention."

When the crowd stopped cheering, he continued:

A couple of weeks ago our Republican opponents took a bold stand by promising they would never commit this great country to a stupid war. Big Fly and I have talked about Ebenezer Cohen's "no more stupid wars" speech and the truth of the matter is that we could not agree more. We join with Ebenezer Cohen and General Dozier in their stand that America should not fight any more stupid wars. I know it is rare for candidates to agree on anything, but we think Ebenezer and General Dozier are exactly right on this issue and we thank them for elucidating it so clearly.

Civility in a presidential campaign? Agreement on an issue by the candidates? The end of the world as we know it must be right around the corner. Tell the Baptists that the Antichrist is lurking in the shadows.

Day 612

Not sure why, but we left South Dakota and drove over to Minnesota the other day. I will miss the Badlands.

Eb and General Dozier got an unexpected endorsement today. The National Association of Atheists (NAA), which is holding its national convention in Santa Fe, New Mexico, announced that it was "wholeheartedly" recommending that its 8 million members vote for the Republican candidates. This is the first time in its over 100-year history that the NAA has endorsed a Republican candidate for president.

When we got the news of the impending announcement, I sat in the RV with Hannah and Suzanne and watched the NAA president speak on the Atheist 2 Channel:

Although the NAA has traditionally endorsed Democratic candidates, we could not help but note that Dr. Davis went to a Catholic grade school, Catholic high school, and Catholic college and that Mr. Washington attended private Baptist schools as a child. Plus, Mr. Washington is a Baptist minister. We simply can't imagine two men with this background being sympathetic with the issues that are important to us.

Conversely, we note that General Dozier attended public schools as a child and graduated from West Point. Likewise, Mr. Cohen attended public schools. We would prefer that the men who run our country not be brainwashed from childhood in educational institutions that promote fairy tales and ignore reality. We recognize that General Dozier is a practicing Episcopalian and that Mr. Cohen is a Jew. However, at least these two men have not been raised in the sheltered cocoon of so-called "Christian education." Plus, we have never seen Mr. Cohen wear that funny Jew hat. We believe these two men are more likely to make rational decisions based on the facts as presented and are less likely to rely upon "the power of prayer" or other superstitious mumbo jumbo.

We remember with horror how previous presidents have started wars because they claimed they "were led by the spirit" or because they felt "God had called" them to do so. We recognize and celebrate the right of every American to exercise their religious beliefs. We would prefer, however, that our leaders exercise their good judgment, rather than their religious beliefs, when making important national decisions.

I asked Hannah if this endorsement hurt Eb. "I don't think so," she said. "It's not like the far Christian right voters are lining up to vote for a Jew for president. I mean, we did kill their Savior, after all."

"What about the Christian value of turning the other cheek?" I asked.

"Apparently, that does not apply to killing the Messiah, Junior," she responded.

Fortunately, Suzanne appeared at this point and announced that she had made some Clinton Gold brownies. I decided to eat a few and stop worrying about politics and religion for the day.

Day 618

Fairman's write-in candidacy is at a fever pitch. The top ten Hate Millionaires organized rallies all over the country today. CNN estimated there were over 15 million people at the rallies. The radio personalities appeared in person at several of the rallies and Fairman appeared via a satellite feed. CNN also reported that the popularity of the write-in vote issue has caused the stock prices of the Hate Millionaires' public companies to skyrocket.

Steinbach appeared at the New York City rally, where he basically took credit for the Fairman candidacy and the national fervor it has created:

Samson Fairman is just the man this country needs. He is a brave and independent Christian warrior who has defeated the infidels of Islam. He is a capitalist who has made his fortune without help from the government. He is a good family man. What more can we ask for, America?

The crowd cheered and Steinbach continued:

I have spoken to my good friend Samson Fairman and he has assured me that one of his first priorities as your new president will be to have Junior Jennings arrested, tried, and executed for treason.

The crowd roared even louder.

Suzanne could see I was not too happy with the crowd cheering for my execution. She took my hand and said in a soothing voice, "You realize this is all part of the plan, right?"

"I suppose," I told her, "but that does not mean I have to like it. And I'm getting kind of tired of being called a traitor."

Suzanne kissed me on the cheek and said, "You can handle this, Junior. I know you can." I gave her a dubious look and then Suzanne gave me that Southern Girl smile that has worked on men since before the War of Northern Aggression. It had absolutely no effect on me. Well, OK, maybe a little. And then she made me a margarita and that helped some, too.

Day 620

Still in Minnesota. Still in an RV.

Today was a good day. Surprisingly so. The Dallas Cowboys News Channel covered a charity golf tournament sponsored by Henry the Hammer to benefit the families who lost loved ones or had children injured in the White Only Settlement Massacre. Surprisingly, there were a number of black football players there. I'm guessing the Assassin, who was the Hammer's cosponsor, was responsible for the attendance of black players at a golf tournament to benefit a racist community.

The Hammer spoke to a female reporter for the Dallas Cowboys News Channel who was as tall as the Hammer's belly button. He said:

This is all about the kids. Nobody should hurt kids. Red and yellow, black and white, all kids is precious in God's sight. You can argue about lots of stuff, man, but can't nobody argue about the kids being special. We need to keep the kids safe. Even Bubba Connolly agrees with that. Bubba's here, you know. He is a dirty-playing, illegal chop blocking son of a gun, and a terrible golfer, but he is here at my tournament to help the little racist white kids.

The Hammer was asked if the tournament was a political statement, given the write-in candidacy of Samson Fairman, who was responsible for the White Only Settlement Massacre. He responded:

> *You know, I set this tournament deal up a couple of months ago, because I know Chuck Norris. We go deer hunting together sometimes. I have been really busy in the weight room lately and I had no idea that the guy who blew up the little racist white kids was running for president. Can he do that? Can you blow up people and then run for president? Isn't blowing people up against the law?*
>
> *I don't keep up with current events–type stuff the way I should, but I talked to my good friend Sammy Assassin Johnson about this. The Assassin, like me, is a defensive player, and hates illegal chop blocks. Unlike me, he is as black as an Almond Joy. But we both agree that kids should not be blown up, even if they are racist white kids. That is why the Assassin is here and that is why he has brought with him a bunch of other black Negro NFL guys.*
>
> *There is a time for everything. There is a time to say something and there is a time to keep your mouth shut. The Assassin and I figured this was a good time to speak up.*

At this point the Assassin walked up, holding a beautiful little white girl with bandages on both of her arms. The contrast in skin tones was dramatic— Almond Joy and vanilla ice cream. Somewhere an AWP grandmother was fainting. The Hammer put his arm around the Assassin and spoke: "The Assassin and I have talked to the NFL players union and the union has agreed we can make this statement."

The Hammer pulled out a piece of paper, glanced at it as if about to read it, then handed it to the Assassin.

The Assassin read, in his incredibly deep voice:

The union is appalled that a man responsible for the death of hundreds of people, including many children, is being hailed as an American hero worthy of the presidency. Our message to the American people is a simple one. If you elect Samson Fairman as the next president of the United States, the union will boycott the upcoming NFL season.

The Assassin then kissed the little girl on the top of her head as she smiled up at him. "Y'all have a nice day," he said to the camera.

Hannah, who was watching the television with me, turned to face me with her mouth wide open. The expression of total surprise on her face was priceless. Then she started to move her lips, but nothing came out. Then everybody's cell phone started to ring. I could hear people in the front of the RV cheering.

"Junior!" Hannah exclaimed. "This is really good news I suppose, but this was not part of the plan. I repeat, we did not plan for this or anticipate this! How did this happen?"

"Welcome to my world, Hannah," was all I could say.

Day 623

The last few days have been really exciting around here, but for once it's not about me, which is kinda nice. I say it's not about me, but I guess that is not exactly true. To be more precise, it's not ALL about me. Nobody seems too concerned about whether I blew everybody up, or whether I am about to be killed. It's kind of like I am on vacation, or maybe spring break, from my life.

People all over the country are in an uproar over the election. The catalyst, of course, was the Assassin's announcement that the NFL players would boycott the next NFL season if Fairman was elected. This announcement has apparently turned sports fans who don't give two hoots about politics into fire-breathing radicals.

Rallies and/or riots have taken place in virtually every city that has an NFL franchise. A few protesters have criticized the football players, but for the most part the rallies have focused on urging people not to vote for

Fairman. Signs like Save Our Season: Anybody But Fairman were prominently displayed at the rallies.

The airwaves have been saturated by the rantings of all sorts of "experts" weighing in on this issue. Dr. Mark Isbell, a Miami psychologist, opined that the players are engaged in "fan blackmail" that is harming the country's psyche. Dr. Isbell elaborated:

> *The players' threat to boycott is simply irresponsible. My phone is ringing off the wall. Miami Dolphins fans are beside themselves with grief and worry that Fairman will be elected and there will be no football. My colleagues across the country report the same concern. The major drug manufacturers tell me they are running out of antidepressants because we are prescribing so much. Since when did football players become politically active? Whatever happened to the good old days when football players spent their off-season taking illegal drugs and hanging out with prostitutes?*

Joseph Sanders III, a Washington, D.C., lobbyist, said in an interview with the Dallas Cowboys News Channel: "Henry the Hammer is a certified political genius. He has raised the art of campaign politics to new heights. He definitely has a future in political consulting after his football and porn movie careers are over."

The RV has been a beehive (no pun intended) of activity. Eb checks in every hour or so. Suzanne is on the phone with people in New York and working on her spreadsheets. When Hannah is not quietly talking on the phone, she is walking around with a big smile on her face. I have to say that I have never seen everybody so upbeat in the RV.

The top ten Hate Millionaires and Fairman are not giving up, however. They are still promoting rallies (although the rallies are smaller) and the Hate Millionaires are still ranting and raving and making up stuff. Today one of the hate jocks said that the Assassin was gay and that the Hammer was a pedophile. Another said that a recent study showed that over 80 percent of active NFL players suffered from brain damage. "How can you make a decision on who to elect as president based upon what a brain-damaged guy who probably took basket weaving in college says?" railed Leah Myer, who I believe is number five or six on the top ten Hate Millionaires list. Myer is a liberal-leaning Hate Millionaire and usually at odds with Steinbach, but apparently she thinks it is in her financial interest to align with Steinbach on the Fairman candidacy.

Today the other shoe fell. Or more precisely, two other shoes. First, P. Julius Whitworth, the albino power forward for the Seattle Fog, appeared at a press conference in New York City with Stevie "Manchild" Wingard and Larryarnold Reems to announce that the NBA players union had decided to take a stand with their NFL brothers. Manchild, a seven foot three inch center who played for three years at Harvard and earned an economics degree before bolting to the NBA for the big bucks, stated:

> *The NBA players union is not a political entity, per se. The union is dedicated to the economic well-being of its members and the stability of the NBA. We don't endorse candidates or support particular ideologies because we are well aware of the negative economic ramifications these types of decisions can manifest.*
>
> *However, the NBA players union is a union of men who share strong beliefs in the sanctity of family and the notion that all children have a fundamental right in this great country to grow up free of fear and abuse. Samson Fairman intentionally killed the white children in Idaho. That is simply wrong, under any moral or economic model.*
>
> *Plus, we have run the numbers. From an economic standpoint, it makes sense for the NBA players union to join with the NFL players union. So, our message to America is that if Samson Fairman is elected president, we too will boycott.*

P. Julius Whitworth added:

> *Since I am one of the three non-European or Canadian white players in the league, I feel confident that I am the only NBA player with a vacation home in White Settlement, Idaho. I have seen firsthand the horrible destruction caused by Fairman. I appreciate my NBA brothers for taking this stand.*

Larryarnold Reems, who I believe joined the NBA after his sophomore year in high school, declined to comment. He did fist-bump the other two players at the end of the press conference, however.

The Major League Baseball players union did not hold a press conference. It just sent out an e-mail that said: "There will be no baseball if Samson Fairman is elected president. Enjoy your year off without any professional sports, America. Spend time with your kids, and catch up on your reading and lawn work."

After she read the e-mail from the baseball players union, Suzanne got on the telephone and talked for over an hour. Finally, I heard her say, "OK, make the play." When I asked her what she was doing, Suzanne smiled and said, "Making a ton of money, Junior. A ton of money. You are going to have a bunch more money to give away."

Better than a poke in the eye with a sharp stick, as Senior was fond of saying.

Day 627

Have you figured out the big plan yet? Remember when Dale Piper dropped by the RV in the Badlands and proposed six really illegal plans to help Eb and me? And we chose a mostly legal plan instead?[101]

Well, the mostly legal plan was to sell short as much stock of the Hate Millionaires' public companies as we could get our hands on. The Israelis bought hundreds of thousands of shares. Suzanne used my endorsement money to buy a bunch as well. Once we bought the shares, the mostly legal plan was that Dale Piper would use his contacts to get the Securities and Exchange Commission to announce a fraud investigation into all the Hate Millionaires' companies. The shares would drop like a rock, and we would make a killing. A financial killing, that is.

The plan was designed to accomplish two purposes. First, Eb and the Israelis would make a ton of money to fill up their campaign war chests, so they could continue their quest to win the presidency. Second, the Hate Millionaires would be discredited by the fraud investigation, and by extension and association, so would Fairman.

The plan worked, although not in the way we anticipated. Once the NFL, NBA, and MLB players announced that they would boycott if Fairman was

---

101   See Day 589.

elected, the jig was up for the Hate Millionaires. NOBODY wanted an entire year without professional sports. And, NOBODY wanted to be associated with anyone who was linked to a year without professional sports. The major sponsors for the Hate Millionaires' radio shows pulled their advertisements, and many of the radio stations canceled their contracts with the Hate Millionaires. This meant the Hate Millionaires were silent, at least for a while. And the value of the stock in the Hate Millionaires' companies tumbled. And we made a bunch of cashola.

So as it turns out, we did not do anything even partially illegal. The SEC fraud announcement never happened. I wonder if that absolves us of the fact that we INTENDED to do something partially illegal. Have to ask Pete that question when we meet up again.

And by the way, today is my birthday. Happy thirty-second birthday to me. Suzanne made my favorite meal: chicken fried steak, mashed potatoes, and fried okra. Hannah made me a chocolate cake, my favorite dessert.

And to top it off, all three of the unions sent me a birthday present. The NFL guys sent me a gold Super Bowl Tier 1 championship ring with my name engraved on it. The MLB players sent me a case of fancy rubbing oil stuff that helps with sore muscles. I was confused about the gift until I read the attached note:

Junior, we know you're a Man on the Run, and we also know you're not in the best of shape, so we thought you could use this stuff. The relief pitchers generally use it because they are never in shape. Also, we know you are helping the Cohen/Dozier ticket and so you and all of your friends will need this stuff when our buddy Big Fly kicks your collective butt! Seriously, stay safe. When this is all over, we will work on getting you some World Series tickets.

The NBA guys sent me a basketball autographed by P. Julius Whitworth and a bottle of fancy men's cologne. The attached note was from Larryarnold Reems. It read:

Junior dude. Manchild was working on his new book and told me to take care of your birthday present. I got you an autographed ball

signed by Julius because he is a white guy and so are you. Although,
just between you and me and the brothers on the corner, that dude does
NOT jump like a white boy, you know what I mean? I be just a tiny bit
suspicious about old Julius.[102] I also thought you might like some of my
signature cologne, Reverse Slam. It really works with the ladies and I
figure you need all the help you can get in that department, you know
what I mean? I mean a man girdle, seriously?

Even in victory, even on my birthday, the critiques continue. Thanks, guys, for everything. Who would have thought that sports unions could affect a presidential election?[103]

Day 632

The last few days have been a little slow, I'm not gonna lie. Now that the revised Dale Piper plan has succeeded beyond our wildest dreams, the troops have relaxed. We know Fairman, Robert Earl, and the fartwa folks are still out there, but for some reason the sense of urgent concern that has dogged us for months has abated. I'm sure it will come back soon enough, but for now I am enjoying my lowered heart rate.

Today I sat in front of the television and watched the Christian Education Is a Right! rallies. In a classic example of politics making strange bedfellows, people in favor of Christian schools rallied across the nation today in support of the DEMOCRATIC candidates for president. Normally, of course, the Christian education folks support the Republican candidates because they believe that the Democrats are liberal heathens who hate Christians and support public schools. But the NAA's endorsement of Eb and General Dozier, plus Eb's status as a Christ killer, have pushed the Christian educators into strange and unexplored territory.

I have to say that the Christian Education Is a Right! rallies are the most organized and efficient rallies I have seen in a long time. Certainly better organized than the Fatty Pride Parade in Missoula.

102   See Day 154, footnote 44.

103   The unions' boycott threat is now widely known as the Triple Play. The Triple Play strategy was used in several more elections until it was outlawed by Congress.

The rallies, regardless of the locale, follow a similar protocol. The preachers, reverends, pastors, etc., marched in front, followed by Christian educators. These two groups carried signs that identified them, like Christian Educators of Round Rock, Texas, for example. Following these two groups of marchers were the kids, beginning with the preschool kids and continuing (in age-appropriate order) through high school. Each school had a professional-looking sign, like Hutto, Texas, First Evangelical Spirit-Filled Assembly of God in Christ Early Development Preschool, for example. The parents of the kids marched with them, and many of the parents carried hand-painted signs. Many of the hand-painted signs purported to give the views of God and/or Jesus on education. The most prevalent signs I saw, in no particular order are:

(1) Jesus Was a Christian Educator;
(2) Jesus Died for Christian Education;
(3) Jesus Loves Christian Educators;
(4) God Created Christian Brains;
(5) God's Will Is America's Educational Destiny; and
(6) God Protects Christian Educators from Jewish Politicians.

After the kids passed by, row after row of football players, wearing their helmets and uniforms, marched in lockstep. The football players were from the religious colleges located nearest to the city where the rally was being held. For example, in the Nashville, Tennessee, rally, the football teams in the East Jesus Division of the Jesus Is Lord League marched in support of the Education Is a Christian Right! cause.

Behind the football players marched incredibly clean-cut college-aged men and women wearing business casual attire and carrying professionally made banners. According to Suzanne, who watched the coverage of the rallies with me on CNN, the banners were primarily quotations from the Bible. The final banner in each rally read: If God Is For Us, Who Can Be Against Us? Suzanne told me that line is from Romans 8:31. She really knows her Bible verses.

Although the Christian Education Is a Right! rallies were well organized and definitely got their point across, they were also a little bit boring for my taste. I guess when you are on the run from the law and trying to avoid being blown up, your boredom threshold goes up a few notches.

The only deviation from the relative boredom of the Christian Education Is a Right! rallies occurred at the end of the rally in Los Angeles. Apparently some unapproved folks slipped through the barricades and were able to walk behind the scripture banners with some hand-painted signs. My favorites were:

(1) WWVD—What Would Vishnu Do?;
(2) Jehovah Kicks Allah's Butt; and
(3) Junior—Will You Marry Me? We Could Bee Very Happy!

I think I will end today's entry on that upbeat sign.

Day 636

Since we are approaching the end of both a year and a decade, there are a bunch of Best of the Decade lists out there. I always enjoy these compilations, and since nothing much is going on here in the RV, I thought I would give you my take on the winners. If you don't care what a Man on the Run has to say about the decade, that's fine. Just skip on over to the next entry.

The first thing I would like to mention is that my girlfriend Mandy/Sandy is listed at number ten on the Hottie Girlfriends of the Decade list. I feel so proud. And to think when I started this trip everyone thought I was gay.

I am also proud that my buddy Pete checked in as the number four Hot Wingman of the Decade. I miss you, buddy.

I don't see Veronica's name on the Top Ten Media Movers and Shakers of the Decade list, so I predict we will be hearing from her about that, particularly since the now broke and disgraced Clarke Steinbach is on the list. I am guessing the list had already been prepared before the professional sports unions messed up old Pierre.

Number three on the Where in the World Did This Guy Come From list is our old buddy Eb. Eb is described as "the best-looking hunk to run for the presidency in years." If they only knew.

The God of the Decade, in a landslide, is Allah. In fact, Allah has been voted the God of the last three decades. I'm pretty sure that as long as the oil flows in Saudi Arabia, Iraq, and Iran, and the Islamic terrorists continue to prosper, Allah is going to be the leader in the God clubhouse for the foreseeable future. Vishnu was a distant second on the God of the Decade list, followed by Odin, Michael Jordan, and Jehovah. Jordan had a good decade because Nike reissued a bunch of his jerseys and shoes. I predict Jehovah will likely continue to lag behind on this list as long as the oil flows in Saudi Arabia, Iraq, and Iran, and the Islamic terrorists continue to prosper.

Number two on the Terrorists of the Decade list is Al Mutsapi, the black seven-foot-tall African Quaker terrorist who messed with America's manhood. I am a little surprised that Al lost out to Dr. Hakim, the female Afghan doctor who caused a bunch of Muslim guys' privates to fall off. Al did a lot of creative things, and Dr. Hakim was pretty much a one-hit-wonder kind of terrorist. I am guessing Dr. Hakim got the nod because she was perceived as a sort of trailblazer who was protecting women against male oppression.

I have to admit I am a little peeved at the Man of the Decade list because Senior is not on it. Not anywhere. The list includes a Brazilian soccer player; a deaf *American Idol* winner; a blind, gay, transgender midget who won two Academy Awards for portraying a blind, gay, transgender midget;[104] and a college professor who wrote the definitive work on the *I Love Lucy* television series. And the guy who helped cure AIDS and saved the Israeli nation from destruction couldn't beat out these folks? What a world we live in.

And to top it all off, the *Burger King New York Times* Man of the Decade is Sheik Faisel Omar Saeed Al Zahrani from Saudi Arabia. The sheik is also the third-richest man in the world because of his oil income. The sheik is so rich that he actually bought the nuclear-contaminated wasteland formerly known as Israel from the Iraqis and Iranians. Iraq and Iran did not care about cleaning up the mess caused by the nuclear fallout and were glad to make money from the destruction of Israel.

The sheik travels the world with his wives and his harem, gambles, and basically has a great time. He also openly and proudly praises Islamic terrorists who blow stuff up all over the world. The *BKNY Times* article stated that while awarding the sheik the Man of the Decade award "might be controversial because of the whole blowing-people-up deal," the *BKNY Times* was "properly following strict journalistic guidelines by ignoring discriminatory racial and religious distinctions" in reaching its conclusion that the sheik deserved the award.

---

104   Junior was criticized for a number of years for not using the term "elevationally challenged" in Day 636, but "midget" and "dwarf" have recently been approved as descriptive terms by the Congress of People Under Four Feet (COPUFF).

I can tell you that Senior REALLY HATED this sheik guy. I will explain more about it later. Have a good evening. See you next year.

Day 640

Well, the new year is starting off with a bang. We went back to South Dakota today. Not my first choice, but then again, I was not consulted. We drove the RV to Mount Rushmore, the big sculpture of the heads of President George Washington, President Thomas Jefferson, President Theodore Roosevelt, and President Abraham Lincoln. I had never been there before, so it was kind of cool to see it in person. The park surrounding the sculpture was closed, but Hannah showed the park ranger some papers and he let us in.

When we got up closer to the sculpture I could see Eb and General Dozier with their security contingent. A photographer was taking a bunch of pictures of the candidates in front of the sculpture. I stayed in the RV, since I am still a wanted mass murderer and traitor.

When the photographer finished taking pictures, another RV drove up next to the Republican candidates. To my great surprise, Kevin Davis and Big Fly Washington jumped out of the RV and shook hands with Eb and the General. Smiles all around and, at least from my vantage point in the RV, genuine smiles and not fake politician smiles. Then, amazingly, they each put on a red, white, and blue "Peace Bee With You" cap and waved to my RV. Hannah said, "Junior, they are waving at you. They are offering you a big thank-you for your help. You can wave back, but you can't get out of the RV."

"But can they see me waving at them?" I asked.

"Probably not, but they know you are here," Hannah said, as if talking to a four-year-old. Suzanne than walked up to me and touched me on the arm and said, "It's for the best, Junior. If you go outside it could cause problems for all of them. Aren't the caps pretty?"

So I waved back.

What happened next is unprecedented in the annals of America's presidential elections, as far as I know. At least I don't remember studying anything like this in my political science classes at UT.

All four guys sat at a table in front of the monument. Eb and Davis sat in the middle. General Dozier sat next to Davis and Big Fly sat next to Eb, which is not how you would have expected them to line up. Hannah turned on the television in the RV and we watched as the really cute CNN political reporter with amazingly big lips proclaimed: "We are going live to Mount Rushmore in South Dakota for a special announcement by the candidates for the presidency." Davis spoke first:

Hello, fellow citizens. My name is Kevin Davis and I am the Democratic candidate for president. Sitting next to me is General Dozier, a man I greatly admire. He is the Republican candidate for vice president.

Eb then spoke:

My fellow Americans. My name is Ebenezer Cohen and I am the Republican candidate for president. Sitting next to me is the Reverend Bobby Washington, whom many of you know as Big Fly. Reverend Washington is the Democratic candidate for vice president. I did not know Reverend Washington until the campaign, but I have come to respect him greatly as a sincere and talented human being.

Davis spoke again:

We have something important to say, but we want to keep it brief. I will do most of the talking, but don't read anything into that. We did rock, paper, scissors and I lost, so I get to explain what is going on here.

The four of us want to tell the country that we all like and respect each other. We are not going to scream and holler at each other and say bad stuff about the other side during this campaign. We differ on several issues, but we agree on many more. I think Eb would be a fine president and he believes I would do a good job as well.

Eb leaned over to the microphone and said, "That is exactly correct, Kevin." Davis continued:

So, America, how about it? Are you with us? Can we stop the hateful nonsense and discuss the issues like civilized human beings? All four of us hope that our great country can unite as a peaceful people and proceed with a sane and reasonable election. Thank you for your time.

Then all four guys stood up, joined hands, and raised their hands in unison. As the camera panned out, each of them hugged each other.

The cute CNN reporter with the larger-than-life lips then appeared on the screen. Her mouth was wide open, like the bald guy in that Screaming Guy painting,[105] and her eyes looked vacant. After an uncomfortable five seconds or so, she touched her earpiece, refocused, and spoke: "Our crack research team is looking into this, but in all likelihood we have just witnessed a unique historical event." She touched her earpiece again and smiled. "I have just been informed that certain news outlets have reported that the scene we just witnessed may have been a hoax. We will continue to pursue this story. Now back to our regular broadcast."

Unfortunately for CNN and all the other news outlets, this was no hoax. We really do have four decent guys who are running for office. I wonder what the news guys are going to do with this. Can we have a presidential campaign without a daily dose of salacious allegations of unseemly behavior? Guess we will find out. (And yes, Dr. Hoover, I had to look up "salacious" to make sure it meant what I thought it meant.)

Day 646

It just now occurred to me that we have been in month twenty-two for a few days now and I have not mentioned it. Sorry for the late notice. I hope I have not messed up your calendar.

Things have changed since my last entry. We are no longer in the RV, which quite frankly is OK by me. It is a great vehicle, but hanging out with the same people for twenty-four hours a day can wear on a person after a while. So, Suzanne and I are now staying in a really cool lakefront penthouse in Chicago.

Yes, that Chicago, the Hog Butcher for the World, the City of the Big Shoulders, and the home of the Chicago Cubs, who have not been in the World Series since 1945. Although Hannah did not specifically say this, she

---

105 Likely a reference to *The Scream* by Edvard Munch.

implied that the penthouse is owned by the same Israeli mafia guy who owns the fancy Aspen house we stayed in. Oh, Aspen. Really miss that place.

I forgot to mention in my end-of-the-year entry that Al Mutsapi finished first in the final WCFL standings. The rest of us just could not compete with the Big Boy wee-wee weapon. I saw a few WCFL experts on CNN complaining about my "inability to finish." Oh well. This year everybody starts with a brand-new slate, so hopefully I won't even be a participant.

Today Suzanne and I sat around and watched a bunch of college football bowl games. Just another benefit of hanging out with a Southern Girl. Suzanne was bummed that the Crimson Tide was not playing in a bowl game, but all in all we had a great time eating chips and queso and tamales and drinking margaritas. Speaking of Alabama football, I have never talked to Suzanne about the strange Alabama tailgate party I witnessed.[106] Need to do that at some point.

The Rose Bowl National Championship Game Presented by the United States Department of Legal Drugs was a thriller. The Boise State Broncos, as the defending national champions, were a big favorite, but they lost in triple overtime to Second Hilltop Holy Spirit Baptist College, the winner of the East Jesus Division of the Jesus Is Lord League.

The Baptists' win is historic. It is the first national football championship won by a team in the Jesus Is Lord League. Boaz "Buckwheat" Trimble, the Crusaders' head coach, was euphoric in his postgame interview with the sideline reporter, a dark-haired beauty with soft blue eyes. He said:

> *Well, young lady, those Boises are fighters, no doubt about it. Plus, I believe everything happens for a reason. But our God is a mighty God, regardless of what that blasphemous God of the Decade report says. He gave us a great game plan and I think we executed it pretty darn good. I mean, if God is for your football team, who can be against it?*

The reporter tried to ask Buckwheat another question, but she was drowned out by the "Jehovah Kicks Butt!" cheer that reverberated throughout the Rose Bowl. As the camera panned over the stadium, the visual was quite dramatic. Half of the fans were standing and screaming: "Jehovah Kicks Butt!" which is

---

106 See Day 400.

the official copyrighted cheer of the Jesus Is Lord League. The Boise State fans, however, were sitting in their seats, smoking the free Clinton Gold provided by the game's sponsor, the United States Department of Legal Drugs.

The postgame coverage then shifted to the Boise State locker room for the traditional interview with the losing coach. Amazingly, Veronica was conducting the interview. I don't know how she got this gig. I am pretty sure she knows nothing about football:

Veronica: Coach, what exactly is a Boise?

Coach: Veronica, as you well know, you can't win 'em all. I would like to thank the United States Department of Legal Drugs and the Rose Bowl Committee for taking care of us big-time while we were here. And, really, I mean this Clinton Gold they gave us is really, really good . . . stuff.

The coach took a long drag on his Clinton Gold. He looked pretty mellow:

Veronica: Coach, why do they call this the Grandaddy of Them All? Is there a Grandmomma of Them All? Seems a little sexist to me.

Coach: Veronica, you raise an interesting question. I know there has been a lot of discussion that the champion of the Jesus Is Lord League could not have made it through the Big 20 Conference undefeated, like we did, but hey, that's the way it goes. Football coaches don't make the rules, we just get our boys ready to play. Until we have a playoff system, these arguments will always exist. But hey, that makes more stuff for you reporters to talk about, right? And by the way, Veronica, really sorry about that Top Ten Media Movers and Shakers of the Decade list. Can't believe Steinbach made it and you didn't.

Veronica: Back to you, Bud.

Suzanne informs me that the Israeli Mafia guy's penthouse is well stocked with Clinton Gold. Before I sign off, I would also like to thank the United States Department of Legal Drugs. Peace.

Day 650

I'm sure you are concerned about my safety, so I will fill you in on why we are in Chicago and not continually surrounded by the Mossad security guys. The consensus of all the security experts is that Fairman and the MFM are lying low for now, and the fartwa folks are clueless about where I am. Hannah moved over to Eb's protection team.

Our fancy penthouse is in a well-guarded building. It also has a bunch of electronic security, and there are roaming teams of Mossad agents who keep tabs on Suzanne and me when we leave the penthouse.

The Man of the Decade was in the news again today. Sheik Al Zahrani is spending billions of dollars to clean up the nuclear contamination in Jerusalem. CNN broadcast a report today showing the sheik walking around the ruins of what used to be Jerusalem. There were bulldozers moving dirt and debris. In the background were those big cranes that appear whenever tall buildings are being built. The reporter said that the sheik was rebuilding Jerusalem so people could once again live there.

The reporter, one of those foreign correspondents with a cool English accent, stated:

> *I spoke to the sheik about who would live in the rebuilt Jerusalem. He told me the city would be an Islamic holy city and that Jews and other infidels would not be allowed to live in or visit the city. The sheik also told me that he had watched the American college football championship on television recently and that he was amused by the strange and boorish "Jehovah Kicks Butt!" chant. "I seriously question the efficacy of the American college educational system," he told me. "Have the Americans been paying attention for the last several decades?"*

I know I have said this before, but at some point I need to explain the deal about Senior and the sheik.

Suzanne says we should enjoy Chicago while we are here, so we are going out to visit some cool museums. The Assassin sent me a Kansas City Almonds cap the other day, so that will be my disguise du jour. Be back later when I am more cultured. Smoke 'em!

Day 653

Welcome to day 653 of the I May Be An Accused Mass Murderer But At Least I Am Cultured Tour. Did the museum thing today. Went to the Art Institute of Chicago, the Field Museum, and the Museum of Contemporary Art. Lots of cool paintings and stuff. Two things of note.

First, there was a big protest at the Art Institute. The Art Institute brought in an exhibit of Madonna and Child paintings. Even if you are not a Mary and Jesus fan, still some pretty cool stuff. If you will excuse a non–art guy making an obvious observation, the whole mother-and-child deal is one of those universal connections that transcends time, religion, and culture. OK, I may have ripped off that line from the brochure for the exhibit. But still, pretty amazing stuff.

About the protest. I don't know if you non–art folks know this, but a lot of the old paintings portraying Mary and the baby Jesus show Mary's naked breasts. Some show Mary breastfeeding the baby Jesus.

Apparently some folks don't think this is appropriate. There were over 100 people outside the Art Institute protesting the Madonna and Child exhibit. They had several catchy chants, including "No boobs! No boobs!" and "Cover Mary's Mammaries! Cover Mary's Mammaries!" The most prominent sign read: The Bible Is Not R Rated!

Since I am not all that knowledgeable about the Bible, I asked Suzanne, who can quote practically any verse in the Good Book, what she thought about the controversy. "Anybody who thinks the Bible is not R rated has not read it," she said. "The Bible is racier than practically every soap opera that has ever been on television. Well, except for the porno soap operas, I suppose."

When I asked Suzanne about the whole topless issue, she responded, "As far as the boobs go, I frankly think it's kind of weird that all of those old-timey *men* (she emphasized this word) painted Mary's naked boobs, but I think Christendom will likely survive. I mean, we know she had them and she nursed Jesus with them, so what's the big deal?"

I will go with the Southern Girl's opinion on this, for the record.

The second exhibit I want to mention is the *Rise and Decline of the Credit Card Industry* exhibit at the Field Museum. It is too bad the curator did not check with me before she put the exhibit together, because I could have filled in some facts for her. Instead, dear reader, you get the benefit of my personal knowledge on this scintillating topic.

As the credit card exhibit points out, once upon a time there were more than 200 credit card companies in the world. The credit card industry was one of the most lucrative business sectors in the United States. Indeed, several credit card companies even purchased professional sports teams. The exhibit goes into great detail about the NFL's controversial decision to prohibit Credit Corp., Inc., from renaming the Arizona Cardinals the Arizona Visas.

As I'm sure most of you know, there are only a few credit card companies in the United States now and the Big Daddy credit card company in the land of the free and the home of consumer debt is Apache Credit Card Co., Inc., owned by you-know-who. The exhibit shows some of what Senior did to take over the credit card industry, but I thought you would like to know how it all came about. As they say in the murder mysteries, here is what happened.

Senior had offices all over the world, but his main office was in El Paso. His primary personal secretary was Rose Franks, who was in the El Paso office. Rose handled Senior's extensive travel arrangements and a lot of his personal business. She also supervised Senior's secretaries in all the other offices.

After years of near-perfect service, Rose's work performance suffered a dramatic decline. She screwed up Senior's travel plans on a number of occasions and forgot to pay a bunch of Senior's personal bills. My mom got incredibly upset when Rose forgot to pay the electric bill and the power was shut off at the family home in Dallas. In August. August in Dallas with no air-conditioning is not pleasant. Mom gave Senior an earful about that mistake.

Like I mentioned earlier,[107] Mom was the boss of Senior, so when Mom yelled at Senior, he took action. Which meant, more often than not, that he told me to fix the problem. "Junior," he told me, "your mama's Apache blood is boiling over, and I can't fade that heat. I need you to talk to Rose and figure out what in the world is going on with her. I don't want to fire Rose,

---

107   See Day 490.

because frankly, she knows where all the bodies are buried. Please fix this for me. And hurry!"

So I talked to Rose. Rose's problem was her credit card debt. Rose's elderly mother needed round-the-clock caregivers and although Rose made good money for a secretary, she could not keep up with her mom's medical expenses. So Rose started charging up her credit cards, and when she maxed out those cards, she got new cards and maxed out the limit on the new cards as well. Rose was getting several phone calls a day at the office from collection agencies, and it was driving her to distraction. She was a complete wreck, and her work performance suffered accordingly.

When I told Senior what the problem was, he told me to tell Rose he would personally pay for her mother's care, as consideration for all the good work Rose had done for him over the years. He then continued, "And just get one of our lawyers on staff to negotiate with the credit card companies and reach a compromise on the debt. Pay the debt from my personal bank account, Junior, and tell Rose we can reach an arrangement later on how she can pay it back."

And that would have been that, except none of the credit card companies would waive their late payment fees, their fees for paying only the minimum amount for more than six months in a row, their default fees, their over-the-limit fees, their intercharge fees, their fees for Internet purchases, and their using-your-credit-card-to-pay-for-your-sick-mother's-medical-bills fees. OK, I made that last one up.

When I told Senior about the fees, and how Rose's actual debt paled in comparison to the fees, plus the outrageous 38 percent interest rate Rose was paying, Senior got on the phone and started talking to lawyers and congressmen. He spent a full day on the project and came away totally defeated. "This is unbelievable," he told me. "All this crazy stuff is legal. These credit card companies can do whatever they bloody well please. And the Republican Party has supported these leeches every step of the way. Today, I am embarrassed to be a Republican."

Senior was not used to losing. He said, "Go ahead and pay off all of Rose's debt, Junior. And call up that do-gooder Democratic congressman from Austin and tell him to get to El Paso next week and bring every good idea he has about credit card reform."

The "do-gooder's" name is Sean Flammer, a young flame-throwing liberal from Austin, the only place in Texas that would elect a black, superliberal Democrat to Congress. It took me a long time to convince Flammer that I was on the level, because Senior normally did not give left-wing true believers like Flammer the time of day.

The meeting with Flammer was one for the record books. Senior told Flammer he wanted to change the laws relating to credit card companies and Flammer told him it could not be done. When Senior asked why, Flammer said: "Because of people like you, Mr. Jennings. Rich Republicans like you are so committed to making money that you don't care about the common man. When you want to do something that seems unfair or possibly illegal, like charge a fee that most rational people would consider usurious interest, you simply get your Republican whores in Washington to issue a regulation that makes the fee legal. That insulates the fee from any sort of state law scrutiny. There is absolutely no way anybody, even you, can undo what has happened up there. There's just too much money to be made screwing over normal folks."

Senior, as you might expect, did not take this well. He and Flammer yelled at each other for about forty-five minutes. At one point, Rose even called security because she thought they were having a fistfight. When they had both calmed down a bit, Senior turned to me and smiled. "I like this do-gooder, Junior. The boy has spunk."

I could tell Flammer was about to object to being called a "boy," so I held up my hand in a "he did not mean it that way" gesture, and Flammer, to his credit, did not say anything. I felt sure that, given time for reflection, Flammer would realize that Senior was not any kind of a racist.

Senior then spoke to Flammer. "Sean, could I make money running a do-gooder credit card company that did not charge crazy fees and usurious interest?" When Flammer said, "Certainly," Senior countered, "Ready to put my money where your mouth is?"

And that is how Sean Flammer became the first CEO of Apache Credit Card Co., Inc.

The credit card exhibit prominently features Flammer as the "Father of the Fair Credit Card," which is an accurate designation because Flammer is the guy who created and structured the company from top to bottom. Senior contributed all the money, of course. Senior's only requirement was that the credit card be named Apache Rose.

The other credit card companies did not go quietly. There were a lot of threats and a lot of lobbying, but it did the companies no good. The exhibit goes into great detail about the congressional hearings that took place, so I won't repeat all of that here. My favorite tactic, which the exhibit does not mention, was the federal court lawsuit alleging that Senior's plan not to charge fees and high interest compromised the nation's security and exposed the country to foreign terrorists.

The end result was that the existing credit card companies could not compete with a company that charged no fees and a reasonable interest rate. The death knell for the other credit card companies took place about a year after the Apache Rose was introduced, when Apache offered a balance transfer option. Hundreds of millions of dollars were transferred, and the established credit card companies had no balances on which to levy fees or interest.

Like he did when he took over the telephone industry,[108] Senior made a lot of enemies when the Apache Rose took over the credit card business. The exhibit includes a number of videotaped interviews with credit card executives who lost their jobs, as well as folks who lost money when the stock of the credit card companies tanked. Gary Witt, the founder and CEO of Credit Corp., Inc., was particularly irate:

> *I realize everything happens for a reason, but I don't understand why Mr. Jennings had to stick his nose into our business. When I met him at one of the congressional hearings, he told me it was just not moral to charge people the fees and interest we charged. I told him, straight out: "I am a God-fearing Methodist, Mr. Jennings. You don't even go to church. How can you call me immoral?" Plus, the fees and interest were all legal! How can it be immoral if it's legal? I'm broke now. Had to sell all three of my houses. I hope that someday Mr. Jennings gets his comeuppance.*

---

108   See Day 437.

Hmm. Another Methodist who is angry at Senior. I wonder where Mr. Witt was when everyone was exploded in New Mexico? Another potential suspect? Maybe I should tell Dr. Jaska about this exhibit.

Day 659

Still in Chicago. Cold. Weather people say it's the coldest winter in almost fourteen years, but hey, I am in a cool penthouse most of the time, so I can't complain. Plus, they have really good pizza here.

Watched a few hours of the Addiction Channel today. Pretty depressing. Mesmerized by a story about a successful trial lawyer who got addicted to Extreme Facebook Two and wound up losing his practice and family. He is in his second rehab stint at a Facebook addiction facility.

The Facebook addiction story was sad, but not as disturbing as the texting and iPod addiction story. The segment showed a bunch of teenagers in texting and iPod withdrawal. Their screams were horrific.

On a more positive note, I watched General Dozier on the Victims' Channel give a speech to the Christian American Victims of Islamic Terrorism Convention in Washington, D.C. I know Eb has the general speak to these types of groups because the general has walked the walk and can therefore talk the talk, and because, well, the general is a Christian and not a Jew. After some brief opening generalities, the general quickly got to the point:

> *I am sick and tired of watching Americans being blown up by Islamic terrorists. I can tell you, however, that from a military standpoint it is virtually impossible to stop every Islamic lunatic who wants to harm Americans unless we blow up every country where Islamic folks live.*

The convention exploded in applause and the general quickly held up his hand:

> *Let me finish my thought, people. I am not advocating blowing all of those countries up. We can't do that.*

The crowd became silent again and the general continued:

The only way to stop Islamic terrorists is to take away their funding. Without petrodollars, the terrorists cannot concoct elaborate schemes to blow things up in America. For years, America's problem has been that we need oil, so we don't go after the rich oil sheiks who support the terrorists. Indeed, several decades ago, after the oil embargo that almost bankrupted our country, Congress passed a law known as the Don't Kill the Golden Goose Act. This law prohibits any attempt by American law enforcement agencies or the military to arrest, prosecute, capture or terminate rich Arab oil sheiks who fund and support Islamic terrorists. Because of the Golden Goose Act, vermin like the recently crowned Man of the Decade travel freely across the world and thumb their noses at the greatest democracy in the world. These sheiks know we won't harm them, so they continue to fund and support people who blow up Americans.

Ebenezer Cohen and I are committed, therefore, to repealing the Golden Goose Act if we are elected. Plus, I have spoken to Kevin Davis and Big Fly Washington and they concur with this strategy. Therefore, regardless of who is elected, the Golden Goose Act will be repealed as soon as possible after the inauguration. America will then aggressively pursue Mr. Sheik Man of the Decade and any other rulers, sheiks, prime ministers, and presidents who fund Islamic terrorists.

There will be those who say this strategy is risky because the Golden Gooses of Islam may cut off our oil. Let me just respond by saying that the protection of our citizens and the preservation of our national pride is worth the risk. So to the Sheik Man of the Decade and those like him, fair warning—your life clock is ticking down to zero. I suggest you start looking for a cave in the Afghanistan or Pakistan mountains. I hope your wives and harem girls like it there.

Everyone at the convention roared. Even on television, the noise seemed louder than a jumbo jet taking off. The camera showed people dancing, crying, and hugging each other. The general left the stage to the sound of "USA! USA! USA!"

Wow. Looks like the ball is now in Sheik Al Zahrani's court, now. I like the idea of repealing the Golden Goose Act, but I think it is safe to predict that some stuff will be blowing up soon. I hope the four candidates know what they are doing.

If the sheik and his buds cut off the oil, I'm headed straight to Texas. Don't want to be up here in the winter with no heat.

Day 663

I feel like I'm back in limbo again, but I can't complain. Although I'm now in month twenty-three of my See America As A Criminal Tour, I'm staying in a cool lakefront penthouse with a beautiful Southern Girl who is a good cook, makes good margaritas, and likes to watch sports on TV. All in all, better than a slap in the belly with a wet fish.

Suzanne and I get along really well. To this point, nothing romantic has occurred. I am not sure if that is a good thing or a bad thing. She is a wonderful woman and she has taken care of me with a fierce loyalty that is unexplainable. She keeps telling me that I am special and that I am meant for great things. We'll see.

Hannah and the Mossad guys told me that Eb, General Dozier, Kevin Davis, and Big Fly all just want me to lie low until the election is over. Once the election is over and we know who is in charge, they will help me out with my mass murder, treason, and fartwa problems.

Speaking of the candidates, their cooperation and civility on the campaign trail is causing problems for the usual suspects. Camille Eslick, a lawyer/commentator on the Democrats Are Stupid Channel, opined today that a civil presidential campaign was likely unconstitutional:

The United States Constitution doesn't provide for a pleasant and boring election. This great country of ours was built on conflict. Only libelous vitriol and contentious campaigning will refine the issues and present a clear choice for the American electorate. I am so ashamed of Ebenezer Cohen and General Dozier for not getting down in the gutter and dog cussing their opponents. I can't believe the Republican Party I have come to know and love has sunk this far.

Eslick's counterpart on the Republicans Are Stupid Channel, Timothy Palu, blamed the lack of animosity on the rich Republicans:

This is clearly a rich-versus-poor issue. The Republicans have all the money and don't want to share it with the rest of us. The Republican candidates know that if they preach the "let's all get along" message, the poor and destitute in this country will fail to realize they are being taken advantage of by the multinational corporations that own the Republican Party, and they won't rise up to protest. Kevin Davis and Big Fly need to realize that the only way for the people to fully participate in a presidential election is for the candidates to say mean, false, and hurtful things about their opponents. Otherwise, nobody will pay attention to the election except the people who actually care about or understand the issues. And that would be terrible for this country! In fact, it may actually undermine the nation's security and expose us to terrorist attacks.

In what appears to be a related matter, the Television Network Channel reported today that the Democrats Are Stupid 2 Channel, the Republicans Are Stupid 2 Channel, and the Bad Stuff about the Candidates Channel are now off the air. Simply not enough content to keep the channels going.

Gotta go. Suzanne just hollered and said P. Julius Whitworth sunk a four-pointer, the game between the Seattle Fog and the Chicago Bulls is going into overtime, and I should come watch it with her. She already has the margaritas and chips and queso waiting. Thank you, Jesus. Thank you, Lord.

Day 670

Just finished working out. This cool penthouse has a workout room with an antigravity, oxygen-enriched treadmill. You run on the treadmill but your knees and ankles don't hurt because they don't bear any weight, and your lungs get extra oxygen. The Israeli mafia must make some serious bread for our benefactor to have one of these babies. The room also has a bunch of huge televisions to watch and take your mind off the torture you are subjecting your body to. One of the screens appears to be permanently connected to a porn channel. I had to turn this screen off—I found it difficult to run while watching porn.

Right now I am sitting in the sauna. I was unaware until just this moment that you could rig a sauna so that you could watch television and work on your computer without electrocuting yourself. I just found the Riot Channel. The soccer fans in England are in their fourth day of rioting after the announcement that a sheik has purchased the Arsenal Football Club and will move it to Saudi Arabia to play in the Arab Premier League. There are now only five teams left in the English Premier League. There used to be twenty-five teams. All the rest are now in the Arab Premier League.

The Man of the Decade is the commissioner of the Arab Premier League. He told the Riot Channel reporter:

> *This is really just a dollars-and-cents matter. My cousin was able to buy the Gunners for cash. The team's owners are in a cash crunch. To all of Arsenal's fans in England, the Arab Premier League has a pay-per-view channel that will show tape-delayed games in England. I urge you to consider buying the League Pass Option. It's the best value.*

When the Riot Channel reporter asked the Man of the Decade about General Dozier's Golden Goose speech, the sheik replied:

> *I try very hard not to get involved in American politics, especially since America's policies tend to change on almost a daily basis. I will say, however, that my cousins and I are exploring our potential options with regard to purchasing most of the NFL and NBA teams when America runs out of fuel. It will be very difficult to run these leagues in America without oil. I suspect we will visit again once the riots in America start. Have a pleasant day.*

The Man of the Decade is a cool customer. I expected him to threaten terrorist attacks after General Dozier called him out. The sheik's threat to purchase American pro sports teams is much more subtle, but it will nevertheless strike a note of fear into most Americans.

My skin is starting to prune up here in the sauna. More later.

Day 678

Got a weird e-mail today from Clayton Singletary, my Nazi Lowrider buddy in Afghanistan. The e-mail read:

Junior. Hope you are well. Things are OK here. The government keeps sending us money, drugs, and women, so the boys are happy. We have a disagreement here and there, usually over a woman, but all in all this is a fine place, and certainly better than prison. Since we know that you're the architect of "Are You a Badass?" the boys frequently express their gratitude for your existence. You would not think that Nazi-loving criminals would be grateful folks, but surprisingly they are.

Anyway, the reason I'm sending this missive is that the other day we were attacked by some local yokel guys who thought they were badasses. They were not. We killed all but one and this guy stayed alive only by screaming over and over that he had a message for Junior. He said that the word on the terrorist grapevine is that Sheik Al Zahrani is the guy behind the New Mexico explosion. Apparently the sheik thought Senior was a threat to him and had him killed. Had nothing to do with the president.

The stool pigeon also said there is a prisoner in the Moline Islamic Detention Facility in Illinois who knows more about the New Mexico explosion and is willing to talk to you. I have it on very good authority that nothing worthwhile happens in Moline. Be very careful.

Huh. I guess we can add the sheik to the list of folks who could have blown everybody up. I can tell you Senior really hated the sheik, for a number of reasons. At some point I need to discuss Senior and the sheik.

For now, I think I need to consult with my superagent. I would like to go to Moline and talk to the terrorist. Need to talk to Suzanne to see if and how that can be arranged.

Day 683

The antigravity, oxygen-enriched machine is a great deal. I ran for over an hour today and my knees and ankles don't hurt a bit.

I was a little surprised to see that the huge TV in the workout room that I thought was permanently connected to porn is not permanently connected to porn. My guess is that Suzanne changed the channel when she worked out earlier today.

So instead of porn, the TV was locked into some sort of religious channel lockdown kind of deal. I flipped through the remote and was given a revolving selection of the Salvation Channel, the Grace Channel, the Prayer Channel, the Forgiveness Channel, the Fruits of the Spirit Channel, and the Redemption Channel. No porn in sight. In fact, no pretty women, naked or clothed, anywhere.

I was about to turn the TV off and watch a tape-delayed Arab Premier Soccer League game when I saw a familiar, unpleasant face on the Redemption Channel. It was our old friend, the guy with a face still made for radio, Clarke Steinbach aka Pierre Smoot.

Unfortunately, it appears Pierre has successfully reinvented himself. Instead of a bankrupted former top ten Hate Millionaire, Pierre is now an incredibly rich and successful Christian talk show guy. The interview went something like this:

Interviewer: So, Mr. Steinbach, the last time many of us saw you, you were speaking at a rally in New York City in support of the presidential candidacy of Samson Fairman.

Smoot: My real name is Pierre, so you can call me that. Clarke Steinbach was an alias forced upon me by Satan, the great deceiver. I have given up that false persona.

Interviewer: Well, Pierre, here on the Redemption Channel we focus on stories of second chances and well, redemption. How did you go from being controlled by the devil to being led by the spirit of the Father?

Smoot: It's an amazing story, really. After the whole Samson Fairman and professional sports boycott debacle, I found myself broke and friendless in South Dakota. I was drinking a lot.

Interviewer: Yes, those of us in the Christian entertainment business were aware of your debauchery in South Dakota. We also heard stories of lewd behavior with minors.

Smoot: Well, those stories are untrue, I can promise you. Illicit lies promulgated by the evil one to ensnare me and to prevent me from realizing my God-given potential as a radio host supporting God's people and our country's soldiers.

Interviewer: So what happened, Pierre?

Smoot: Well, believe it or not, I was watching the Rose Bowl National Championship Game Presented by the United States Department of Legal Drugs between Boise State and Second Hilltop Holy Spirit Baptist College. I was rooting for the Fighting Boises, because I had money on them. And when the Fighting Boises missed a chip shot field goal in the third overtime to lose the game, I was enraged. I was throwing stuff, breaking bottles of booze, totally out of control.

Interviewer: Sounds grim, Pierre.

Smoot: I was at the lowest of the low. I felt I had nothing left to live for. I knew that Guido, the big guy who works for my bookie, would come by soon and break my knees because I couldn't pay off the bet. And then, from the television, I heard this amazing sound. It was the sound of thousands of grateful voices cheering "Jehovah Kicks Butt! Jehovah Kicks Butt!"

Interviewer (quickly): A copyrighted cheer of the Jesus Is Lord League.

Smoot: Yes, of course. And the cheer filled me up. It filled my heart and my soul. I felt like I was floating. I looked up and I saw a vision of an *angel. The angel said, "Pierre, you can change. You can be redeemed. Stop being filled with hate. Be filled with Jehovah's love and peace. You can tell others. Go forth!"*

Interviewer: *Wow. What a great story.*

Smoot: *Isn't it? Now I know without a doubt that everything happens for a reason. There was a reason why my radio career failed, I lost all of my money, and I became a drunk. God wanted me to fail so I could turn my life around and make a lot of money as a radio host supporting Him.*

Interviewer: *Amazing. So what did you do?*

Smoot: *Well, I started off slow, with just a one-hour radio show on one small station in South Dakota. I called the show the Jehovah Kicks Butt Radio Hour. I had to change the name, of course, when I got the cease and desist letter from the lawyers representing the Jesus Is Lord League. I did not fully understand at the time the importance of our nation's copyright laws. I tried to change the name to the Jehovah Kicks Bottoms Radio Hour, but the lawyers objected because that still violated the spirit of the JKB copyright.*

Interviewer: *Of course. So what is your program called now?*

Smoot: *After a lot of prayer, and several court-ordered mediations with the Jesus Is Lord League lawyers, I changed the name to the Jehovah Tramples All Radio Hour. The show is now a three-hour show and we are syndicated all over the world. I'm proud to say that I'm now rich again, and that the show broadcasts Jehovah's awesome power and might even in countries controlled by Islamic terrorists. Jehovah is truly great and I can't tell you how happy I am to be rich again. Being poor really sucks.*

Interviewer: *So, another redemption story of success. Pierre Smoot turned his life around and found both redemption and a bigger bank account. Now a message from our sponsor, Salvation Skin Cream.*

Well, that's too bad, isn't it? I guess the upside is that old Pierre is probably not starting his show off with the pithy "Today Is Day 683 of the Junior Should Be Dead By Now Watch." At least I hope not. Enough for today. Maybe tomorrow will be happier.

Day 687

As I'm sure you have realized by now, dear reader, I had a pretty good gig going up until about 687 days ago. Sure, I got tired of being Senior's gofer, and my self-respect was not always the highest, but hey, I was raised in a loving family that was incredibly wealthy. I had no serious needs that were unmet. I had a best friend. I had a financial and emotional safety net. I was never going to starve, freeze in the winter, or die from heatstroke in the summer.

Because my life was hunky-dory, I never worried about the state of the world. I was not upset or frightened when I heard about wars, earthquakes, floods, or revolutions.

In short, I was a self-absorbed, rich, Ugly American. Have I made that point clear enough?

Anyway, today I was reminded again of my selfish Ugly Americanism (I know, probably not a word, Dr. Hoover) when I visited Asid Abdul al-Banna in the Moline Islamic Terrorist Detention Facility. As a quick aside, the "Are You a Badass?" program saved America even more money when we started arresting and convicting a bunch of terrorists, because we did not have to build any new jails for them. We just used a few of the jails that had become empty when the gangs left to be foreign badasses.

Back to Asid. He was born in Khost, Afghanistan, the ninth of twelve children. The public school he attended only went to the fourth grade. Asid joined the Jihad Against American Greed (JAAG) primarily because the organization fed and clothed him. I learned all of this by reading the report on Asid that the Mossad security guy gave me as we drove to Moline.

Asid was sitting alone in a small room when I arrived. He was in shackles. My Mossad bodyguard was sitting outside the room, but he could see us through a large one-way window. I know it makes no sense that a wanted criminal like me could simply walk into a jail and visit with a convicted terrorist, but hey, very little of the last 687 days has made sense, right?

I don't know why (although maybe it's because I am an Ugly American), but I have never given much thought to the regular foot soldier terrorist type. I know who the biggies are (Abu Abu Mohammed Mohammed and Alberto Gonga Mutsapi, for example) because in many ways they seem to possess larger-than-life personalities—kind of like the movie stars who win best actor nominations. The run-of-the-mill terrorists, the guys who generally get blown up, are more like the key grip or the best boy kind of guy—important to the production, but fungible.

Asid is a small, slender man. To describe Asid using American sports stereotypes, he looks like a good glove, no-hit utility infielder, or possibly a high school long-distance runner. He does not look like a superstar.

Let me interject here that there is absolutely nothing wrong with being a key grip or a utility infielder instead of a movie star or a quarterback. And I am not saying that just to be nice. Although Suzanne does her best to make me feel like I am an All-Pro NBA power forward, I'm pretty sure I am just a water boy in the grand scheme of things.

Asid spoke excellent English. We talked for over an hour. Asid said that he was talking to me only because his brother had been captured by very strange men in Afghanistan and Asid was promised that if he cooperated, his brother would not be killed, but would instead be sent to Moline. Asid said he would prefer to die and go to Paradise, but since that was not going to happen anytime soon, he would like to be with his brother.

Here are the highlights of our conversation:

(1) Sheik Al Zahrani planned and funded JAAG's attack five years ago on Trinity Exploration's Rebecca #1 offshore rig in the Gulf of Mexico;
(2) Asid was supposed to die in the attack but the detonator on his bomb pack malfunctioned;
(3) Sheik Al Zahrani planned the attack for a day he believed Senior was going to be on the rig;
(4) The purpose of the attack was not only to kill Senior and destroy the rig, but also to create an environmental disaster in the Gulf; and
(5) Sheik Al Zahrani wanted to kill Senior because he considered Senior to be the biggest threat in the entire world to the success of radical Islamic terrorism.

Asid said that because he has been in jail since the Rebecca #1 attack, he does not know for certain if Sheik Al Zahrani was behind the New Mexico explosion. However, Asid said that it would not surprise him. "All I can say, Joshua," said Asid, "is that the sheik had a severe case of both fear and absolute loathing when it came to your father. The sheik was actually a bit irrational when he talked about your father. This was very unusual, because the sheik was normally very matter-of-fact when it came to discussing and planning attacks. I got the definite impression the sheik would do whatever it took to eliminate your father."

And yes, I found it a bit strange that Asid called me Joshua. Kind of weird that a terrorist is the only person I know who calls me by my real name.

I am now back in the penthouse. Asid is still in jail. Senior is still (I think) dead. And the sheik is still the Man of the Decade.

I have been thinking about this all night and I still don't know what to think, so I am just going to hit the sack. More later.

Day 688

Still in the Windy City. I am excited because I have never before been downtown in a really big city on Ethnic Heroes Day. I never went to downtown Dallas to watch the Ethnic Heroes Day parades because I did not want to fight the traffic. Since I am still in a cool lakefront penthouse here in Chicago, all I have to do to watch the parades is look out the big picture window.

Did you know that Ethnic Heroes Day came about because of Senior? I'm pretty sure you didn't. I realize I'm writing a bunch about stuff Senior did, but he is my dad, after all.

It also just occurred to me that the history major is sort of writing a history book here. In a way, I am providing you, dear reader, with a behind-the-scenes look at certain historical events. That's actually kind of cool. So even if I do end up dead and/or disgraced, I have provided my readers (if I end up having any) with at least a modicum of benefit.

Some of you may remember from your history classes in school that there used to be this big holiday called Martin Luther King Day, to celebrate the life of the great civil rights leader. Then, the federal government created another national holiday, General Deanna Villarreal Day, to celebrate the life of the first Hispanic female five-star general to win the Congressional Medal of Honor.

Soon after General Deanna Villarreal Day was instituted, public pressure was applied to have a "Day" for a specific hero of each of the ethnic minorities in the country. It wasn't long before we had a bunch of these kinds of holidays. When I was a kid I thought this was a great deal, because I got out of school for all of these holidays.

As I have mentioned before, Senior had companies and employees all over the world. Although Senior could be tough on his upper-level managers, he was a great guy to work for if you were a regular working-class Joe who punched a time clock. Senior's employees got great retirement benefits and more time off for vacations than virtually all similarly situated employees working for Senior's competitors.

However, the increasing number of national holidays for ethnic minority heroes eventually drove Senior crazy, because the time off from work hurt Senior's bottom line. The holidays particularly hurt Senior in industries where he competed against companies in foreign countries, because these companies did not have to give their employees time off for all the ethnic hero holidays.

Senior checked with his lawyers, who told him it was against the law not to give his employees time off for the national holidays, and there was absolutely nothing Senior could do about it. "Lawyers are useless most of the time," Senior told me on more than one occasion. "Generally they just tell you what you *can't* do. They rarely think creatively and figure out ways to help you do what you need to do to help your business."

Senior then tried to figure out a way to solve the problem without lawyers. First, he hired a bunch of smart Ivy League economists to prepare a report that quantified how many man-hours were wasted and how much money was lost because of the ethnic hero holidays. The numbers were staggering.

Senior, as only he could do, got an audience with the vice president of the United States and showed him the numbers. The vice president told him: "Senior, I know the numbers look bad, but let's face it—most of the people in this country don't care about those numbers. The people *do* care about celebrating American heroes. Do you realize that each of those ethnic hero holidays was created by an Act of Congress? Do you propose that this president go to Congress and say that he wants to repeal each and every ethnic hero holiday? That would be political suicide. I cannot advise the president to do that."

When the vice president refused to help, Senior came to me and said, "Junior, it is clear to me that rationality will not carry the day on this issue. I need an irrational, nonsensical approach. Got any ideas?"

Yeah, I know that sounds bad, but I took Senior's question as complimentary of my ability to paint outside the numbers. And so Senior and I agreed that if our country's leaders were not ready to accept the truth, we should give them a lie they were predisposed to believe. And so we did. Sit back and enjoy. This is a pretty good story.

Senior used his contacts and his money to hire a first-rate team of accomplices. I can't give you their names because I don't want to get them into trouble. Instead, I will identify them by their occupation or specialty. In no particular order of importance, Senior hired:

(1) a Stanford University Arabic Studies student working on her PhD;
(2) a retired State Department bigwig;
(3) a Hollywood screenplay writer; and
(4) an Islamic terrorist.

I realize hiring an Islamic terrorist sounds a bit unbelievable and is possibly illegal, but this particular terrorist was believed by his compatriots to be dead and he had helped our government on several projects and he was basically retired anyway and . . . well, it's a long story that is not strictly relevant here. If I have time later, I may fill you in on this guy's deal.

Anyway, Senior sent me and these four folks to his ranch outside Marfa, Texas, in the Chihuahuan Desert. There aren't many people in and around Marfa. I think the last census determined that there was less than one person per two square miles in the area.

Senior's primary instruction to Team Marfa, as we called ourselves, was "know your audience." Our audience was President William Carroll, who made a ton of money as a Wall Street business lawyer representing multinational companies before he transitioned into politics. President Carroll was also a devout Baptist who began every day of his presidency with a thirty-minute devotional and prayer meeting with his staff.

Virtually all of President Carroll's cabinet members and close political confidants were also dedicated Christians of one stripe or another. President Carroll's concession to diversity on his staff was that while you had to be a Christian, you did not have to be a Southern Baptist.

So Team Marfa pondered this question: "What semi-irrational and nonsensical theory or idea would convince a corporate lawyer/devout Baptist

president to ask Congress to repeal each and every ethnic hero holiday?"
After much wrangling and gnashing of teeth, the answer was clear: the Minutes of the Board of Directors of the Babylonian Guard.

At that time the Babylonian Guard (BG) was the most powerful and
feared Islamic terrorist group in the world. And one of the supposed reasons
for the BG's success was its organizational structure. According to our retired
State Department bigwig, the U.S. intelligence services believed the BG was
actually structured like a corporation, with officers and directors. The BG did
not call these guys officers and directors, but their role was similar to officers
and directors in a corporation. Team Marfa's Islamic terrorist said that the
U.S. intelligence services were full of warm camel poop, as usual, but that was
OK. As long as everybody that mattered *believed* the BG was structured like
a corporation, that is all we needed.

Some of you probably already know this, but when the board of directors
of a company meets, a record of what they do at the meeting is typed up for
posterity. I know this firsthand because one of my first jobs for Senior when
I graduated from college was to review the board of director minutes for all
of Senior's companies and prepare an executive summary for him to read. A
truly boring job. The minutes themselves were boring to read and summariz-
ing the minutes was even more boring.

Team Marfa decided that the BG's board of directors met once a month
and that we should write up two years' worth of minutes. So, we had to come
up with twenty-four separate sets of minutes. We relied upon our PhD student and Islamic terrorist to actually type up the minutes, since nobody else
on Team Marfa knew Arabic.

Our Hollywood screenwriter suggested we come up with a mission statement for the BG board. The team's Islamic terrorist said no self-respecting terrorist organization had a mission statement, but we all agreed to give it a shot
since President Carroll might be swayed by an incendiary mission statement.
So,[109] the beginning of each set of minutes noted that the Board of Directors of
the Babylonian Guard recited in unison the following mission statement:

*The Babylonian Guard will work ceaselessly, selflessly, and tirelessly,
with the help of Allah, to take over the world by subverting the morals of*

---

109 *Junior* has been criticized by English teachers and literary critics because more than
240 sentences begin with the word "so" or "well."

the infidel Christians, destroying the economies of the infidel Christian countries, and controlling the media in the infidel Christian countries.

The minutes for each meeting contained, among other things, a description of the reports given on each prong of the mission statement: (1) subverting morals, (2) destroying economies, and (3) controlling the media.

From my perspective, the mission statement was the key to drafting the minutes. Once we decided on the mission statement, we were able to structure the minutes around the three prongs of the mission statement. That made the minutes much easier to write.

I realize this entry is getting a bit long, so I will just summarize what we said about the ethnic hero holidays in the BG minutes:

(1) The BG planted information in the media that promoted the proliferation of the holidays, particularly Tunisian Hero Holiday and Algerian Hero Holiday;

(2) The BG, through various political action committees, donated money to politicians to get the ethnic hero holidays passed;

(3) The ethnic hero holidays were crippling the American economy, and various Arab companies were siphoning off business from American companies hamstrung by the holidays;

(4) Illegal drug use, teenage pregnancy, and divorce in the United States had increased since the inception of the holidays, and church attendance in the United States had decreased; and

(5) The BG moved illegal materials and infiltrated suicide bombers into the United States on the ethnic hero holidays because security at the borders and the airports was less vigilant on the holidays.

We also played up the fact that in the last two years, five different terrorist incidents in America took place on an ethnic hero holiday. The BG minutes reflected that the terrorists specifically planned these incidents months in advance for an ethnic hero holiday and that the BG believed America was most vulnerable to attack on an ethnic hero holiday.

Finally, and this was my suggestion, the minutes reflected the BG's opinion that President Carroll's devout Southern Baptist beliefs made him a weak leader who did not have the cojones to repeal the ethnic hero holidays. I don't know what word we used for cojones, or if there is such a word in Arabic. That is just my paraphrase of what the minutes said, if you get my drift. We also threw in a bunch of other stuff that had nothing to do with the ethnic hero holidays, so our target audience would be less likely to smell a rat.

Once the minutes were written, Team Marfa's Islamic terrorist and PhD student worked together to plant them with a radical Arab student group at Cal Berkeley, and the State Department bigwig used his contacts to get the group busted. There was a lot more to it than that, but that is the gist of how we got the minutes into the hands of the administration. I should also point out that our Stanford student, like most Stanford students, hated Cal Berkeley and strongly suggested we dump the minutes there.

It only took two weeks for the administration to react. I don't know for sure why President Carroll did not specifically mention the Minutes of the Babylonian Guard in his nationally televised speech explaining that he would ask Congress to repeal all the ethnic hero holidays for national security reasons and create one Ethnic Heroes Day in which America would celebrate all of its ethnic minority heroes. I have a hunch why, however, based upon the following quotation from his speech:

> *Let me say this to the enemies of our God-fearing country. Don't for a minute think that our devotion to Jehovah almighty is a sign of weakness or frailty. I am ready, as a man and as the president of this great country, to fight and die to preserve the United States of America and the religious freedoms our citizens enjoy.*

My guess is that President Carroll did not publish the Minutes of the Babylonian Guard because it would not have done his political career any good for the nation to know that Islamic terrorists questioned his presidential cojones.

So, dear reader, now you know the real story behind Ethnic Heroes Day. A little "new history" for everyone from the history major. I'm not sure anybody will really care about this, but here it is anyway.[110]

---

110 After *Junior* was published, the revelations of Day 688 sparked a significant controversy. Both the Babylonian Guard and former president Carroll denied the existence of the Minutes of the Babylonian Guard. The three living members of Team Marfa then each published best-selling books about the minutes. Dr. Taylor Chase, a professor of Arabic Studies at Columbia University, included several drafts and the final version of the minutes in an appendix to her book *Gods, Terrorists, and Cojones: Hero Worship in the 21st Century.*

Gotta go. The parade for Cheyenne Indian Heroes is marching by. I want to see if there is a float or one of those big balloons honoring Lame White Man.

Day 690

I realize I have put this topic off a few times, but today I need to discuss the terrorist attack on the Rebecca #1 rig. The attack is all over the news today because it is the five-year anniversary of the crime. CNN is running a clip of some Arab bozos in some bozo Arab country celebrating the anniversary. One of them is carrying a sign that CNN translates as: "Senior is dead now just like his oil well."

And before you say anything, I am *not* going to apologize for calling these guys bozos. I will likely call them much worse before this entry is over.

Before the New Mexico explosion, the day the Rebecca #1 was attacked was easily the worst day of my life. Fifty-five of Senior's employees were killed when a bunch of low-life bozos on a skiff boarded the Rebecca #1 on a Sunday morning when most of the workers were attending a church service on the rig. The bozos had machine guns. When the machine guns ran out of ammo, the bozos blew everything and virtually everybody up.

Remember when I said Senior did not go to church much?[111] Well, for some reason Senior was at church with Mom and the girls that day. I don't remember what the occasion was, but I'm sure the only reason he was there was that Mom made him go. And Mom had an ironclad rule that Senior could not take his cell phone to church.

So yours truly got the call and had to walk into the church building, pull Senior out of the worship service (drawing an evil glare from both my mom and the pastor), and give him the horrible news. And then I watched my dad sit down on the front steps of the Highland Park Community Church, put his face in his hands, and cry. Watching my dad break down like that was the most devastating sight I have ever witnessed, until Day 1 of this diary, when I watched the caskets of my mom and sisters being lowered into the earth.

I need to take a break. Be back in a few.

OK, I'm back. I managed to get Dad away from the church steps before the media arrived, and we took one of his jets to the Louisiana Gulf Coast to see what was left of the Rebecca #1. There wasn't much left, and what was left was on fire. After several fruitless hours of talking to law enforcement

---

111 See Day 446.

and government counterterrorist "experts," Senior and I left the site and then visited the family of each man and woman killed on the rig. Fifty-five houses. Fifty-five grieving families. Fifty-five apologies.

Over the course of the next two weeks or so, Senior and I went to fifty-five funerals. Fifty-five sermons about heaven and God working in mysterious ways. Fifty-five graveyards. Fifty-five burials.

Need another break.

Back again. When we finally got back to El Paso and got our bearings again, Senior told me that he was tired of grieving and wanted "to kick some Arab ass." Senior called a bunch of the people he knew in the government and they, predictably, told Senior to hold his water and let the feds take care of finding and prosecuting the culprits.

Senior, of course, ignored this instruction. He did not, to my knowledge (trial testimony again), participate in hiring or paying folks to blow bozo Arab stuff up. Senior told me, however, that he was going to do something that everybody would hear about, and when they heard it, their ears would vibrate. I now assume he was referring to the oil deal and that the oil deal is still in play, but I don't really know for sure. It is certainly possible that Senior's death also killed the oil deal.

I hope to give you more info on the oil deal as we go along, assuming I live long enough. That's all for today. I need another break.[112]

Day 694

Month twenty-four, and a funny scene on TV today. The Second Hilltop Holy Spirit Baptist College football team went to the White House today for the traditional photo op that the national champs get with the president. Uncle Ken held up a number 2 Second Hilltop football jersey with his name on the back and smiled for the camera. Each member of the football team

---

112   Day 690 is one of the most famous and oft-quoted entries in *Junior*. Numerous scholars have pointed out that Junior's inability to write Day 690 without taking several breaks reflects the pain Junior felt about describing his mother's death twice—once metaphorically when the Rebecca #1 was destroyed, and later when he recalled the events of Day 1. Day 690 is also required reading in many U.S. medical schools and graduate psychology programs as an accurate description of how grief affects the human psyche. After *Junior* was published, "bozos" entered the American lexicon as a term for terrorists.

sported a "Jehovah Kicks Butt!" cap. President Uncle Ken, however, did not have a cap on his head.

The scene was humorous to me because I know how much Uncle Ken hates publicity stuff like that and I could see the "why me?" look in his eyes. What made the spectacle even funnier was the commentary provided by our friend Veronica after the ceremony was over. As I think I mentioned when I wrote about the national championship game earlier, Veronica knows nothing about sports. I don't know why she is providing post-photo-op comments, but she is. Here is what she said:

There was a bit of controversy today at the White House because President Strickland refused to wear the "Jehovah Kicks Butt!" cap provided to him by the Second Hilltop football team, even though the team provided the White House with a copyright violation waiver letter signed by the general counsel for the Jesus Is Lord League. Although the president's press secretary stated that the president prefers not to wear ball caps because they are not "presidential," several members of the Second Hilltop contingent expressed concern that President Strickland was disparaging their religious convictions, and that this was especially troubling given Allah's repeated victories in the God of the Decade contest.

I am reliably informed that the jersey given to the president usually has a number 1 on it. When I asked Dr. David Gloier, the dean of Christian Symbolism at Second Hilltop, about the numbering issue, he told me the following.

A pleasant-faced, gray-haired man of approximately sixty years of age appeared on the screen and spoke:

We gave it a lot of thought, Veronica. We could not give the president a number 1 jersey because, obviously, only God is number 1. And by God, I mean Jehovah, of course. We considered the number 3, but that number obviously refers to the Trinity and the day our Lord and Savior rose from the grave. The number 7 is also a popular number but that is how many days it took Jehovah to create the universe. After much praying and several meetings, we decided the number 2 was appropriate.

Veronica appeared on the screen again. She was smiling and wearing a "Jehovah Kicks Butt!" cap. She continued:

Well, this trip was not a total loss. The Second Hilltop players told me that they were really disappointed I did not make the Top Ten Media Movers and Shakers of the Decade list, so they gave me the cap intended for President Strickland. Back to you, Bud.

Day 699

Something really cool happened today. Cool to me, at least. Clarence Sims telephoned and said that the University of Texas had expressed an interest in working a sponsorship deal for the Man on the Run logo. The Texas Longhorns football team with my logo on their jersey! That is about the coolest thing I have ever heard of. I told Clarence I would have to check with my superagent Suzanne, but that I thought we could probably work out a deal.

When I went to tell Suzanne the good news, she was putting on her coat. I asked her where she was going, and she got real evasive. After I badgered her for a while, she finally said, "Junior, it's Sunday. Up until I met you, I went to church almost every Sunday. I am not blaming you at all. I just miss it. I know you're not a church guy, and I know it seems weird that a girl who supported her lazy drugged-out boyfriend by stripping wants to go to church, but that's just how it is. One of the security guys is going to take me, so it won't be dangerous."

When I told her I would go too, she seemed surprised, but pleased. I think. You can never tell for sure with a Southern Girl.

We wound up in a small church out in one of the suburbs. I have no idea how or why Suzanne chose it. I did not see a big sign out front so I don't even know if it was Baptist, Methodist, or some other Protestant sliver. Anyway, we sang hymns, and Suzanne really seemed to enjoy it. She knew all the words to the songs without even looking at the little songbooks in the pews.

The only semi-uncomfortable part of the service came during the sermon. The congregation has a custom of choosing a pew at random and having the people sitting in that pew read the Scriptures chosen by the preacher for the sermon. And, of course, our row was chosen.

There were five folks in our row. I was sitting on the end, which meant I read the last few verses. The verses were from a book called Isaiah. The only reason I remember that is because I am a big basketball fan and way back in the day there was this great point guard named Isiah Thomas who played for the Indiana Hoosiers and the Detroit Pistons, and he was from Chicago. And we are in Chicago now. Coincidence? At this point in our story, who can tell? Anyway, I digress. Back to the church.

We read the Bible verses from the preacher's Bible. So when I finished reading, I had to take the Bible up to the pulpit and give it to the preacher. I felt like everybody's eyes were glued on me as I walked up the aisle. And I did not have a hat or my man girdle on. I kept waiting for someone to scream: "Call the police—it's Junior the mass murderer!" but nobody did. Instead the preacher commented on how well our row read the verses. I am guessing he does that every week, but he sounded so sincere. I guess preachers need to be able to sound sincere.

After church was over, the Mossad security guy, who was not at all pleased about my walk down the aisle, drove us all over the city to make sure we weren't being followed. I don't think Suzanne even noticed. She spent the whole time reliving the service, like we had just been to a great movie or concert or ball game or something. She clearly had enjoyed herself. And, she kept touching my arm.

This is definitely an interesting development.

One of the security guys just told me that because all of those people at church saw me, we definitely need to leave Chicago tomorrow. I told them that was OK with me, and my vote was that we go someplace warm. Any guesses where we end up next?[113]

---

113   Junior's visit to a church in the Chicago area has never been confirmed. A number of researchers have attempted to locate and identify the church mentioned in Day 699, without success. Some scholars have speculated that the Day 699 Bible Reading Incident, as it is known in the *Junior* literature, was fabricated by Junior to mask his real destination on Day 699. These scholars point out that both vice presidential candidates were in Chicago on Day 699, and therefore contend it is likely that Junior met with one or both of them on this day instead of attending a church service.

Day 704

Our buddy Sheik of the Decade was back in the news today. Said he expects the rebuilt Jerusalem to be ready for occupation in about nine months. We are now in month twenty-four of the I May Be An Accused Mass Murderer But At Least I'm Not A Bozo Sheik Tour. I wonder if I will still be around by month thirty-three?

Today we are in the Show Me State. That means we are in Missouri, for those of you not conversant with state slogans. Suzanne and I are on our own again, although there is some sort of monitoring device on the car that lets the Mossad guys know where we are. We are driving a really boring car. I'm ashamed to even tell you what it is. The Mossad guys said we needed to look normal and driving a boring car like this one would keep us from being recognized.

It's kind of like Suzanne and I are on vacation. The Mossad guys told us that the MFM is in hiding and the feds are busy on higher-priority issues, like trying to keep bozo terrorists from blowing stuff up. So, our job is more or less to keep a low profile and keep moving so we won't be easy to find.

I told Suzanne about how much fun I had driving by tourist sites in Tennessee and imagining what they would be like. Suzanne was polite, but it was clear she thought that was a really stupid way to see a state. Oh well. Guess we will do something different. Frankly, that's OK. I really enjoy hanging out with Suzanne and she will undoubtedly make the trip more fun.

We are currently at a gas station in Elmer, Missouri. I am stopping a lot more for potty breaks in Missouri than I did in Tennessee.

Day 710

Suzanne is one of those people who wants to help everybody. She finds it hard to say no or turn away. The Red Head Vets episode is a good example. As you may recall,[114] Suzanne pretty much shamed me into talking to those guys. And that turned out to be a good experience, I admit.

However, as I mentioned in the previous entry, our orders are to keep a low profile. And talking to strangers would seem to run counter to those orders. I explained that to Suzanne. But, dear reader, if you have been paying attention, you know that Suzanne doesn't always follow my instructions. In

114 See Day 471.

fact, she rarely follows my instructions. And that is why tomorrow the world will know we were, for a few days at least, in Missouri.

The whole thing started out innocently enough. Did you know that the population center of the United States is in Missouri? I know this seems like a bit of a tangent, but hang with me. In looking at our tourist guides, we learned that the population center of the United States is near Cuba, Missouri. Wait, it gets even more boring. According to the United States Census Bureau, the population center of the country is the point at which an imaginary, flat, weightless, and rigid map of the United States would balance perfectly if weights of identical value were placed on it so that each weight represented the location of one person on the date of the census.

Has there ever been a nerdier tourist attraction? Because we were driving an incredibly boring car and trying to maintain a low profile, I thought it would be a good idea to see an incredibly boring tourist attraction. And so we did.

It was getting dark when we left the population center of the United States, so we stopped in an AT&T Budget Motel in Bland, Missouri (keeping with the boring mantra here), for the night. As I checked us in (we had fake ID), Suzanne wandered around the lobby area and found out that the local American Legion was having its monthly meeting. For those of you who don't know, the American Legion is a patriotic veterans' service organization. I know in El Paso the local American Legion post does a lot of good work helping the homeless.

Suzanne, of course, wanted to go into the meeting and thank the veterans for their service to our country. It wasn't easy, but I was able to convince her that since we were supposed to be keeping a low profile, maybe that was not such a good idea.

After we had been in our room for a few minutes, Suzanne announced she needed to go to the store for some "essentials." One of the things I have learned on my See America As A Wanted Criminal Tour is to not ask what that means. So, I gave her the boring car keys to the boring car and sat down in front of the television to see what kind of movies you can download in Bland, Missouri.

I had the movie selection for the evening narrowed down to three when Suzanne arrived, with David "Pig Butt" Bennett in tow. I'm sure, dear reader, that you know who Pig Butt Bennett is, but when he showed up in our room I did not recognize him, and Suzanne had no idea who he was either. Suzanne brought him into our room because she found him sitting outside the motel in a pair of gym shorts and a T-shirt, shivering in the sub-thirty-degree night. Suzanne, as I may have mentioned previously, likes to help people.

After Suzanne explained why she brought this really stinky, barely clothed guy into our room, he looked up at me and said, "What do you want with me, Junior? I never did anything to you. Please don't hurt me, Big Man. I was just looking for the American Legion meeting." And that was the beginning of three very weird days.

I asked the man what his name was, but he could not tell me. He just kept repeating that he wanted to go to the American Legion meeting. The dude was not violent, and he seemed to enjoy being warm, so we just kept him in the room with us. After a few hours, Suzanne convinced him to take a shower and get cleaned up. That helped all of us, because the stink factor was off the table.

On the second day, when he still could not tell us who he was, Suzanne called Hannah and we figured out a way to use an application on the computer to take the guy's fingerprints and send them to the Mossad guys. Within hours, we learned that our visitor was the famous Pig Butt Bennett and that Pig Butt had some posttraumatic stress issues that could be handled with medication. A few hours after that, we had the medicine Pig Butt needed.

On the morning of the third day, Pig Butt was in his right mind again. Suzanne bought him some new clothes and cut his hair, and Pig Butt looked really good. Nothing like the crazy, stinky, half-naked dude that Suzanne had dragged into our room.

It is not often you get to meet a genuine American hero, so we spent the rest of day three in Bland, Missouri, talking to Pig Butt about his life and asking him questions. I could tell he did not like talking about himself, but he was doing so as kind of a payback for our helping him out.

I knew Pig Butt got his nickname in the Army Rangers because he grew up on a pig farm here in Missouri, and of course Suzanne and I (and everybody else in America) knew that Pig Butt won the Congressional Medal of Honor in Portugal III. Pig Butt filled us in on a few more Army Ranger actions but said they were still top secret so we had to keep them under our hat. I agreed to do so, but they are so cool and so dramatic I am tempted to break my promise.

Pig Butt also told us about the dark side of war and how after he left the Army he had a hard time being with other people and spent a lot of time by himself. His wife left him because she could not handle his personal demons, and Pig Butt said he did not blame her in the least. He was not easy to live with.

Pig Butt said he still raised pigs and had a farm in the vicinity. He was not sure how he had gotten off his meds. We told him that we had contacted the military folks in charge of this stuff and they had promised to send someone to check on him once a month.

Pig Butt said that was great, but he would like to repay us by traveling with us and acting as sort of a bodyguard, because he knew there were people looking for us. Suzanne and I thought having a Congressional Medal of Honor winner protect us was a great idea. But when we checked with the Mossad guys, they said Eb thought Pig Butt could help us more by telling people how we had helped him—sort of get out the message that Junior is a good guy so that people would be less likely to believe I was a mass murderer when I came in from the cold after the election.

Suzanne and I talked it over, and although we REALLY wanted a competent bodyguard, we decided to go along with Eb's plan.[115]

Pig Butt also agreed, and Eb's publicity folks set up an interview between Pig Butt and some real important television news personality for tomorrow afternoon, right here in our room in Bland, Missouri.

So, it is time for us to go. We need to be on down the road when Pig Butt gets interviewed tomorrow. Adios.

Day 712

Well, the weather did not cooperate. The big-time news network guy in New York City that was supposed to interview Pig Butt got snowed in. And the last-minute replacement? You guessed it—our old buddy Veronica Wells.

Veronica was in Missouri covering a sex scandal[116] involving the governor of Missouri, the leading scorer on the University of Missouri's women's basketball team, and the head football coach at the University of Missouri, so she was just a hop, skip, and a jump from Bland. And to her credit, Veronica was on her best behavior. She asked very professional questions and actually listened to Pig Butt's answers.

---

115 This agreement is known in the *Junior* literature as the Missouri Compromise.

116 Commonly referred to as the "Show Me, Show You Scandal."

Veronica was also very respectful. I don't know if Eb's guys told her that she better not blow this scoop, or if Veronica was showing respect for Pig Butt's service to our country, but either way, she did a good job. She even threw a batting practice fastball question right into Pig Butt's wheelhouse:

Veronica: Mr. Pig Butt, sir, is there anything else you would like to say to our viewers?

Pig Butt: Yes, thank you Ms. Wells. War is necessary, but war inevitably and invariably scars those of us who survive it. My soul has been irretrievably damaged by war. I hear voices. I am beset by demonic urges. When Junior and Suzanne found me, I was dirty, downtrodden, and possessed by hundreds of personal demons. Junior and Suzanne took care of me, got me the medicine I needed, and restored my soul. If not for Junior and Suzanne, I would probably be dead now.

I have been around many evil men. You can't fight in wars without being around evil men. And I can tell you without a doubt that Junior is not an evil man. He has a good soul. So please, America, give the guy a break. Let him live a normal life. Let him be. Just let him be.

Thanks, Pig Butt.[117]

Day 715

Do you want the good news first or the bad news first? We'll start with the good news—we are no longer driving the really boring car. The bad news? We are no longer driving the really boring car because somebody blew it up.

When Suzanne and I left Bland, Missouri, we decided to keep going south and we wound up in Damascus, Arkansas. You know Damascus, Arkansas, I'm sure. It is just south of Bee Branch, Arkansas, and a few miles northwest of Guy, Arkansas.

We did not intend to wind up in Damascus. As we drove on the road to

---

117   The Bland Interview has consistently been ranked in the top 100 journalistic events of the twenty-first century.

Damascus in our very boring car, this huge thunderstorm hit, with these magnificent flashes of lightning. Neither one of us could see out of the car because the rain was so intense. Plus, it was nearing midnight, so we stopped in Damascus and spent the night.

The next morning we drove into Conway, Arkansas, just in time for Toad Suck Daze, a festival that features, among other things, the World Championship Toad Races. I had never been to a toad race before, and we had no particular place to go, so we hung around and enjoyed the festival. Quick fact—toads are not fast.

I was actually kind of mellow when Suzanne and I left the festival grounds for our car—I had drunk a few beers and was relaxed and not at all concerned that someone may have tracked us from Bland to Conway. Suzanne mentioned she was a little chilly, so I pointed the key fob deal at the car from a distance to start it up and get the heater going—and the boring car exploded.

So much for mellow. I assume the MFM is back in the game again—we know Fairman likes to blow stuff up.

We are in a different car now. Sammy the Assassin is driving us somewhere. He just sort of showed up out of nowhere. Big surprise, huh? More later.[118]

Day 718

We are now in Oklahoma. Remember "Whores for Scores"?[119] I can promise you that virtually every citizen of this fine state does. And I assume the Crankens Sooner Troopers are still running around here somewhere and would be happy to blow up a Jennings male. OK!

Actually I am probably very safe, because we're in the Tulsa Queer City of Refuge. As you probably know, the QCRs were created back when the airborne strain of AIDS was killing a bunch of people and all the gay folks were looking for a place to hide from the vigilantes. The idea for the QCRs did not originate with Senior (the prime minister of Israel, of all people, thought it

---

118   Critics who contend *Junior* is not factually accurate point out that the book never explains how the computer disk containing the book survived what is referred to in the *Junior* literature as the Conway Boring Car Explosion.

119   See Day 585.

up), but Senior worked with the leaders in the gay community and the government to make the idea a reality.

The purpose behind the QCRs was to provide a safe haven for homosexuals during the airborne AIDS pandemic. The feds set up barricades around certain sections of a city for homosexuals to live in and prohibited troublemakers from entering. It was obviously more complicated than that, but that is the gist of it.

Although the cure for AIDS made the QCRs unnecessary, a lot of folks decided they liked living in a QCR. So several QCRs became permanent municipalities, with their own government, police force, etc. The Tulsa QCR grew until it occupied over half of Tulsa, which is why there is a Tulsa QCR, Oklahoma, right next to Tulsa, Oklahoma.

Suzanne and I should be relatively safe in the Tulsa QCR because, as should be obvious by now, the gay community loved my dad. Also, the MFM and most of the other folks who are or may be trying to kill me are notorious homophobes who would not come anywhere near a QCR.

I made that last statement knowing full well you may also consider me a homophobe, since I said early on in this tome that I wanted to make it clear that I'm not gay.[120] As we drove into the Tulsa QCR, I mentioned to the Assassin that I had never been in a QCR before. The Assassin said, "They are actually very nice. I always visit the San Francisco QCR when we play the 49ers. Great restaurants and shopping. I'm seriously considering buying a condo in the SFQCR so I can spend more time there in the off-season." I must have looked a little stunned that a badass NFL linebacker would have a vacation condo in a QCR, because the Assassin looked at me a little crossly and said, "Don't get your panties in a wad, boy. No matter how straight you are, you are still gay to somebody."[121]

The Assassin dropped us off at a small hotel. We checked in like two happy folks on a vacation, although we still used our fake ID. As I write this, Suzanne is calling a restaurant the Assassin recommended to see if we can get a reservation. More later.

---

120 See Day 31.

121 This statement is the sixth of the Seven Conundrums in *Junior*. It is known as the "Straight Is Still Gay Conundrum."

Day 722

Welcome to month twenty-five of the I'm Still Not Gay But Right Now I'm Living In A QCR Tour.

It's kind of weird here. People smile and nod at us as we walk down the street. They act like they know us. I can't decide if people here are just really friendly, or if they know I'm a wanted mass murderer and they are by their smiles implying that they know who I am but I don't need to worry because they are not going to turn me in. (I realize that was a real ugly sentence, Dr. Hoover, but I think I will just leave it like that.)

The Assassin called today to see how we were. I told him we were good. And I would have told him we were good even if we were living in a rat-infested tenement and eating week-old cat food. Don't want a reprise of the panties-in-a-wad episode. The Assassin is kind of scary when he gets angry.

The Assassin said the word on the intelligence street is that the bad guys don't know where I am—everyone assumes I am still hiding somewhere in Arkansas. In fact, the Assassin said he has paid a few guys to go to Arkansas and pretend they are Junior fartwa hunters. These fake fartwa fanatics have been interviewed by several Arkansas television stations and they are telling anyone who will listen that they believe Junior and Suzanne are in Arkansas.

The Assassin also told me that I should meet with Dickie Marsh, a petroleum engineer who has worked in Trinity Exploration's Tulsa office for as long as I can remember. The Assassin said Dickie would call me soon to set up a time and place to meet.

"Try to enjoy yourself, Junior," the Assassin told me. "Everybody is working to keep the bad guys away and we all think you should be safe in the QCR. There is plenty of stuff to do there. Restaurants, movies, Broadway shows. In fact, the World Cup starts this week and lasts for a month. Watch a bunch of soccer on television. You could do worse. Like get blown up." The Assassin then laughed his "I'm a badass NFL linebacker and you're not" laugh and hung up the phone.

Day 727

Dickie Marsh is a pretty old guy (probably between fifty-five and sixty) who has been with my dad from virtually the beginning of Trinity Exploration.

Although Dickie is a salaried employee, I know he has personally invested in some of Senior's drilling prospects and has come away a millionaire several times over. Dickie likes to ride his Harley, tell dirty jokes, and laugh a lot. He is loud and profane, and he had enough credibility with Senior that he could get into shouting matches with Senior and not get fired.

I don't know Dickie all that well because he worked in Tulsa and I rarely had any interaction with the Tulsa office. So we spent the first few minutes of our meeting today in an awkward social dance as Dickie did his best to tell me how sorry he was about Senior and I tried to express appropriate thanks.

Finally, Dickie took a huge swig of his beer and got to the point. "Junior," he said, "I know you were involved in the oil deal in the beginning, but have you been able to keep up with it since the New Mexico explosion?"

I told Dickie that I had not. "Well," he continued, "it appears to be working. I have been monitoring the progress of the oil deal very closely and it appears to be on schedule. Before Senior . . . died, he told me that if anything happened to him, I should report to you about the oil deal. I have followed your travels in the news, but it wasn't until the Assassin told me you were in the Tulsa QCR that I felt comfortable checking in with you."

"Thanks," I told him. "I'm not sure what I'm supposed to do with that information, but maybe it will become clearer to me as this whole thing plays out."

Dickie took another swig, grimaced, and continued. "Need to tell you something else, Junior."

When he paused, I interrupted: "He knew, didn't he? Senior knew he was going to be blown up."

Dickie massaged his forehead like he had a headache and said, "I can't be absolutely sure, Junior, but I think so. As you know, the primary Trinity folks on the oil deal were Johnny Soul, Rebecca Milner, Herman Tyler, and me. We met with Senior once a week without fail and we were supposed to meet with Senior at the reservation the day after the rally. Anyway, Senior called me a few days before the meeting and said that under no circumstances were any of us to come to the reservation. And that's when he told me to report to you if something happened to him. He also made me promise that if the oil deal worked, you would get the credit. I have thought a lot about that conversation over the last couple of years. I could be wrong, but it seems to me that if the oil deal works, and you get the credit, there won't be many people who will want to see you arrested. Most folks will want to give you a medal."

"Dickie," I asked, "did Senior give you any indication who was going to kill him?"

Dickie finished his beer with one big swallow, softly belched, and said, "No, but it's pretty freakin' clear, isn't it?"

"Yes, it is," I replied.

Day 730

Kind of in a routine now. I get up in the morning and Suzanne and I work out together and have a nice breakfast. We then go "do something," like visit a museum or some other touristy thing. Suzanne then either (1) goes shopping, (2) goes to the spa for a massage, manicure, or some other such thing, (3) does her superagent duties, or (4) does some combination of 1–3. While Suzanne is doing 1–4, I either take a nap or go downstairs to the hotel bar and watch the World Cup on the huge television hanging above the bar.

Quick note on Senior and soccer—he hated it. Thought it was a boring game played by "little bitty guys who would be playing flute in the marching band during halftime if they lived in Texas."

I know I have told you a bunch of Senior success stories, but you probably don't know that Senior tried, and failed, to keep America from becoming a soccer power. After one of America's many World Cup disasters, there was a big push by ESPN, which owned the television rights to the World Cup, to encourage America's best athletes to take up the sport. The television network threw a ton of money at the initiative, including millions of dollars for college soccer athletic scholarships.

Behind the scenes, Senior threw every roadblock he could think of in front of ESPN's soccer push, but even Senior was not strong enough to beat the Worldwide Leader. "You just watch," Senior told me when it was clear that ESPN was going to have its way, "the Longhorns are going to lose some really good defensive backs because of those Connecticut Yankees."

Senior, as usual, was right on the money. The USA beat England today, 5–0. Quandre Ramonce Dunn, a former high school all-state cornerback from Port Arthur, Texas, who turned down a full ride to play football at the University of Texas to instead join the USA soccer development team, scored all five goals in the first half. The USA team spent the second half of the game passing the ball around and playing keep-away from the Brits.

Today, as is the case most every day, I was the only guy in the bar watching the soccer games. I don't know if that is because most folks are at work or because people who live in or visit the Tulsa QCR don't care for soccer (we are still in Oklahoma, after all, where real football is king). Anyway, since I am the only guy here on a consistent basis, the bartender and I have struck up a friendship. His name is Zack. After a few days of dancing around the topic, I just admitted who I was. He hasn't killed me or turned me in yet, although maybe it's because I am such a good tipper.

Zack, like a lot of bartenders, is a good listener. Since it is generally just me and him at the bar, he also talks a lot to me. Zack has been in trouble with the law a bunch. He grew up in a gang in Los Angeles and spent several years in jail. In a weird twist of small worldism, Zack says that when I stayed in one of the secure areas in Afghanistan I met his brother. Zack is a small guy, shorter even than me, but he looks lethal. I would not want to meet him in a dark alley.

Zack says he thought seriously about joining his brother in Afghanistan, but that would mean he would never see his mother or sister again, and he did not want to live like that. Zack's brother had a bunch of money saved up from his criminal deeds, so he gave Zack the money to move his mom and sister out of L.A. Zack says he chose Tulsa because they have some cousins here.

As I was settling my tab today after the soccer games were over, Zack said, "Tell you the truth, Junior, Tulsa is boring as dirt, and the Tulsa QCR is even worse. Most jobs I can, you know, at least flirt with the chicks. Flirting with girls in the QCR, of course, is just a waste of time. But for me, at least right now, boring is good. I need to just lie low and stay out of trouble for a while." I told him we were in the same boat, at least on the lying low part, and that I would probably see him tomorrow.

Back in the room now. Suzanne left me a note saying she was getting a seaweed aloe artichoke mud facial. Sounds disgusting. Think I will take a nap. Over and out from the TQCR.

Day 735

Today was a good day. Suzanne surprised me on our morning outing. She told me that we were going to a museum about the American West, but instead we wound up at an eye hospital. The Tulsa QCR, it turns out, is where a bunch of well-known eye surgeons and specialists who also happen to be gay decided to live. These guys (and gals) created this really advanced high-tech hospital to help people with vision problems. And these guys really like me because Suzanne sent the hospital a bunch of my endorsement money.

A couple of the doctors actually cried when they met me. One of them said, "You know, Junior, most folks can't afford what we do here. Generally speaking, we can only serve the very wealthy. But Suzanne gave us several grants and told us to use the money on surgery and treatment for middle- to low-income families. Because of you, there are people who were blind who now can see. This is so amazing! You changed these people's lives forever. Thank you so much for your generosity. You are a special man."

The doctor then gave me what I anticipated would be a real awkward hug, but instead turned out to be a very nice moment. I have never had a grown man cry on my shoulder before. The man's tears of joy were so genuine that I teared up a bit myself. Then I hugged Suzanne and thanked her for picking this place to send some of the money to.

When we returned to the hotel, we received more good news. According to CNN, the most recent polls show that Eb has drawn into a virtual tie with Dr. Davis. If the election were held today, the winner would likely win with no more than 51 percent of the vote. Although I think Dr. Davis would make a fine president, I'm glad Eb has a fighting chance at victory. I don't think Eb will win, because Senior does not want him to win, but I'm proud of Eb for making the race close.

Suzanne just called me from her room. Says we need to leave soon to make it to the Asian fusion Cajun seafood restaurant that is getting great reviews. I may need to start working out twice a day. Eating at all of these great restaurants is fun, but fattening. More later.

Day 738

Did you know that Tulsa, Oklahoma, hosts one of the biggest gun shows in the world? Me neither. Knowing that there are thousands of gun nuts (and I say that with love) just a few miles away salivating over thousands of guns does not make me feel very safe. You would think Junior fartwa hunters would be first in line at one of the biggest gun shows in the world.

I learned about the gun show because I got a call from the Assassin this morning. The Assassin said that the Hammer would be in Tulsa to sign autographs at the gun show and he wanted to drop by the TQCR to say hey. Although I am not sure that is such a great idea, because the Hammer sticks out like, well, like a 525-pound white guy with a shaved head and a neck the size of a truck tire, I can't refuse to meet the Hammer. Don't get me wrong, I like the Hammer. I'm just a little worried that he will attract Junior fartwa hunters and other undesirables.

Headed down to the bar to see the Hammer now. Will report back later.

I'm back. It was good to see the Hammer. The Hammer said that he was also a little nervous hanging around all those guns, but that the gun show paid him a bunch of money to sign autographs and be nice to the customers. I asked the Hammer if he had ever been to the Tulsa QCR before and he said, "No, but I like the Boston QCR a whole lot. They have some great seafood and Italian restaurants there. I almost always go to the BQCR and eat a few good meals when we go up there to play the Patriots."

Remembering my conversation with the Assassin on the subject of NFL players and QCRs, I tried to nod and keep my face neutral. Didn't work. The Hammer smiled and said, "Junior, I can tell you are surprised, and to tell you the truth, I avoided the QCRs for years because the gay boys just made me nervous. But good food is good food, you know what I mean?"

It was hard to argue with that logic. While we were eating our dinner, the Hammer got to his reason for coming to see me. "Junior," he said, "I've been asked to deliver a message to you. The message is that the prime minister of Israel up in New Jew Dakota is dying of some disease. I am not supposed to tell you who gave me this message. Sorry."

I frankly did not know what to say. We both sat in silence for a few minutes. I was very sad, because the prime minister is a good guy. And I was more than a little curious as to who gave the Hammer the information and why the source of this bad news had to remain anonymous.

Eventually the waiter came and we had to order, so we moved on to other topics. We discussed football, the World Cup, and the worldwide manhunt for me. The Hammer then asked if I was still traveling with "that pretty 'Bama girl." When I said I was, the Hammer replied, "That's good, Junior. It is not good to be by yourself. Two are better than one. I know I really hate it when I beat the left tackle a few times in the game and then the other team double teams me with the left guard or the tight end. It's a lot harder to beat two people."

Given the way my life has worked for the past 738 days, I have been pondering the Hammer's unsolicited advice for the last thirty minutes or so. Is someone trying to tell me something here?

Day 739

The Hammer's news about the prime minister still has me bummed. I don't have many people on my side, and it looks like one of them will be gone soon. That really sucks.

I just reread the previous paragraph. That was pretty selfish, huh? Let me try that again.

The Hammer's news about the prime minister still has me bummed. The prime minister is a really good guy who risked his personal safety and his reputation to help me. I will always be grateful to him for that. He has a really hard job as prime minister and I'm sure dealing with me did not make it any easier. I hope he is not in any pain.

I suppose that's a little better, anyway. I have tried to get in touch with Hannah and Jehu to talk about the prime minister, but they have not returned my calls, e-mails, texts, etc.

Suzanne suggested I go down to the bar and watch the USA–Brazil World Cup match. I don't think she even follows soccer, so I'm not sure where she got the idea. She said maybe watching the match would take my mind off the prime minister for a few hours.

I have decided to take Suzanne's advice. I have also decided to bring the computer with me and see where this entry goes.

OK. Down in the bar now. Zack the bartender asked if I was OK. Said I seemed a little down. Could not tell him about the prime minister, so I just said I was not having a particularly good day. Zack did not press it any further. He gave me a Queer City Lager, turned up the sound on the TV, and went to find me some snacks.

The announcer for the soccer match is saying that Team USA is so good that its reserves could easily beat every other team in the tournament, with the possible exceptions of Brazil and Saudi Arabia. Saudi Arabia, according to the announcer, has significantly improved its team over the past two decades by offering millions of dollars to the best soccer players in South

America, Africa, and Europe to convince them to become naturalized Saudi citizens and play for the Saudi national team. The financial package basically insures that the players will be set financially for life, as will their children, grandchildren, and great-grandchildren. And that is why the players on the Saudi team have names like Schneider, Torrez, Eto, and Dokic.

Zack's back. Brought me some peanuts and some chocolate-covered pretzels. Zack says he has missed me the last few days. Says it's not as much fun to cheer on the dear old US of A by himself.

Quandre Ramonce Dunn just scored. The crowd is alternately chanting "USA!" and "QRD!" When QRD got the ball in front of Brazil's net, three Brazilian defenders converged on him. QRD faked one of the defenders out of his jockstrap (wonder how you say jockstrap in Portuguese?). The other two Brazilian players (smaller guys Senior might have referred to as flute players) bounced off QRD like bullets off Superman. USA 1, Brazil 0.

For those of you who are not soccer fans, you should know that there are no time-outs in soccer. The clock is always running, which means no commercials until halftime. Since commercials are crucial to the Worldwide Leader's balance sheet, small print advertisements periodically appear in one corner of the television screen, and there is almost always a running script at the bottom of the television screen. The script at the bottom of the screen currently reads: "The deadline for entries in the Jerusalem Homesite Lottery expires in two days. Submit your entry now. Jews and other infidels need not apply."

QRD just headed in a corner kick. A Brazilian hung on each of his arms, but QRD was still able to elevate and get his noggin on the ball. USA 2, Brazil 0.

Zack says he has watched almost all the World Cup matches. Says the Saudi Arabian team is really good. Says the Sheik of the Decade has promised to buy each player on the Saudi team either a private jet or a luxury yacht if the team wins the championship. The player gets to choose.

The Brazilian who lost his jockstrap earlier just walked up and kicked QRD in the groin. QRD seems unfazed. The Brazilian is given a red card and kicked out of the game. He walks off the pitch shaking his head and talking to himself as the fans boo. The camera pans the crowd. Even the green-clad Brazilian fans are booing.

Zack tells me that QRD's mother really wanted him to attend UT on a football scholarship so he could get a college education. She refused to allow her son to join the USA soccer development team unless the United States Soccer

Association guaranteed that QRD would receive a college degree. So the USSA arranged for QRD to be enrolled at Georgetown University in Washington, D.C., since the Georgetown campus is close to where the players on the development team live and practice. When QRD went on the road for matches, he had personal tutors travel with him so he could keep up with his schoolwork.

QRD just served up a nice high pass to Eugene "Tree" Nettles, who headed it into Brazil's goal. Tree is a six-foot-eight-inch leaper from Oakland, California, who was an all-American power forward in high school. The young man broke Duke's heart when he turned down a basketball scholarship to join the soccer development team. Tree has serious hops.

When QRD sent the pass into the box, Tree and two five-foot-eight-inch Brazilian defenders jumped. Guess who won? The announcer repeated the appropriate cliché for the situation: "You can't coach height, Bud." USA 3, Brazil 0. Halftime.

Zack and I are visiting. He is cheering me up a bit, telling some pretty funny jokes. He just invited Suzanne and me over to his place to watch the USA–Saudi Arabia final. Says he asked for the day off for two reasons. First, so he can watch the game. Second, because the hotel is hosting a big-time dog show of some sort. Says the dog owners are lousy tippers and only want to talk about pet grooming and breeding—topics he does not know or care much about. Told Zack I would check with Suzanne, but it sounded like a good idea as long as there weren't a bunch of people there, given my infamous face and fartwa status. Zack says just family and a few friends will be there and they would all be cool about the wanted for mass murder and treason thing.

Game is over now. I did not provide a running commentary of the second half because it was simply not very interesting. QRD did not play in the second half because the USA coaches were concerned the Brazilians would try to hurt him. Final score: USA 6, Brazil 1. Brazil's goal, which came in the eighty-eighth minute, was the first goal Team USA has surrendered in the entire tournament.

QRD is being interviewed by one of those semi-snotty English soccer "experts," who just asked QRD about the rumor that the Sheik of the Decade has offered him a multimillion-dollar contract, a yacht AND a private jet AND his own personal oil well to play for the Saudi team in the next World Cup. QRD gives an interesting answer, which I will do my best to replicate even though I am not a fast typist:

I realize I should be polite about this offer, but to be honest, it is offensive to my sensibilities as a black man, a Christian, and an American. Sheik Al Zahrani believes I am an infidel—so why would I want to help him win a soccer game at any price? It's interesting to me that the sheik considers himself better than the rest of us merely because he was born in a country that has significant petroleum deposits. The sheik did absolutely nothing to gain his wealth—it was all given to him. In my book, that does not make the sheik a successful man that we should idolize or look up to. I will not sell myself to a man who, to quote one of my favorite lines from my 20th-Century History class at Georgetown, "was born on third and thinks he hit a triple."

The limey was silent, clearly confused by the baseball reference, so QRD continued:

In addition, I have been following the American presidential election and it appears to me that the sheik's arrogant reign of terror may be coming to an end in the very near future. I applaud the candidates' announcement that the Golden Goose law will be repealed.

Finally, let me say that I love my country. My country has given me opportunities that someone like me would never have had in Saudi Arabia. My goal is to win the World Cup for my country. I look forward to beating the sheik's ringers in the final. Then I will go back to my country, America the beautiful, and finish my doctoral dissertation. Thank you, and have a nice day.

With that, QRD flashed the University of Texas "hook 'em horns" sign, said, "Hi Mom!" and walked off the pitch.

That guy would have been hell on wheels on the cornerback blitz.

Day 740

Still alive. Still hanging out in a QCR with a beautiful, Bible-quoting waitress/stripper/superagent. Still, I assume, under a fartwa. Still grateful.

No World Cup matches today, so I decided to take a nap. Suzanne woke me up from a really nice dream. "Your computer's beeping," she said.

I figured it was a message from Hannah about the prime minister, but when I turned the computer on my father's face appeared. "Took you long enough," I muttered to myself as I hit the play button.

My father's always-exuberant voice filled the room:

Hello, son. Sorry it's been so long since our last communication. If you are listening, it means things are still going according to my plan, at least for the most part. It was difficult for me to plan for every contingency and I had to factor in that you would be faced with hard choices and decisions that I could not account for.

For example, I knew you would not like being on your own, so I assume you are still with Pete. If Pete is not around for some reason, my guess is that you are with a strong, smart, beautiful woman.

I looked at Suzanne, who smiled and blushed. The disembodied voice continued:

Anyway, Junior, thanks for hanging in there. I believe we are nearing the latter stages of all this. I can't tell you exactly when your mission will be accomplished, but you are closer to the end than the beginning, I promise.

I wish I could say you are no longer in danger, but I can't. You need to really be on your toes for the next few months. There are people out there who want to do you harm. Pay particular attention to the Muslims, Junior. They are vicious and fearless and at some point they will come after you, if they haven't already.

Also, please do me a favor. Please go see the prime minister before he passes. Tell him he did a great job and I really appreciate all of his assistance.

How about QRD? Would have made a stud cornerback for the Horns. Would have brought absolute mayhem on the cornerback blitz.

Love you, boy. You are a great son.

The screen went blank. I looked at Suzanne, who was vigorously crossing herself. "Hey," I said, "I thought only the Catholics did that crossing thing. You aren't a Catholic. You are a born and raised white trash Alabama Protestant."

Suzanne looked at me with wide eyes. Not Southern Girl wide eyes, but scared out of your mind wide eyes. She sputtered, "I just did not know what else to do, Junior. I'm pretty freaked out right now."

A number of flippant comebacks bounced around in my brain, but I managed to keep them there. I just held Suzanne while she cried. And thought about fearless Islamic terrorists.

Day 752

Today I relaxed and hung out in the hotel. The *Burger King New York Times Book Supplement* came today and it contained a section on what it called "Junior Books."

Just as an aside, before I get to the supplement, let me say that I think Burger King has done a great job with the paper. I remember when the *New York Times* was about to fold and there was a big public debate about what to do with the paper. A lot of folks laughed when Burger King bought the paper, but my guess is that McDonald's and Taco Bell are kicking themselves about now. The paper has been a huge financial and critical success and Burger King's Whopper sales have gone through the roof. Every time the *BKNY Times* breaks a story, the television announcer says: "According to the *Burger King New York Times* . . ." and everybody who hears that thinks, somewhere deep in the carnivorous section of their brain: "WHOPPER!"

Actually, a Whopper sounds pretty good about now. Anyway, back to the supplement. The supplement identifies four "Junior books": (1) *The Confessions of Peter Running Horse*; (2) *The Story of Mandy: Life on the Run with Junior*; (3) *The Veronica Wells Story*; and (4) *The Junior Myth*.

Pete's *Confessions* focuses primarily on our torrid love affair. The reviewer called it a "quixotic journey into the miasma of the criminal gay syndrome." If I knew what that meant, I would probably be angry. I remember when, seems like years ago now, I was peeved because the Gay and Lesbian Network reported I was gay and Pete thought it was funny.[122] Well, Pete, buddy, how do YOU like it? Miasma, indeed. Miss you, man. And I DO love you. You know that.

---

122 See Day 31.

The most amazing book is *The Story of Mandy*, since, of course, she does not even exist. The book is described as a "whimsical journey of love, eroticism, and danger." If you were to read *Confessions* and *Mandy* back-to-back you would think I am the greatest lover of all time, because *Mandy* is mostly about hot sex while the feds or MFM are outside shooting at us. At least *Mandy* portrays me as a vigorous and studly lover, so the book is not a total loss.

I would question whether Veronica's book could even be called a "Junior Book" since the book is about, as you would expect, Veronica. The plot is similar to the screenplay Veronica gave me earlier. The reviewer says that Veronica "discovered" me, whatever that means, and that "if not for Veronica, Junior would never have exploded onto the national stage." I don't know if the reviewer's "explosion" reference is an attempt at a pun or not.

The Junior Myth posits that I don't even exist—that I am a figment of everyone's imagination. The reviewer described the book as a "crushing critique of the Junior phenomenon, based upon a detailed and scathing analysis of the frankly unbelievable events surrounding the purported son of Joshua Jennings, Senior." If they only knew the half of it.

Hannah finally called me and we talked about the prime minister. She was really upset. Said she had taken leave from guarding Eb to watch over the prime minister. I found that curious, but I did not comment.[123]

Hannah said she called because the prime minister wanted to see me in the next couple of weeks. Said the Mossad guys are working on a plan to make that happen. Said she would be back soon with details.

Suzanne just yelled that we need to leave or we will be late for the revival of *Oklahoma!* which is opening tonight in one of the fancy big theaters here in the TQCR. Since I am just a boy who can't say no when a pretty girl tells me to do something, I need to end this entry. Later.

Day 764

Welcome, a few days late, to month twenty-six of the All Hell Has Broken Loose And I Am No Longer Just Relaxing And Lying Low In A QCR Tour. It has been twelve days since my last entry. So much has happened, it's hard to know where to begin. I will try to hit the highlights and add stuff that maybe you have not read or heard about in the media.

---

123   This entry is cited, along with Day 320 (*see* footnote 68) by scholars who contend that Hannah was the prime minister's daughter.

Things started to go seriously south the night of the World Cup Final. Suzanne did not want to go to Zack's house to watch the match. First, she said she really wanted to stay and watch the dog show. I told her I would not miss the World Cup Final for a dog show. Then she got to her real reason.

"Junior," she said, "this is such a bad idea. Nothing good can happen by being Zack's guests at the party tonight. Who knows what kind of person Zack is? You don't know anything about Zack other than that he is a little man who talks to you and serves you drinks during soccer games." I don't know why Suzanne made such a big deal about Zack being short. I refrained from mentioning that Zack also gave me tasty snacks, because Suzanne was really upset.

In a rare moment for me, I withstood Suzanne's arguments. I told her Zack had made a big deal about the invitation, I had told Zach I was going to his house today, and I did not want to go back on my word. I told her she did not have to go if she did not want to. Thank Painted Woman[124] she decided to go with me.

Then the cabdriver got lost on the way to Zack's house. Zack told me that he lived on Sycamore Street. When I told the cabdriver we wanted to go to Sycamore Street, Suzanne muttered, "Naturally." I still don't know why she reacted that way and I was too afraid to ask at the time. Anyway, there are three different Sycamore Streets in Tulsa. Don't ask me why. By the time we arrived, the party was in full swing. You could smell the Clinton Gold from the street as we left the cab.

Suzanne tried to talk me out of attending the party even as we walked from the cab to the house. "You don't know these people, Junior. This is not a good idea."

When we arrived at the house, everybody was in a good mood because it was halftime and Team USA was already ahead 3–0. QRD had scored two goals and assisted on the third. The most amazing aspect of the game, according to the television analysts, was the total dominance on defense by the USA. The Saudi offensive players (Brazilian-and Spanish-born nationals), who were magicians with the ball, found it very difficult to penetrate the USA defense, and on the few occasions they did, the USA goalie stuffed their shots. The USA goalie is Johnboy Camp, a six-foot-four, five-tool baseball

---

124 Painted Woman is a goddess worshipped by the Chiricahua Apache.

prospect from Texarkana, Texas, who turned down a huge contract offer from the Boston Red Sox to play soccer for his country.

We spent the rest of the game enjoying ourselves and cheering on the team. The game was never in doubt, so Suzanne (who had loosened up a bit) and I spent time visiting with Zack and Zack's family and paid less attention to the game as it played to its conclusion.

When the other partiers started shouting "USA!" and "QRD!" over and over again, I went back over to the TV to watch the last few minutes of the game. The score was 7–1 and QRD was being taken out of the game to thunderous applause.

Then everything got crazy. Remember when I mentioned earlier that the Worldwide Leader ran a script at the bottom of the screen for advertisers?[125] Well, as the crowd at the stadium and the partiers at Zack's house on Sycamore Street screamed "USA!" and "QRD!" over and over, the following appeared at the bottom of the screen:

Al Jazeera reports that Junior Jennings has been killed in a hotel explosion in the Tulsa, Oklahoma, Queer City of Refuge. The Jihad Against American Greed has claimed responsibility for the attack, making the following statement: "The infidel Joshua Jennings, Jr., has now joined his infidel father in hell. Allah Akbar!"

In a bizarre confluence of images, the script ran over and over at the bottom of the screen, just below the images of the celebrating USA team. It looked like the players were celebrating my untimely demise.

The cheering in Zack's house stopped and everybody, Suzanne included, looked at me as if to confirm I was still among the living. Then, as one, everyone reached for their cell phones. Somehow, Suzanne and I had both left our phones at the hotel. I pleaded with everyone NOT to let the world know I was there. I explained that although they had a cool scoop, if they told the world our little secret, the next explosion would likely be right here in this house.

The partygoers stared at me for about thirty seconds, trying to decide what to do. Then, everybody's cell phone began to ring. I heard snatches

---

125   See Day 739.

of rap songs, rock-and-roll songs, gospel songs, various animal noises, and other mechanical ring tones as the partiers held their phones in their hands and looked at me. Finally, one of the young men looked at his phone, then at me, and said, "It's my momma. She's probably wondering if I was in the explosion. I've got to tell her I'm all right. Sorry, man." As he took his call, all the other partiers did the same.

For some reason, I looked at the television again. QRD was being interviewed, but someone had muted the sound. The script at the bottom of the screen now read:

> *CNN reports that Joshua Jennings, Jr., has been killed in a terrorist explosion in the Tulsa, Oklahoma, Queer City of Refuge, along with his waitress/stripper traveling companion. The Methodist Free Militia has claimed responsibility for the explosion and released the following statement: "The criminal Joshua Jennings, Jr., was executed today in the Tulsa Queer City of Refuge, a shameful modern-day Sodom. The criminal was a friend of perverts. The fartwa is satisfied."*

I looked at Zack at that point and told him that Suzanne and I needed to get out of Dodge and that he should tell his guests to go home immediately. Zack agreed.

At that point I should have borrowed Zack's phone to call or text somebody like Hannah or the Assassin, but I was just too freaked out to think straight. Zack fully understood that he was in danger if I stayed around, so he loaned me his car and Suzanne and I drove out of the Tulsa QCR.

We wound up on I-44, which is the first big road I saw, and headed west. Suzanne was crying, and frankly, I could not think of anything to make her feel better, so I just drove. I concentrated on keeping Zack's car on the road and under the speed limit. We stopped in Bethany, Oklahoma, near Oklahoma City, for gas. At that point, Suzanne had calmed down a bit. We talked and mutually decided that we should buy a cell phone and let someone know we were not blown up. Since Suzanne was known by the world primarily as my "waitress/stripper traveling companion," we decided it would be safest if she bought the phone.

The Assassin and the Mossad guys were relieved when they heard from us. Hannah set us up in a small motel in Bethany where nobody asked questions, and we waited for another Mossad guy to drive the pony car up from Florida, where it has been sitting since we left Florida for Aspen. Hannah was insistent that I needed to drive the pony out of Bethany. I still don't know why. I hope Zack gets his car back.

Amazingly, the world still thinks that Suzanne and I are dead. I say "amazingly," because I was sure the folks at Zack's party would eventually let the word slip that we were at Zack's and not blown up. So to the folks at Zack's, thanks a bunch.

Although the original news reports focused on Suzanne and me, the emphasis quickly shifted once it became known that all 300 dogs staying at the hotel for the dog show were blown up, as well as forty gay seniors from a Tulsa QCR assisted-living center who were having dinner in the hotel's restaurant. The day after the explosion, the Dogs Are People Too Channel debuted a four-hour documentary that described the life and times of each dog killed, complete with both still pictures and video of each animal, and interviews with the pet's owners, or if the owners were also killed in the explosion, interviews with relatives of the owners. The documentary ran twenty-four hours a day for a week.

Three days after the explosion, the senior senator from Oklahoma held a tearful press conference at the bomb site and declared that she would introduce legislation, retroactive to a date before the explosion, making the killing of more than fifteen show dogs a federal crime punishable by a mandatory prison sentence of no less than twenty years. The senator said she would call the bill "Alfie's Law," after a bluetick coonhound killed in the blast. "The loss of these fine animals," she said, "is an affront to everything that is good and decent in this country. This will not stand."

Five days after the explosion, the United States attorney in Oklahoma City indicted Samson Fairman and the Methodist Free Militia for hate crimes under federal law, since both gays and seniors qualified for hate crime protection. She said that the normal penalties would be doubled, because the hate crimes statute had a "twofer" provision that applied in this situation. She also said she was still trying to determine if any of the victims was a member of a racial minority. Although the hate crimes statute did not contain a "threefer" clause, the United States attorney was certain that one could be implied from the legislative history.

For some reason, the United States attorney did not indict Fairman for killing Suzanne and me. Must have been an oversight.

Seven days after the explosion, the American Association for Retired Persons and the Gay American Association for Retired Persons announced that they would pay a $5 million reward for the capture of the Sheik of the Decade, "dead or alive." Nick Bessett, a crusty veteran of two of the Vietnam wars and the president of the AARP, gave an interview on the Senior Channel in which he stated: "Those towelheads should know better than to mess with American seniors. We can still kick ass."

Yesterday, all 102 senators sponsored a bill that would immediately repeal the Golden Goose Act.

I realize that this is becoming sort of a useless tradition, but once again, let me sincerely apologize for getting people killed. I had no idea this was going to happen. The experts told me we were safe in the TQCR.[126]

When we got the pony car, I drove it south out of Bethany into Texas, which is where we still are. Although I'm glad to be in Texas, and glad to have the pony car back, I feel really guilty about the victims of the Tulsa QCR explosion. Be back later.

Day 768

My latest "death" has spawned a God controversy. The MFM broadcast a press conference yesterday in which three hooded men explained the details of how the MFM tracked me to the Tulsa QCR and planted the explosives that killed me. One of the hooded men stated:

We are confident that we killed the criminal Joshua Jennings, Jr. We are even more confident that Jehovah, the true God of the only righteous believers, guided us on this important mission and gave us steady hands and determined hearts to do our duty. Those lousy Arabs

126 Scholars have debated whether Junior intentionally did not apologize for getting the show dogs killed, or if the failure to mention the dogs was just an oversight.

did not kill Junior Jennings. The Arabs are liars and their god is not a real god.

Fairman did not appear to be one of the three hooded men. Fairman has not said a word publicly since the explosion.

The Jihad Against American Greed responded today with a similar press conference on Al Jazeera. The JAAG had four hooded men instead of three. The leader spoke in English that was clearer and easier to understand than the MFM spokesman's. He gave a professional-looking PowerPoint presentation that provided pictures and video of how the explosions were set and detonated.

The spokesman then concluded:

> *We think it is humorous that American Methodists have claimed credit for the assassination. Methodists have absolutely no track record of successful violence, whereas the followers of Allah, praise be to his name, have a rich history of random and brutal murders. It is obvious that once our attack on the infidel Jennings succeeded, the Methodists simply piggybacked on our success and tried to claim credit. We have compared the timing of our announcement that the infidel Jennings was dead with the Methodists' announcement. There is no doubt that our announcement came before the Methodists'.*
>
> *Plus, the idea that Jehovah somehow assisted in the explosion is ludicrous. Jehovah, if he even exists, is a small, insignificant god compared to the mighty Allah, praise be to his magnificent name. To paraphrase Sheik Zahrani, have you Americans been paying attention for the last three decades? What has Jehovah done for you lately?*

Pierre Smoot weighed in from South Dakota to show his support of the MFM:

> *I think it is laughable that there is even a dispute over whether the followers of Jehovah are capable of extreme and cruel violence. Has anybody out there read the Old Testament lately? What about the Crusades? Come on, people! Show your pride in Jehovah! Jehovah Tramples All!*

My favorite pro-Jehovah response came from none other than Buckwheat Trimble, the coach of the college football national champion Second Hilltop Holy Spirit Baptist College Crusaders:

> *Was Allah asleep during that World Cup final? On vacation? Taking a leak? Did the Arab terrorists notice how that game turned out? I'm not a soccer expert, but I believe a 7–1 score in soccer is considered an old-fashioned butt whipping. And what about QRD? Boy could have been a force on the cornerback blitz.*

I wonder what the pro-Jehovahs and pro-Allahs will say when they learn that their gods let them down and the infidel/criminal is still alive and eating really good Mexican food in Austin, Texas? Let's don't tell them yet.

Day 770

Still in Austin. Still dead, as far as most of the world is concerned. Still eating good Mexican food.

We have a new entry in the "Who killed Junior?" contest. Remember when I mentioned that one of the top-ranked criminals in the Criminal Fantasy League was the QCR Killer?[127] Well, it turns out HE killed me.

CNN released a video today of a man sitting in a chair. He is holding a dog in his lap. The man's face is blacked out, and his voice is altered by one of those mechanical contraptions that makes him sound like an alien robot in one of those movies from the 1960s.

"You can call me the Patriot Avenger," he began. The dog, which appeared to be some sort of poodle mix, barked at the mention of the name and interrupted the voice. The Patriot Avenger paused and then continued:

> *For years now I have been trying to weed out the weak sisters in this great country of ours. I have traveled from QCR to QCR, a man on an important mission, eliminating the dress-wearing boys whose very existence threatens our nation. Am I the only one to notice that when*

127 See Day 253.

we decided to protect these deviants with special laws like "hate crime" legislation, and when we decided to give them their own freaking cities for goodness' sakes, that our country has gone downhill and the camel jockeys have taken over?

As a quick aside, let me also say that I would prefer to be called the Patriot Avenger (he paused while the dog barked again) in the World Criminal Fantasy League standings, instead of the QCR Killer. I understand why I was given the QCRK moniker, but now that I have identified myself I would prefer to be known by my correct pseudonym.

Anyway, back to the issue at hand. I killed Junior and his smoking-hot girlfriend. I tried to work it out to where the stripper/waitress/girlfriend was not around when the explosion happened but stuff happens, know what I mean?

Let me say that I had no particular ax to grind with Junior, although I was a little peeved that he was ahead of me in the final fantasy league standings last season. I killed Junior primarily because I just happened to come across him in the Tulsa QCR when I was planning to kill someone else there. I figured I could use the fartwa money.

I think it's funny that the Methodists and the camel jockeys are arguing over whose god killed Junior. Clearly, there is no god. Has anybody been paying attention to the world lately? If there was a god, would the world suck as much as it does? Wake up, people!

I'm not surprised that the camel jockeys claimed responsibility, since they can't move their lips without lying, but I'm disappointed in the Methodists. It is clear to me that the Methodists claimed responsibility so they would not have to pay me my fartwa reward. I am consulting with my attorney to determine the appropriate legal action to pursue against the Methodists.

I'm also sending proof of my work in the Tulsa QCR to the WCFL for verification. I would ask the WCFL to send it on to the various media outlets so that my claim of responsibility can be verified.

Let me add that I'm also claiming responsibility for the forty old gays. That should be worth a lot of points. I am pretty sure a bunch of them were racial minorities, so I claim "threefer" credit.

Finally, I did not kill the dogs. My explosives were aimed solely at humans. The camel jockeys, who are very indiscriminate when it comes to blowing stuff up, must have killed the dogs. The Patriot Avenger (dog barks) loves animals and would never harm them.

Suzanne says there is a message for me on the other computer[128] so I guess I'll quit for now. I hope the WCFL docks the Patriot Avenger big-time when I resurface alive and well. Actually, I hope he is arrested and convicted for killing people in the QCRs. Maybe put him in a cell with Big Rico.

Day 772

I'm sure it is no surprise to you, dear reader, that the message I mentioned in the last entry was from you-know-who. Because of that message, I am now headed south to Baja, Texas.

Thought I would give you an update on the presidential election. One of the weird things about this election is that the candidates are not seeking endorsements from the usual suspects, and that is ticking the usual suspects off.

For example, none of the candidates accepted the invitations of the following groups to attend their convention and beg for an endorsement:

(1) American Chamber of Commerce
(2) National Education Association
(3) Veterans of Foreign Wars
(4) NAACP
(5) American Business Council
(6) International Association of Fire Fighters

The candidates' failure to curry favor has caused a big problem for these organizations, which plan their national conventions with platform demands and candidate prostration in mind. According to CNN, these organizations

---

128 The *Junior* literature is replete with articles on the number of computers Junior used, the capabilities of these computers, and where and how Junior obtained the computers. See *Supernatural Computing: An Existential Analysis of Junior's Hardware*, by Sarah Amanda Butler.

have had to scramble for substitute entertainment, which has been a boon for second-tier musical and magic acts.

The CNN report had numerous quotes from the head honchos of these organizations, the gist of which was: "We can't believe the way the candidates are treating us. We could help these guys win the election if only they would make us a few promises. What has happened to the presidential elections we have come to know and love?"

In response to the CNN story, the candidates issued the following JOINT statement:

> *All four of us believe it is counterproductive and unseemly for men who are campaigning to lead the most powerful country in the world to crawl on bended knee to special-interest groups of any stripe or persuasion. We are open to everyone's ideas, but we will be beholden to no one. We intend to lead this country by doing what is best for the entire country, not certain groups of people who believe their interests are more important than everybody else's. Thank you for your consideration and don't forget to vote.*

Wow. Way to go guys! I wonder if Senior had all of this in mind when he arranged this entire mess. Probably.

Suzanne and I are taking a leisurely drive down to Baja, pursuant to our instructions. Not in a big hurry. I am once again waiting for my passenger to return from a restroom break. We are in the pony car.

Since everybody assumes we are dead, we are less concerned about being seen, but I am nonetheless wearing a cap. The cap of the day is El Mercado Manuel Jorge Guerra's Taco Shack. Just writing that sentence makes me hungry. Need to sign off and find a taco stand.

Day 775

As Suzanne and I drive around Texas, I see a bunch of oil wells and refineries and other oil-and gas-related stuff and it reminded me of the oil deal, so I thought I would tell you a little bit more about it.

After the attack on the Rebecca #1, Senior called in Wally Douglass and Frank Scott, his go-to lawyers in Houston who I wrote about earlier.[129] Wally and Frank, unlike most lawyers, are incredibly creative and the three men tossed ideas back and forth until they settled on a plan they called "The East Texas Solution." The runner-up plans were called "The High-Perf Scenario" and "The White Oil Subterfuge." If I have time I will give you more details on the meeting and what was discussed.

Senior then brought in his best Trinity Exploration people from around the globe and everybody (including Frank and Wally) stayed in a conference room for five days straight, leaving only for trips to the bathroom and to the hotel across the street from the Trinity El Paso office for sleep. Dickie Marsh, Rebecca Milner, Johnny Soul, and Herman Tyler are Trinity's best people when it comes to petroleum geology, petroleum engineering, oil and gas production, oil pipelines, oil storage, computer programming and modeling, and anything else related to getting the stuff out of the ground and getting it to market, and they all provided ideas on how to implement the East Texas Solution. As I have mentioned earlier,[130] the really rich guy with the really big boat and General Dozier were also consulted.

I wish I could say I played an important role in the planning of the East Texas Solution, but I did not. I mostly just got everybody coffee and took orders for the food that was brought into the conference room. I did sit in on all the meetings, however, and I can tell you I have never seen Senior so focused.

Senior's only real complaint with the East Texas Solution was that it would take at least five years to properly implement. I remember when Senior left the room for a bathroom break during one of the long sessions with Wally and Frank, Wally leaned over to me and said, "Junior, your daddy really has the red ass for these Arab guys, but something like this just takes time. I don't know if Senior has the patience for this. We both know from experience that patience is not one of Senior's better things."

---

129 See Day 140.
130 See Days 164, 395.

Which, of course, was true. But here we are, five years later, and it appears that the East Texas Solution is on the verge of successful completion, at least according to Dickie Marsh. Hold on to your hats.[131]

Day 779

Stopped for lunch today in Laredo, Texas. After some really good Mexican food (have you noticed a pattern to my food consumption, dear reader, since I have been in the Lone Star State?), Suzanne and I saw a sign for the World's Only Exorcism Museum. It is not often that you get to see the "world's only" anything. Plus, exorcisms must be important, since there are by my count at least 300 movies about exorcisms.[132]

I really wanted to stop at the museum, but Suzanne had no interest. "That kind of stuff creeps me out, Junior," she said. "Even though I think most of that stuff is either Hollywood make-believe or Catholic hoodoo, I do believe the devil exists and I am not all that interested in looking for him, even in a museum."

I managed not to comment on the "Catholic hoodoo" reference, although I was certainly tempted to remind her about her Catholic crossing reaction back in the QCR.[133] But try as I might, I could not get her to go into the building with me. So I put on my dark sunglasses and my Palestine High School Wildcats cap and made a solo visit to the exhibit. Luckily I was just in time for a tour, so I joined a group of about fifteen other souls interested in exorcism.

---

131   Day 775 is the subject of some debate. Some scholars see Day 775 as being in conflict with Day 690, in which Junior does not appear to have a great deal of knowledge about Senior's plan of revenge against the perpetrators of the Rebecca #1 attack. Most scholars, however, view Day 775 as simply an elaboration and amplification of Day 690 and note that Junior was clearly upset when he wrote Day 690 (the "need a break" language), which could explain the failure to include a more complete version of events relating to the creation of the East Texas Solution.

132   *Junior* has been criticized in some quarters because when the book was written there were only 228 English-language exorcism movies. Most scholars, however, consider the 300 number an approximation. Three years after *Junior* was written, the number of English-language exorcism movies in existence stood at 325.

133   See Day 740.

Our tour guide was Former Father (FF) Michael Farley, the owner of the museum. FF Farley, it turns out, was one of the priests who lost his job when the Vatican took Senior's advice and "let the nuns run the show."[134] The Catholic Church had sued all the former priests who used the FF designation for copyright and trademark violations, but the court threw out the lawsuit, finding that the church had not properly copyrighted either the word "former" or the word "father."

In his introductory remarks to the tour group, FF Farley noted that "everything happens for a reason" and that his termination from the priesthood when the nuns took over was obviously God's way of steering him to create this museum.

FF Farley began his tour with a little history on exorcism. First, we saw an exhibit showing Jesus "casting out demons," with excerpts from the Bible explaining what Jesus did. FF Farley then gave a detailed description of the practice of exorcism in the Catholic Church and virtually every other religion. He even showed us copies of exorcism PowerPoint presentations created by the Catholics and the Lutherans and other religions that their priests followed in conducting exorcisms.

After seeing pictures and testimonials regarding several of the more famous exorcisms, including the exorcisms of Anneliese Michel, Robbie Mannheim, and Ellen DeGeneres, FF Farley showed us pictures and videos of exorcisms that HE had conducted in South Texas over the past few years. FF Farley then explained that he had formed a for-profit deliverance ministry, Texas Demon Exterminators, that had successfully conducted hundreds of exorcisms in the greater Laredo area.

"Make no mistake about it," FF Farley opined. "The devil is real, he is powerful, and he is living among us today. Anybody who disagrees with me on this issue has simply not been paying attention lately. Could the world be in such a mess if the devil was not interceding on a daily basis?

"Consider, for example, Junior Jennings. The man blows up the president and then he completely avoids capture for this terrible crime, even though the entire United States government is looking for him! Only the devil is powerful enough to accomplish this. Yes, the devil is definitely helping Junior Jennings."

I was about to say something, but fortunately a little old woman walking with a cane spoke up. "But Former Father Farley, the camel jockeys killed

Junior the other day. I heard about it on the television. Are the camel jockeys more powerful than the devil?"

"Trust me on this," FF Farley replied. "Junior is not dead. He is still among us, traveling throughout this great Christian nation, doing his best to destroy our faith and our values. I can't explain how I know this. I just sense his presence, his very evil presence." FF Farley then looked at me, or at least I think he did. Maybe I was just a little nervous by that point.

FF Farley then gave each of us one of his Texas Demon Exterminators business cards and said that if we came across friends or relatives who were exhibiting signs of demon possession, to give him a call. He said that his service was particularly helpful in resolving unhappy marital situations and in assisting parents with troubled teens.

When I got back to the pony car I related all of this to Suzanne. To her credit, Suzanne did not say, "I told you so," although I am pretty sure the Southern Girl expression that she hit me with perfectly conveyed that sentiment.

I'm going to go out on a limb here and say that the devil, if he exists, is not helping me. I think Senior is in charge here, and since he is my dad and I have known him all my life, my considered conclusion is that Senior is not the devil.

Plus, if the devil does exist, the opinion of this wanted criminal on the lam is that the devil is too busy creating and perpetuating wars, plagues, New York banker–induced financial crises, and reality television shows to worry about my measly existence. And no offense intended, dear reader, but I have my doubts about whether the devil is all that concerned about the events of your day, either.[135]

So watch out for your neighborhood deliverance ministry. Peace.

Day 782

Welcome to month twenty-seven of the They Still Think I'm Dead But I'm Not Tour. The Methodists and the Muslims are at it again. The dispute over who blew me up in the Tulsa QCR has escalated. The MFM released a cartoon showing a pudgy, big-nosed Muhammad holding a checklist entitled "Blowing Stuff Up To-Do List" on which the phrase "innocent show dogs"

---

135   This paragraph is known as the Satanic Corollary to the Day 248 Theory of Unimportance.

was checked. The sheik's boys retaliated with a crude drawing showing Jesus riding on a donkey with the question "What Would Jesus Do Without Allah's Oil?" written beneath it. When these guys find out I'm alive (which is inevitable, I'm afraid) I may have to find another bunker to hide in. The "who killed Junior?" debate has escalated into the latest round of the "whose God is best?" contest.

Pursuant (I really love this word) to our instructions in the message from you-know-who, Suzanne and I are still driving around South Texas before we eventually make it down to Baja, Texas. Today we drove northwest from Laredo to the area near Eagle Pass, Texas, which is located on what used to be the border of Texas and Mexico.

I'm sure, dear reader, that you have heard of the Eagle Pass Massacre, but until you come here and see the 1,713 "graves of craving" just north of town, it is hard to fully appreciate this tragedy. The whole evil stupidity of it all just hits you in the face like a brick.

Remember when I mentioned earlier that I was meeting with Mexican bank presidents, Mexican drug lords, and Mexican generals when Senior's cell phone went dead and he had to buy a phone by himself?[136] Well, both Senior and I had a bunch of meetings with these guys, and others, in an attempt to figure out a way to save Mexico from imploding. Obviously, we were not successful.

Senior was one of the first guys to realize that the Mexican banking system would likely collapse if his plan to legalize certain drugs in America became a reality. Because of his connections in the American banking community, Senior knew that the largest Mexican banks were little more than money-laundering operations for the Mexican drug gangs and that once the drug money dried up, the banks would fail.

Senior and I explained our concerns to the Mexican bank presidents, generals, and drug lords, but they either didn't care or they didn't believe that Senior could get the legislation passed. We tried to set up a meeting with the president of Mexico, but he refused to see us. I'm pretty sure, however, that the drug lord we met with who was also the Mexican president's cousin reported the substance of our meetings to the Mexican president.

---

136   See Day 437.

Senior, never one to miss a business opportunity, decided that if the Mexicans would not listen to him, he would make some money off the situation. The major Mexican banks were desperately in search of additional funds, so Senior put together a consortium of Texas lenders to assist the Mexican banks in maintaining their liquidity. The catch was that the banks had to put up a ton of reserves as collateral for the loans, and the collateral had to be put in a bank that Senior owned in El Paso.

Sorry. I started off talking about the evil stupidity of the Eagle Pass Massacre and veered off to the banking issue. More on the banking deal later.

What you may not know about the Eagle Pass Massacre is that Senior and I worked very hard to try and prevent it. In addition to the banking issue, Senior and I also talked for hours to the generals, drug dealers, and bankers about the anger that Americans (particularly Texans) felt regarding the violence on the border caused by the drug trade. People were being brutally murdered virtually every day on both sides of the border in drug-related crimes. Texans living on the border were armed to the teeth and jumpy. We explained that the Texans on the border were not afraid to take chances and would eventually retaliate, and it would get ugly.

Senior even offered some creative financial incentives to the generals and the drug dealers if the drug dealers would move their operations further south. Looking back, it was probably illegal for Senior to do this, but he was determined to do whatever he could to prevent more loss of life on the border.

The generals seemed to understand this issue, and were certainly amenable to financial inducements, but the drug dealers were running the show and they could not have cared less. The drug dealers basically said that Americans were chickens and that if any Texans bent on revenge crossed the border they would be carved up and returned to Texas in trash bags. I have to say that the Mexican drug dealers I dealt with were not very nice people. They were not only poopheads, they were very mean and scary poopheads. I was not sorry to see them go down hard.

So the people in charge in Mexico (i.e., drug lords, generals, and bankers) were caught off guard when a group of South Texas ranchers crossed the border at Eagle Pass and killed ten members of a Mexican drug gang in retaliation for the drive-by shooting of the Eagle Pass High School homecoming queen during the homecoming parade. The ranchers shot the gang members in broad daylight in the town square of Piedras Negras, then strolled back across the bridge into Eagle Pass.

The people in charge in Mexico were caught even more off guard by the American reaction to the killing of the gang members. The Mexican government filed a protest with Washington, which was ignored. The United States secretary of state opined that violent retribution was not the policy of the current administration, but that the federal government would not intervene in what was essentially a Texas state criminal law matter. The Texas attorney general declared that the alleged crime fell within the ambit of federal criminal law, and so she was powerless to intervene. In other words: ". . . and the horse you rode in on, Mexico."

Then we all held our breath and waited. Senior and I called our Mexican contacts repeatedly to try and prevent more bloodshed, but they refused to take our calls.

When the reprisal came, it surprised all of us. The Piedras Negras drug gang, instead of attacking the heavily protected Anglo citizens of Eagle Pass, decided to murder the unarmed Hispanic residents of a poorly constructed *colonia* just north of Eagle Pass. The gang members attacked at midnight, using machine guns, machetes, and hand grenades. The cowards killed everyone, women and children included.

Senior felt guilty about the massacre, even though he did absolutely nothing to cause it and worked very hard to prevent it. He purchased land and created a cemetery for the graves of all the victims. Senior also paid for tombstones and funerals for every person that was killed.

The tombstones are called the "graves of craving" because of an entry found in the diary of Carolina Mendoza, one of the victims of the massacre. Ms. Mendoza, a nineteen-year-old young woman who worked as a maid, wrote: "This life is not easy, but I came here because I crave peace and safety. I am tired of the violence and oppression in Mexico. I crave happiness and a chance to work hard. I crave security. I crave a better life. Thank you, God, for giving me a chance to come to America. I really love it here and I believe things are going to work out for me."

Suzanne and I sat in the pony car this evening on a small hill overlooking the cemetery. The "graves of craving" are well maintained, thanks to Senior's money. The grass is green, which is not an easy feat in South Texas. Flowers are everywhere.

After I told Suzanne the backstory that I just provided to you, dear reader, she took my hand and looked me square in the eyes. It was not a Southern Girl look. At least I don't think it was.

"Junior," she said, "this is not your fault. You and your dad did everything you could. These graves are a testament to the power of evil. Your father, even with all his power and influence, was unable to prevent this tragedy. Sometimes, the bad guys win. Sometimes the bad guys even beat Senior. That's just the way it is."

I confess I have never thought about the Eagle Pass Massacre in those terms. I guess she is right—the bad guys beat Senior and me and as a result a bunch of innocent people were killed. I have lost many times in my life, but it is hard to admit Senior could lose to a bunch of poophead drug gangbangers.

I tried to put a positive spin on the whole thing, telling Suzanne that EVENTUALLY the good guys won because the drug dealers were wiped out when the Mexican drug trade died. Suzanne pointed to the cemetery and succinctly put the kibosh on that argument: "Eventually did not help Carolina much, Junior."

Ouch.

Assuming I am on the good guys' team, I am cautiously optimistic that the good guys will EVENTUALLY win whatever contest is currently in play. From a selfish perspective, however, I am a little concerned about when exactly that victory will occur and whether I will be around to enjoy it, or whether I will be like Carolina. That's it for tonight. Adios from Eagle Pass.

Day 786

Stuff is starting to happen. The bozos blew up a church in Birmingham, Alabama, in which Big Fly Washington was scheduled to speak. Nobody was hurt, because Big Fly's schedule was changed at the last minute and the service was canceled. Apparently the bombs were set on a timer to explode when Big Fly was making his speech.

Two bozos were arrested in a Miami hotel room located across the street from an Eb Cohen fund-raiser. Both had rifles.

Even more interesting, thirty bozos were killed when they unsuccessfully tried to blow up oil wells in Yemen and Oman. Why is that more interesting? Let's save that for later. Can't give everything away yet.

The bottom line is that the bozos are starting to push and take chances. I predict things are going to get hairier and scarier before they get better. If they get better.

Still waiting on the signal from you-know-who that we should cross over into Baja, Texas. Still eating lots of good Mexican food, although I have been supplementing the Tex Mex with a bunch of barbecue. I love Texas, but it is not good for my waistline. More later.

Day 790

I have risen from the dead again, thanks to Former Father Farley. FF Farley gave a press conference today in Houston. He was wearing a cap that read "Texas Demon Exterminators," along with a phone number and website address. Sitting next to FF Farley was our old friend Veronica Wells. Naturally, Veronica began the press conference with a self-aggrandizing opening statement:

> *I have never believed Junior was killed in the Tulsa QCR show dog massacre. Consequently, I have continued to diligently investigate this important issue. When Triple F called me, I immediately came to Texas to review his information, and sure enough, I have uncovered another in my long line of Junior scoops. And for those of you who enjoyed my recent best seller The Veronica Wells Story, good news! I am currently working on a sequel that will include a detailed account of my work on this latest blockbuster event. And now let me introduce you to Former Father Michael Farley, or as I have come to know him, Triple F. Take it away, Triple.*

FF Farley looked like he had died and gone to heaven. He was clearly enjoying the attention, even though he appeared a bit overwhelmed. FF Farley swallowed a few times and then spoke:

I used to be a Catholic priest. As you know, there are no more Catholic priests in America. For several years after being let go by the Church, I struggled for direction and purpose, although let me quickly add that the rumors of drunken binges and eating disorders are completely untrue, or at least severely overblown.

Anyway, when I was at my lowest point, God saved me by leading me to the devil. Everywhere I turned, I saw evil, sin, and hopelessness. God opened my eyes to all the suffering and depravity in the world and showed me that the devil is a powerful force on earth and that I should focus my energies on defeating the devil. God showed me that the devil lives in all of us and has control over the vast majority of us. God called me to help Him defeat the devil.

So, I started Texas Demon Exterminators . . .

FF Farley took off his cap and showed it to the camera.

. . . and began conducting exorcisms in the greater Laredo area. This deliverance ministry became modestly successful, which allowed me, with God's help and direction, to establish the World's Only Exorcism Museum in Laredo. God also called me to have security cameras installed around the museum to protect the exhibits and to assist in business development for the deliverance ministry.

Anyway, about ten days ago I was giving a group tour in the museum and I sensed a powerful source of evil in the group. I should point out that my evil sensor is highly developed and I can sense evil in virtually everyone and in any situation and context. For example, I sense a very strong presence of evil in the group assembled here today.

The camera panned to Veronica, who frowned slightly. Triple F continued:

Anyway, after the tour concluded, I could not shake my sense that the devil had a personal representative in the tour group. So I reviewed the tapes from the security cameras and saw a man who, although he had on a cap and dark glasses, was chubby enough that he could have been Junior Jennings. Let me state for the record that I never thought Junior was killed in the show dog massacre because I believe Junior is filled with the devil's spirit and is receiving direct assistance from the devil. Anyone who thinks differently is simply not paying attention.

After reviewing the tapes, praying, and consulting with my securities attorney, my intellectual property attorney, and my accountant, I called Ms. Wells. Our respective counsel negotiated for several days, and then I agreed to show Ms. Wells the security tapes. We consulted with numerous experts, and there is no dispute that Junior is the man on the tapes. And so here we are.

I hope my discovery puts to rest the dispute over which god killed Junior. Obviously, the Methodists and the Muslims have some explaining to do. And as far as the so-called Patriot Avenger is concerned, he should just be ashamed of himself. In fact, I publicly offer my services, at a substantial discount, to the Patriot Avenger. The man is in desperate need of an exorcism.

Finally, let me add that all of this proves once again that all things happen for a reason. Clearly, God had all the priests in America removed to set in motion the events that have led to this press conference. Y'all have a nice day, and give me a call if you have any deliverance ministry needs.

I turned off the television when Veronica began to hawk her "Junior: The Devil Made Me Do It" T-shirts and coffee mugs.

Day 793

Still in Texas. Just another day in paradise.

Been getting lots of phone calls and e-mails from folks, now that I'm not dead again. Big Foot called to let me know that after the TQCR explosion there was a run on Man on the Run gear because people thought it would become a collectible and more valuable in a couple of years. Big Foot was upbeat: "The Assassin called me soon after the explosion and said you and Suzanne were OK, but he said not to call until the world knew you were not dead. So good to hear your voice again, man. Tell Suzanne we made a bunch more money for your charities."

Sister Flannery sent me an e-mail. After giving me updates on a few of God's Elect, she wrote: "Mother Superior Hookenstein says Triple F is yet more proof that Senior was right about who should be in charge. I have no idea what she is talking about. As for me, I knew you weren't dead. I have to admit, though, I was getting a bit worried when you did not resurface and prove the weird Methodists and the crazy Muslims wrong. Be careful, and stay away from dog shows."

I also got e-mails from the Hammer, the snow globe girls, and Dickie Marsh. Dickie's e-mail said simply: "EAST TEXAS." The Hammer went into great detail about his current weight lifting regimen and then wrote, almost as an afterthought: "Glad you were not blown up with those poor dogs. Why would anybody blow up dogs? The Assassin told me to tell you to go down to Mexico. Didn't Mexico disappear?"

Day 800

Welcome to Baja, Texas, the largest state in the union. I know, it looks a lot like Mexico. We are out in the middle of nowhere in the Chihuahuan Desert, which, according to something Suzanne found on the computer, is the most biologically diverse desert in the world. More fun facts to know and tell from the Man on the Run. We are staying at the hacienda owned by Presley Kimball. Yes, that Presley Kimball, the Christian rock-and-roll star. Suzanne is beside herself.

You know when you read about certain famous people and they are described as "just normal people like you and me"? Well, Presley is not like that. He is different. Walks, talks, acts different. I hesitate to come right out and say that Presley is a self-absorbed diva who cares only about himself, but I won't hesitate to say that I don't particularly enjoy his company. Suzanne, however, hangs on to his every word like it is gospel.

And of course, that is part of the problem. I have never been a big fan of bombastic, heat-seeking Christian rock music. It just seems oxymoronic to me. Suzanne, my Bible-quoting superagent, loves Christian rock and roll.

Sorry about the insecure jealous-like tangent. I will try to write the rest of this entry like a grown-up wanted criminal and not an eighth-grader.

Presley is an acquaintance of the Assassin. The Assassin arranged for us to stay here. I think Presley and the Assassin met at one of those remote island resorts that caters to incredibly rich and famous people who don't want to be mobbed by their fans.

Presley's hacienda is also very isolated. To get here we had to travel over some fairly rough terrain. I switched the pony to off-road capability and even then we had a tough go of it. About five miles out, the road turns into basically a cow path that leads straight to the hacienda. You can't sneak up on Presley's place.

Presley, of course, flies here on his private plane. A private airstrip is situated within the perimeter of the fenced-off acreage surrounding the hacienda.

We've been here for five days. Presley was here to meet us and we hung out for a few days, and then Presley flew to Nashville for the Christian Music Awards. He asked us to go with him. I said no thanks, but I'm pretty sure Suzanne wanted to go.

I'm sitting in one of Presley's dens. At least I think it's a den. You wouldn't think a person would have more than one den, but this room is not a bedroom, a bathroom, or a kitchen, so I'm calling it a den. There are a bunch of gold and platinum records on the walls, as well as a huge poster from Presley's Be Humble Tour. The picture on the poster is of Presley wailing away on his guitar, long blond locks flowing.

Presley said I could use this room as an office during our stay, which is very nice of him. I have been communicating with our friends over the past few days, but nothing seems to be happening. I appear to be safe in Baja, at least for now. No indications that the bad guys know I'm down here.

That's it for now from the hacienda. Don't forget to be humble.

Day 803

Still at the hacienda. No big news to report. Presley due back in a few days from Nashville.

Suzanne is developing a nice tan. She hangs out at the pool every day. Presley has some servant-type folks who wait on us hand and foot. Suzanne really likes the sweet iced tea they bring to her while she works on her tan.

Yesterday was Prohibition Rescission Redux, when everybody celebrates the anniversary of the legalization of drugs in the United States. Lots of parades, lots of pot smoking. Suzanne and I decided it would be un-American not to join in the celebration. Not surprisingly, Presley had a lot of stuff here in the hacienda for us to celebrate with.

Since the legalization of drugs in the U.S. was a major factor in the creation of Baja, Texas, I guess now is a good enough time to fill you in on a little of what I know about that subject. As I wrote earlier, both Senior and I recognized back in the day that Mexico was in trouble. We were, of course, not alone. Anybody who was paying attention knew there was a big problem down here.

Three months after the decriminalization legislation was passed by Congress and signed by the president, I got a phone call from one of the Mexican drug dealers I had negotiated with. For a brutal, vicious drug lord, he was semi-straightforward. He said the infighting among the drug gangs had concluded, and that the two surviving drug gangs had joined forces with one of the generals and they were going to try and depose the president of Mexico and take over the country so they could access the country's treasury. The drug guy told me this because he thought that maybe Senior could somehow prevent the gangs from taking over the government.

I told Senior, who told the president of the United States, who told us to stand by. And so we did. As did our country. And simply watched the proud country of Mexico disintegrate.

Senior has been given a lot of credit and/or been assigned a lot of blame for Mexico's collapse, but the truth of the matter is that he initially tried to save the country from itself by meeting with leaders in the government to discuss the problems facing the country. They told him to get stuffed. Then Senior and I met with the drug dealers, bankers, and generals, with similar results.

At that point, it became business as usual for Senior. As I have already explained, he loaned money to the biggest Mexican banks to keep them afloat. Senior also loaned money to the state-owned oil and gas monopoly, as well as the state-owned power-generation companies and mining companies. He also bought large interests in the biggest Mexican agricultural conglomerates. Senior knew he could make money on the back end when everything in Mexico went south. You can call that predatory if you wish, or you can simply call it good business. The Mexican companies were more than happy to take Senior's money.

Once the banks started to fail, the fate of Mexico was essentially sealed. The drug dealers were not pleased to discover that the vast majority of their deposits were not in Mexico, but were actually in Senior's bank in El Paso as security for the loans taken out by the Mexican banks. A bunch of Mexican bankers turned up dead.

When the Mexican banks could not make their loan payments, Senior and his consortium of Texas banks took control of the Mexican banks and essentially shut them down. And soon after that happened, the drug gangs and their general of choice mobilized their forces and took over the government in Mexico City. It actually wasn't that difficult. The army was not getting paid, and the drug dealers promised to pay the soldiers when they took control.

Senior knew the country would not last long with the drug dealers in control of the treasury. Senior decided that to protect his business interests in the Mexican companies he had invested in or loaned money to, he needed to get the competent people who ran these companies out of harm's way. He also knew, of course, that if these folks got out of Mexico the companies would not be able to operate, which would even further accelerate the demise of the country.

So Senior and I created a sort of Mexican Underground Railroad to get these folks out of Mexico. Senior owned a bunch of hotels in Texas, Arizona, and California along the border, so the refugees and their families stayed free of charge in the hotels while their native country fell apart. The feds and the state governments knew what we were doing and looked the other way. Nobody was too crazy about letting these folks come over, but nobody wanted blood on their hands. And plus, the people coming over the border were top-notch professionals and everybody knew we would need them to eventually go back and help run things when the craziness ended.

I need to emphasize here that although Senior believed Mexico had to hit rock bottom before it could recover as a nation, he never wanted to have America take over the country. That was all D.C. The feds in charge at the time saw a wonderful economic and military opportunity in Mexico. They wanted Mexico's oil, gas, and other minerals, and they wanted the land buffer against potential invaders and terrorists that Mexico provided. Plus, to be honest, I think a lot of folks thought that the land in Texas south of San Antonio was virtually Mexico anyway. Why not just annex the whole enchilada?

When the drug dealers in charge of the government asked Senior and me to come to Mexico City to visit about the state of the country, I told Senior it was a bad idea to go. I figured they would just kill us. However, Senior said we would be safe, and it was important that we go. The feds in D.C. were also on board with our trip, because they wanted to hear our firsthand account of what was going on. Plus, the feds could have cared less about what happened to us.

I don't know what I expected, but I never expected that the drug dealers would offer to sell Mexico to us. But that is exactly what they did. The drug dealers wanted a bunch of money so they could leave the country and live happily ever after, and they were willing to do anything to get it.

When Senior told the administration what was going on, there was a big debate in Washington. Should the United States negotiate with the drug dealers and buy Mexico, or should the United States simply send an army down there and conquer the country? It would not have been difficult to defeat Mexico militarily. Most of the soldiers had gone home after the drug dealers took over.

Senior told the president that if he sent troops to Mexico, Senior would ream him out in the press and do everything in his power to make sure he was not reelected. Senior's threat prevailed, and Senior negotiated on behalf of the United States to buy Mexico.

I know there have been many books written about the negotiations and how the price was calculated, so I won't repeat all of that here. What you may not know is that when it was all said and done, Senior lost money on the deal. He gave up security interests and preferred loan positions in a number of Mexican companies to keep the companies afloat and to avoid even more hardships for the employees who worked for those businesses.

There are also some interesting and unreported stories on the vote by the citizens of Mexico to approve the sale, and how Baja, Texas, came to be chosen as the name for the new state. If I have time, I will fill you in on those facts later. Enough history for today. Adios from Baja, Texas.

Day 808

OK. Remember when I was semi-rude about Presley the other day? Well, hand me a knife and fork because I may have to eat those words.

Presley came back from Nashville yesterday. His latest album, *Righteousness Rocks*, won the album of the year award. He let Suzanne hold the trophy. She nearly fainted.

I was sitting in the Be Humble den last night after dinner when Presley came to see me and asked if we could visit. "Junior," he said, "I know you don't like me all that much, and I know I'm kind of a diva sometimes, but we need to talk about some stuff. You don't remember this, but you and I have met before."

I told Presley that I would probably remember meeting a famous musician, and he said, "When we met, I wasn't famous and I wasn't much of a musician. We shook hands at my father's funeral in the Mount Zion Baptist Church in LaPlace, Louisiana, about five years ago. Daddy was killed on the Rebecca #1. You attended the funeral with Senior."

As I mentioned previously, Senior and I went to fifty-five Rebecca #1 funerals. I did not remember shaking hands with Presley and I told him so, although I also told him I was very sorry about his dad.

Presley continued. "Anyway, after the funeral your dad and my mom struck up a conversation. Senior was so nice to Mom. It turns out that you and I were born only a few months apart, and apparently Mom told Senior she was worried about what I would do with Dad gone. I had flunked out of college and I was just working odd jobs around town.

"A few days after the funeral, Senior called me and asked me what I was going to do with my life. I told him that I loved to sing in the Mount Zion choir and that it would be great if I could go back to college and get a music degree so I would be qualified to teach high school music and maybe be a choir director for a church. Senior worked it out for Trinity Exploration to pay for my tuition and books."

Presley was in tears as he continued. "Your dad saved me, Junior. Going back to college was the best thing that ever happened to me. I learned how to play the guitar and how to write songs. And even more important, I discovered that I can reach others for God with my music. I truly believe that God put Senior in my life to save me from a life of misery and uselessness and to use me to tell others the good news about the kingdom of heaven."

Presley was clearly sincere. His tears and expression of gratitude were obviously heartfelt. Nevertheless, it took everything I had to refrain from telling him that I did not think that God blew up his dad and fifty-four other people on the Rebecca #1 so he could be a Christian rock-and-roll star. I know that's tacky, but that's what I was thinking.

Then Presley surprised me. "Don't get me wrong, Junior," he said. "If I had my way, the explosion would never have happened and my dad and the others would still be alive. I would be a walking, talking odd-job-doing failure forever if it could bring my dad back."

That was when I knew that I would need some chips and salsa to help me digest my previous statements about Presley. And then it got even more complicated.

Presley paused and looked around before he spoke again, as if to make sure nobody else could hear. "Junior," he said, "I believe in God and all, but I am not one of those crazy prophet-like guys who claim to get visions and messages from God, you know what I mean? I'm just the lead singer in a Christian rock-and-roll band."

Presley paused and looked around again. I had a pretty good idea where this was going, so I looked around as well. Thought maybe I should call up those nice servant people on the house intercom and order up some chili con queso, maybe even some jalapeños, to spice up my meal of poorly chosen words.

Presley saw me looking around and paused for a second or two, then continued. "Anyway, the deal is, what I really mean to say is that, well, about a year ago I met the Assassin at the Pink Turtle Resort in Barbados. He gave me a computer disk and said that it was important that I watch it. Your father, even though he had been blown up in New Mexico, was on the disk! Senior said he was very proud of me and that my dad would be proud as well. Senior said there might come a time when I would have an opportunity to help you and that he would really appreciate it if I did so. And now you're here. This is just so weird."

Presley shook his head and looked at the floor. After a minute or so I broke the silence by telling Presley I was really grateful to him for taking Suzanne and me in, even though we were being chased by the Muslims and the Methodists. Presley looked up as if he had forgotten I was there. "Actually, there's more to it than that," he said a bit absentmindedly. "Follow me."

I followed Presley down the hall to what appeared to be yet another den. He pushed a button on a console and a screen descended from the ceiling.

Presley pushed another button and a huge picture of Presley playing a guitar appeared on the screen. His guitar was spitting fire and a bright red light radiated around his head. Above Presley's picture were the words: "The Let Him Be Tour." Presley smiled. "Tour starts tomorrow, bro."

Senior strikes again. With a Baptist.

Day 815

Welcome to month twenty-eight of the Being In Baja Is Okay But I'm Ready To Leave Now Tour. The good thing about hanging out in Presley's place is that we are probably safe here. We are so isolated that it would be difficult for Methodists or bozos or fartwa guys to sneak up on us out in the middle of nowhere. The bad thing about hanging out in the middle of nowhere, however, is that it can get kind of boring.

In fact, I am so bored that I'm going to attempt to watch the Masters golf tournament in Augusta, Georgia, on television. I know I'm going to alienate a bunch of folks here, but can there be an event in the entire world that is more pretentious and boring than the Masters golf tournament? Set your watches. I will be back after today's coverage or my nap is over, whichever comes first.

Here I am again, much sooner than I anticipated. I was nodding off when the whispering announcer who was going into excruciating detail about the way the grass was cut on the course was interrupted by screaming and the sound of gunfire. Seems that three bozos who were trying to blow up the eighteenth green were gunned down by Georgia state troopers. No nonbozo casualties, which is great. So the Masters may NOT be the most boring event in the world today, although it still has my vote as the most pretentious. I don't know what the leader board says, but at least we know that the Georgia state troopers lead the bozos 3–0. Way to go, Georgia state troopers.

It's interesting to me that of all the strategic targets the bozos could choose to hit, they selected the Masters. I'm not sure why the destruction of the Masters rates high on the bozos' list. I mean, as long as nobody is hurt, I am perfectly fine with the Masters course being blown to kingdom come. I know a bunch of rich, old white men would be really upset, but would anybody else really care?[137]

OK. They have removed the dead bodies of the bozos and play is continuing. I guess I need to give the Masters folks credit for efficiency. Very little time was wasted in bozo removal.

Now the announcer is whispering something about the imported sand that is used in the sand traps and how the golfers are using sand wedges with a special alloy that allows the golfers to displace more sand with a lower loft angle. The golfer about to hit his sand wedge has taken four practice swings, hitched up his pants three times, and thrown grass into the air twice to check the wind. Now he is complaining because someone is talking in the gallery. What I wouldn't give for a cornerback blitz right now. I am now going to either take a nap or blow my brains out. If there are no more entries, you will know which option I chose.

Day 819

Still around, so I guess you can conclude that I did not blow my brains out. No longer in the hacienda, however. Got an e-mail from the Assassin telling us to drive to Mexico City, the capital of Baja, Texas. Before we left the hacienda, Presley called and we had a nice talk. Presley said the tour was going well—sold-out dates at every arena. He also said the Let Him Be Tour merchandise was selling like hotcakes, so there should be thousands of people wearing Let Him Be Tour caps, T-shirts, and sweatshirts. Can't hurt, right? I

---

137 Two years after *Junior* was published, Augusta National Golf Club, a private all-male country club where the Masters golf tournament was played, filed for bankruptcy. According to bankruptcy court filings, the members of the club could no longer play golf due to the side effects of Big Boy, the male enhancement drug sold by Alberto Gonga Mutsapi, the Swaziland terrorist. When the members stopped paying their dues, the club was forced to file for bankruptcy. The club was purchased in bankruptcy by Mitchell "Chicken Man" Young, who made his fortune with a chain of popular chicken and waffle restaurants. The Chicken and Waffle Open has taken the place of the Masters on the PGA circuit.

considered asking Presley if he had been sued yet by Veronica, but I did not want to spoil his good mood.

One of the more interesting consequences of the transformation of the country of Mexico into the fifty-first state of Baja, Texas, is the shift in population. Everybody was worried that millions of poor and uneducated Mexicans would travel north across the border, but that didn't happen. Once they became American citizens, most of the folks in Mexico decided to stay where they were—why leave their homes when they could enjoy the advantages of American citizenship in their hometowns?

To the surprise of the so-called experts, the biggest population migration was from north to south. Millions of Anglos crossed the Rio Grande and moved to Baja. They moved for a number of reasons, including cheaper real estate, untapped markets for the manufacture of goods and the provision of services, and to be a part of a new beginning. Baja, Texas, was the new hip place to be, whether you were an artist, tradesman, lawyer, or entrepreneur.

And our instructions from the Assassin were to meet up with one of the most successful Anglo transplants to Baja, Texas: Nico Dempster. A little background may be necessary here.

When Senior negotiated the treaty that resulted in the sale of Mexico to the United States, he insisted on a clause that required all laws, regulations, and public signs in Baja, Texas, to be written in both English and Spanish, that English be taught as the primary language beginning in elementary school, and that fluency in English be a mandatory requirement for high school graduation in Baja, Texas. This clause is identified in the treaty as the New Language Covenant.

Senior refused to use the translators provided by the feds when he was negotiating with the drug dealers because he did not trust the feds. Instead, he took Nico with him to translate.

Nico was a Spanish teacher at El Paso Coronado High School, and on the side he taught Spanish to business executives. Senior did not bother to learn the language himself, but he required all the Trinity higher-level management types in Texas to learn it. Nico, who has the gift of gab and superior entrepreneurial instincts, convinced Senior to hire him to teach the Trinity executives.

Nico did a great job with Trinity's executives and Senior trusted Nico, so

Nico got the job of translating during the treaty negotiations. Nico, a friendly and engaging guy, made a bunch of friends and contacts during the negotiations. And he parlayed those contacts (and his association with the great Joshua Jennings, Sr.) into a number of profitable gigs and contracts.

For example, Nico founded a company that was given the contract to implement the New Language Covenant. This was a huge endeavor. Every law, every regulation, every traffic sign, every public communication from the government had to be translated into English. Plus, a new English-language curriculum had to be developed for the school system. Nico made a ton of money on this project and received rave reviews for his efforts. Nico is now incredibly well connected and serves on several powerful governmental committees in Baja.

There was a lot of construction on I-35 as we approached Mexico City, so we did not arrive at Nico's place until well after dark. After Suzanne and I got settled, we sat in Nico's living room and had a drink. Nico was effusive: "I can't tell you how great it is to see you again, Junior. I've been reading about you, of course, and it's hard not to notice all the television coverage of your exploits."

When I commented on his nice digs, Nico said, "All because of your dad. I was a high school teacher with a small apartment in El Paso, but with your dad's help, I was reborn as a sort of government language implementation specialist. Everybody in Baja, from the bigwigs to the normal folks, loved and revered Senior, and since I was his translator I was able to pick up a bunch of business and contacts."

We talked for a few more hours before we called it a night. Nico said he was told to expect us, but he did not have any messages for us, so I guess we will just hang out here and see what happens.

To tell the truth, I kind of like it here in Mexico City. I wasn't that crazy about coming here, because I remember how awful it was in the city when the drug guys were in charge and we were negotiating the treaty. But now that I have seen the revitalized city, I can testify that it is a real nice place. Clean, safe, the whole nine yards.

Getting kind of tired, so I guess I should hit the sack. Wind is picking up—blowing pretty hard right now. Hope they don't have hurricanes in Mexico City. I'm done. Buenas noches.

Day 823

Still in Mexico City awaiting further instructions. Today was another strange day, bozo-wise.

According to CNN, ten bozos were killed today at a women's volleyball match at the University of Texas in Austin. The bozos walked onto the court with weapons drawn and were promptly mowed down in a hail of gunfire from every direction. The students in the stands, UT's volleyball coach, even the referees were packing heat. The bozos did not get a shot off.

I find this weird on several levels. First, why would the bozos attack a women's volleyball match? No offense to volleyball buffs, but you would think the bozos could find a more high-profile sporting event to mess up. I realize their attempt to bomb the Masters was unsuccessful, but you would think they could find something more significant than a regular-season women's volleyball match. At least wait for the playoffs.

Second, how could the bozos not know about the Texas law allowing concealed weapons on college campuses? It's the only one in the country and it has been ridiculed worldwide as an extremely bad idea. I thought the bozos were better informed and prepared than that. Seems like the bozos may be losing their edge. My speculation (and hope) is that the East Texas Solution is having its desired impact on the bozos.

Let me go ahead and add for the record that I still think the law allowing guns on campus is a really stupid idea. My guess is, however, that since the law clearly saved a bunch of people from being killed by bozos, the law is here to stay and will soon be implemented in other states.[138] Suzanne says we are late for our lunch appointment with Nico. Gotta run. East Texas!!

---

138 The Texas gun law referenced in Day 823 was repealed the year after *Junior* was published because of a gun battle that took place at Kyle Field on the Texas A&M University campus during a football game between Texas A&M and the University of Texas. A Texas A&M cheerleader, who allegedly believed he was being attacked by Bevo, UT's longhorn steer mascot, pulled a pistol and shot the animal five times. Students from both schools then opened fire. Although there were no human fatalities, both Bevo and A&M's collie dog mascot were killed, and a number of students and football players were injured. When it was determined that Luke Ward, the all-American quarterback for the Longhorns, and Bud Wymore V, the all-American defensive tackle for the Aggies, were wounded by gunfire and out for the rest of the season, the Texas legislature met in emergency session and repealed the gun carry law.

Day 827

Remember when I wrote about the brutal and vicious but semi-straight-forward drug lord who called to give us a heads-up about the plan to depose the Mexican president?[139] Well, apparently he is the reason I am in Mexico City.

Nico took me to visit with Julio Perez today. We met in the Mexico City Petroleum Club. As a quick aside, my guess is that there was not a petroleum club in Mexico City before Mexico became Baja, Texas. In Texas, virtually every city with more than 50,000 inhabitants has a petroleum club. Stands to reason that if Mexico changed its name to include Texas, the capital city needed its own petroleum club.

Julio, as you might have guessed, is a survivor. He is the only drug king-pin in Mexico who hung around and survived the transition from Mexico to Baja, Texas. The only other big-time pre-Baja drug guys who are still alive are the ones who split with the money.

According to Nico, Julio is still around because he has a valuable skill that is in demand in Baja—he knows how to grow marijuana. You may not know this, but one of the biggest problems Senior faced when he was try-ing to convince the feds that legalizing pot was a good idea was figuring out where the United States would get the stuff. Nobody wanted to deal with the Colombians or the other huge drug cartels. Senior had to bring in a bunch of agricultural experts who said the weed could be grown in the United States. And after Senior's law was passed, the states where the marijuana could be grown made a ton of money selling it to the feds.

When Baja joined the union, it also wanted to harvest a big marijuana cash crop. So Julio, one of the few living experts in the state, also became a valuable commodity.

I met Julio in a small private dining area located on the third floor of the club. Nico, who was not invited to the meeting and who made it clear he did not want to attend the meeting, waited for me on the first floor at the club's well-stocked bar. When I arrived in the private dining room, Julio placed a small box on the table and flipped a switch. "Frequency jammer," he said. "Don't want anybody listening in."

---

139 See Day 803.

After some brief small talk, Julio got right to the point: "I owe your father big-time, young man. Everybody down here wanted to kill me once the sale was concluded, but Senior protected me and told the government folks that I could help bring in a bunch of money growing the locoweed. He even set me up with some land that he foreclosed on when the banks all tanked. So not only did Senior save my life, he made me a rich man."

Like I mentioned before, Julio had been a brutal and vicious man, pre-Baja. I wasn't sure how much he had changed, if at all, and I was more than a little uncomfortable sitting alone in a room with him. As we talked, I kept wondering if the Methodists would pay him fartwa money for killing me.

Julio smiled, as if he was reading my troubled mind. "I know you are the Man on the Run and the Muslims and Methodists are chasing you, but you have nothing to fear from me. Not because I am a particularly good man, because I am not. I will never do anything to harm you because I fear your father, Junior. He was a hard man. Even if Senior is dead, and I am not totally convinced that he is, I know that Senior's arm is long enough to reach out and wring my neck if I even *think* about hurting you.

I just nodded, and Julio continued. "Two weeks before he was killed, Senior came down to my grass farm to visit me. We walked in the fields by ourselves and talked about many things. We talked about family. We talked about life and death. One of the things that linked me with Senior is that Senior and I knew something about the Baja sale that nobody else knew. It was a secret only he and I shared. Right before he left my grass farm to head back to El Paso, Senior told me that there would come a time when I would need to tell you the secret. And I think the time has come."

So Julio told me the secret. Now I have to figure out what to do with it. More later.

Day 831

As I mentioned earlier, Mexico City is a place where hipsters like to hang. This means that there are plenty of artsy events here, like movie festivals, art shows, and stuff like that.

I am alone at Nico's place. Suzanne is at a Jane Eyre movie festival. She was there yesterday as well. Did you know that there are over 200 Jane Eyre movies? I hope Suzanne is not going to watch them all.

I haven't talked much about the election lately because nothing much has happened. The candidates talk about the few issues they disagree on, pose for pictures, and kiss babies, but really, there are no big headlines. At least until yesterday, that is.

Remember when I said that Eb did not know much about sports?[140] Well yesterday, Eb's lack of sports knowledge and, to be honest, his own naïveté, may have cost him some votes.

If you are even a casual sports fan, you have probably heard of Paul "The Hose" Vineis. The Hose is one of the best left-handed pitchers in baseball. His fastball regularly hits the 100 mph mark. Unfortunately, the Hose is also a wretched excuse for a human being. He has a long track record of abusing girlfriends and spouses, drunk-driving convictions, bar fights, and all sorts of other bad stuff.

Despite his off-the-field activities, the Hose has made a very good living as a pitcher. He has been suspended a few times, and spent time in anger management, sex addiction, and alcohol rehabilitation clinics, but he always manages to make it back to the field. A lefty with a 100 mph heater is given a lot of second chances.

Two days ago, however, the Hose messed up big-time. He was pitching in Los Angeles against the Dodgers, and the umpire behind the plate called twenty-four straight balls. The Hose charged the umpire and started yelling at her. The umpire let the Hose vent for about ten minutes and then finally tossed him.

That would have been that, but one of the television cameras caught the Hose uttering what the media has described as "a virulent anti–blind gay transgender midget slur." I don't know what the Hose said, because all the replays of the incident block out the Hose's mouth so you can't read his lips.

Yesterday, the league fined the Hose $1 million and suspended him for the rest of the season, without pay. And to top it off, the Hose is being prosecuted under California state law for a verbal hate crime, which carries a minimum two-year jail sentence.

Kind of a long intro to Eb's problem, but like I have said on many occasions, I have plenty of time here. Anyway, trust me when I say that Eb has never heard of the Hose, and also does not know that the term "hose" is

140 See Day 474.

baseball slang for a pitcher's arm. And apparently Eb's people did not prep him for the slur controversy, because he was totally blindsided by reporters as he left a rally in Green Bay, Wisconsin. Here's how it went:

Reporter: Mr. Cohen, please give us your thoughts on the Paul Vineis suspension. Should he be kicked out for the entire season?

Eb: I thought I had memorized the names of all of Green Bay's players. Does Mr. Vineis play for the Packers?

Reporter: I'm talking about the Hose, Mr. Cohen.

Eb: I apologize. I thought we were talking about a football player. Where does a garden hose fit into this question?

Reporter: Paul "The Hose" Vineis is a pitcher for the San Antonio Sheriffs. He has been suspended by Major League Baseball for uttering a virulent anti–blind gay transgender midget slur against a female umpire. He is also being prosecuted for a hate crime under California law. Do you think that is fair, Mr. Cohen?

Eb (clearly treading water while he thinks and waits for help from his handlers): I see, a baseball pitcher. San Antonio. Can you tell me what the baseball pitcher said?

Reporter: I don't know what he said, exactly. And even if I did, I could not repeat it out loud, because then I might be prosecuted for a hate crime as well.

Eb: I see. Can somebody whisper to me what Mr. Hose said?

One of Eb's aides whispered in Eb's ear. Eb now looked more confused than ever.

The reporter pushed: Well, Mr. Cohen?

Eb: I confess I have no idea what that phrase means. I have never heard it before. That's a virulent slur?

Reporter: Apparently so. Are you saying the Hose did nothing wrong?

Eb: First, let me say that I respect everyone's right to live their lives within the confines of the law. If the umpire wants to live the blind gay transgender midget lifestyle, that is certainly her business.

Reporter: Actually, I don't think the umpire is blind, gay, transgender, or a midget. I think it would be hard for an umpire to be blind or a midget. Anyway, do you agree that the Hose should be kicked out of baseball and sent to jail for uttering the virulent anti–blind gay transgender midget slur, even though the umpire is definitely not blind or a midget but could possibly be a gay transgender?

Eb: I know it's not nice to say bad things about people who are different from you. We teach our children in this country to respect others and treat them with dignity. Mr. Hose was definitely wrong to utter a slur, and I am assuming here that what Mr. Hose said is, in fact, a slur, because I honestly don't know.

Reporter: Granted, but you have still not answered my question. Should the Hose be kicked off the team and go to jail?

The camera swerved back to Eb, and you could see he was thinking. He still looked good, still had that presidential vibe about him. But the Eb that answered the question was not the presidential Eb, but was instead the fat Eb who got beat up every day after school:

Eb: When I was a youngster, the kids at school made fun of me all the time. I was overweight, so they called me fatso. I was not good in sports, so they called me a spaz. I learned to read later than most of the other kids in my class, so they called me stupid. I wore glasses, so they called me four-eyes. When I was in high school I never had a date, so they called me a loser. These words were hurtful and painful and made me cry on more than one occasion.

But my parents told me not to feel sorry for myself. They told me that sticks and stones might break my bones, but names could never hurt me. I know that is simplistic and a bit untrue because names can hurt you, but I think the principle is sound. Having been an underdog myself, I will always root for and protect those who need protection, but I have to say that putting someone in jail for calling someone a name seems a bit over-the-top. Aren't there more important things for our police to do?

Reporter: What about the Hose's suspension and $1 million fine? Is that wrong?

Eb: I don't know baseball's rules and I am sure the commissioner is doing what she believes is in the best interest of baseball. But my associate just told me that Mr. Hose has done a lot of illegal things like hitting women and driving under the influence of alcohol, yet he was never suspended for a full season for those actions. Given those circumstances, the punishment for saying mean words seems a bit harsh, don't you think?

Reporter (turning away from Eb and facing the camera, clearly pleased): It appears that presidential candidate Eb Cohen has just criticized and called into question the constitutionality of California's hate crime jurisprudence and has also opined that the commissioner of Major League Baseball is a complete moron. We will continue to follow up on this important story as it develops.

Looks like the media has finally found an election controversy. And all because a lefty couldn't find the strike zone.

Day 835

Is it rude to tell a woman that you don't want to hear anything more about Jane Eyre for the rest of your life? Is that worse than telling her that her jeans do, in fact, make her backside look big? The things you contemplate as a Man on the Run.

Eb's Sticks and Stones Speech has, not surprisingly, drawn both praise and criticism. I think it is safe to say that Eb and General Dozier will not get many votes from the blind gay transgender midget community, but the experts say most of those votes were going to the Democrats anyway.

Eb caught a huge break, however, when five professional lip readers hired by CNN to analyze the Hose's tirade published a transcript of what the Hose said. Here are just a few of the highlights:

(1) "My dead grandmother can see better than you!"

(2) "You are a slimy _____ (derogatory term for a woman's, you know, private parts)!"

(3) "That call was worse than the Japs' decision to bomb Pearl Harbor!"

(4) "You are stupider than a drunk Baptist trying to explain creationism!"

(5) "The lead in the Helen Keller movie has already been filled!"

(6) "The short bus has arrived, you stupid retard. Time to leave!"

(7) "Have you been to the proctologist lately? Because I think you need to get your eyes checked!"

(8) "Aren't you an Auburn graduate? I didn't think they could count to twenty-four!"

The Hose also took virtually every deity's name in vain, including, but not limited to, Jehovah, Jesus Christ, Allah, Vishnu, Elvis, Thor, and Michael Jordan.

Now, believe it or not, the focus of the national debate over the Hose has moved from his virulent anti–blind gay transgender midget slur (which most people did not understand anyway) to the Hose's rant against everyone else in the world. Christians, Muslims, and the followers of the other gods that the Hose cursed are boycotting all Major League Baseball games. Buckwheat Trimble, coach of the national champion Second Hilltop Holy Spirit Baptist College football team, is quoted on CNN as follows:

> *How is it possible that Major League Baseball will suspend a player for uttering an alleged blind gay transgender midget slur, but does absolutely nothing when the man takes God's name in vain? Does Major League Baseball care more about the blind gay transgender midget community than Jehovah almighty? Is there a better example of the inane inconsistency of worshipping the creature rather than the creator?*

Major League Baseball also received complaints and/or threats of boycotts from

(1) the AARP (for the dead grandmother quote);

(2) every women's group in existence, along with the American Gynecological Association (for the you-know-what reference);

(3) the Japanese Players Subcommittee of the Major League Baseball

Players Union ("The Pearl Harbor reference is strategically and historically inaccurate, and is offensive to every Japanese-born player. We suggest that an equitable punishment would be to give every Japanese hitter who faces the Hose for the next two seasons four strikes instead of three.");

(4) the Baptist Convention of America ("The Hose's comments reinforce the conclusion that the Antichrist is among us and the rapture is near.");

(5) the Helen Keller National Trust ("Major League Baseball, by and through its authorized representative, has violated federal trademark law by using Ms. Keller's name without permission in an entertainment setting wherein patrons are charged a fee for entry.");

(6) Mothers Against Churlish Comments ("MACC suggests that Major League Baseball require the Hose to attend MACC's seven-week sensitivity training workshop.");

(7) the Association of Colorectal Surgeons ("The Hose is apparently unaware that the proper name for this specialty is, and has been for many years, colorectal surgery. No hard feelings on our part, however. In fact, we offer to provide the Hose with a thorough exam, free of charge, during the seventh-inning stretch of any game of his choosing."); and

(8) the Auburn University Ex-Students Association ("Actually, it is the University of Alabama's graduates who get confused when the math involved exceeds the number of fingers and toes.").

I wonder what Jane Eyre would make of the Hose's comments? Whaddya wanna bet there will be a panel discussion on this topic during tomorrow's festival?

Day 839

Fortunately, I think Suzanne is getting tired of the Jane Eyre festival.

To be forthright with you, I have a sense of foreboding that is difficult for me to shake. In many respects, I have been the beneficiary of fortuitous circumstances, but it has become obvious that I am up against a formidable enemy and that the end result of this adventure is anything but a foregone conclusion. I realize that forewarned is forearmed, but I can't foreclose the possibility that Senior did not foresee everything. I really don't enjoy being in the forefront. Forever is a really long time.[141]

Day 843

Welcome to month twenty-nine of the Forget What I Said About Foreboding Tour. I know that four days ago I got a little weird and halfway predicted disaster. Remind me NEVER to do that again. I am now officially retired from the predicting business.

I feel pretty safe now because Suzanne and I are on a cool plane that is flying us out of Baja, Texas. In fact, I am riding in my pony car inside the plane. That's how big the plane is. Suzanne thinks it is pretty silly to sit inside a pony car inside a plane, so she is in the regular passenger section of the plane.

Another thing I don't plan to do again anytime soon is rag on Jane Eyre. If it wasn't for old Jane, the bozos likely would have got me. Suzanne begged me to go to the last day of the Jane Eyre festival, because an expert panel was going to have a roundtable discussion and rank the top fifty Jane Eyre movies of all time. I told Suzanne I really needed to wash my socks instead, which she did not find humorous at all. After thirty seconds or so of the Southern Girl "I Can Make You Miserable and We Both Know It" stare, I relented.

And so when the bozos blew up Nico's place with four well-placed bazooka rounds, I was not there to get exploded. Fortunately, neither was anybody else. I assume Nico has homeowner's coverage. If I owned an insurance company I think I would start issuing a Junior rider that voided any coverage if I was staying in a covered property.

I think it's safe to say the bozos are on my trail. I don't know if the bozos want to kill me because (a) I am Senior's son, (b) they think I am part of East Texas, (c) they want to show the Methodists and Jehovah up, or (d) just for

---

141 Day 839 is the last entry for month twenty-eight. Every entry in month twenty-eight (815, 819, 823, 827, 831, 835, 839) is four days apart. Month twenty-eight, particularly as it culminates in Day 839, is recognized as the genesis of the literary convention of "four shadowing." Since the concept of "four shadowing" is considered by many literary critics to be one of the few acts of creative genius by a twenty-first-century American author, there is considerable debate over whether Junior actually wrote the entries in month twenty-eight.

general purposes. I guess at this point the "why" is not the most important thing. The most important thing is just to get away from them and stay away.

And so that is why I am in my pony in the plane on the way to North Dakota. Next stop, New Jerusalem. Shalom.

Day 848

Spoke way too soon. Didn't quite make it to North Dakota. In fact, did not make it past Louisiana. Hanging out in Baton Rouge.

Just a few minutes after I finished up the previous entry, Suzanne told me to come watch the television in the passenger section of the plane. What I saw was more than a bit disturbing.

The program was called *The Blessed Hunt for Junior Jennings*. The moderator, who spoke heavily accented English, explained that forty bozos (my word, not his) had been tracking me for the last five months with the express purpose of "wreaking Allah's vengeance on the infidel son of the infidel father." The Sheik of the Decade's name was not specifically mentioned, but is there any doubt who is funding these guys?

The production quality of the film fell somewhere between a cheap porn flick and a wartime documentary. It was a pretty gritty effort, but the dedication and fearlessness of the bozos jumped off the screen. These guys have no doubt that their god is going to help them kill me and they can hardly wait to get it done. In fact, since they all want to be next in line for the kill shot, they have to roll dice to determine who gets the next assignment.

Another interesting thing about the film is that it documented in detail the bozos' failure (at least to date) to accomplish their goal. The bozos were so sure they had us in Conway, Arkansas, that they left the scene to escape capture and were 100 miles away when the explosion occurred. They did not know the cheap, boring car we were driving had a remote start function. And for some reason the bozos did not know that Suzanne and I had left our hotel in the TQCR before they blew it up. Pretty sloppy, it seems to me. How could you miss that?

The segment of the film on the Masters debacle was a bit confusing. It was hard to tell if the bozos went to Augusta because they thought I was there or because they viewed the tournament as an affront to Allah. There was a lot of guttural screaming about rich white suppression and golf-playing infidels.

The bozos were able to track me to Austin (hence the women's volleyball attack) and then down to Mexico City, so they are clearly good at finding me. So far, thank goodness, they are not very good at killing me. It's weird that the film has been released already, since all it really shows is the team's failure to accomplish its goal. I have to wonder if the sheik sent the first team after me.

I officially take back the previous sentence. Having twenty-five or so (the film did not make clear how many of the forty are still alive and hunting me) dedicated bozos still looking to kill me is a bad thing. They WOULD have killed me in Mexico City if not for Jane Eyre.

And basically, that is why the plane stopped in Louisiana. *The Blessed Hunt for Junior Jennings* freaked the smart people out. The smart people figured the bozos might anticipate a trip to New Jerusalem. We are holed up in Baton Rouge until the smart people figure out what to do next.

Day 853

Did you know that Baton Rouge means "red stick"? Apparently, back in the really old days, if you came upon a settlement of Indians that had a red stick outside their village it meant the Indians would just as soon kill you as look at you. At least that is what the guide book that Suzanne is reading says.

We are still in Red Stick because it's a safe enough place to hide while the smart people manipulate the airwaves. General Dozier gave a speech to the Veterans of Asian and African Wars and Near Wars, which produced the following sound bite for the news networks: "I'm done tiptoeing around this subject. It's high time we find these jokers and just flat-out smoke their asses." Dr. Davis was a bit more statesmanlike: "I realize the men in the documentary contend they are fulfilling a religious directive, and I realize that in America we respect religious diversity. However, murder is against the law. These men need to be brought to justice."

In addition to the sound bites critical of the bozos, there were also a surprising number of pro-Junior comments, mostly from folks associated with the charities Suzanne has sent money to. Thanks, guys.

Then, of course, there were all the crazies. The crazies did not seem to care much about me one way or the other, but they were royally peeved that the towelheads/camel jockeys/sand (fill in the blank of your favorite racial or sexual-orientation slur here) had the nerve to come to America and try to kill an American citizen and/or blow up American sporting events.

So I guess the groundwork has been laid. Every American who watches television or peruses the Internet (and I am guessing that is everyone) knows that there are some bad Arabs out there who need to be put down like rabid dogs. As far as the bozos are concerned, there now is a red stick next to every city.

Day 856

The smart people have decided to shake things up. Suzanne and I are in South Carolina. Why? Because the smart people don't think the bozos will look for me here, since I have never been to South Carolina and have no connections here. Also, the smart people say that South Carolinians REALLY hate anyone that even looks like an Arab and that any bozos who try to cross over into South Carolina will be shot at the border.

So Suzanne and I are back in the pony car and driving around the Palmetto State. The smart people have also decided it would be a good idea if we had a bodyguard, so my good friend Pig Butt Bennett is now traversing the great state of South Carolina. Pig Butt is following us in a pickup truck decorated with a bumper sticker that reads: My Daughter Is a United States Marine and Can Kick Your Son's Butt. We are blending right in.

We did something today that the smart people probably would not have approved of, but it made Suzanne happy and I have learned that it is very important to make your travel companion happy. Even though we are supposed to be traveling incognito and under the radar, Suzanne has been keeping up with some of her friends on Wide World Interactive Facebook Plus. It turns out that one of her very best friends in the world, Jamie Kay, is an exotic dancer in Greenville, South Carolina. So Suzanne and I patronized the Southern Comfort Lounge in Greenville while Pig Butt sat in his pickup in the parking lot to watch for bozos.

Now let me say for the record that I did give this excursion some thought and I figured that if the bozos somehow survived execution at the South Carolina state border, they would almost certainly not look for me in a strip club.

I mean, those guys can't even look at fully clothed women, right? Their heads would probably explode if they came into a strip joint.

We arrived at the Southern Comfort Lounge just in time for Jamie's performance. According to Suzanne, Jamie is well known in the Greenville metropolitan area for her Palmetto Dance, in which she removes palmetto tree branches wrapped around her buxom body while dancing to a medley of Allman Brothers songs. The palmetto is the state tree of South Carolina, so Jamie is considered somewhat of a patriot in these parts. I have to say, Jamie gave a moving performance.

I underestimated the positive effect that visiting the Southern Comfort Lounge would have on Suzanne. It did not occur to me until Suzanne and Jamie started visiting that Suzanne has gone months without talking to a single friend of hers. She was clearly aching for some female companionship. After the first few minutes of their conversation, both women completely forgot I was there. I did not want to interrupt their reunion, so I just, you know, watched some other dancers so as not to make the ladies feel bad that they were totally ignoring me. Sometimes you just have to put others' needs before your own.

Would you believe me if I told you that watching more than three hours of "exotic dancing" can get boring? Yeah, I didn't think so. But the truth of the matter is that I got a bit sleepy in hour three. Maybe it's because my excitement threshold has risen a bit from being on the run from the law and wanted for mass murder and treason.

The ladies decided it would be a great idea to enjoy a "spa day," so we all (Pig Butt included) checked into a fancy hotel that featured a famous spa called the Body and Soul Holistic Transcendental Life in Balance Longevity Spa. Pig Butt and I shared a room and the ladies shared an adjoining room. Again, checking into a fancy hotel and spa may not have been the smartest move, but Suzanne was so excited and happy I just could not refuse.

Pig Butt and I declined spa treatments. We stayed in the room, played cards, and watched some sports on television. Pig Butt's asleep now, snoring softly.

Watching Suzanne with Jamie reminded me of how weird my life has become. It has been forever since I just hung out with a friend and relaxed. Kind of lonely.

OK. That's enough self-pity for tonight. Need to save some for later entries. Good night from the Palmetto State.

Day 857

I don't know if Suzanne is a mind reader, sneaking peeks at my computer,[142] or just very empathetic, but she showed up in my room this morning saying she had a treat that would make me feel a lot better. A lot of things went through my mind when she said this, but the Fit for a King Spa Day was not one of them.

Today I was wrapped, facialed, manicured, pedicured, saunaed (wet and dry), barbered, shaved, plucked, hot springed, exfoliated, and bathed in wine. Then to top it off, I lay on a slowly vibrating table while a beautiful woman stretched out all of my muscles, gave me a vigorous massage, and poured some sort of fantastic-smelling lotion on me. My skin felt like it was breathing pure oxygen. That doesn't make any sense, I know, but my entire body was tingling.

When I saw the bill for my King Spa Day I noted out loud that the cost of the lotion alone could probably keep the Red Head vets in pizza and beer for a year. That was a really stupid thing to say (even though it was true) because I hurt Suzanne's feelings. I immediately apologized and she seemed to forgive me.

Suzanne smiled and said, "You know, Junior, I love those vets, but there is only one of you. And you have given up so much for everyone and not asked anything in return. Do you have any idea how much money you have given away?"

I told Suzanne no and when she told me the amount, I admit I was stunned. I had no idea the endorsements were doing that well.

Then she kissed me on the cheek, which stunned me even more. You can never tell with a Southern Girl, but I don't think it was a sisterly kiss.

Been quite a day. Pig Butt's asleep again. Goodnight from Greenville from the King for a Day.

---

142 Since Suzanne allegedly did not understand the Chiricahua Apache language, the meaning of this statement is unclear.

Day 860

Today started off as a pleasant day. Suzanne and Jamie went shopping, so Pig Butt and I hung out in the room and watched the NFL draft on television. We saw a bunch of very big men in very brightly colored suits, many of whom thanked their Lord Jesus Christ for their draft status. The best part of the whole thing was when two of the television draft experts got into a fistfight over the accuracy of their mock drafts.

My pleasant day was interrupted, however, by a strange commercial. Rifleocity, a gun manufacturer based in (where else) South Dakota, announced it was initiating the Junior Chase Cup, a contest in which the bozos (my word, not theirs) and the MFM would compete to see who could kill me first. Not only me, but also Suzanne and any other "known associates of Joshua Jennings, Jr." The winner would receive a bunch of money, a ton of Rifleocity products, and "a significant endorsement contract for the promotion of Rifleocity and the modern, upscale-weaponry lifestyle."

Pig Butt, who had been slightly dozing when the commercial came on, became fully awake when he heard about the Junior Chase Cup and started cleaning a gun. I had not actually seen his gun before. It was a pistol.

For some reason, I hadn't really focused on the fact that our bodyguard would have a gun. Stupid, I know. Pig Butt saw me staring at the pistol and said, "I've got a rifle, too. Think that will be enough?" I had no idea, but I said sure, two should be enough.

"You know, Junior," Pig Butt continued, "you seem like a really good guy to me. You helped me and you have helped a bunch of people with your endorsement royalties. Why do all these people want to kill you? Who did you tick off?"

It was a very good question, one I have been pondering for approximately 860 days. And I still don't have an answer.

Day 865

No longer in South Carolina. Thanks for the Palmetto Dance, the King Spa Day, and the bozo-free zone, guys. Had to leave South Carolina because the smart people found out we were hanging with Jamie Kay, Suzanne's stripper friend, and were not pleased. Turns out Jamie is not exactly a model citizen.

Hannah called me yesterday and the conversation went something like this:

Hannah: Junior, why didn't you tell us you were spending time with Jamie Kay?

Me: Hello to you too, Hannah. How long has it been since we talked? Maybe about a hundred days or so? How are you? I'm fine, thanks for asking.

Hannah: It's been kind of busy here, Junior.

Me: Yeah, and I have just been goofing off, trying to avoid being blown up by Methodists and bozos. By the way, do you know what the current score is in the Junior Chase Cup?

Hannah: But you have not been blown up, have you? What does that tell you?

Me: Trust me, we don't have enough time for that discussion, Hannah. Why do you care that I am hanging out with Jamie Kay?

Hannah: Because she has a rap sheet as long as your arm. Prostitution, assault and battery, shoplifting, vagrancy, you name it, she has probably done it. You should be more particular about who you associate with, Junior. We are trying to sanitize your public persona so you can come in from the cold when the election is over, and you go hang out with a stripper and prostitute?

Me: You know, Jamie has been really nice to Suzanne and me. She showed us the sights here in South Carolina and took us to some great restaurants. When she found out I liked barbecue, she hooked us up with some guy out in the countryside who cooked up some of the best pork ribs I have ever eaten. It's kind of nice to have someone show us some old-fashioned hospitality.

Hannah: And the Palmetto Dance? You consider that old-fashioned hospitality?

Me: Jamie may not be an angel, but she has been very attentive to us, particularly Suzanne. Every day, Jamie has gone out of her way to be helpful. Suzanne really needed a boost, and Jamie provided that. Suzanne is much happier, which means I am much happier as well. When is the last time you guys did something hospitable for me?

Hannah: You mean outside of saving your life?

Me: Not really the same thing, Hannah.

Hannah: Junior, you are really not making sense, but I don't have time to argue anymore right now. The Southern Comfort Lounge, where Jamie Kay plies her trade, is run by a crime syndicate. This means the Southern Comfort is under constant audio and video surveillance by law enforcement. This means, by definition, you are not flying under the radar, like we asked you to do. So you need to leave the Palmetto State, pronto.

Me: Can you at least say please?

Hannah: Good-bye, Junior.

I guess Mossad agents are not used to saying please.

So we are on the road again. The fugitive, the stripper, and the war hero. (Dibs on that phrase, by the way. It sounds pretty good).[143]

Not sure where we will end up yet. More later. I hope.

Day 873

Month thirty of the Laying Low But No Longer In The Palmetto State Tour is now upon us. Several things to report. First, I know you probably know this, but lots of stuff happens in between my entries. I don't write everything down because, well, I'm just lazy. I was never a great student, in part because I often

---

143   One year after *Junior* was published, Presley Kimball recorded and released an album entitled *The Falsely Accused, the Southern Girl, and the Pig Farmer.* The album went quintuple platinum and won three Grammy awards.

did not turn in my work on time. Plus, when you are not a good writer to begin with . . . well, you get the picture, right? Let's hope that the next alleged mass murderer/treasonist who runs from the law for 873 days is a better and more motivated author.

Anyway, on the things-to-report side, there may be problems in the New Old Jerusalem. The Sheik of the Decade has postponed the results of the housing lottery. Something about a "delay in the final environmental reports" on the city. Right. The sheik has always been known as a big environmentalist.

Dale Piper dropped by the other day. Turns out he and Pig Butt go way back. The three of us sat around and drank beer and I listened to Dale and Pig Butt swap war stories. Dale said he wanted me to know he was off the case, now that it looked like the bozos (my word, not his) had probably blown everybody up on the reservation, so the DOD no longer needed him to work his magic. I appreciate what Dale did, but frankly I am glad he has moved on. A scary dude.

Pig Butt took Suzanne and me to a shooting range run by one of his old Army Ranger buddies. Said we might need to defend ourselves if push came to shove. Suzanne was a much better shot than me. Pig Butt's army friend got both Suzanne and me a pistol. So now I am an armed fugitive. I REALLY hope we don't need to use these guns. I'm just as likely to shoot myself as a bozo or a Methodist.

Speaking of bozos and Methodists, our old friend Samson Fairman surfaced the other day. Frankly, he looked terrible—kind of gaunt and sad. He read the following prepared statement:

I have dedicated my life to protecting the American way of life that Jehovah has given us in His divine wisdom. I have made mistakes, which I regret. Primarily, I regret the killing of the show dogs in Tulsa, Oklahoma. That was a terrible error, for which I take full responsibility. I have decided to take a leave of absence from my role as the leader of the Methodist Free Militia, effective immediately. I will continue to act in an advisory capacity when needed, particularly in regard to the Junior Chase Cup. Again, I am truly sorry about the dogs.

Who would have thunk it? The beheader of Abu Abu Mohammed Mohammed brought down by show dogs.

Presley Kimball checked in. The Let Him Be Tour has been a commercial and critical success. Presley says a famous director has been filming the tour and a movie about the tour is in the works. The Let Him Be Two Tour is a foregone conclusion.

Pig Butt just arrived with some pizza. We are in North Carolina. More later.

Day 876

Can I say something about smart people here? How are you going to stop me, right? I have a lot of respect for smart people, because I am not a really smart guy. I am not stupid (most of the time), but if there was ever a smart people draft, I would, at best, be an undrafted free agent.

I have trusted the smart people to guide me on this trip, and they have done a great job. I'm still alive, which is proof that the smart people are on top of things. But I'm convinced that, generally, we are just not as smart as we think we are. I think history bears me out on that point. Someday, if I survive all of this, I may write a brilliant essay on this subject, but for now I guess I will just have to leave you with my unsupported opinion: Even the smart guys screw it up sometimes.

Why the rant on smart people? Well, the smart people have decided that since we are in North Carolina anyway, we should head over to Seven Devils and hang out with Sister Flannery, Mother Superior Hookenstein, and God's Elect. I really think that is a superbad idea, because if the bozos are tracking me and they catch us in Seven Devils, the sisters and the kids will be in harm's way.

If the bozos catch me and kill me somewhere out on the road, then that is just how this weird adventure is supposed to end. I will be killed even though I am absolutely innocent. If they track us to Seven Devils and hurt the sisters and the kids, however, then I am guilty, guilty, guilty.

We are still driving around North Carolina and so far have not gone within a hundred miles of Seven Devils. We will see how this dispute between me and the smart people plays out.

I realized the other day that I have never told you the big secret that Julio Perez, the scary drug guy, laid on me in Mexico City. Would you like to know what he told me? OK, you twisted my arm.

Basically, Julio told me where all the money that the United States paid the Mexican drug dealers for Mexico is hidden. Somehow, Senior and Julio figured that out. Some of the money is hidden in a cave, but most of it is in a bank account. And Senior and Julio know the secret passcode for the account. According to Julio, Senior wanted me to know about the money. The question is, what am I supposed to do with $100 billion?

Day 880

I guess I shouldn't rag too hard on the smart people, because they set up Veronica to do a nice puff piece on yours truly. A little background first.

When all the endorsement money started rolling in, Suzanne came to me and said she wanted to cure a disease with the money. I told Suzanne to get in touch with Dr. Jaska to see what she was working on. That may seem a little strange, given Dr. Jaska's position as head of the Blue Ribbon Commission to Figure Out Who Blew It All Up, but I knew that Dr. Jaska knew that I didn't explode my dad. And, she is the smartest of the smart people I know.

Anyway, Dr. Jaska was working on a cure for sickle-cell disease, a blood disorder that messes up a person's red blood cells. So, Suzanne gave her a bunch of endorsement money and Dr. Jaska created a machine that somehow filters a person's blood and fixes the red blood cell problem. I'm certain that a smart person would say I did not describe that right, but the end result is that the machine is going to save a bunch of people's lives. Is that cool or what?

Another cool part of this deal is that Suzanne sent the money to a nonprofit foundation that Dr. Jaska founded, so the machines are donated FREE to hospitals. Granted, the machines are very expensive to manufacture, so there are only a few in existence, but I know for a fact that whichever candidate wins the election is going to support the project with massive federal funding.

OK. Background over. Today the Veronica Network ran a special feature presentation entitled "Junior Saves the Day: How a Wanted Criminal and Fugitive from Justice Fixed Our Blood." Excerpts follow:

> *Veronica: The laws in our country require us to be color blind, but disease does not respect man-made law. For example, sickle-cell disease is a blood disorder that strikes black people. The disease has killed millions of people worldwide, mostly in Africa, but it also affects a number of black people here in the United States. I am a black*

woman, and I have friends and relatives who have been stricken with this disease. Possibly because of my race, but more probably because of my popularity, prestige, and integrity as a newscaster and journalist, I have been given the honor of breaking this amazing story. A cure has been developed for sickle-cell disease. And even more amazing, we have Joshua Jennings, Jr., a man despised literally by millions, a man who has been hunted by the authorities for 880 days, to thank for this cure.

It is hard to imagine anything more important to survival than blood. The life of every creature is in the blood. There is power in the blood. Blood is elemental. Blood is basic. Let's hear from Dr. Grayson Jaska, who came up with the cure for sickle-cell disease.

Dr. Grayson Jaska: I have been working with a number of scientists for years on a potential cure for sickle-cell disease. Although we were close on the science side of the equation, I knew it would be decades before we would have the funding to complete our project. Then, totally out of the blue, I was contacted by a representative of Junior Jennings and offered copious amounts of money to complete our research on the cure for sickle-cell disease. I am a woman of science and not of faith, but I have to say Junior's help was nothing short of a miracle.

Veronica: Can you tell us how the cure works?

Dr. Grayson Jaska: I don't want to bore your viewers, Ms. Wells, but basically, the machine we have developed literally repairs a person's red blood cells. The bad blood goes into the machine and good blood comes out of the machine.

Veronica: So will sickle-cell disease soon be a thing of the past?

Dr. Grayson Jaska: Yes, although it will take some time. I predict that within fifteen years virtually all semblance of the disease will be eradicated.

Veronica: Do you find it ironic that the cure has come about as a result of the efforts of a wanted criminal?

Dr. Grayson Jaska: To be honest, Ms. Wells, I have heard the word "irony" misused by journalists and broadcasters so many times I am not really sure what the term means anymore. I will say this, though, if you will allow a scientist to attempt a little literary license. Blood will tell.

Veronica (obviously confused): Blood will tell what, Dr. Jaska?

Dr. Jaska (patiently): I worked closely with Joshua Jennings, Sr., on the AIDS cure. He was a great man, a man of vision. I don't know Joshua Jennings, Jr., well, but the young man clearly has his father's heart when it comes to helping others. That is what I meant when I said that blood will tell. Junior has first-class blood.

Veronica (still obviously confused): OK, thanks, that's great. Bloody good, if I can also use a literary license, although I may need to check with my lawyers to make sure I am not violating any copyright laws.

I guess that's enough. There was more, obviously. Thanks, smart people. Hopefully, the "literally millions" of people who despise me have been reduced by at least the number of folks who have sickle-cell disease or who know people who do. And thanks, Dr. Jaska, for the first-class-blood remark. Really made my day.

Day 883

The Patriot Avenger, one of my almost killers, is back in the headlines today, although this will likely be his last day in the spotlight. This morning the PA's lawyers filed a federal court lawsuit against Rifleocity, the company sponsoring the Junior Chase Cup. The PA contends that Rifleocity breached a fiduciary duty it owed to him by excluding him from the Junior Chase Cup and only making the contest available to the Islamic terrorists and the MFM. He also alleges that Rifleocity tortiously interfered with his prospective reward proceeds, violated the Federal Fairness in Contests and Lotteries Act, and violated his First Amendment rights.

According to the expert legal analyst on the Lawsuit Channel, "the First Amendment claim may actually have legs, because the Patriot Avenger declared he did not believe in God, and the other two contestants are clearly identified strongly with their religious beliefs. Plus, the lawsuit was filed in the United States District Court in San Francisco, which has a rich history of protecting First Amendment rights."

The PA made news this afternoon that will moot his claims, however. Turns out he made the mistake of messing with a bunch of senior citizens in the Phoenix QCR.

I was not aware of this, but the Gay AARP (GAARP) and the AARP are holding a joint national convention for the first time ever. The Phoenix QCR won a highly contested bidding process for the convention. Thousands of senior citizens are slowly puttering around the PQCR complaining about the government and the current generation and whatever else old people complain about. I am guessing the Luby's restaurants in Phoenix are making money hand over fist.

According to the news reports, the PA had planned to blow up the opening ceremonies of the convention, which were scheduled to be held in the Cialis Desert Inn. From a WCFL perspective, it was a stroke of brilliance, because the PA would have received a ton of extra points for killing old and gay people, with some minorities thrown in. He likely would have built a WCFL lead nobody could overcome short of a nuclear blast.

The PA, however, was tripped up by a nosy and perspicacious Arizona State criminology student putting herself through school working as a hotel maid. (And yeah, I stole that big word from the TV news report.) When Ashley Naomi, the Sun Devil student/maid, found the PA's notes on projected WCFL point calculations as she cleaned his room, she knew exactly what was going on and rushed to the main ballroom at the hotel to alert security. The security detail found the PA in a custodian's closet with enough explosives to blow up the entire hotel. The PA also had his poodle-mix dog with him.

The PA, whose real name is/was Doug Dash, managed to escape from hotel security, but he ran into the hotel ballroom where all the old people were congregating. That was his last mistake. I'm not sure exactly how the geezers recognized Dash as the Patriot Avenger (maybe it was his dog), but when they did, it was all over but the shouting. Before the security guys could stop them, the old folks literally stomped the PA to death. The poodle mix was unharmed.

Nick Bessett, the president of the AARP, was quoted as follows: "As I believe I said after the TQCR bombing, people should know by now that you don't mess with America's senior citizens, because we can still kick ass, as we proved today. I admit that my preference was to kick some towelhead ass, but this Patriot Avenger punk will do for now."

I don't believe I can add anything to that, so I will sign off for now.

Day 887

I have deferred to the smart people. We are at Seven Devils. Suzanne really wanted to come, which influenced my decision. We have been here a few days now and nothing bad has happened yet.

Our welcome when we arrived was surprisingly low-key. Sister Flannery took the three of us to Mother Superior Hookenstein's office and she assigned us each a room and a list of chores. I received a small smile from the mother superior, but that was about it. I'm not saying I deserved a hero's welcome or a standing ovation, but I was a bit taken aback by the lack of overt friendliness. Maybe the mother superior somehow read what I wrote about her being the kind of girl who could not get a date. Wouldn't put it past her.

Pig Butt, who goes by the name of Mr. Bennett here, is in hog heaven, if you will excuse the obvious pun, for two reasons. First, it turns out Pig Butt loves kids. His wife left him before they had kids, and Pig Butt has always wanted a big family. So Pig Butt is having a great time hanging out and playing with God's Elect.

Second, the sisters grow a bunch of their own food, so there is a long list of farm chores for Pig Butt to do. "It's not as much fun as pig farming, Junior," he told me, "but it's good to break a sweat working the land."

Suzanne, unbeknownst to me, has a cosmetology license, so I guess she is now my hairdresser/waitress/stripper/superagent traveling companion. She is putting her cosmetology training to good use by giving haircuts to all the kids. And it could just be my imagination, but Mother Superior Hookenstein's hair does not look as gray as it did when we first arrived. When I asked Suzanne about that, she invoked the hairdresser-client privilege.

And what about me, the guy with a history degree and limited skills? I got foot duty.

According to Sister Flannery, one of the biggest problems in an institution (my word, not hers) like this is that the kids' feet are subjected to all sorts of nasty bacteria. Plus, foot washing is not a priority for God's Elect. So once a year, there is a campus-wide foot washing, toenail clipping, and antibacterial applying. Every single God's Elect foot has to be thoroughly washed. Every toenail has to be properly clipped. And then every foot has to be dipped into some really strong (and foul-smelling) goo that kills every germ that is still hanging around. As you might suspect, it is not a job that anyone is really excited to do. Which is, of course, why the mother superior decided that now was a good time to handle this once-a-year chore.

"Junior," Sister Flannery told me, "you are once again the answer to prayer. I have been praying since the last foot cleaning that I be spared this chore, and then, providentially, you show up! God is great, isn't He?"

I suppose I don't mind being the answer to prayer, but why can't I be the answer to an "If only I had a good man to love and spoil rotten" prayer by a beautiful woman who is a great cook and loves to watch sports on television? Oh well, I guess answers to prayer can't be choosers.

Washing the feet wasn't horrible, but I don't recommend it as a career choice. It is pretty stinky work and all the bending over has kinda thrown a kink in my back. Plus a couple of God's Elect did not really understand the importance of my project and were reluctant to participate. I tried to explain that later they would thank me, but that logic did not go over very well. Some of God's Elect can run pretty fast.

More later from the land of clean feet.

Day 888

Today was the annual awards banquet here in the land of God's Elect. It was a ton of fun, although a bit long, since every kid got an award for something. There were awards for singing, drawing, kickball, finger painting, Scripture memorizing, and on and on. Lots of applause, lots of happy faces.

Suzanne got a blue ribbon for haircutting and Pig Butt got the Farmer of the Year award. And yes, I received the coveted Best Foot Washer award.

After all of God's Elect were put to bed, Suzanne, Pig Butt, and I were invited to the mother superior's office. Sister Flannery was there as well. We had a real nice visit. The mother superior had lost a bit of her frostiness, which I attribute in part to Suzanne's hair-color work.

Mother Superior Hookenstein talked in glowing terms about how much our endorsement money had helped God's Elect and how grateful she was. It was the speech I thought she would give when we first arrived.

I did my best to "aw shucks" it all off and "be humble," as my good friend Presley Kimball always advises. "For now," I said, "I guess giving the money away is just what we keep doing until the election is over and/or until I am not being chased by Islamic terrorists or Methodists."

The mother superior got a bit serious at that point. "What you do is definitely important, Junior, and you have been an absolute do-gooder machine for the past ten months or so. Tell me, how does that make you feel?"

I had to be honest—she was a mother superior, after all: "Good, but not as good as I thought it would, to tell you the truth."

The mother superior smiled, as if I was a dull child who had finally figured out the answer to an easy question. Then she said, "What you do is more important than who you are, Junior, unless who you are is more important than what you do."[144]

Day 900

Looks like we will need to leave Seven Devils. Three bozos were killed when they made the mistake of giving Jamie Kay a standing ovation after her Palmetto Dance. The other patrons in the Southern Comfort Lounge saw the Arabs stand and assumed they were about to witness a terrorist attack, so they shot the men. No charges were filed.

Don't want to risk the bozos following us here, so we are about to make an "appearance" somewhere far away from God's Elect so the bozos will come after us. The smart people aren't crazy about this idea, but I'm pulling rank. More later.

Day 904

Welcome to month thirty-one of the Surely This Has To Be Over Soon Tour. You, dear reader, have the advantage over me. You can tell by peeking ahead if we are almost finished. I, on the other hand, can't tell how many pages are left in this literary classic.

---

144 This statement is known as "The Mother Superior's Conundrum," the last and most famous of the Seven Conundrums in *Junior*.

My gut tells me the end is near, so I should go ahead and tell you about the oil deal. When I say "the end is near," I'm not speaking in terms of Baptist end-of-the-world, horrible Antichrist stuff, so don't freak out. I'm not predicting disaster for me or for the world in general. In fact, today I feel pretty lucky, like maybe this will all turn out OK.[145]

Those of you out there who are oil-and-gas-type folks or know a lot about Texas history may have already figured out what the East Texas Solution is. If so, congratulations. You can skip ahead to the next entry. For the rest of you, read on.

First, let's recap what was going on when the East Texas Solution was conceived. The bozos had just blown up the Rebecca #1, killing fifty-five Trinity employees. Senior was fit to be tied. He wanted to hurt the bozos bad. Specifically, he wanted to get back at the Sheik of the Decade. Senior knew that, short of a war, there was no way he could kill enough bozos to stop the sheik's terror tactics. And he knew that as long as the Sheik of the Decade and his counterparts in Iraq and Iran had control of all that oil, there would always be petrodollars to fund bozo attacks.

So, Senior decided to just take the bozos' oil. East Texas–style.

Now, a little Texas history from your favorite history major. In 1930, a guy named Dad Joiner discovered oil at 3,536 feet on the widow Daisy Bradford's farm in Rusk County, Texas. Joiner's well was the first well drilled into what was later designated as the East Texas Oil Field. The East Texas Oil Field is the largest oil field in the United States, if you don't count the Johnny-come-lately Alaskan fields.

The primary oil-producing formation in the East Texas Oil Field is the Woodbine Formation. The Woodbine Formation was so prolific when the East Texas Field was initially discovered that virtually anybody who could get a well drilled into the formation found a bunch of oil. Wells were drilled everywhere. In fact, at one point there were forty-four wells drilled in one city block in the city of Kilgore, Texas.

The oil produced by the East Texas Field was critical to the Allied war effort in World War II, so the world's largest oil pipeline at that point in time was built to transport the oil from Texas to refineries in the Philadelphia area. Dubbed "Big Inch," the twenty-four-inch pipeline was 1,400 miles long.

---

145 This is the last reference to luck in *Junior*, and like all the other references, it is found in a day associated with the number thirteen (9+0+4=13).

Eventually, the major oil companies gobbled up most of the good leases in the East Texas Oil Field, cutting out many of the local, small-time operators. Some of the local guys responded by drilling on land next to the majors' leases, and then deviating their wells underground to tap into the productive Woodbine Formation on the big boys' leases. This technique was dubbed "slant hole drilling." Since it was all done underground, it took the major oil companies decades to figure out what was happening.

The slant hole drillers took an estimated $100 million worth of oil from the major oil companies, and many of them used this money to become leading citizens in their communities. When the jig was up and the authorities brought criminal theft charges against the slant holers, not a single one of them was convicted. The citizens of East Texas were not about to convict their local heroes for sticking it to the major oil companies.

Senior knew about the history of the East Texas Field and decided, based in part upon Frank and Wally's advice, that the best way to get back at the sheik was to slant-hole the heck out of the bozos. The East Texas Solution was a huge undertaking that I can't begin to describe here, even if I understood it all well enough to explain it, which I don't. The gist of the deal is that Senior, under the protective cover of mounds of confusing lawyer-generated paperwork, created and funded hundreds of companies that drilled wells just across from the borders of Iraq, Iran, and Saudi Arabia. Once the wells were approved by the local country's regulatory authority, the wells were secretly reopened and directionally deviated underground across the border into the oil-producing formations that Allah had allegedly bequeathed to the bozos. The deviated wells then sucked Allah's oil out of the ground as hard and as fast as they could.

Senior's people also built several huge underground oil pipelines to move the oil thousands of miles away to underground storage facilities. In homage to the East Texas Field, one of the pipelines was named "Biggest Inch."

Although most of the discussions in Senior's office regarding the East Texas Solution were over my head, I do remember that a big issue was how to keep the bozos from finding out what was going on. And this is where General Dozier's involvement became important.

Remember when I said General Dozier was involved in the oil deal?[146] Well, General Dozier was the army's go-to guy in the event the United States

146 See Day 395.

decided to invade the bozos. This meant the general was continually briefed on the situation in bozo land. And it turns out that General Dozier had a computer-hacker guy who could sneak into the computer systems the bozos used to monitor their production and reserves. General Dozier used his hacker to check on the reserves in Iraq, Iran, and Saudi Arabia because he did not trust the reserve information published by those countries.

Senior knew about General Dozier's access to the bozos' computer systems (no big surprise) and asked the general if he could provide technical assistance for the East Texas Solution. General Dozier was happy to oblige and instructed his hacker to manipulate the reserve information in the bozos' computer systems so they would not realize what was happening until it was too late.

So there you go. You now know about the oil deal that I have been referring to, either directly or indirectly, since virtually the beginning of this adventure. As I know I mentioned somewhere,[147] the oil and gas pros thought the East Texas Solution would take about five years to pull off, and we have passed the five-year mark. This means Allah's oil should be almost completely sucked out of Saudi Arabia, Iraq, and Iran by now and safely sitting in the storage facilities.

The whole thing seems unbelievable, I know. But Senior is/was one of those guys you should not tick off. Because Senior knows all about payback.

Day 909

Pete called today. It was really good to hear from him. We had a long talk. We talked about a lot of things, including whether it made sense for him to join up with me again. Pete offered to come travel with me, and I could tell he meant it.

Pete has been doing a lot of stuff with the tribe back in New Mexico. In fact, he has become kind of a big dog within the tribal leadership. Obviously he is working in the background, since he is still officially a person of interest in the New Mexico explosion and a possible target of both the Methodists and the Muslims.

I told Pete it made more sense for him to stay on the reservation. The tribe needs him more than I do, at this point. I had to tell him three times to stay

---

147 See Day 775.

there before he agreed. Pete kept saying that he loved me and he wanted to help keep me safe, but I told him Pig Butt was here and could handle that issue.

Our conversation was, to be honest, incredibly painful and emotional. I'm pretty sure I hurt Pete's feelings. Pete asked, "Big Man, will I ever see you again?" I told him sure, but we both knew I was talking out of my backside, because there is no way either of us knows how this will end up.

So, Pete, if it turns out that it doesn't turn out like we hoped, you were the best friend a guy could have. I love you. But, you know, not in a gay way.

Day 915

Hello again. Pursuant to my plan to keep the bozos away from God's Elect, we have been visible in a number of different locales over the past fifteen days or so. With the Mossad's travel assistance, Suzanne, Pig Butt, and I have been in Cleveland, Ohio (Rock and Roll Hall of Fame and Museum), Seattle, Washington (Jimi Hendrix Museum—finally!), Wheaton, Illinois (Billy Graham Center Museum—at Suzanne's request), and Washington, D.C. (Arlington National Cemetery—Pig Butt knew several guys buried there). The Mossad guys made sure that pictures of the three of us at all of these places made it into the mainstream media. So I am pretty sure the bozos won't be going to Seven Devils, even if they somehow figured out we were there at one point in time.

Now that the bozos are hopefully confused about where we are, the plan is to go visit the prime minister. Jehu called and said the prime minister was fading, so we need to get up there quickly.

Day 918

Back in New Jerusalem. Back at the New Hotel King David.

Let's see, now. The last time I was here, Eb was a chubby stutterer. Now, Eb is number three on the Where in the World Did This Guy Come From list and in a dead heat for the presidency.

The last time I was here, Pete was here with me. Now, Pete is back at the reservation and my companion is a beautiful Southern Girl cosmetologist/stripper/waitress/superagent.

The last time I was here, only the feds were after me. Now, I am also being hunted by crazy Methodists, fartwa enthusiasts, and fanatical Muslims.

The last time I was here, the prime minister of Israel was healthy and vigorous. Now, he is dying.

The Mossad guys took me to the prime minister's house last night. Suzanne and Pig Butt stayed here at the hotel. We have a nice big suite here.

Jehu and Hannah were both with the prime minister when I arrived. The prime minister asked them to leave. Hannah resisted at first, but eventually she left. I think she had tears in her eyes.

The prime minister was dressed in a suit, like this was some sort of a formal meeting. He sat stiffly upright in a wheelchair, but he looked like he should have been wearing pajamas and lying in bed. The prime minister was gaunt and pale and obviously in pain. Since what we talked about may be important, I am going to write down as much as I can remember. Frankly, I don't know if what was said is important or not. But the prime minister is a very important guy and I don't want to mess up if part of my job is to record what we talked about.

Believe it or not, the first thing we talked about was my love life. The prime minister commented on how pretty Suzanne was and asked if we were "a couple." I told him I did not know. He laughed and said that if my love life was anything like his, I would find out the answer to that question when Suzanne told me that we were a couple. The prime minister then kind of rambled a bit about his wife and family. Said he had a really smart father-in-law. Not sure what that was all about.

We also talked about food. "You know, young man," the prime minister said, "in the first Exodus, Jehovah rained manna from heaven. In our current promised land, we eat hamburgers, tacos, fajitas, and pizza. A big improvement, don't you think? I think the Christians' sophomoric 'Jehovah Kicks Butt' cheer is ridiculous, but I must admit that I am incredibly grateful for the food Jehovah has provided for us here. I think that deep-dish pizza is especially heaven-sent. We have a place here in New Jerusalem called Eglon's Fat Boy Pizza. When I eat that pizza I feel like I will never die. And if it wasn't for your father, I would never have eaten deep-dish pizza."

After we talked about food for a while, the prime minister seemed to drift off. He wasn't asleep. He just seemed to be lost in thought. When the prime minister refocused, he seemed surprised to see me for a second, then he recovered. "You know, Junior," he said, "I owe you an apology. When you first came to see me, I said you were not a son of a bitch like your father, or something to that effect.[148] To be honest, that was not a compliment. I knew Senior had big plans for you, although I did not know exactly what they were, and when I met you way back when, I had serious doubts about whether you had the chutzpah to pull it off. Obviously, I was mistaken. You have survived all of these months and accomplished a great deal. So I take back my previous statement. You ARE a son of a bitch, just like your dad."

Not knowing what else to say, I thanked the prime minister of Israel for calling me a son of a bitch.

Then the prime minister continued. "And while I'm at it, let me also apologize for my people. Hannah told me that the Jewish charities were not properly thanking you for your contributions. Frankly, I can't explain their lack of discernment on this issue. Although I obviously can't reveal everything to them, I have told my people how important you are to the success of our nation and how you have helped Eb in so many ways. I have even written letters to the charities involved. But for some reason, when it comes to you, what I say and write does not appear to matter to many of my people. I can't explain it, except to say that I fear our people may have lost the capacity for gratitude. I had hoped that we could enjoy the milk and honey of this country without falling prey to its tendency toward selfishness, but my hopes have not been realized. You deserve more respect from the chosen people, Junior. Maybe it will come later as everything plays out. I certainly hope so."

Before I could ask the prime minister to explain to me how "everything plays out," he moved on to another topic. "But as for me, Junior, I am incredibly grateful for everything your father has done and everything you have done. It has been miraculous."

I thought the prime minister was referring to Senior's work in allowing the Israelites to take over North Dakota, and I commented on how it must have been hard for him to adjust to the cold weather. At that point in the conversation the prime minister's eyes shone brightly as he smiled, and for just a moment, he did not look terminally ill. "Oh, Junior," he said, "I am not talking about North Dakota. North Dakota is bupkes compared to what is

148 See Day 78.

coming next. I only wish I could be around to see it." Then he zoned out on me again.

When it appeared that the prime minister's apparent trance would continue indefinitely, I went to the door and invited Jehu and Hannah back into the room. Hannah looked at the prime minister, shook her head, and said, "He does this more and more frequently now. Sometimes he is gone for thirty minutes or more."

As Jehu fussed with the prime minister's wheelchair, the prime minister looked at me. It was only then that I remembered what Senior wanted me to say. I wasn't even sure the prime minister really knew who I was, but I just blurted out: "Mr. Prime Minister, my father asked me to tell you that you did a great job and he really appreciated all of your hard work."[149] The prime minister smiled and a tear rolled down his cheek, but he did not respond. And then Jehu rolled the prime minister's wheelchair out of the room.

Day 921

Some good news today, I think. The Securities and Exchange Commission has announced a fraud inquiry regarding stock purchases and sales by Franklin Icks, the president of Rifleocity. I suspect our old friend Dale Piper may still be on the case after all.

We are no longer in New Jerusalem. For the last several days we have been hanging out on a sheep ranch. Don't know why, other than Hannah knew the people here and said we should be safe here. I don't want to tell you the name of the place, just in case things don't end up well. Wouldn't want the nice folks here to get into any trouble.

I did not get off on the right foot with the nice sheep guys. Things are really busy here and we eat in shifts. For some reason, Suzanne and I wound up eating with a bunch of the sheep guys' kids. Suzanne really liked eating with the kids. I thought the kids were OK, especially if you are fond of squirming, spilling, and screaming.

Anyway, the kids were not eating most of their food, and so I fed a bunch of the scraps to the border collies on the ranch that herd the sheep. The border collies seemed hungry and really grateful.

---

149 See Day 740.

A tip from your favorite Man on the Run. If you are ever on a sheep ranch, absolutely do NOT take the children's scraps and feed the scraps to the border collies. Sheep guys really do not like that. Apparently it messes up the dogs' stomachs and affects their ability to herd the sheep. My bad.

The reason things are so busy is that we are in the middle of sheep-shearing season, which they tell me is the sheep rancher's equivalent of the farmer's harvest time. In other words, this is a very important time of year for the sheep folks. This is when the sheep folks figure out how much money they will make for all of their sheep-raising efforts. A bunch of certified sheep shearers are here. I had no idea that you could get certified as a sheep shearer.[150]

Pig Butt, as usual, is very helpful. His pig-farming skills apparently translate quite well into sheep ranching. The sheep ranchers are very grateful for his help. Plus, he knew enough not to feed the border collies.

As I have said on numerous occasions in this rambling account, I have limited skills. So most of my duties here have involved trash duty and cleanup, things I could not mess up very badly. I also play with the dogs, who like me because I gave them the dinner scraps.

Anyway, today I finally did something that made the sheep people happy. Totally by accident, of course.

The dogs and I were wandering around in the wilderness, a couple of miles from the barns and stuff where the sheep shearing and other important work was going on. I had no particular plan—I was just kind of goofing off and contemplating what I would do once we had to leave the sheep ranch.

Just as I was about to turn around and head back, the dogs started barking and going crazy and ran into the bushes. To be honest, my first thought was that a Junior fartwa hunter or a crazy Muslim sent by the Man of the Decade had found me, and I wondered if maybe I would be safer with pit bulls or Doberman pinschers than with border collies.

To my relief, the border collies had found a sheep, not a crazy Methodist or Muslim. The sheep had hurt its leg somehow and could not walk. So I picked it up and carried it back to the main house. I had to take a bunch of breaks along the way because the sheep was heavy, although I may have

---

150 Some scholars point out that Junior refers to a "sheepstorm" in Day 1 (sometimes translated as "sheep shearing," see Day 1, footnote 1) and question Junior's apparent lack of knowledge regarding the sheep-ranching business. See *Junior: Sacrificial Lamb or Wolf in Sheep's Clothing?* by Paige Wilder Webre.

omitted that part of the story when I arrived. As far as the sheep people know, I may have carried the sheep on my shoulders all the way without a break.

I was totally blown away by my reception when I arrived back at the main house. Everybody stopped what they were doing to shake my hand or give me a hug. The sheep shearing actually stopped for thirty minutes or so and everybody of legal drinking age hoisted a cold beer and toasted my retrieval of the lost sheep. And all for just one sheep. It was pretty cool, and it made me feel like I was contributing after all.

So now I have a standing invitation to come back and be a shepherd guy, as long as I don't feed the border collies. More later from your favorite Shepherd on the Run.

Day 925

You know when things have not been going your way, and then some good things happen, and you want to believe that the good things are a sign that everything will be all right after all, but deep down inside you have this sinking feeling that maybe you are misreading the signs, and you should not get your hopes up because if you do, you will just be even more disappointed when things don't work out? (Not a good sentence, I know, Dr. Hoover.) I am not a big believer in signs, mostly because the people I know who think they can interpret the signs of the times are almost always disappointed. Generally, I don't look at what is going on around me and try to interpret or predict what will happen next.

However, if I WAS a believer in and/or interpreter of signs, today would be one of those days that would make me think this is all going to work out after all.

Dr. Jaska held a televised press conference today. She said a lot of stuff, but here are some of the good parts:

Dr. Jaska: I am pleased to announce that the Blue Ribbon Commission to Figure Out Who Blew It All Up has reached some conclusions. The commission has concluded that Sheik Faisel Omar Saeed Al Zahrani is responsible for the New Mexico explosion that took place over two and a half years ago. When I say "responsible," I do not mean Sheik Al Zahrani was present in New Mexico when the explosion occurred. In fact, we know that Sheik Al Zahrani was at the Cannes Film Festival in Cannes, France, when the explosion occurred. However, we have evidence that Sheik Al Zahrani planned and funded the attack in New Mexico, and that the primary target of the attack was Joshua Jennings, Sr. This evidence includes the sworn testimony of individuals with knowledge of the attack, as well as transcripts of taped telephone conversations, copies of e-mails and text messages, and bank records that establish that Sheik Al Zahrani funded the attack.

FBI Director Matthew Lopez (interrupting): And for the record, the sworn testimony was not obtained through torture in the United States of America or on any United States military installation in Australia or Antarctica.

Dr. Jaska (looking annoyed): Since the Golden Goose Act has been repealed, and our legal counsel has determined that the Golden Goose Act would not prevent prosecution relating to the explosion, our government has been in contact with our good friends in the Saudi Arabian government and requested permission to speak with Sheik Al Zahrani. Unfortunately, Sheik Al Zahrani seems to have disappeared. The Saudi Arabian government has informed us that they, too, are looking for Sheik Al Zahrani and have not been able to find him. Apparently, Sheik Al Zahrani, two of his bodyguards, and three of his wives cannot be located.

FBI Director Matthew Lopez (interrupting again): We have issued a worldwide "be on the lookout for" alert for the sheik. The Saudi Arabian government has issued a similar warning, because the Saudis want to talk to the sheik about some oil-production irregularities in their country. The governments of Iraq and Iran also have issued notices regarding Sheik Al Zahrani. When we asked them why they wanted to talk to the sheik, those governments told us to mind our own beeswax.

Dr. Jaska (smiling just a bit and looking less annoyed at the interruption): I am also very pleased to announce that we have found absolutely no evidence that Joshua Jennings, Jr., had any involvement in the explosion. We no longer have any interest in talking to Joshua Jennings, Jr., about the tragedy in New Mexico. On a personal level, I want to apologize for any harm or trauma we have caused to Mr. Jennings, and I hope he will soon be able to mourn the loss of his family in peace, without worrying about being arrested by the authorities or killed by crazed vigilantes. Surely everybody realizes by now that Junior is just the innocent son of a famous man, and he has done nothing to deserve the hatred and vitriol that has been directed at him. And finally, again on a personal note and not on an official level, to Samson Fairman and the Methodist Free Militia: Shame on you. You should know better.

FBI Director Matthew Lopez: Let me also add on a personal level my thanks for the help of Dr. Jaska and the commission. I know this took longer than we thought it would, and some of you out there thought we could have done better with Dr. Ravindra Svarup Gupta, but hey, this is government work, and things sometimes move slowly. Plus, since Dr. Gupta recently lost his title as the longest-running champion on Triple Jeopardy, maybe he isn't as smart as we thought after all. And for all you Methodist Free Militia members and Junior fartwa enthusiasts, I hope this announcement today will convince you to stop your persecution of Joshua Jennings, Jr. From your perspective, there is absolutely no need to try and shoot, stab, or blow up Junior Jennings. As for the Islamic terrorists who are stalking Junior, I have no idea what your perspective is, but it seems to me that since the sheik is missing there is no need for you to continue to hunt Junior Jennings, either. The FBI requests as nicely as we can that you just go back home. Pretty please.

Pretty good stuff, huh? It only took 925 days, but now at least the feds don't think I blew everybody up. So the history books will not blame the explosion on the Apaches, which is something I have been worrying about from Day 1.

I wonder what Samson Fairman is thinking about right now. Does he feel remorse for killing all those people while trying to kill me, when it turns out I was innocent all along? My guess is no. I suspect he wanted to kill me because the information I broadcast about his nefarious deeds in Pakistan cost him the Republican nomination for president. The hunt for me as the great exploder was just an excuse.

I hope I am not speaking too soon, but it seems to me I should not have anything to worry about, at least Methodist Free Militia–wise. So Fairman, if this book ever gets read, I want you to know that I believe you are a slime-bucket. You were rich, comfortable, and everybody spoke highly of you. And what did you do? You blew up innocent people. So I hope you get what you deserve. I hope there is a little mourning and weeping in your future.

Don't misunderstand me, dear reader, I am not asking anybody to go hurt Fairman. My hope is that maybe Fairman will reap just a tad of what he sows. I am not sure exactly what that means, other than whenever a bad guy got into trouble, my mother would say that he was just reaping what he had sowed. Watch out for the Reaper, Fairman.[151]

Day 930

I suppose I should mention the election again. We are finally getting close to voting time. Despite the best efforts of the Hate Millionaires and the political reporters, there have been no scandals on either side. I don't know if the Mossad guys have given up on finding dirt on Davis or Big Fly, but it seems to me if there was any dirt there they would have found it already.

Two or three days ago all four candidates boarded a train, and they will travel together throughout the United States in the weeks leading up to election day. The press secretaries for both sides agreed to call the train the Unity Train. The candidates are going to make joint appearances and give joint speeches to promote the nation's unity and celebrate the peaceful transition of power. Believe it or not, the last stop on the tour is the Apache reservation where everybody got blown up.

---

151 Samson Fairman is not mentioned again in *Junior*. Six months after *Junior* was published, Fairman's wife turned him in to the authorities after a domestic altercation at their home. Fairman was charged with numerous felonies associated with the explosions at the Sisters of Mercy and Charity Convent in Montreal and White Only Settlement. He committed suicide in jail before he could be tried on any of the charges.

One of the unexpected side effects of this nonconfrontational election is that the candidates don't need to raise as much money. No need for expensive attack ads when everybody loves each other. This means the really rich people who usually try to buy favors and ambassadorships have extra money to spend elsewhere. The *BKNY Times* has reported that charitable giving is up 20 percent and that private jets are selling like hotcakes.

I am guessing that the Blue Ribbon Commission's findings will make it that much easier for whoever wins the election to give me a stamp of approval so that I can officially come in from the cold. Suzanne is still skeptical that the politicians will help me, but that is part of what makes her such a great agent, I suppose.

Speaking of Suzanne, she has been fielding a number of endorsement opportunities for me. It seems that now that I have been cleared by the Blue Ribbon Commission, companies want me to endorse their products. Unfortunately, most of the opportunities are for diet programs that would require before and after pictures. I have instructed my agent to respectfully decline those opportunities for the time being.

That's it for now. I need a double bacon cheeseburger.

Day 933

Welcome to month thirty-two of the I May Be A Son Of A Bitch But At Least I Am No Longer A Wanted Criminal Tour. In reviewing the last few entries, I noticed that I have not told you where I was. Since we left the sheep ranch, Suzanne, Pig Butt, and I have just sort of been traveling around. We don't stay in the same place for more than a day or two. For the most part, we've been driving around the northeastern part of the country, because Suzanne has always wanted to see it. For the past few days we have been in Maine.

Some more good news—looks like the Junior Chase Cup has been discontinued. Rifleocity, the gun manufacturer who came up with the idea, filed bankruptcy yesterday. The news report did not specifically say why, but my guess is that the SEC fraud investigation was probably a big reason. So thanks, Mr. Piper.[152]

---

152 This is the last reference to Dale Piper in *Junior*. Scholars have not been able to agree upon who Dale Piper was, or if he even existed. There are no military or civilian records indicating that a man named Dale Piper, with a military, defense, or consulting background, lived in the United States during this time period.

Got an e-mail today from Mary Haught. Mary is a wills and estates–type lawyer in El Paso. I know Mary because she is very involved in philanthropic stuff in El Paso and is on the board of directors for the Assassin's children's home. Mary's e-mail said that now that I am no longer wanted by the feds, she needs to talk to me about Senior's estate. This is a surprise to me, because I did not think Mary was Senior's estate lawyer. I thought Senior used some hotshot guy in Dallas.

I confess that over the last 933 days I have not thought about Senior's estate even one time. Now I have all sorts of questions, like who has been taking care of Senior's estate for the last 933 days and how it has been operated.

My exoneration by the Blue Ribbon Commission has proven to be a boon to our friend Veronica. Veronica has been on the talk show circuit, taking credit for her declaration way back when that I was innocent and that everybody should just let me be.[153] Veronica's Let Him Be products are selling faster than she can produce them, and she has added a line of "Shame on you, Samson" T-shirts. I wonder if she has permission from Dr. Jaska for that line.

If in fact my life is about to get back to somewhere close to the normal human being line, and I realize that is a big "if," I wonder where Veronica will go from here. Most of her successful stories have been about yours truly. She can't ride that horse forever. So what's next? Movies? Politics? Porn?[154]

I am sitting on a picnic table on a dock facing the Atlantic Ocean. Suzanne and Pig Butt are standing in line for what is supposed to be the best lobster sandwich in Maine, according to Suzanne's guidebook. I am hungry—can hardly wait. More later.

Day 937

Well, I have been accused of a treasonous mass murder I did not commit, chased by Methodists, assisted by snow globe girls, alternately criticized and

---

153 See Day 58.

154 Junior's speculation about Veronica Wells's future proved to be either prescient or simply a lucky guess, depending upon your point of view. Ms. Wells appeared in several first-run movies after *Junior* was published, receiving generally poor reviews. She then served two terms as a United States senator from her home state of Louisiana. Upon retiring from the Senate, she formed a movie production company that produced pornographic documentary films.

praised by nuns, and despised by millions. You would think I would be incapable of surprise at this point. But you would be wrong.

Today I was informed during dinner by my Alabama white trash Protestant superagent that we are a couple. When I asked when this happened, Suzanne said, "At least four or five months ago, Junior. I can't believe you didn't know. Everybody else knows." I looked at Pig Butt, who was trying real hard not to laugh as he nodded and ate his fried chicken.

I am not saying I am unhappy about this. Just surprised that it happened and I did not even know it.

Also received an e-mail from Sister Flannery today that said simply: "Congratulations! See, I was right, wasn't I?"

I am not sure what Sister Flannery is congratulating me for. I assume she is congratulating me because the Blue Ribbon Commission has totally exonerated me, but who knows, maybe she is congratulating me because I am now one-half of a couple.

Anyway, if this ever gets read, Sister Flannery, thanks for your help. Best of luck with God's Elect.[155] I think that is all for now. I need to take a break and contemplate my new status.

Day 940

Well, it worked. The East Texas Solution is officially a success. Dickie Marsh sent me an e-mail yesterday that read:

Pay attention to the news. General Dozier's computer geek just removed the hocus-pocus hacker stuff from the Arabs' reserve data. The Arabs now know exactly how much (or little) oil they have left. They suspected before, but now they know how bad it really is. They have plenty for their own needs, but absolutely nothing for export. That is all over for them.

---

155 Although there was a Seven Devil's Home for God's Chosen in North Carolina when *Junior* was written, the true identity of Sister Flannery has never been conclusively determined. After *Junior* was published, Mother Superior Hookenstein was contacted by the *BKNY Times* for a comment and stated simply: "No comment." Junior's description of the events at Seven Devils was the basis for *Let the Nuns Run the Show*, an award-winning Broadway musical that ran for over a decade. Mother Superior Hookenstein was played by Mitzi Hyatt of Big Boy fame. Ms. Hyatt won a Tony Award for her performance.

Sure enough, the world knows today that the bozos are virtually out of oil. It's all over CNN and all the other channels. The Democrats Are Stupid Channel credits President Uncle Ken's economic policies for this good news, although it does not say exactly how these policies brought about this result. The Republicans Are Stupid Channel says the economic and social policies proposed by Eb and General Dozier caused the bozos to run out of oil. The Baptist News Channel reports that the Antichrist is here and the end of the world is imminent.

President Uncle Ken presided over a news conference today in the Rose Garden. He assured the American people that the United States was prepared for this contingency and had billions of barrels of oil in reserve. What the president didn't say was that those billions of barrels belonged to Allah five years ago and that Senior had stolen them from the bozos and transported them via pipeline to secret locations guarded by the U.S. Army.

When asked whether he had been contacted by the leaders of Saudi Arabia, Iraq, and Iran, Uncle Ken said, "I have received queries regarding emergency economic assistance from each of those countries. I have assured our friends in those countries that I will inform the new administration of their requests. I think it makes more sense for the new president to deal with this issue, don't you?" President Uncle Ken said it with a totally straight and sincere face, but you could hear the reporters laughing in the background.

When General Dozier was asked about the situation, he said, "I am just as shocked as all of you. I thought those countries had enough oil to supply the world for decades to come." When a reporter asked how, if elected, Eb's administration would handle requests from Saudi Arabia, Iraq, and Iran for economic aid from the United States, General Dozier began, "I assume we will be able to work out an aid package for our friends in those countries . . ." and then the general started laughing and could not stop for several minutes. After he regained his composure, the general began again, "No, seriously, we will do our best to help . . ." and then he burst into laughter again.

CNN reports that impromptu parades/rallies/riots are breaking out all over the United States. The film footage shows a lot of Jehovah Kicks Butt! and Allah Sucks! signs. People are dancing in the streets and waving American flags.

So, it's been a good day. Hoorah for our team. Senior pays back the Sheik of the Decade.[156]

Day 945

The fallout from the East Texas Solution continues. Banks are foreclosing on real estate developments all over the Middle East.

The Riot Channel, however, is making money hand over fist, because there are riots everywhere in bozoland. Without our oil money, the bozos are having a hard time keeping the lights on, and folks are not happy. Iraq, Iran, and Saudi Arabia have each called out their army to quell the disturbances, with limited success. Stuff is blowing up. Sheiks are getting out of Dodge.

The members of the Saudi Arabian World Cup team held a press conference in which they complained about not being paid. The Manchester United Channel reported that yesterday was payday in the Arab Premier League and none of the players received a paycheck. The announcer cried tears of joy when he discussed the possibility that the soccer teams would return to England.[157]

And me? I am hunkered down with my better half and Pig Butt in Vermont. I am just kind of waiting around and hoping the good news continues. I don't want to get my hopes too high. Pig Butt helps keep me grounded. He cleans his guns every day and gives Suzanne and me daily shooting lessons. "It ain't over till it's over" is Pig Butt's motto, and I am inclined to follow it. He is a Congressional Medal of Honor winner, after all, and the bozos are still out there. We still need to keep watch and be on our guard.

---

156 Although the word "luck" is not used in Day 940, scholars have found significant the fact that such a momentous and positive event occurred on a day associated with the number thirteen (9+4+0 = 13), and have constructively implied the word "lucky" as part of this entry.

157 The Arab Premier League was disbanded just a few months after this entry was written, and the former English Premier League teams quickly moved back to England. The date the Arab Premier League folded is now celebrated as a national holiday in England.

Day 950

Decided to celebrate the success of the East Texas Solution by traveling down the Kentucky Bourbon Trail, which, according to Suzanne's guide book, "features six distinctive distilleries nestled in the lush scenery of the Bluegrass." Unfortunately, the previous sentence is not entirely correct. We are in Kentucky, but Suzanne prohibited a celebratory journey down the Kentucky Bourbon Trail. NOW, I feel like I am officially one-half of a couple.

We are in Kentucky to meet up with Mary Haught, the wills lawyer I mentioned earlier.[158] Why Kentucky, you ask? Well, I decided it was not a good idea to go to El Paso, since the bozos might be looking for me in Texas. Mary was coming to Lexington, Kentucky, anyway to interview a witness in a probate dispute she is working on, so we drove down from Vermont.

Mary and I met in her hotel room. Suzanne and Pig Butt stayed down in the lobby. Generally, here is what occurred:

Mary, after a few minutes of small talk: Senior came to see me a few weeks before the explosion and told me he wanted to change his will. He brought with him the will prepared by his attorney in Dallas. Senior said he wanted to make a few changes, and he did not want to use his regular lawyer, because the lawyer's secretary was good friends with your mother and had a big mouth.

Me: I never saw either will. I don't recall ever discussing anything with my parents about their estate planning.

Mary: Senior told me as much. Anyway, Senior told me that he was suffering from a terminal illness and that he needed to amend the estate plan and give some specific instructions.

Me: Didn't that seem a little suspicious to you? I mean, Senior didn't look sick, did he?

Mary: Senior did not look sick to me, but his motivations were irrelevant to me and it was none of my business. My job, as long as he was competent, was to make the changes he wanted.

---

158   See Day 933.

Me: So what did he change?

Mary: First a little background on what has happened since the explosion. Your mother was named as the first executor of your father's estate. Since she was unfortunately killed in the explosion too, the executor job was supposed to fall to you as the successor, but you were obviously not in a position to perform. The second successor executor is Samuel Johnson.

Me: The Assassin?

Mary: Correct. Mr. Johnson and I have been working together with the probate court to manage Senior's significant estate. The probate judge, who was a good friend of your father's, has bent over backward to give us leeway while we wait for your legal predicament to be resolved one way or the other.

Me: Well, I hope that will be soon.

Mary: As do I. Anyway, there is one instruction from Senior to your mother, in her role as executor, that neither Mr. Johnson nor I understand, and we decided I should talk to you about it. Mr. Johnson was concerned that the resolution of this issue could not wait until your legal status has been fully resolved.

Mary then showed me the instruction in question. It read: "Rebecca—After the Arabs' oil dries up, tell Junior to give the Mexican money to the Jews. Junior will know what I am talking about."

Day 953

Still wandering around in Kentucky. The smart folks figure the bozos will not be looking for us here.

I have placed several calls to the prime minister and sent several e-mails to request a meeting so we can discuss the Mexican money. The prime minister has not called me back. For the life of me, I can't figure out why Senior wants me to give the Mexican money to the Jews.

I did figure out one thing, however, that makes me feel better. I have been mad at my dad since virtually Day 1 of this bizarre journey because I thought he knew about the explosion and he allowed my mom and sisters to be blown up with him. I mean, Senior always seems to be one step ahead, so surely he knew Mom and the girls would be at the rally on the reservation, right?

Well, upon further reflection, maybe not. Senior's instruction about the Mexican money was written specifically to my mom. That clearly means Senior thought Mom would survive him. So, I'm sorry, Dad, for doubting you. I know you loved Mom and the girls and would never have put them in harm's way. Mom and the girls probably just flew up there to surprise you.

Suzanne just yelled to come over to the television. Be right back.

Very sad news. The prime minister has died. Don't feel like saying anything else at this point.

Day 959

I could not go to the prime minister's funeral, but I watched it on television. Eb gave a wonderful speech. He recited all the prime minister's accomplishments and concluded by saying that, despite these accomplishments, the prime minister was the most humble man in Israel.

I feel like I have watched Eb grow up before my very eyes. Eb has matured from a stuttering nebbish into a true statesman and leader. The campaign has done wonders for him.

The Sheik of the Decade is back in the news today. The Real Estate Network is reporting that the sheik borrowed a bunch of the money he used to purchase blown-up Israel from Iraq and Iran, and he has stopped making his loan payments. The lenders, a consortium of New York banks, are in a pickle because even though the sheik allegedly cleaned up the radioactive fallout in Jerusalem, there is no way that the real estate value of Israel comes even close to what is still owed on the loan. The New York lenders are looking at a catastrophic loss. Naturally, they are making overtures to the feds for help.

General Dozier was interviewed on the Banking Network and asked whether the Democrats would consider federal help for the bankers who loaned money to the sheik if the Democrats won the election. "Sure," the general responded, "we would consider that, for about ten seconds. Then we would seriously consider filing federal criminal indictments against these parasites for aiding and abetting the man who killed President Carrier and all the other good folks in

New Mexico." As we get closer and closer to the election, General Dozier has lost all pretense of political correctness. I am not complaining; it just seems a bit odd for the general to restrain his natural tendencies for months of campaigning, then let it all hang out right before the election.

CNN, following up on the Real Estate Network report, says that the Saudi Arabian government has frozen all the sheik's assets it can find, but financial experts are opining that it is likely impossible to locate and freeze all the sheik's assets all over the world, because he simply has too many. The Accountant and Actuarial Network is reporting that independent accountants who worked for the sheik are being questioned by Saudi authorities and, in some instances, being offered financial incentives to cooperate.

Guess that is all for now. Rest in Peace, Prime Minister.

Day 962

Remember when I said that the Unity Train's last stop was the Apache reservation where all of this started?[159] Well, the candidates arrived at the reservation today, took a tour, and met with the tribal leaders.

And then they had a press conference, and things got a little bit crazy. General Dozier spoke first:

Eb is about to say something that is a bit unusual. Some of you may not like it. We have talked about it, and I am fine with what he is about to say. This will be a win-win for everybody.

Then Eb spoke:

I always like to have General Dozier introduce me when I am about to say something that some folks may not like. You guys always get such expectant looks on your faces, and you start punching numbers on your cell phones.

---

159   See Day 930.

The crowd gave a brief, nervous laugh. Eb continued:

> *First, let me say how much I love this country. Campaigning has brought me in contact with many wonderful people and I have to say that we are blessed as a country to have so many fine citizens. But, after a great deal of thought, I have decided to stop my campaign for the presidency. I urge all of you to vote for Kevin Davis and Big Fly Washington. They will make a great team and will lead this country admirably.*

Eb paused to take a breath. Some people in the crowd began yelling "No! No!" Reporters shouted questions.

Eb raised his hand and began again:

> *Let me try to explain this and I think I will answer most of your questions. First, my health is fine. Second, there is no impending scandal out there. Third, nobody is forcing me to do this.*

The questions and shouting continued until General Dozier stood up and glared at everybody. When the noise stopped, Eb continued:

> *I am proud to be an American. I am also proud to be a Jew. I have been asked to serve as the next prime minister of Israel. I think it is a job I need to do. I am convinced that Dr. Davis will be an absolutely great president and that my highest and best use at this point in time is to serve the Jewish nation.*

There was a bunch more, but I will leave it at that. I think the general is absolutely correct. This is a win-win. The United States gets a great president, and Israel gets a great prime minister. And don't think for a moment that I have not realized this is probably exactly what Senior intended. Senior wanted Eb to mature through the crucible of the election campaign and be in place to lead Israel when the prime minister passed away. (And yeah, Dr. Hoover, I had to look "crucible" up just to make sure.)

Seems to me there could have been an easier way for Senior to do this than getting blown up and pointing the feds at me as the main suspect, but there you go.

So it looks like we will all live happily ever after.

Day 965

You knew, dear reader, that I was being sarcastic with my "happily ever after" line in the last entry, right? I really was.

Well, I clearly should not have said that, even in jest. Because we almost wound up about as far away from happily ever after as you can get. The good news, for you excitement junkies who may have been bored lately due to the lack of stuff being blown up, is that this entry is right up your alley.

It turns out the smart people were not as smart as we hoped. The bozos somehow figured out we were in Kentucky. And yesterday, they found us.

As you know from previous entries, Suzanne likes to go to church on Sunday. She has, to her credit, abstained from churchgoing at my request because of all the hoopla the Chicago churchgoing incident created. Yesterday was Sunday, and Pig Butt decided Suzanne might like to go to Bible World, a Christian theme park located here in Kentucky. Pig Butt and I figured that if we dressed appropriately, we could enjoy the park in relative anonymity and Suzanne could get her Jesus buzz (do NOT tell her I said that).

So we drove to Bible World, and of course it was closed because it was Sunday and no self-respecting Christian theme park is going to make its employees work on the Lord's Day. I can't believe I did not think of that.

I am not sure if I have mentioned this, but Suzanne, Pig Butt, and I have been riding around in Kentucky in a white panel van. The smart people figured there were so many white panel vans out there, we would not be noticed.

The first bullets shot by the bozos ripped through the side of the white panel van as we sat idling in front of the padlocked entrance to the Bible World parking lot. Pig Butt screamed at us to hit the deck, and he gunned the van through the chain. In just a few seconds, we were inside the park. I was on the deck and did not see what Pig Butt did, but I learned later that he threw a grenade at the front entrance as we approached and drove the van right through one of the ticket-taking stalls. I don't know where the hand grenade came from.

Pig Butt parked the van behind Noah's Ark and gave Suzanne and me both guns and hand grenades. I'm not gonna lie. I was scared to death. I glanced at Pig Butt. He had a smile on his face as if he was about to eat some chocolate cake. With vanilla ice cream on top. Suzanne, on the other hand, appeared to be possessed. Her normally sweet and placid face was contorted into a frightening scowl and she was muttering to herself, using words that I have never heard her say before and cannot repeat here. I thought at the time that we might need to get in touch with Former Father Farley.

We peeked through the windows of Noah's Ark and saw fifteen bozos walk into the park. They were carrying automatic rifles and looked very confident. They were not seeking cover.

Suzanne, still muttering, started to jump out of the second-story window of Noah's Ark and, I guess, charge the bozos. Pig Butt held her back, although not easily. He put a finger to his lips, then picked up his rifle and shot five bozos. It took five seconds. The other ten bozos took cover and began to return fire.

We left Noah's Ark quickly, which was good, because the bozos pretty much destroyed it with automatic gunfire and hand grenades. They even shot the rainbow hanging over the ark.

The Garden of Eden was close by, so we ran inside. Suzanne immediately left us. Pig Butt said, "Junior, you stay with me. I can't control Suzanne. She's got the bloodlust real bad. I've seen it before. Normally it happens to a guy after his buddy gets shot, though. I have never seen anybody get this amped-up at the beginning of a battle. If we survive this, I suggest that you NEVER cheat on this woman."

He still had the chocolate-cake smile on his face. I was not smiling.

Pig Butt and I hid behind an exhibit called the Tree of Life and waited. Pig Butt pointed across the way to the Tree of Knowledge of Good and Evil exhibit and waved. "She's back there," he said. "Just wanted to make sure she did not shoot us."

Two bozos, wary this time, crept into the Garden of Eden. They passed an exhibit where a guy in a fig leaf was surrounded by animals. The guy was writing on a chalkboard. The chalkboard was filled with the names of animals.

Suzanne, screaming, leaped out from behind the Tree of Knowledge of Good and Evil and began shooting. She clipped one of the bozos on the shoulder but totally missed the second. Pig Butt cleaned up, saving Suzanne's crazy hide. Suzanne shot each bozo twice more, even though they were clearly dead. She then ran off again. Pig Butt looked at me and produced an unhurried smile. "Ten minus two equals eight," he said.

We decided to follow Suzanne. She led us to the Red Sea. The water in the Red Sea was actually red. As we approached the Red Sea, I could see on the other side of the water a mannequin wearing a beard and carrying a staff. I assumed it was Moses. Then a bozo stepped from behind Moses and started shooting at us, screaming, "Allah Akbar" over and over again. Fortunately the bozo was a terrible shot, because we had no cover. Pig Butt shot him and the bozo fell into the Red Sea, where he landed on top of a statue of a horse and rider partially covered by the red water.

Suzanne joined us. She appeared to be significantly less crazy. "I'm OK now," she said. "It's just that whenever I think of someone trying to hurt you, Junior . . ." Suzanne's next words were drowned out by an explosion that sent the Red Sea high into the air. We were drenched by the water, but unharmed. Pig Butt sent a few bursts in the direction of the explosion and then led us away from the Red Sea.

Then nothing happened for about ten minutes. We walked slowly by the Ten Commandments and David killing Goliath, but saw no bozos. As we crawled by the Burning Bush exhibit, however, we took fire and had to take cover behind the Rock of Ages. Fortunately, it was a really big rock.

Pig Butt yelled, "They are shooting at us from the City of Jericho!" Suzanne got that crazy look in her eyes again and said, "Stay here for five minutes and be prepared to shoot at Jericho. I can take care of this!" Then she ran off.

Pig Butt shrugged and shoved another clip in his rifle, still no concern on his face. "Get ready, Junior," he said. "This should be interesting." And it definitely was.

I laid my rifle on the Rock of Ages and aimed at the City of Jericho. I heard Suzanne scream, "Now!" somewhere off in the distance, and the walls of the City of Jericho fell outward, exposing the bozos. We shot and killed all seven bozos in about ten seconds. I say "we." I assume I may have hit one. And that was it. No more bozos.

I'm curious. How many of you anticipated that the walls of Jericho would fall down? I assume some of my readers know enough about the Bible to fig-ure out that was what was going to happen. Suzanne certainly knew the Bible story and guessed there was probably a switch somewhere that caused the walls in the exhibit to fall down. Pig Butt also knew the story and was ready to blast away when the walls fell. Like the bozos, I was not up to date on my Bible stories and was totally surprised when the walls came tumbling down.

We are now in a different vehicle and are no longer in Kentucky. I sincerely apologize to the owners of Bible World for messing up your park. If you will send me a bill, I will pay for all the damages.[160]

Day 969

The Mossad guys tell us they think we killed the last of the bozos chasing us here in America. That's good. I have never been a big gun guy, but I have to admit I am glad I had one in Kentucky. Or more specifically, I am glad Pig Butt had a gun.

Now it looks like I may be safe from future bozo attacks as well. Clayton Singletary, my old friend from Secure Area 88 in Afghanistan, is on CNN explaining that the Nazi Lowriders killed the Sheik of the Decade by mistake. I am cautiously optimistic that there are no other sheiks out there who want to fund Junior hunters.

"We had no idea who he was," Clayton told the CNN reporter. "Our guards just saw two guys with guns trying to sneak through one of the gates. Standing orders here are to shoot first and ask questions later. It wasn't until we found one of his wives outside the gate and talked to her that we realized we had shot the Sheik of the Decade and his bodyguard. Don't mind telling you we had a little party at that point. You can tell the Smithsonian guys that we can send a few body parts for their terrorist exhibit if they are interested. Free of charge."

CNN also interviewed the sheik's wife, who spoke flawless English. She did not seem all that upset about the loss of her husband. "My husband," she said, "unfortunately became a bitter man when the oil disappeared. He blamed Allah for his troubles. My husband was never very good at accepting

---

160   The Bible World theme park that was destroyed in Day 965 was not rebuilt. Instead, it was renamed Jehovah Kicks Allah's Butt Park. Guided tours are given showing the damage caused by the gun battle, and where each Islamic terrorist was killed. The gun battle is also re-created by actors for tour groups.

responsibility. It was never his fault. I tried to talk to him many times about this character flaw, but he refused to view himself rationally."

Is it just me, or shouldn't one of the richest men in the world have a wife who isn't a nag? You would think the sheik could find a woman who would not criticize him about his character flaws. I guess it doesn't make any difference now, since the guy is dead. I won't miss him.

I switched the television to ESPN to watch some highlights and saw my old friend the Hammer being interviewed. The Hammer was dripping with sweat. In fact, the Hammer's sweat was dripping on the head of the small woman who was interviewing him. She did not seem to notice. She was a real pro.

I expected to hear the Hammer discuss the Cowboys' prospects for the upcoming season. Instead, the woman asked him about the death of the sheik. The Hammer paused, wiped sweat off his face, and said:

You know, little lady, Senior Jennings was a good friend of mine, so it don't hurt my feelings none that the Arab guy is dead. Plus, it makes me happy that the Arab guy had a witch for a wife. One more thing before I hit the shower. The stuff about the sheik guy blaming Allah for his troubles? How lame is that? I don't get it when people ruin their lives by doing stupid things and then they blame Allah or God, or Jehovah, or whoever. What a loser.

I think I will give the Hammer the last word on the sheik. Thanks, big guy.

Day 972

Got a phone call from Eb today. I had sent him a congratulatory e-mail back when he accepted the prime minister job. I did not expect to hear from Eb for a while, because I figured he would be really busy prime ministering.

After some pleasant preliminaries, Eb said, "Remember when we first met on the New Sea of Galilee?"

"How could I forget? We met on a very nice yacht. You stuttered a lot and told me that you wanted to get the Republican nomination for president."

Eb laughed and said, "Yes, I was quite the compelling candidate. Do you remember what I told you, other than that I wanted to be president?"

"Not specifically."

Eb continued, "I do. I said that the prime minister insisted that I meet with you in person to give you this information and that you would know what to do."

"That does ring a bell, now that you mention it. And I had no clue what you were talking about."

Eb sighed. "Well, Junior, pretend we are sitting on the yacht again. When I took over as prime minister, Hannah gave me an envelope. She said the prime minister wanted me to open the envelope after I took office. The letter inside the envelope is addressed to me and has a lot of important information and advice. One of the pieces of advice reads: 'Call Junior about Jerusalem. He will know what to do.' So I am calling. Do you know what to do?"

And then I remembered that Senior wanted me to give the Mexican money to the Jews.

Day 980

Election day is finally here and although the result is a bit anticlimactic, everybody seems really happy. Lots of parades. Lots of happy people on television talking about what a great country we have and how great it was to have a campaign where candidates did not scream and holler and say bad things about each other.

I guess not everyone is happy. Just for grins, I checked the Democrats Are Stupid Channel and the Republicans Are Stupid Channel. Blank screens.

The newly elected President Davis gave a great speech in which he praised Eb and General Dozier and talked about "our wonderful tradition of a peaceful transition of power." He also made good on his promise to bring me in from the cold:

Let me digress for a moment here and talk very briefly about Joshua Jennings, Jr. Mr. Jennings is a fine young man who was unfairly accused of a serious crime. As we all know now, the New Mexico explosion was orchestrated by Sheik Al Zahrani, whose head is now displayed in the Smithsonian's Islamic Terrorist Severed and/or Mutilated Body Parts Exhibit. One of my first acts when I am officially inaugurated will be to

*issue a blanket pardon for Mr. Jennings. So I ask the American people
to let Joshua be. Just let him be.*

Thanks, Mr. President.

Day 982

If Eb wasn't a hero before, he is certainly one today. CNN announced today that Eb has just signed a deal to buy Israel from the banks left holding the bag when the sheik stopped making his loan payments. The price: $95 billion in cash.

The Banking Network reports that the sale was a complete surprise because the state of Israel has been running on a financial shoestring since moving to North Dakota. The experts can't figure out where the money is coming from, and Eb has refused to comment on the issue, other than to say: "The Lord has once again helped us.[161] God's people are going back home."

The Nuclear Fallout Network reports that while only Jerusalem is habitable at this point, recent advancements in the cleanup of nuclear fallout will make it possible for the majority of Israel to be habitable within two to four years.

In a related story, the FBI has announced the capture of the drug cartel kings who sold Mexico to the United States. Actually, most people don't realize yet that the arrest is a "related story." Another scoop from the history major.

Day 990

Well, this is the last day of month thirty-three. Thought I would shake it up this month and mention the last day rather than the first day of the month.

Suzanne and I will be leaving in a few minutes to fly to Jerusalem. The original one. Eb has invited us. There is going to be a big parade and celebration for the Jews' homecoming in the City of David. (And yes, Suzanne told me that Jerusalem is also called the City of David.)

Pig Butt has gone back home to his pig farm in Missouri. He had to hire an agent to field all the inquiries regarding movies and books based upon

---

161   Hebrew scholars have noted that Ebenezer means "stone of help."

his life, and endorsement opportunities. Thanks for saving my life, Pig Butt. I owe you.

I am looking forward to seeing Jerusalem. I have never seen it before. Suzanne says we should stay a couple of weeks. We are going to celebrate my thirty-third birthday next week and Suzanne says it would be fun to have a party in Jerusalem. That's OK with me. The Assassin says we can deal with Senior's estate when I get back.

Suzanne says we need to leave for the plane in five minutes. She has also told me that we need to discuss our wedding plans during the flight, so I will likely not be able to write on the plane.

That's OK, because I think we have come to the end anyway, haven't we? Looks like all the issues have been resolved, and my participation in Senior's grand plan is no longer necessary. Thanks, dear reader, for hanging with me. I know it has been a long book. But now, I guess it is finally finished.

Hold that thought. Note to self—I just remembered that back when I started this I said I was going to tell you why Pete called me Big Man.[162] When things settle down in Jerusalem I will tell you that story.[163] Suzanne is giving me the Southern Girl stare, so I need to go. Peace.

---

162 See Day 2.

163 This is the seventh, and last, "note to self" statement in *Junior*.

Afterword

Joshua Jennings, Jr., and Suzanne were honored guests in the Jerusalem Homecoming Parade, riding in a convertible with Prime Minister Cohen. Junior was given a key to the city.

Junior and Suzanne disappeared the day after the parade and have never been seen again. Their disappearance remains one of the biggest mysteries of the twenty-first century. Seven years after the Jerusalem Homecoming Parade, in accordance with Texas law, Joshua Jennings, Jr., was declared legally dead by the probate court of El Paso, Texas, so his estate could be administered.

After Junior was declared legally dead, the Harvard University Life Criticism Department conducted a seminar on Junior's life. Jana Mars, the head of the department, gave Junior's life five stars, calling it "easily the most exciting and influential life of the twenty-first century, even if he did seem a little henpecked there at the end."

Dean Wilkerson, Jr., PhD
University of Texas at Fayetteville, Arkansas

Acknowledgments

Thanks to Cathy and Gina for the typing and the encouragement. And thanks to the Assassin, who listened to me as I blathered on about this project.

Ray Donley

About the Author

Ray Donley's childhood dream was to play point guard in the NBA. When that dream died, he became a lawyer, a profession in which foot speed and fast twitch muscles are not a prerequisite to gainful employment. After writing factually accurate and mostly boring legal briefs for thirty years, Ray decided to write a novel so he could just make stuff up. He researched, as lawyers do, and determined that what the world needed was a novel that combined his interests in the Bible, sports, cosmic cause and effect, silly religiosity, and movies where things get blown up. Ray lives in Austin, Texas with his wife, who is also an attorney. Their two wonderful daughters attend college.